LIST OF CHARACTERS

Fictional Victorian characters

Olwen Malkon of Swindale Hall

Her father and brothers, Oliver and William. Deceased

The Reverend and Mrs Malkon, Alfred and Edmond Malkon. Olwen's uncle, aunt and cousins

Susan. Maid

Celia Goodfellow and Augusta Dudley. Olwen's former governess/companion and her friend

Joyce. Maid

Dr John Osbourne. Physician

Herr Professor Brandt. Visiting professor at St Hilda's House

Dr Nicholson and Dr Linton. Medical officers at St Hilda's House

Mr and Mrs Percy. Retainers at Swindale Hall

Reagan. Self-styled keeper of Swindale woods

Inspector Redman and his constables. Police

The Bishop

★

Fictional historical characters

Ælwyn (Wyn). Ælfwald's daughter

Oshere, (Heri). Grandson of Modig

Modig. Ruler of the land north of Hadrian's wall

Bri. Heri's companion

Historical figures

Ælfwald. King of Northumbria

Ælf and Ælfwinne. King Ælfwald's sons

Osred. Nephew of King Ælfwald

Eanbald I. Archbishop of York

Æthelred. Deposed former king of Northumbria

Sicga. A nobleman in the court of Ælfwald

PROLOGUE

S he woke and the dream, uncanny, fled.
  But it left a lingering tail.

She rose and went to the window, pushing up the sash, and felt the night air, cool upon her face, and her pulse began to steady. The moon was full, and in its pale light the orchard trees turned to silver, with the ings spreading either side of the river, ethereal and lovely. Somewhere a fox barked and was answered by its mate from beyond the garden wall, where the church tower could just be seen. The air blew gently through the open window, spring-scented, and she closed her eyes and went on standing there, still troubled by the dream, until she grew chill. Shivering, she opened her eyes—

And stared out upon an altered scene.

She leaned forward. All was quite changed! The lawns and borders had gone, the brick walls and glasshouse had vanished, the orchard had become a woodland, and the trees, no longer arrayed in their spring finery, were shedding autumn leaves. She must be dreaming still for the moon, rising above the treetops, was now not a silvery orb but a huge harvest moon, and it hung there, blood red, in the night sky.

She looked over to where the church tower should be and found that it too had disappeared. In its place was a small wooden building, encircled by a wall and, in the pasture beyond the wall, a pale horse stood, its head turned towards her. And then she saw them, shadowy figures gathering close, and knew that their coming was because of her, and was afraid.

SARAH MAINE

The Awakenings

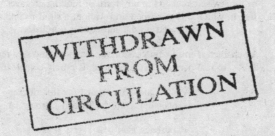

HODDER

First published in Great Britain in 2022 by Hodder & Stoughton
An Hachette UK company

This paperback edition published in 2022

1

A CIP catalogue record for this title
is available from the British Library

Paperback ISBN 978 1 529 38514 4
eBook ISBN 978 1 529 38513 7

Typeset in Plantin Light by
Palimpsest Book Production Limited, Falkirk, Stirlingshire

Printed and bound in Great Britain by Clays Ltd,
Elcograf S.p.A.

Hodder & Stoughton policy is to use papers that are natural,
renewable and recyclable products and made from wood grown
in sustainable forests. The logging and manufacturing processes
are expected to conform to the environmental regulations of
the country of origin.

Hodder & Stoughton Ltd
Carmelite House
50 Victoria Embankment
London EC4Y 0DZ

www.hodder.co.uk

CHAPTER I

That was the first time that Olwen's odd dreams elided with reality. Until then they had been strange, haunting and disjointed, but they had at least remained within the boundaries of sleep. It felt as if she had been dreaming every night since the drowning – fractured images, desperate sequences and always a sense of urgency, a frantic striving to save a situation that was already lost.

This, perhaps, was what grief did. It took over the mind and paralysed the body.

The fever and chill she had developed upon departing from Swindale Hall, her erstwhile home, had proved a godsend; it gave her a reason to stay in her own room for much of the day, keeping away from a household that had offered such a chilly welcome. Her room was at the back of the vicarage, and it became her refuge. She lay abed now and rolled over, tangled in the sheets, and stared vacantly at the narrow bookshelf that housed a handful of books hastily gathered up upon departure, the remainder left behind in her larger, more congenial room at Swindale. 'There's no space for more,' her aunt had told her. 'You must adapt to having rather less accommodation than you're used to. . .' and be grateful. The unspoken words had echoed through the hall of the vicarage that first day when Olwen had stood, forlorn and defeated amongst her valises. 'Besides,' her uncle had added with a genial, unconvincing smile, 'we have books aplenty here!' Collections of sermons, no doubt, or dreary treatises, not the novels and stories that Celia had brought with her to Swindale.

Standing in the draughty vicarage hall Olwen had pleaded her cold, and been allowed to retire.

'You will soon be well again.' Her aunt's tone brooked no other possibility.

Celia would have known how to bring comfort, Olwen thought. Celia would have been resolute in the face of these disasters. But Celia was gone, along with all that was familiar. The drownings, so swiftly followed by Father's decline had left her devastated, thrown completely off-balance, numbed by it all, too stunned to think.

And alone, quite alone. . .

She had not known that Celia would leave her, but her aunt had told her the day after the funeral when she was already gone, her employment no longer a necessary expense. 'We've no room in the vicarage for a governess you've long outgrown,' she had told her. 'I can't imagine why your father kept her on for so long.' Because she was her friend, Olwen had wanted to wail, because she made things all right. Celia had been her mentor, and her rock. But the triple tragedy that had befallen her family had been beyond even Celia's ability to mend and Olwen's protests had gone unheeded. And it seemed that, with Celia's departure, her misery was absolute. Her uncle no doubt *meant* to make her feel welcome but he stressed rather too frequently that he was now responsible for her, her legal guardian, and that he was fulfilling his Christian duty in a wholly laudable manner, consistent with his standing in the parish. Olwen suspected that her aunt's welcome was grounded in avarice rather than empathy, and as for her cousins – Alfred seemed to watch her, like a predator biding his time, while Edmond guilelessly accepted her arrival with indifference.

Closing up Swindale Hall after the funeral had mostly been undertaken while Olwen tossed in her bed, fever-ridden and incapable of rational thought. Mrs Percy, bless her, had seen to it all, suffering stoically the curt commands of her aunt, who had taken it upon herself to play the mistress.

Which she was not, of course. Swindale Hall belonged to Olwen.

And yet the thought of living there again was inconceivable.

Olwen rolled onto her back and stared up at the ceiling. The place would be forever tainted by what had occurred there and she dreamed of it some nights, standing empty and hollow. In one such dream her brothers had sprung from under dust-sheeted furniture, dripping wet, shrieking with mirth at a prank well-played, 'We *knew* we could fool you.' And she had woken, daring for an instant to hope, only to slide back into despair as her reasoning returned. Sometimes in the dreams she heard her aunt's voice: 'There really isn't space, you know. . .' and it was not of books that she spoke. Or she would turn and see Alfred standing, framed in the doorway, staring back at her, his features too deeply shadowed to read. And yet, amongst the anguish and the sorrow, her dreams sometimes stirred in her a strange yearning, a longing, and she would glimpse a hillside, catching the scent of bluebells on the wind.

But last night it had been different, and she was left feeling unsettled and disturbed. A waking dream. . . Did such a thing exist? Or had grief brought her to the point where dreams and reality merged at the margins of consciousness? Since arriving at the vicarage she had exaggerated her illness in order to extend her solitude, but perhaps she was fevered still. . . And yet today was the day she had been told that she was well enough to go for the first time to Sunday service, and she sensed that any special pleading would fall upon deaf ears.

She dressed slowly, brushing her hair with care then twisting it into a knot at the nape of her neck and stared at herself. in the mirror, barely recognising the bruised expression and her dark-encircled eyes. And last night's dream stayed with her. . . She went downstairs, troubled by it, and pushed open the door to the dining room where breakfast was being eaten. The vicar looked up, greeting her with bonhomie, 'Ah! My dear child.' His wife gave her an appraising nod, and Edmond offered a vague smile. There was no sign of Alfred, for which she was grateful.

The scale of disquiet that the dream had engendered, however, was completely eclipsed by what she felt halfway down the aisle of St Helen's Church an hour or so later. And it changed everything. The fear came from nowhere, unheralded and shocking. She had entered the church through the porch, noting how the spring sunlight shafted through the lancet windows, lighting vases filled with pussy willow and sweet-smelling jonquil before pooling on the stone-flagged floor, and she had only taken a few steps before it struck her.

Fear without substance, all-consuming and real. . .

Grabbing the polished filial at the end of the pew, she turned in distress to Edmond, clutching at his arm and trembling. Startled, he sat her down. 'What's wrong?' he asked.

She shook her head, bewildered.

'Olwen? You draw attention to yourself.' Her aunt, behind them, hissed angrily and thrust a bottle of smelling salts under her nose.

Parishioners were flowing into the church as they did every Sunday but they came to an unexpected halt, their progress blocked, while those already seated craned their necks to watch the little drama unfold. The circumstances of Olwen Malkon's arrival in the village had sustained gossip for the past fortnight and here she was, on her first appearance, behaving in such a diverting manner. The personification of youthful grief, the women thought, dewy-eyed and maudlin; how well black became her, their men decided, imagining how they might comfort her.

'I cannot stay,' she whispered up to Edmond.

His mother answered for him. 'Nonsense. We set an example, Olwen, it is expected.'

'But I cannot,' she repeated, her eyes still on her cousin. And it was a plain fact. She could no more take a step forward than she could fly up to the rafters or perch on the rood screen. People were squeezing past them, taking their seats then twisting round to watch as the organ's welcoming melody faded to swell again in the opening chords of the first hymn. Her aunt, pink-cheeked with annoyance, hissed at her again, gesturing to their pew at the front where, by now, they should be seated, hands folded in dutiful attention.

Setting an example.

'I need air.' Brushing aside the smelling salts, Olwen got to her feet, meeting the woman's outraged eye. 'Forgive me, but I cannot stay.' Her palms were clammy and her heart thumped alarmingly.

'*Nonsense!*' her aunt repeated. 'You must—'

She broke off as a quiet voice spoke from behind. 'Can I be of assistance, Mrs Malkon?'

The woman turned and gave a tight smile. 'You're very kind, Dr Osbourne, a passing faintness, nothing more. . .'

'I need air,' Olwen insisted, desperate now and gulping, hemmed in by Edmond and her aunt. The smelling salts had cleared her head enough to sharpen the sense of menace.

'And air you shall have.' The doctor's tone was firm. 'Make way, if you will,' he said, then lowered his voice and cocked an eyebrow at her aunt, 'or I reckon you'll have a scene on your hands.'

The woman bit her lip, aware of the growing buzz of interest, and conceded the ground. 'Edmond, you go too.' But Olwen had already slipped through the gap the doctor had created and was half-running back up the aisle, head down, oblivious to the curious stares. The doctor strode after her and Edmond, delayed for a moment by his mother, followed.

She reached the porch and stood there, gasping for air, her palm against the wall, while, behind her, the organ brought the congregation to its feet, and to order.

'D'you feel sick?' The doctor stepped in front of her and studied her face. She shook her head. 'Dizzy?' Another shake. 'Good. Take off your bonnet.' She tugged at the ribbons and he took it from her, tossing it onto the close-cropped grass, his eyes still on her face. 'I'd loosen that crêpe collar if I were you, it looks too tight.' It was, and she did. 'Good. Now breathe in through your nose, deeply and slowly, while I count to five.' He counted. 'Out through your mouth. And again. One, two. . .'

Edmond emerged from the porch. 'All right now, coz?'

'. . . three, four. . .' The doctor waved him to silence. 'Let it go. And again. One, two. . .' Confident fingers took hold of her wrist and he stared ahead as he noted her pulse, then smiled for the first time. 'Calming nicely. Slow breathing helps. Always remember that. Are your stays too tight?'

Edmond guffawed. 'Is that all it was?'

The doctor gave him an even look. 'In my view, tight stays account for much that bedevils their wearers.' Turning back to Olwen, he gestured to a tabular tomb, dark with velvety moss. 'Sit a minute.' He shrugged out of his jacket and folded it for her to sit upon. 'D'you have anything to drink on you?' he asked Edmond.

The youth proudly patted his pocket. 'Brandy.'

'Excellent.' He snapped his fingers for it and Olwen, now seated, had recovered enough to appreciate the expression on her young cousin's face as he surrendered his flask.

'I don't drink brandy,' she remarked. 'Nor do I wear my stays too tight.'

The doctor took the flask and sniffed its contents. 'Pleased to hear it.'

'Neither am I given to swooning and making an exhibition of myself.'

He handed it to her. 'So what brought that on, d'you suppose? Take a drop, it'll do you good.' And while the brandy lit a fire in her throat, the hymn came to an abrupt end as if the congregation could suddenly see right through the nave wall and had been shocked into silence by the outrageous tableau they made. The vicar's niece, in full mourning clothes, sitting, bare-headed, on a tombstone, sipping brandy, no less, with a stranger who stood there in his shirtsleeves, discussing her stays.

'That's better,' the doctor said; the little smile had not escaped him.

'Mama said we should slip in at the end of the hymn,' Edmond said, glancing back towards the porch.

Olwen's smile vanished. 'No.'

'No?' The doctor explored her face. 'Why not?'

'I simply can't.' She looked aside, avoiding his scrutiny, and studied how the yew trees cast a dark shadow on the walls of the ancient chancel. Sentinels of the dead, someone had told her, heartwood red, sapwood white, the embodiment of Christ's blood sacrifice. She swayed a little as the fog of fear came close.

'Oh no you don't.' The doctor reached her in a stride. 'Head down, between your knees.' He recovered the brandy flask from her limp grasp and passed it to Edmond.

'She went quite white!' her cousin exclaimed.

Olwen felt the doctor's hand on her head, pressing it down firmly until her forehead was almost on her lap. Her stays bit in savagely and the pain dispelled the fog. She tried to straighten but he held her there. 'Give it a minute. Blood to the brain. Best thing.' He spoke in short phrases as if she was a simpleton. Again she tried to straighten and this time he removed his hand. 'It would be unwise for her to go back in,' he said, addressing Edmond. 'I'll stay. You go.'

Edmond looked uncertain. 'I think Mama would want me to remain as well. . .'

'By all means.' The doctor sat himself on another gravestone and said nothing more, his attention apparently taken by two ring doves who were circling a small square stone water-filled trough, tails fanned out in courtship, cooing softly.

'You can both leave,' said Olwen. 'I shall be perfectly all right out here in the fresh air until the service has finished.'

The doctor gave her a brief smile. 'I've a professional obliga-tion to remain but – ' he gave Edmond a considering look '– there's no need to deprive Mr Malkon of the benefit of his father's sermon.'

Edmond grinned and pulled the brandy flask from his pocket again, offering it to the doctor, who waved it aside. 'I get 'em on a daily basis.' He raised an eyebrow in query, gesturing with it towards Olwen.

This amused the doctor. 'Miss Malkon, would you find another drop beneficial?'

Olwen shook her head, meeting the humour in his eye. He was some ten years or so older than Edmond, darker in colouring, and an inch or two shorter, although her cousin was an unusually tall youth. The doctor was broad shouldered, having grown to full manhood, and had an assurance that, for all his posturing, Edmond, at eighteen, had yet to acquire. Like herself, the doctor was newly arrived in the village, having come down from Edinburgh to replace an ageing colleague, while Olwen's home was less than ten miles away.

Except that it was home no longer, closed up and empty. The thought overwhelmed her again. Shutters at the windows, dust sheets on the furniture.

Home now was the vicarage.

'May I ask how long it is since your father died?' the doctor asked after a moment, and she frowned, though doubtless the whole village was aware of her circumstances; it was only to be expected.

'Almost three weeks.'

'So little time,' he said gently, then added, 'Grief does strange things to us, Miss Malkon, to the body and to the mind, you cannot separate the two.'

'And the boys just a few weeks earlier,' Edmond said, furtively taking another nip from his flask. 'Poor little chaps.'

The doctor looked across at her in enquiry, but she did not enlighten him, not trusting herself to speak of it. He made no further remark, but she was aware of his eyes dwelling on her a moment before his attention returned to the doves, whose courtship was progressing well. Male chest feathers were puffed out and cooing was now interspersed with courtly bows. The birds' behaviour seemed to engross the man, allowing Olwen, in turn, to study him. Carelessly dressed, he wore his dark hair a little longer than was fashionable but his beard was neatly trimmed and there was a strange intensity to his expression as he watched the doves. In the short time he had been in the village he had gained a good deal of respect but also a reputation for bluntness and a contempt for well-loved remedies. He had expressed quite freely his reservations about his predecessor's practices – medieval, he had been heard to call them – but the villagers had liked old Dr Thomas and opinions about his successor were divided.

As if conscious of her scrutiny, he snapped back to attention. 'Did you eat breakfast this morning?'

'Yes.'

'What did you have?'

'A boiled egg and some toast. And tea.'

'Hmm,' he said, and then addressed Edmond again. 'I expect your mother's becoming concerned, you know. If you were to slip back in, as she suggested, you might signal to her that all is well.'

Edmond looked back at him. 'How? I can hardly signal from the back to the front as she'll be facing the altar.'

The doctor's lips twitched. 'Aye, that's a difficulty. But if you were to wait until she turns, as she doubtless will, you could give her a signal. A nod will do. And a smile.'

'And then come out again?'

The doctor shook his head. 'You'd be better staying put. Though at the back of the church you'll be well-hidden from your father if you choose to doze.'

Edmond, having all his life been told what to do by strong-minded individuals, could recognise an order when given one, even if it did run counter to an earlier, more formidable, one. 'And you think that would be best?'

'Your mother will be consoled.'

Edmond took a final swig from his flask and pocketed it. Olwen doubted that her aunt knew of the flask's existence but, as in all things, Edmond aped his older brother. 'You'll be all right, will you, coz? With just the doctor here?' She nodded, wishing they would both go and leave her in peace, but that seemed too much to hope for. On the path, in a spot of sunlight, avian courtship had reached its climax and the female dove crouched in submission while the male, triumphant, raised his wings and mounted her. 'Oh, I say,' Edmond aimed a boot at the pair, who flew off in a flutter of outrage. 'I'll go then,' he said.

The doctor grinned as he vanished inside the porch and he was smiling still when he turned back to Olwen. 'Are your uncle's sermons long?' he asked.

'I don't know. I've not attended church here before, except once, some years ago.'

'Well, I reckon you've maybe three quarters of an hour's peace and while I'll not pester you with questions, I wonder if you *can* explain what happened just now?'

Sitting here, in the dappled sunshine, it was hard to recall, let alone explain, the feeling that had come upon her. But he did not press her and, perhaps because of that, she made an attempt. 'It was a feeling. . . an awful sense of dread, of fear almost. . .' She stopped. 'And I knew that I could not. . . must not. . . go any further into the church.'

'Must not?'

She shrugged and said nothing more, having no words to explain.

'Has it happened before?' She shook her head. But she sensed again the deep unease that last night's dream had engendered. He paused as if considering, then asked, 'Did you attend your father's funeral?'

'Yes, but that was not here, it was in the little chapel on the estate.'

'No such feelings there?'

'No.'

He said nothing more but let his eyes roam over the churchyard before turning back to her, his head cocked to one side. 'Grief can be delayed, you know, for weeks, months or even years and it takes many different forms. The mind puts up its own defence, producing a sort of numbness, until gradually it's able to confront such sad events, but reaching the point of acceptance is never easy.'

He spoke gently but without the pitying tone that others used, and for that she was grateful. But she had had no thoughts of her father, nor of her beloved brothers, as she entered the church, for she knew if she dwelt on *their* loss, despair would overwhelm her. No, this sensation had been of threat, of danger targeted very directly at herself, and had been accompanied by that strange intense ache of longing.

The doctor was awaiting a response but she had nothing to say to him. He had been so quick to make his diagnosis, so sure of himself. And he knew nothing of her dreams. 'I suggest that coming into the church brought back the distress of the funeral,' he went on, warming to his theme. 'You had, perhaps, blocked it, delayed it, so to speak.'

'Perhaps,' she said, not believing him.

He continued to study her. 'Are you taking anything to help you sleep? Laudanum or some other potion?'

'Only at first, my aunt gave it to me.'

He frowned. 'Resist her! Dreadful stuff. Poison. And are you sleeping better now?'

'It varies. I dream—'

'That's inevitable. And dreams reach deep. Are you taking any other pills or preparations, something for your nerves, perhaps?'

'No.' What of the promise not to pester, she wondered.

'Good. You can't imagine how many ladies dose themselves with substances they cannot begin to understand, addressing some spurious or imagined ailment, and do themselves real mischief. I'd one patient in Edinburgh who thought nothing of adding several ounces of laudanum to a glass of sherry every night to help her sleep, then wondered why she was fatigued and bewildered during the days. Nothing I could say persuaded her that the wretched stuff was killing her.'

'And did it?' she asked, momentarily diverted.

'It will, but for now she lives on in a serene torpor.'

'Perhaps, then, laudanum is exactly what I need.'

He smiled a little. 'Life's adversities are to be confronted, not evaded, Miss Malkon. There're no easy way past them, but given time they tend to resolve.' His brow furrowed again. 'Your cousin suggested you've suffered other recent losses?'

'Yes,' she said, and turned away again. To speak of the drowning would be her undoing. . . She focused instead on the doves, which had returned to the same spot of sunlight beside the hollowed stone and resumed their interrupted courtship. He had only to ask the local gossips if he wanted to know more.

'Then you've a great deal to endure and some disorder of the emotions is only to be expected,' he continued, 'and that can be every bit as debilitating as a physical ailment. They say the body rules the mind but the opposite is also true. Remember, deep slow breathing helps and putting your head down between your knees controls faintness by bringing—'

'Blood to the brain,' she finished for him.

He raised his eyebrows, amused again. 'Exactly,' and the male dove, having invested sufficient time in courtship, cut short the nuptial niceties and briskly mounted the female. The doctor glanced at them. 'Pregnancy can produce the same symptoms, of course?'

She almost gasped with shock, and her irritation vanished. How horrified her aunt would be! But the man, apparently unconcerned by conventions of polite behaviour, simply smiled back at her. 'Not in this case, of course. Would you like to walk a little, perhaps, just around the church? You could take my arm.'

CHAPTER 2

A gravel path ran through the churchyard past tightly packed gravestones, moss-covered or blackened with age, the lettering wind-blasted into illegibility. A landscape of the dead, she thought, where generations of villagers lay side by side, long forgotten, their earthly conflicts forever unresolved. Some stones stood upright, others had bowed in the face of storms or collapsed into earlier burials creating an undulating surface to the ground. A wall ran atop a low bank, encircled by a ditch where half-opened marsh marigolds provided a splash of colour, while the hum of bees gave a promise of renewal. She had shaken out the doctor's jacket before handing it back to him. 'My predecessor was keen that I understood the antiquity of this lovely church,' he had said as he pulled it on, apparently indifferent to its creases, 'and I expect your uncle has done the same.'

He picked up her discarded bonnet and gave it to her but she carried it, ribbons dangling, enjoying the breeze in her hair as she walked beside him. 'I've had it from both of them. Dr Thomas came often to the hall, and would sit for hours with Papa discussing the local antiquities and monuments; a gentleman from the museum in York often joined them.' The past had been for her father more compelling than a present cluttered with children who, having lost their mother so young, might have hoped for rather more of his attention. 'It's very ancient, I believe, although I have forgotten the details.'

'Then my duty is clear. Next to deep breathing nothing is more beneficial to the mind than a distraction, no matter how dull.' He cleared his throat and clasped his hands behind his back. 'St Helen's Church appears in the Domesday Book – ' his mimicry of old Dr Thomas was shockingly accurate and she dropped her eyes to hide a smile – 'but there's every reason to believe its foundation is earlier.'

'What reasons are they, Doctor?'

He gave her a slanting look. 'D'you hope to catch me out?' he asked, before continuing in the same tone. 'Surviving fabric suggests that the current nave is older than the chancel, while the antiquity of the chancel arch supports the idea that the earlier church was also a two-celled structure. The porch is later—'

'Clearly.' He gave a mock frown at the interruption and she felt her spirits lightening.

' – and the aisles are thirteenth century additions. A foundation date in the Dark Ages is possible, and the postulated two-celled structure might itself have had an earlier, presumably timber, predecessor.'

Last night's dreams flashed across her mind and was gone. 'How do you know?'

Her sudden tension passed unnoticed. 'I don't. No wait, yes, there was a reason. . . Some fragments of carved stones, I believe, aye, that's it, they turned up during recent restoration work, embedded in the south wall. Quite extraordinary, in fact, have you seen them?' She shook her head. 'Come now, and have a look.'

Intrigued by this man, who looked far too bohemian to be a doctor, she allowed him to lead her between the gravestones to a shady corner where scythed grass had been piled in a sour-smelling heap. Bits of broken gravestones, chipped vases and other debris had been dumped there too and would soon be screened by nettles. 'They're amongst all this, as I remember. Wait there, if you will, there's broken glass and all sorts.' He left her and began rooting amongst the decaying heap, turning and examining the different stones, apparently unconcerned about the toll on shoes and trousers. 'If old Thomas is right about their antiquity, then they really ought to be inside the church. . . Aha! Here's one.' He rolled a broken fragment of stone towards her, turning it to expose a surface on which was carved an arch under which sat an enthroned figure, staring fixedly ahead. 'Apparently

there's some debate amongst scholars who. . . Oh Lord—' He
let go of the stone, yelping as it fell on his foot, and caught her
just before she fell. 'Breathe,' he commanded, in a very different
tone. 'To my count. One, two, three. . .' She did as he bid, holding
onto him, fighting giddiness and a rising panic.

Unnoticed by either of them, a figure had appeared on the
path, dressed in riding breeches and a topcoat. 'Olwen?' the man
called out. 'Whatever's going on?'

She released herself from the doctor's grip, recognising Alfred
with dismay. 'My cousin,' she murmured and straightened, aware
suddenly how this must look, the two of them, in a dark corner
hidden from the church door.

But Alfred was already striding towards them, crushing prim-
roses underfoot. 'Who's that with you?'

She pulled herself together, not liking his expression. 'Do you
know Dr Osbourne? Let me introduce my cousin, Mr Alfred
Malkon.'

The doctor nodded, unperturbed. 'How d'ye do? If you'll go
to the other side, Mr Malkon, we can get your cousin safely back
onto the path. And then she can sit again for a moment and—'

But Alfred had taken possession of Olwen's arm, blocking the
doctor with his shoulder. 'Why aren't you in church with the rest
of 'em?' he asked, throwing him a dark look as they went back
through the gravestones.

'I had a funny turn so I came outside—'

'Where you had another one, eh?' Once safely back on the
path, Alfred scrutinised the doctor, his expression very much like
his mother's. 'But what were you doing right over there, in that
corner?'

Only by a slightly heightened colour did Dr Osbourne betray
a recognition that the question was perhaps a reasonable one. 'I
was showing Miss Malkon the carved stones retrieved from the
walls of the church.'

'Why?'

'Because I asked to see them.' Alfred's manner was objection-
able and Olwen felt her hackles rise. Not only had he a sharper

wit than his brother, he had a nastier mind and would likely have said more had not the church bells rung out, signalling the end of the service. The congregation began to emerge from the church and the vicar positioned himself at the door, his wife beside him, greeting each of the departing faithful with a handclasp and a smile.

Edmond slid out behind them and, catching sight of the little group on the path, came forward. 'Feeling better, coz?' he asked her, but turned at once to his brother. 'You're like to catch it, Alf. Mama's not best pleased.'

Alfred Malkon was as tall but leaner than his brother, an altogether more handsome man, but his scowl deepened at this domestic insight. 'I can't imagine why,' he drawled. 'You know Dr Osbourne, I presume. He's been showing Olwen some old stones from the church.'

'Have you? Why?'

'My very question.' Alfred continued to eye the doctor unpleasantly but turned at the sound of his mother's voice.

'Alfred,' she said, coming down the path. 'You've returned.'

'Behold.' He spread his arms wide.

'I expected you last night—' She broke off, recalling Dr Osbourne's presence. 'And how is Olwen now?'

'Miss Malkon?' the doctor deflected the question to her.

'Much recovered, thank you, Aunt.'

'Then I wonder that you did not rejoin us, my dear, when Edmond did.'

Olwen was spared more by the arrival of her uncle, his vestments billowing around him like a cloud of sanctity. 'My poor dear Olwen. You're better now, I trust? And Dr Osbourne, thank you! How timely. . . So kind. Such a sad time. . . Come back to the vicarage and eat with us. Do!' His wife made as if to interject but the vicar was pressing. 'There's a fine joint of beef, I'm told. You'll come, won't you? Such a service to us. . . Edmond, run ahead, would you, and tell them to set another place.' His eye fell on his elder son and he added, with less enthusiasm, 'Two extra places, Edmond. . . tell them two.'

'My dear Mr Malkon.' His wife laid a hand on his arm. 'Dr Osbourne might already have his dinner prepared for him. Or indeed there might be patients requiring his services.' Her smile was brittle, hardly a smile at all.

'Are there?' The vicar stretched his head forward like an earnest tortoise. 'And have you?'

'I've neither dinner set for me nor patients waiting and I'd be delighted to come.' The doctor gave a little bow to Mrs Malkon and perhaps it was only Olwen who caught the irony in it.

CHAPTER 3

The vicar led the way down the churchyard path, sweeping the doctor along, bending to him in close conversation as he held open the gate into the vicarage demesne. The parish of Kirkthorpe lay some twelve miles east of York and it was not a demanding living, in fact it was a very pleasant one, and it had been in his older brother's gift. The parishioners were country folk and either biddable and faithful, or indifferent to his ministry, and the living provided the family with a lovely old vicarage that had settled itself into a pastoral landscape, from where the vicar and his wife continued traditions they had neither the wish nor will to change.

But what was being said with such earnestness, Olwen wondered as she made to follow her uncle, conscious of her aunt's annoyance piercing her from behind. 'Are you given to funny turns, m'dear?' Alfred asked, tucking her arm firmly into his.

She resisted the urge to remove it. 'No. I'm not.'

'Simply an aversion to Pa's sermons, eh? We're in agreement there, hence my unavoidable delay.' She gave him a brief smile. Alfred, without the means to set up his own establishment, was straining at the parental leash.

Since she had arrived at the vicarage Olwen had not joined the family for Sunday dinner but had her meals brought up to her room and had been excused from Sunday service until today. 'You will find it helpful,' the vicar had informed her over breakfast, smiling his most benign smile. 'A time for reflection, during which you'll discover the comfort of Our Lord. And now that you're better you can eat your dinner with us too, can't she, my dear?'

His wife had nodded. 'Susan can't be at your beck and call forever, you know. She has other duties to perform.'

It had been the vicar's benevolent custom to invite one or two of his parishioners to join his family for Sunday dinner each week following the service but he had not done so since Olwen's arrival, on account of their recent bereavements. The doctor, he announced as they assembled at the dinner table, beaming across at his guest, was an entirely appropriate exception. 'Especially given your timely assistance in the church, Doctor, so kind. . . and besides, we've not yet had the chance to welcome you to the village.' And, as he carved the beef, the vicar proceeded to repeat the lesson the doctor had given Olwen on the church's history. 'My late brother, Olwen's father, was fascinated by its antiquity. Dr Henly, of the Philosophical and Antiquarian Society, believes there was an early monastery here, which would explain the presence of those extraordinary carved fragments. Alfred tells me you were looking at them.' He gave Dr Osbourne a swift appraising glance as he passed him a plate. 'Thought to be parts of a free-standing cross, I understand, of Anglo-Saxon date. I've asked a local stonemason to see how far it might be reconstructed.'

The doctor glanced at Olwen, who avoided the look, clasping her hands tightly together under the table as she saw again the drilled eyes of the seated figure staring out into a place beyond that fog of fear. 'The general upkeep of the churchyard must be quite an expense,' he remarked. She sensed him trying to move the subject on and was grateful.

'Oh, indeed it is, my dear sir. And inexcusably hard to find parishioners willing to maintain even their own family graves, let alone help to keep the paths raked and the edges trim.' The doctor's success, however, was short-lived. 'Another such cross has been reconstructed from fragments found at Ruthwell, I'm told, where it once stood to almost twenty feet in height. Imagine that in our own little churchyard.'

From nowhere a picture flew into Olwen's mind. . . a mighty cross standing before a tall and narrow church, looming out of the darkness. . . The image was gone in an instant but she felt

the hairs lift on the back of her neck and looked up to see the
doctor considering her from across the table. That exchange did
not escape her aunt, who pursed her lips and interrupted her
husband's flow. 'You trained in Edinburgh, I understand, Doctor,'
she said. 'Are you Edinburgh born and bred?'

'No, Mrs Malkon. My home is south of there, in a tiny place
called Halterburn, in the Borders, not far from Kelso.'

Olwen looked up, diverted. 'In the land of Walter Scott! I adore
his Waverley novels, I've read them all; they describe such a
landscape.' Her aunt was frowning at her again, having no time
for such nonsense, but the doctor smiled.

'Aye, he paints a grand romantic picture, doesn't he? And I
share the man's enthusiasm, it's a beautiful part of the country,
although he's bequeathed it a reputation for cattle raiding, bloody
feuds and bold abductions.'

'Dear me,' said the vicar, vaguely. 'How dreadful! No wonder
you came south.'

The doctor's eyes sparked with amusement and he opened his
mouth to clarify his remark, but the vicar's wife was before him.
'So what brought you to Kirkthorpe, Doctor?'

'I'm a country man at heart,' their guest replied. 'Having been
in the city since I qualified, experience in a rural practice was
what I wanted.' Alfred gave a snort; in his view, village life was
dull beyond bearing. 'And it brings me close to York where, as
we were discussing earlier,' the doctor nodded to the vicar, 'such
interesting work is taking place on afflictions of the mind.'

So that had been their discussion!

And which of them, Olwen wondered, bristling silently, had
raised the matter. Afflictions of the mind. . . Her thoughts were
certainly disordered, driven by a storm of emotions that swirled
around her head, for sorrow and remorse did not make for an
easy mind.

Afflictions indeed.

How swiftly all had changed, she thought as the vicar reclaimed
the conversation, and she suppressed a sigh. Meals at Swindale
had been so different; her brothers' chatter, interspersed with

their tutor's quiet rebukes and Celia's attempts to distract their father, had given them a vitality. Better still were the days when her father had claimed fatigue, taking his meals in the library, for then restraint had been lifted and the conversation had become more lively and enlightening, with both tutor and governess subtly shaping the young Malkons' opinions and powers of reasoning.

Following his wife's demise, Olwen's inattentive parent had engaged Celia Goodfellow as governess-companion without stirring himself to enquire beyond her excellent references. He had, therefore, remained unaware of the radical and progressive ideas that quiet lady was instilling in his daughter's receptive mind. Olwen was taught to think for herself, to be inquisitive and to challenge preconceptions, as well as learning how to manage a household, guided in practical matters by the experienced hand of Mrs Percy, the housekeeper. Percy, her long-suffering husband, was devoted to his master, dealing patiently with his endless illnesses and complaints. The boys were left to their tutor, an eccentric but broad-minded young man, and in Celia's care Olwen had been happy in a way that she only now fully appreciated when the likelihood of regaining such a state seemed impossibly remote.

Looking around the table, she realised despairingly how complete had been her loss, reduced to the status of a dependant, a poor relation, in terms of position if not of wealth. Her opinions were neither sought nor approved of and any she might express were invariably corrected, while the strictures under which she was expected to live brought daily frustration. Unreasonable as it was, Olwen found it hard to forgive her father for placing her under the guardianship of the vicar. He had done so in a flurried panic when it became clear that he was, after all, quite seriously ill, and the possibility had begun to loom that he would die before Olwen achieved her majority. She had known her uncle, of course, but not well and had always considered him a fool, while her aunt was a shrew whose disapproval of Olwen was thinly veiled. 'She's given far too much licence by That Woman,' Olwen had once heard her telling the vicar, having crossed swords with Celia over several aspects of her upbringing.

Six months, she thought, looking around the table again, and then she would be free of them. She had only to endure. . .

Coming back into the moment, she saw that Alfred was watching their guest with a dark expression while the doctor, she noticed, was encouraging the vicar to continue with what was becoming a second sermon, freeing him to give appreciative attention to his dinner. Perhaps the man had an indifferent cook, she thought, diverted and amused.

'Some more parsnips, Doctor?' her aunt asked, interrupting the flow.

'Yes, do,' urged the vicar, 'they are our own.' But, as if suddenly self-conscious, the parsnips were refused and the table cleared for dessert. 'We grow all our own vegetables and we've a fine established orchard,' her uncle continued, gesturing to the fruit pie that was brought through. 'Cooking apples, eating apples, plums and pears and each year I grow peaches in the hot house.' And then, with a wholly unconvincing start: 'Why Olwen must show you, after we have eaten. Yes, that would be delightful for you! Spring has come early this year and the blossom is well set. Yes, indeed, my dear, you must take the doctor outside after luncheon and show him.'

Her aunt, however, disliked the plan. 'There's a chill to the wind,' she said. 'And it's bad for the digestion to walk straight after eating—'

'No, no, my dear,' the vicar countered gravely. 'If one were to *run* around the orchard then, yes, but surely a walk, or an amble. . .'

Alfred rolled his eyes and looked across at Olwen. 'Which are you inclined to, Olwen, an amble or a run?'

She bit back a smile as the vicar rebuked him. 'She must walk! Alfred. A slow walk, don't you think, Doctor? And take a shawl, Olwen, consider your aunt's advice.' Oh, how absurd it all was, Olwen thought, digging her fingernails into her palm. 'Olwen has nothing whatsoever to detain her,' her uncle assured their guest, and that much was true. 'Go along now, my dear, it will do you good. The early Pearmains are perhaps where you should start.'

'No running, Olwen,' Alfred reminded her as she rose.

The doctor looked across at her with consternation as he too rose. 'If you're quite sure. . .' but the vicar's napkin flapped them on their way.

Olwen led the way through the conservatory and out into the vicarage garden where flower-filled borders edged neat lawns sloping down towards the orchards. A little to one side there was a well-tended vegetable plot, framed by high brick walls. A glasshouse standing against one of these was where the vicar nurtured his peaches, although Olwen had it on Edmond's authority that only one or two were brought to maturity each year and had the taste and texture of blotting paper.

The doctor followed her down a gravel path, saying nothing, and when they reached the trees Olwen stopped and turned to him. 'So, Doctor Osbourne, are you sent to draw me out and determine whether I have an affliction of the mind?'

He did not trouble to deny it. 'That was certainly your uncle's intention, if rather clumsily achieved. And if you'd oblige me by running wildly through the orchard, I might have more to report back than what I've already told him.' Taken by surprise, she laughed. 'Ah!' he remarked, with a twinkle. 'I shall certainly report that laugh; a very positive sign.'

Instantly she frowned at him. 'You might also like to report that I find having my every move, thought and activity monitored and remarked upon quite impossible to bear.'

'An affliction indeed.'

'And if I'm not already unbalanced I soon will be as I cannot live like this, not even for six months.' The bitterness spilled out; she had not meant to expose her feelings quite so openly and made an attempt at levity. 'Unless you will prescribe me daily laudanum.'

'Six months?' he enquired, ignoring her last remark. 'What happens then?'

'I reach my majority and can go home and be my own mistress again.'

'Well, one can endure more or less anything for six months,

even without the deadly tincture. Can you not find something
to occupy your time?'

'A distraction? Nothing, I'm told, is more beneficial to the
mind than a distraction.'

He smiled again, acknowledging the hit. 'Do you play an
instrument, perhaps, or indulge in watercolour painting, or could
you write bad verse like so many do? Any, or all, of those will
do, you know. Set yourself a routine and, if you like, I shall
recommend that you be left alone to pursue such interests.' He
paused and she found her resentment evaporating, but he went
on looking at her, his expression unreadable.

'Shall you attend church next week?' he asked abruptly and
at once fear clutched at her heart and she looked away, biting
her lip. 'Ah,' he said, watching her and then, when she said
nothing, 'You can confide in me, you know, if you wish. . .'

She walked on.

'The mention of the cross fragments during dinner disturbed
you a little, I think,' he persisted, from a pace or two behind her.
'I saw you blanch. Can you describe for me what you felt?'

She carried on through the orchard, saying nothing, conscious
of him following.

Beyond the boundary wall lay the marshy flood plain and
beyond the ings flowed the River Nidd, swollen after the spring
rains. Farmers who grazed their animals there sometimes lost
one or two when the river levels rose suddenly. It was treacherous,
unpredictable land. Today, though, the river flowed tranquilly
through the flat countryside and, on the far bank, black and white
cows had come down to drink, standing ankle deep in the shallows. She halted, looking across at them, and the doctor came
and stood beside her, his hands in his pockets, saying nothing
but following her gaze. 'It was the eyes,' she said, at last, 'the eyes
of the seated figure, they seemed to drill right into me. Piercing
white eyes looking out in the darkness. . .'

'White?'

'They've little white stones, or chalk in them.'

'Have they?' He looked puzzled. 'How do you know?'

She hesitated. 'I'm not sure, but I do.'

'So you'd seen the fragments before?'

'Yes. . .' She felt suddenly confused. 'At least. . . no, I've not. . .'

He frowned. 'Someone showed them to you, perhaps? But in the darkness?' He took a step closer, searching her face. 'Explain, if you can?'

She looked aside. 'I've not seen the carvings until today and yet. . . and yet they were familiar. I have seen them before.'

'Or something like them?'

'Perhaps.' She would not argue, but no, it was that same seated figure, she recognised it with certainty, a deep carving, painted in bright colours, halfway up the shaft of the cross, on a side facing away from the church towards the path, lit by a harvest moon. But if she told him that he would surely think her mad.

'When we're fearful,' he remarked, his eyes still on her face, 'our eyes open wide and our pupils dilate, they too expand. Is there something that you fear, Miss Malkon?' He paused but she made no reply. 'Your uncle says that you often cry out in the night. . . wildly sometimes.'

And at that, blinded by unbidden tears, she turned away and walked quickly back towards the house.

CHAPTER 4

Is there something that you fear?

Olwen considered the question frequently in the days that followed and at night as she lay in her bed longing for the oblivion of sleep, and yet dreading the dreams that she knew would come. They were intensifying on a nightly basis; strange dreams that defied explanation and were beginning to develop an odd, almost episodic coherence to them. Was it her fear for an unknown future which brought them on, she wondered. Her aunt and uncle's expectations of her were well known and hung above her like a dark cloud, while Alfred considered the matter settled between them.

But she did not doubt her ability to refuse him when he came to make a formal offer.

For Celia had taught her to know her mind.

So why, she asked herself, was she haunted by these strange all-consuming dreams?

Tonight she had retired early to her room and lay in bed frowning into the darkness, and wondered again why she had heard nothing from her erstwhile companion. No letters had arrived, her aunt had told her, and Celia had provided no forwarding address. It was very strange, so unlike her, and Olwen would have welcomed her counsel. 'Quiet but firm resolution, Wen, once you have decided upon a matter,' had been amongst Celia's maxims, as she urged her charge to resist her father's matrimonial scheming. 'Avoid producing a drama; it's what they expect but it undermines us and plays into their hands, and so they call us weak and nervy. We're only weak, my dear, if we allow others to be powerful.' Celia herself had been the very embodiment of calm, but determined, rebellion.

When it did come to turning Alfred down, she knew there would be a terrible scene and wanted to avoid him making a declaration until she felt stronger. For now, her mourning black protected her, but one day soon the matter would undoubtedly be raised and she bitterly blamed her father for ever promoting the match. 'I must know you are in safe hands, my dear,' he had said, his skin cold and clammy as he held her hand. The lustre of good health had long departed from his face, and his lip had trembled, but she had refused to submit. 'If not Alfred,' he had persisted, plucking at the bedclothes, 'then Edmond. He's young, I know, but a kindly fellow. A betrothal, perhaps, to give me peace of mind?'

She locked her hands behind her head and stared up at the ceiling. Edmond! How little her father had understood her that he could suggest such a thing.

Celia had taught her that she must determine her own destiny. 'What is so often portrayed as kindly protection, is control thinly disguised. Don't let men fool you with soft words and flattery.' And the doctor. Was he the same? He had been so very sure of himself, so glib, so ready to recommend routine as a cure, urging her to fill her days with genteel pursuits, distract herself from her woes.

But this apprehension, this sense of dread, was surely more than the distress of the moment or a fear of the future. She frowned into the darkness. It was more, surely, than simple grief.

And what if she had told the doctor about her dreams, about her growing confusion between the real and the unreal, of landscapes that blurred and altered in front of her. Recently the stones too had appeared, in fleeting glimpses, in her dreams and even now her mind scuttled away from the thought of the carved figure with its drilled eyes. Sometimes there was a man there, standing beside the cross, demanding obedience from her. And she recalled other scenes that seemed so real, wolf-hounds beside a smoking fire, the sound of roistering men, the clatter of horses' hooves on cobblestones. Once or twice these last few days, she had had strange liminal experiences when she seemed to slip into a state of grief and anxiety that was separate from her own, running parallel and powerful, but quite distinct, and sometimes she would wake, conscious of a sense of expectation, of waiting.

Of hope.

And of a name that hovered there, just beyond her grasp. . .

Should she tell the doctor all of that? He would think her deranged!

She sat up, bent her knees and clasped the blanket tight around them. As a child struggling to come to terms with the terrible loss of her mother, she had taken refuge from the world by concocting stories in her head, insulating herself, playing a central role in dramas drawn from the books she read, adopting bold attitudes and performing heroic acts in exotic or wild locations. Her *alter ego,* her imaginary self, was frequently a person of high rank, often in disguise or in hiding, and was more adventurous and passionate than she could ever imagine being. Some of her inventions would run on in her mind for weeks, becoming ever more engrossing as incident after incident befell her second self, and she had taken great comfort in this parallel, secret life; it became a way of keeping loneliness at bay, of escaping the limitations of her existence. And then Celia had arrived and seemed to understand and had gently, but firmly, encouraged her to delight in the real world instead and the fantasies, having served their purpose, gradually faded away.

But now. . . Now it was as if her *alter ego* had resurfaced and taken command, turning the tables on her, inventing stories over which she had no control but in which she must perform, investing her with emotions more powerful than any she had imagined. It had been a real, visceral fear she had felt that morning when she had looked out of her window, and seen the world change before her eyes.

The week passed without further incident but, as Sunday approached, an uneasiness grew in her again. The very thought of entering the church made her heart thud and her breathing quicken. She found it terrifying to contemplate attending morning service, but her only hope of avoiding it was to claim continuing ill health and, if this was to be successful, she must get her uncle on her side.

And so, before breakfast on the following Sunday, knowing that the vicar would be in the study preparing his sermon, she tripped lightly down the stairs and pushed open the door. He looked up as she entered. 'Olwen!' but his welcoming smile vanished at the sight of her. 'My dear girl, whatever's wrong? So pale.'

She grasped the opening. 'Uncle, I don't feel well at all. My head aches and I. . . I have palpitations.'

He rose in a fluster, papers cascading from his desk to the floor. 'Then we must call at once for Dr Osbourne. He must come,' and he had reached for the bell pull before she could stop him.

'Uncle! No. . . really. If I might be simply be allowed to stay in my room this morning and rest—'

'No doctor?' he said to her, his neck extending. Susan appeared. 'No church? Fetch your mistress, girl.'

Her aunt arrived but showed little sympathy. 'A walk to church, and sitting quietly through the service, will do you no harm whatsoever.' She put a hand to Olwen's forehead. 'You've no fever.'

'But I might cause another disturbance.' Panic was ballooning in her.

The woman's eyes narrowed. 'I trust you will not.'

'Indeed, she *must* not.' The vicar took Olwen's hand, then frowned and turned it over to examine it. 'Why, my dear, your palm is quite clammy. . . On balance,' he said, eyeing his wife with some wariness, 'it might be best if she spent the morning in private worship and contemplation, if she *is* feeling unwell.'

Her aunt was not fooled, visibly torn between wanting to thwart Olwen and avoiding the possibility that her husband's niece might make another mortifying scene. Caution triumphed and Olwen spent an idle morning in her room reading, and staring out of the window, revelling in the knowledge that she was alone in the house. All too soon, though, she heard noises signalling the return of the household. She had closed her book, intending to go down and proclaim herself recovered enough to eat, when a brisk knock came at the door. It opened to reveal her aunt, and behind her, Dr Osbourne.

'Your uncle felt it wise to ask the doctor to return,' the woman said, taking in the book on Olwen's lap, the Bible unopened on the bed. 'Although in my view there's very little amiss.'

Dr Osbourne's jacket was as crumpled as it had been the previous Sunday. 'How are you feeling now, Miss Malkon?'

'Rather better, thank you.'

He stepped across to her and put a hand on her forehead. 'Can you describe your symptoms?'

'A headache, and. . . and palpitations and, at the time, I felt a little fevered but that has passed.'

The lie was swiftly exposed. 'She had no fever.' Ignoring her aunt, Dr Osbourne took Olwen's wrist between his fingers, releasing it a moment later without comment.

'And the headache?'

'Also better.'

He bent then and stared intently into her eyes, switching his gaze from one to the other in a cool professional appraisal. 'You don't wear spectacles?' She shook her head. 'And you've been reading.' He cricked his neck to see the title of the book and she saw his eyebrows raise. 'Have you eaten today?' Another shake and her stomach growled in confirmation. He made no remark but she sensed a smile. 'And have you been outdoors?'

'No.'

He swung round to address her aunt. 'Sometimes the body is simply out of sorts, Mrs Malkon. Might I suggest that I accompany your niece for a turn around the garden to ensure myself that all is well, and that she then eats her dinner as usual? Please convey my thanks to the vicar, and my apologies, but I regret that I am unable to join you today.'

Once outdoors, he walked beside her as before, his hands behind his back. 'Is there anything more that I should know?' he asked.

'No.' He glanced at her. 'I. . . I didn't want to create another scene.'

'Understandable, but why would you?'

She sensed that he was less interested, more detached, than he had been last week. In fact, she doubted that he was taking her seriously at all. She made no reply and he continued in a dry tone he had not used before. 'Forgive me, Miss Malkon, but might I remark that for a young lady who has suffered three recent bereavements, your choice of reading matter is unwise.' She stopped and turned to face him, feeling her blood rise in indignation. 'While I commend my countryman's storytelling skills,' he went on, with a smile, 'I very much doubt that the exploits of Dr Jeykll and Mr Hyde provide an ideal distraction in the circumstances.' He paused, perhaps awaiting some response, but she had clamped her jaw shut. 'Declining food is likely to make you light-headed, you know, so I recommend that you tuck in very heartily to whatever the vicar's excellent cook brings to table.'

She narrowed her eyes at him. 'You believe I contrive to make myself interesting.'

'No, no. I simply suggest that these factors, combined with your understandably disturbed emotions, and a recent feverish cold, might explain your present—'

'In other words, I've only myself to blame?'

He met her furious gaze quite unabashed. 'We speak in confidence, Miss Malkon, but I don't believe you felt ill today. I believe you wanted to avoid going to church, though I'm not exactly sure why.' His expression softened. 'These are difficult times for you, I know, and the mind, when unbalanced by strong emotion, becomes chaotic, and chaos is aptly defined as disorder and confusion. What you require is a period of calm; healing the mind takes time, like any other wounding. I will speak to your uncle and recommend forbearance.' He paused again but she remained silent. 'And so here is my prescription,' he ticked off the points on his fingers. 'Jane Austen for entertainment, good food, regular exercise, followed by a natural, unaided sleep. And now, if you'll forgive me, I'll leave you to enjoy this lovely garden.'

CHAPTER 5

John Osbourne, having reported to the vicar, left the vicarage feeling a little contrite. Perhaps he had been too brusque with the girl, too dismissive. In the course of the week he had learned from his housekeeper the sad story of her brothers' deaths and from her uncle he had just heard a little more, and it had been a tragedy, right enough. Drowned, poor lads, on an ornamental lake almost within sight of their house, the rowing boat sinking through a layer of ice. And their distraught father following them to the grave only weeks later.

No wonder the girl was all to pieces.

Her mother, the vicar had informed him, had died giving birth to the younger boy when Miss Malkon was a girl of nine. 'My brother always was a. . . a. . . a difficult man but after losing his wife he became reclusive, burying himself in his books. He was never a well man and went into a steep decline after the boys' death. So sad. Quite tragic. We did what we could for him, of course—'

'What he'd agree to, that is, given his nature,' Mrs Malkon had interjected, and examining her granite features John had wondered if he had fallen short in his duty towards a young woman left in that harridan's care.

But he was a physician, he told himself, and it seemed to him that Olwen Malkon required emotional rather than medical attention – although she probably got precious little of that. The Reverend Malkon had also confided that she could be an obstinate girl. 'Her governess had rather *modern* views, if you take my meaning.' Any innovative idea of the last fifty years, John reckoned.

His wife had sniffed. 'She was a bad influence on the girl.'

'And is, I regret to say, now living a *most* irregular life.' The vicar had taken out his handkerchief and held it to his nose.

Aye, Miss Malkon was, on all counts, to be pitied, he thought as he closed the gate between the vicarage and the churchyard, but the cold truth was that there was little he could do to improve things for her, other than prescribe some poison to dull the senses – which he would never do. Grief was not an illness, after all, it was a natural reaction to loss, and served a purpose, albeit a painful one. No, it must be endured; let her once fall into the grip of opiates and she was lost.

He had, though, found himself thinking rather more about Miss Olwen Malkon than he ought to have done this past week, and to his embarrassment he had also dreamed of her. It had been a curious dream that for some reason had included her dead brothers, tousled-haired lads, very much alive, their sad fates yet un-signalled. And in the bizarre way of dreams he had given them some trinket to pass on to their sister, a bangle, or some such, and they had exchanged knowing grins at being given the task of go-betweens. He had woken with a vivid image of her wearing it pushed up high on the soft flesh of her upper arm. . .

He frowned, taking himself sternly to task. She was, without question, an attractive young woman and he must take care. Her mouth was perhaps a little too wide but he liked her defiant chin and he had seen her eyes suddenly light with humour, signalling that beneath her current anxieties there was a lively mind. Their colour was essentially blue, he had noted, but looking into them just now they had darkened to an extraordinary, almost violet, hue.

He wandered through the churchyard, musing on the case, passing the spot where the vicar had accosted him earlier that morning, begging him to visit his niece again. Pushing open the church door, he was assailed by the sickly sweetness of the spring flowers – such a contrast with the spartan churches of his home-land – and he strolled down the aisle to the place where she had frozen the week before, recalling the panic in her eyes. Undoubtedly her illness today was a sham, but that episode had been genuine and she clearly feared a repetition. How strange. . .

He surveyed the nave for anything that might have triggered the incident but drew a blank. In places the plaster had dropped away, revealing a wall of roughly coursed stones with others above set like books aslant on a bookshelf, alternating on each succeeding course, zigzagging their way up the tower, herringbone fashion. This must be the ancient work the vicar had described to him but there was surely nothing there to spark her fear. Quite the reverse in fact; the church looked serene and timeless, the flowers and wands of pussy willow adding a gentle mellowness. Never one for the church and its rituals, he had, with native cynicism, recognised that acceptance in this little community would be furthered by his attendance at their church. And it was no hardship, after all, a moment's quiet reflection was always to be welcomed, and he sat for a while in one of the pews.

He had not been entirely frank with the vicar's wife about his reasons for coming south. The patient he had described to Olwen as being hopelessly addicted to laudanum had, in fact, been a senior colleague's wife to whom he had been sent to assess her condition. She was a mature, voluptuous woman whose distress, John had rapidly concluded, derived from boredom and neglect. After one or two visits during which she had refused to consider reducing her consumption of the opiate, she had made unwelcome advances. Tactfully declining her offer of intimacies, he had reminded himself that a heightened sensuality was a common feature of addiction and had concocted a reason for withdrawing from her case. Her husband, however, had appalled him by making it clear that he would turn a blind eye to any 'treatment' he could offer his wife, implying that John's reputation for open-mindedness had recommended him to both himself, and the lady. John had backed away but it soon became apparent that his refusal to be drawn in and provide what his colleague was either unwilling, or unable, to supply himself had not only scuppered his chance of preferment but had made him a powerful enemy.

As he had no influential friends to counter this very active hostility, being of a different class, he had had no alternative but to leave Edinburgh, a disillusioned though wiser man. Sensual dreams concerning Olwen Malkon, therefore, served as a painful reminder of the pitfalls of his profession.

Stepping back out into spring sunshine he pushed these dismal thoughts aside and smiled, remembering her choice of reading matter. He had read the novella himself, intrigued by the dark duality of its characters. It was a fashionable theme these days; literature was rife with twins and doppelgangers, and even medical science had its own angle on the matter. Although tangential to his medical training, he had developed an interest in diseases of the mind and tried to keep abreast of developments in that area. Recently he had read papers discussing how afflictions that manifested themselves in unrecognisable or bizarre conduct need not, as had previously been thought, necessarily indicate a permanently altered state for individual sufferers; out-of-character behaviour might be episodic, intermittent. Doctors in Vienna and Zurich were at the forefront of this new thinking, building on the work of French colleagues, determined that the vagaries of the mind should be better understood. He had read with fascination their insistence that dual, or indeed multiple, personalities might reside in a single afflicted patient and how hypnosis, once generally discredited, had been used, with varying degrees of success, to coax disruptive *alter egos* out of the shadows.

To his shame he had attempted hypnosis once himself, when drunk with fellow students. They had been involved in a lively and increasingly riotous discussion of the method following a lecture on the subject and had recklessly decided to put it to the test. Pooling their resources, they had persuaded an obliging streetwalker to submit herself to an experiment and he had drawn the short straw as the one to conduct the trial. He had made the mistake once of mentioning his mother's Romany blood and had consequently been mocked by some and shunned by others, and amongst his friends he had subsequently been endowed with insights and abilities that he consistently denied. On this occasion, during the experiment, he had somehow managed to put the girl under and, to his profound relief, had also brought her safely back to reason. How much had been a performance on her part, a desire to oblige, he was never sure, and later, when he had come to understand the perils of such procedures, he had felt rather ashamed of the episode.

He strolled on through the churchyard and, hearing voices, turned to see two men over by the compost heap, apparently lifting one of the carved cross fragments onto a wheelbarrow. He went closer. In his dismissal of the girl's symptoms he had forgotten about that second incident. It was the eyes, she had said, drilling into her.

The men straightened and touched their caps as he approached. 'Heavy work, that,' he remarked.

One man spat. 'Vicar's wants them shifting to the vicarage garden but the Lord knows why. Said it was fitting work for a Sunday.' His view was evidently at variance.

'They're of some antiquity, I'm told.' She had reacted oddly at dinner last week too, John remembered, when the stones were mentioned. 'Are there many with carving on them?'

'Can't say. They're half buried.' Sour looks indicated an opinion that they would have been better left that way. The stone in the wheelbarrow was the one John had shown Miss Malkon and he bent to examine it again, pulling out the folding magnifying glass he carried with him. She was right, the eyes of the seated figure were a little alarming with their narrow unflinching stare, and he peered into them.

Frowning, he drew back, then looked again.

Traces of some white substance adhered to the pit of the drilled eye. Chalk? It was just a fleck, visible only under magnification. But how could she possibly have known? He stood there, perplexed, then became aware of the men watching him. 'Fascinating,' he said, with a breezy smile, and walked on through the churchyard.

He continued to puzzle over the matter as he opened his front door, and his thoughts dwelt on Miss Malkon as he ate his solitary dinner, ignoring the pile of patients' notes at the other end of the table. On Sundays the arrangement was that his housekeeper left his dinner in the oven and he would clear away himself, allowing her the rest of the day at liberty. She was a plain cook at best and the half-congealed Sunday dinner was hardly appetising but he ate it and, with his chores done, decided that the task of trying to make sense of his predecessor's chaotic record keeping could no longer be deferred.

He pulled the pile of papers towards him and was deeply engrossed, struggling to decipher the scrawl that described the man's bizarre remedy for Mrs Braithwaite's rheumatism – more folklore than science – when he heard a pounding on the door. He went to answer it and found the vicarage housemaid gasping on the doorstep. 'Please, sir, you must come! It's Miss Malkon, she's fallen and hit her head.'

He reached at once for his jacket. 'Is she conscious?' he asked. 'Bleeding?' He snapped the clip on his medical bag and waved the girl out of the door ahead of him.

'Bleeding a little, sir, and. . . and well. . . sort of conscious, sort of not.'

'Meaning what?'

She turned a scared face to him. 'Comes and goes. Gabbling nonsense. And she rolls her eyes up, and all you can see is the whites.'

Damn! He had not considered epilepsy. But it was a fall, the girl had said. 'Was she alone when it happened?'

Susan nodded. 'She'd gone down to the orchard with her book after dinner. Mr Alfred went looking for her and then came running back.'

'Have they moved her?'

'Mr Alfred said better not to.'

'Good man.'

The vicar was waiting at the front door, wringing his hands, his face contorted with concern. 'I fear she's done herself damage, Doctor! I fear for her faculties.'

'Take me to her.' The wretched man was blocking the doorway.

'She keeps harping on about her brothers. Speaks of a betrayal! I can make nothing of it at all.'

John stepped purposefully forward and the vicar came to his senses and led him through the now familiar house and out into the garden where a little huddle was gathered beside by the glasshouse. The vicar's wife, he noted, was sat calmly on a chair that appeared to have come from the potting shed. 'Are all these people strictly necessary?' he asked, addressing her stonily. 'Perhaps just yourself—?'

'I shall stay,' Alfred said, folding his arms and standing his ground. The vicar also remained.

John shrugged and knelt beside the girl. He spoke her name. No response. Cautiously he examined her head where blood had stiffened her hair. 'Head wounds generally bleed a good deal,' he said, glancing up at Mrs Malkon.

'I said so myself,' she replied.

'You say she came to for a moment?' he asked, dismissing the wretched woman and addressing the vicar.

'Yes, but she made no sense. . . hardly conscious. . . clearly distressed.'

Carefully he felt along the girl's arms and shoulders, watching her face for any response. Nothing broken, it would seem. Slipping his hand beneath her skirts, he rapidly examined her legs for evidence of fractures. The vicar turned away with an exaggerated delicacy; his son, John noted, did not.

'Alfred,' his mother snapped. 'I don't see why you stay.'

'Because the good doctor might require assistance carrying her to the house.'

John glanced at him as he rose to his feet; a cold young man, he decided. His housekeeper, a notable gossip, had spoken of an engagement, awaiting the end of mourning to be announced, but he hoped she was wrong. He straightened and stood a moment looking down at the girl. Judging from the dried blood on her head she must have been lying there for some time, and he glanced up at the darkening skies; she would have to be moved.

'Have you something with which we could fashion a stretcher?'

he asked, turning to the vicar. 'Some planks, perhaps? I doubt very much that her back is injured but just to—' He broke off as the girl stirred, moving her head a little, her brow puckered and her lips parted. He dropped back to his knees. 'Miss Malkon, can you hear me?' She mumbled in response and he leaned close to catch the words. 'You've hit your head, but have you any other pain?'

Her eyelids fluttered open and with a shock he saw what the housemaid had described. Her eyes rolled back into her head, exposing the whites, and her body jerked in some sort of spasm. He put a hand to her arm and found her skin cold and clammy. He repeated her name. 'Can you hear me?' She stilled, and for a moment it seemed as if she did. 'Miss Malkon?' The jerking ceased and her eyes closed again and he saw that she had gone stiff, quite rigid in fact. Damnation. He had badly misjudged this case. He said her name once more but she seemed locked in a trance-like state.

Then he remembered again that unseemly experiment with the Edinburgh streetwalker and rapidly considered his options. A risk, certainly, but it had worked once and he was short of other ideas. He took a moment, trying to remember what he had done to bring the lass back to wakefulness, then glanced up, feeling a drop of rain. It was surely worth a try. 'Miss Malkon.' He spoke slowly,' in a quiet, steady voice. 'Olwen. . . Trust me, it's safe, I promise you.' Why had he said that! Of course, it was safe. 'Come back to us.' He paused, telling himself that she heard him. 'I want you to picture a flight of steps. There are ten steps, *ten* of them, and they are carpeted so your feet will make no sound.' Mrs Malkon made as if to speak but he raised his hand to silence her. By God, he'd look a fool if he failed. 'In a moment I'm going to count you up the stairs, and you'll come with me, and when you reach the tenth, you'll open your eyes, and be here with us.' He paused, looking for relaxation in the rigid muscles but seeing none. 'First step. Take a deep breath at each one.' Even the birds in the orchard fell silent, and the wind had ceased tossing the boughs of the fruit trees. He felt another drop of rain. Dear Lord, let this work. 'Now, breathe in.' Nothing. 'Second step.' Still nothing. 'Breathe, Olwen.' She remained in the same unconscious state but as he reached step six he sensed a change in her. She breathed out in a sigh. 'Well done. Now. . . step seven. Deep breath in. Good girl. Eight. Almost there.' Without a doubt her shoulders were relaxing, her jaw becoming slack. Excitement coursed through him. It was working! 'Nine, Olwen. Just one more step and then open your eyes. Trust me, you're quite safe.' At the tenth step her eyes opened quite naturally as if from a deep sleep and she looked up at him, studying his face. And then, as he watched, he saw her expression change and her eyes flooded with recognition. Overwhelmed with relief, he smiled down at her.

And, as if in response to the smile, she lifted her hand, very slowly. 'Heri!' she said, and caressed his cheek.

CHAPTER 6

John's smile froze. He stood and exchanged a startled look with her uncle. 'Speak to her, Vicar,' he said, more shaken than he could let on.

The vicar knelt heavily beside his niece. 'Olwen, my dear. You fell, poor child, and hit your head but you'll be all right presently.' He took possession of her hand and stroked it awkwardly, turning back to John. 'Should she try and sit?' John nodded and watched confusion flit across the girl's face.

'Uncle?' she asked, in a very different voice, withdrawing her hand and raising it to her brow. 'I fell?'

'Yes, my dear!' the vicar cried. 'But you're all right now, just a little shaken. Can you stand? I think you must, my dear, as I believe it's starting to rain.'

Between them, her uncle and cousin got her to her feet and, with one on either side, they assisted her back towards the house. Mrs Malkon rose, fired a suspicious glance at John, and followed the others without a word, and it was then that he saw that behind the seated woman, laid out on the gravel in an approximation of a cross, were the carved stone fragments brought from the church-yard that morning.

Edmond, who had withdrawn obediently to the orchard, had returned to watch the recovery and now he walked beside John. 'Odd that,' he remarked, glancing at him. 'Her mistaking you.'

'Odd, yes.' Quite unaccountable, in fact. John's mind was working furiously. Was it the sight of the stones that had caused this? 'But she recognised your father straight away.' And thank God she had; it had been a bad moment.

By the time he reached the house Miss Malkon had been

settled in a chair in the morning room, a rug on her knees, and was looking around in a bewildered way. Still pale, he noticed as he crossed the room to her, but her eyes were now alert, and of this world. Susan had been sent for a bowl of warm water and he took it and began cleaning the matted blood in order to examine the wound. She gave a sudden shiver at his touch, and he stopped. 'I'm hurting you?'

'No.'

He resumed, more gently. 'How are you feeling now?'

'A. . . a little confused.' She rolled her head experimentally from side to side.

The cut, when revealed, was not a deep one but he made a pad of lint and wound a bandage around her head. 'Very much the brigand now, Miss Malkon,' he said, peering into her eyes. Pupils behaving normally, no cause for concern there but what an extraordinary colour they were. Quite violet now. 'Some tea, perhaps?' he suggested, addressing the vicar's wife. 'And, I think, a little space. . .' They were all clustered around again. 'I'll stay a moment and speak to you before I leave.' He nodded at the vicar, who took the hint and waved his sons out of the room ahead of him. Susan went for tea but Mrs Malkon stayed put.

Wishing the woman to the devil, John turned to Olwen. 'Can you remember what happened?' he asked. 'Did you trip, perhaps, or come over feeling faint again?' She shook her head. 'Is this the time for your courses, by any chance?'

'No.'

Would she mention the carved stones? 'Can you remember anything at all from before you fell?'

Another little head shake. 'I just woke to find myself lying there, and everyone clustered around me. And. . . some stairs, or steps.'

A guarded look had replaced the confused one and he was intrigued, but could hardly interrogate her further with her aunt sat there, glowering. He glanced at the book that someone had brought up from the garden, noting wryly that his advice had been ignored. 'You'd gone outside to read?' he asked, gesturing to it.

'Yes.' Her chin came up in defiance, which he acknowledged with a brief smile.

'And nothing else hurts?'

'No. I am quite well now, thank you,' she said. There was an unmistakable note of dismissal in her voice and so he rose, gave a few words of advice regarding rest and food, and took his leave.

He encountered the vicar hovering in the hall. 'What did you glean, Doctor?' he asked, beckoning him into the study.

'Very little, I'm afraid. A momentary faintness, perhaps. I think she would remember a stumble or a trip.'

The vicar had the full round face of an ageing cherub, pale and doughy, and it was glowing now with an anxious sheen. 'Dear me. But I must say how grateful. . . how remarkable. . . the way you spoke . . . coaxing her back as you did. Quite extraordinary!' John wondered privately whether she might have stirred then anyway, although she had remembered the steps. 'Most concerning,' the vicar went on, 'that expression. . . her eyes. . . I thought her senses quite deranged.'

'For a moment only. She knew you straight away.' John paused, then grasped the issue. 'Vicar, last week, in the churchyard, when I was showing your niece the carved stones she had another odd attack—'

'An *attack*?'

'A sort of panic. I noticed just now that she had fallen close to where the stones had been laid out and it occurs to me that she might have come across them, unexpectedly, and that the same thing might have happened. I think. . . I really do advise you to move them, or cover them up, until we have got to the bottom of these seizures.' The vicar peered back at him. 'The recently bereaved, Vicar, can have the oddest fancies.'

'I'll see to it straight away. But how peculiar, how very strange! One might expect the iconography to bring comfort rather than distress, but if you say we must, then of course it will be done.' He paused, bafflement writ large on his face. 'And she called you Harry!' he said.

The doctor shrugged. 'Unaccountable,' he agreed and took his leave, promising to visit again in the morning.

But he was not to escape so easily; as he proceeded down the path Alfred Malkon stepped out from behind the bushes. 'How is she?' he demanded.

'Recovering. No real damage done and she's having a cup of tea. Was she just lying there when you found her?'

The young man drew himself up and scowled. 'What are you suggesting?'

'I merely enquire.' This reaction, though, gave John a moment's pause.

'She was,' Alfred said ungraciously, and John made to continue down the path. 'She called you Harry,' he moved to block him again.

'Perhaps I resemble someone of that name.'

The scowl deepened. 'Seemed to know him rather well.'

'She'd hit her head, man!'

'And you called her Olwen!'

John raised an eyebrow. Ridiculous fellow. 'What is you are suggesting, Mr Malkon?' Alfred said no more but the scowl remained. 'Nothing? Then I'll take my leave of you. Good day.'

He continued on his way. Unaccountable, yes, he thought as he strode back towards home, a blow to the head, yes, but there had been such a look in her eyes when she first opened them. If he had been asked to describe it, he would have said it was a look of joy, of relief, and of. . . something much more profound.

Harry, she had called him, but with the *a* softened to an *e* – Herry - as if his mother had spoken it, with her soft Scottish burr.

When the door closed behind the doctor Olwen turned her head away and stared out at the garden. They had told her what happened, she had tripped, they said, and fallen and banged her head. And they had found her unconscious, they said, a little confused when she woke. No one knew how long she had lain there before Alfred found her, and no one had seen her fall.

Her aunt rose and left the room without a word, and Olwen put her head back and closed her eyes.

Trust me, you are safe.

She could still hear his voice, still feel the imprint of his hand on her bruised head. Her pulse began to thud again. Was this what madness did? Scramble the workings of the mind so that nothing made sense? She had opened her eyes and *he* had been there, looking down at her so earnestly – and then he had smiled.

Heri. Stepping out of her dreams. And that was the name that had eluded her.

But the scene that had played through her unconscious mind as she lay on the gravel had not been of him, but of something else entirely. It was a little garbled in her mind now but she remembered that she had been in the churchyard, where the church had been half its current size, encircled by a low wall, and the cross had stood beside the path, towering above her. Her aunt, dressed in a long plain gown, had stood at the churchyard gate while Olwen argued with Edmond, who was playing a role that sat ill upon his youthful shoulders.

'Why are you come, Osred?' She remembered addressing him with that strange name, fear rising in her. 'Do you bring me word of my brothers? I have been asking and asking. . .'

'They are safe,' he had replied, glancing towards the church. 'They tired of their lessons.'

Something was not right, she was certain of it, and she had felt a stab of fear when he refused to meet her eye. The next bit was lost, fragmented in her mind, but she could remember protesting, praying that he did not see the terror in her. 'Did you come simply to tell me this?' She had looked towards her aunt. 'I am forced to remain here, despised by this woman, a virtual prisoner.'

Her aunt stared coldly back at her, saying nothing, and Edmond had shrugged. 'She knows her duty, which is to keep you safe until. . .' The details of the argument that followed had gone but she remembered the cross, standing tall, the carved figure staring back at her with an unflinching coldness. And then someone had emerged from the church and she had recognised Alfred, wearing a long coat, boots laced up his calves, and he had come and stood beside Edmond, his arms folded across his chest in a cold rage as she had sometimes seen him.

She had been consumed by her fear then, lost in a tumult of confused voices arguing and making no sense, but a single thought had cut through. 'I want to see my brothers.'

'Enough!' It was Alfred who spoke and she had seen then that there were other figures in the gathering gloom, closing in. . . It had been as in her dream the other night, the scene from her window! And she saw that they were in awe of Alfred, a circumstance he could only long for in the real world, and her own fear had mushroomed as he replied. 'Osred has already told you – ' He had pulled her arm through his and turned her towards the church. ' – and we wed this day, you and I. We seal the knot.'

A wild confusion had then consumed her. It was wrong, all wrong. A trick! And then she had heard another voice, calling from a distance, saying her name, pulling her back. It was a voice she knew, a beloved voice, reeling her slowly in, leading her up the steps towards him, away from the edge of the abyss.

And at last she had reached him, had opened her eyes and seen him smiling down at her.

Heri.

She had known him at once. He had come at last and so, closing her eyes, she allowed herself to relax, and broken fragments of her other dreams began to come together.

He had come down with the men from Hen Ogledd, the old north, and Modig himself had brought them, long after they were despaired of. They had entered her father's northern stronghold with a proud swagger, stopping in the centre of the hall, where a fire burned in the hearth, eyes swivelling, wary of their welcome. Silence had fallen and the air had tightened. And she had watched from her seat at her brothers' side as all faces turned to her father, Ælfwald the king. She had seen his eyes light with a genuine joy and he rose with a shout of welcome while Modig bent a stiff knee, his men following suit.

Her father came down from the little dais to greet him, gripping the older man's shoulder, bidding him rise, and clasped his hand in both of his. It *was* her father, she was sure of it, but in her dreams he had been a younger, more virile man, dressed as if for a play, with a sword at his side, a man of power and status such as her real father had never been. He had turned back to her brothers who sat, mouths agape in awe of these men who stood tense and proud, and bid the boys join him, and they had come to stand beside him, half-grown puppies, barely reaching his shoulder.

The men who had come with Modig remained on bended knee awaiting word from their own lord before rising, and Olwen had little doubt who would have first call on their devotion if it ever came to a choice between Modig, their lord, and Ælfwald, their king.

It was then that she saw Heri for the first time, standing tall behind Modig, his eyes fixed on her father's face until, beckoned forward, he knelt again and kissed the king's hand. His grandson, she heard Modig say, his heir, his father dead in battle. 'His name is Oshere, but we call him Heri.' Her father spoke a few words to him, then clasped his shoulder too, bringing him to his feet before turning to introduce her brothers to these wild northern allies. The boys gazed with admiration at the tall young man and he acknowledged them with a nod and eyes that glinted, and she watched them glow in response.

In the hall the air slackened, the wolfhounds settled again and her father's warriors relaxed. They made space for Modig's men, offering ale, gesturing to the food, and she was recalled to her own duties, bringing a pitcher of mead and a drinking vessel for their guest. 'Welcome,' she had said, addressing Modig but conscious of the young man who stood beside him, appraising her.

'My daughter,' her father said.

Modig's eyes ran up and down her form, but he greeted her with respect as he took the proffered drink. 'I thank you.' He quaffed it off, smacking his lips, his eyes still on her. 'And might I ask your name, maid?'

'It is Ælfwyn, sir, but most call me Wyn.'

They had stayed but a short while, confirming their fealty to the ruler of Northumbria whose realm, for now at least, encompassed theirs. Wyn had exchanged no further words with Heri, although several times she had caught him watching her in a way that caused a flame to leap in her. And on the day that Modig's followers gathered in noisy preparation for departure, her brothers ran up to her and pressed something into her hand, before running off, laughing. It was an arm ring, the gold still warm from its wearer's body, and she recognised it at once. Looking up, she saw Heri, already mounted, smiling down at her.

'It is perhaps over large,' he said.

She slipped it onto her wrist where it hung loose. He dismounted swiftly then and, taking her arm, he pushed it higher, above the elbow and onto the soft flesh below her shoulder where it stayed like the clasp of a warm hand. 'Keep it there until we meet again,' he said.

She arched her eyebrows at his presumption. 'Do you think we shall?'

There was a clatter of hooves and, at a shout from Modig, the men began to move off. Heri swung himself back onto his horse. 'I'm certain of it,' he said. 'Trust me.' And, without warning, he leaned forward and touched her hair, raising a lock to his lips in a swift caress, then he shortened his rein and cantered after the others, not once looking back.

That touch had stayed in her mind, a sweet and tender moment. And even now she could recall every detail of the hall with the wolfhounds stretched out beside the hearth, the smell of roasting meat, of spilt ale and of men – and she could still feel the tension that had greeted Modig's arrival, see the fur on the grizzled old warrior's collar, the glint of firelight on the weapons of his men, and the other arm rings Heri wore amidst the tattoos on his muscled arm.

Behind her the door opened and she opened her eyes to see
Alfred framed in the doorway.

He came in and closed the door behind him. 'The doctor's
becoming a regular caller,' he remarked, strolling over and taking
a seat opposite her. 'His other patients must feel neglected.'

This was not the man in the long coat whose word commanded
fear but still she found herself tensing. 'I was told it was you who
summoned him,' she said.

'It was my father.'

She picked up her book and opened it. 'I trust I'll not trouble
him again.'

'He called you Olwen.' She pretended to read, ignoring him.
'When he played that odd little game of his, counting you up
some steps, he called you Olwen.'

She did not look up. 'It is my name.'

'He was very free with it.' Still she ignored him and he leaned
closer. 'And who, dear cousin, is Harry?'

She froze, and lifted her eyes to meet his. 'Harry?'

'You called the doctor Harry.' Alfred was watching her intently.
Oh dear God, *had* she? Had she said the name out loud? 'I
can't imagine why.' She wanted to leave the room then, to escape
from him, but he was between her and the door.

'Then you stroked his face – ' he reached out and lightly dusted
her cheek with the back of his hand. ' – in such a touching
manner.' And suddenly the menace of that other Alfred was in
his eyes.

'Then he'd be rather taken aback, I imagine,' she replied,
returning to her book, gripping it to keep her hands steady. What
else had she not been told? 'Are you the guardian of my virtue,
rather than your father? How absurd you are.'

'My father is a fool, Olwen. I'm not.'

CHAPTER 7

That night, as if spurred on by the events of the day, Olwen's *alter ego* returned.

But this dream was of a different time, and in another place. It was early morning and she was slipping past tired guards, accompanied only by her serving woman, modestly dressed to avoid attention. Her father, together with his retinue, had been journeying again, taking his sons with him, testing bonds of fealty throughout the kingdom and collecting tribute, but they had returned to the safety of the old fortress late the night before. All this the dream conveyed to Olwen in extraordinary clarity.

Her woman had brought word of three ships from Frisia that had come upriver on the far reach of the morning tide. 'They've tied up below the bridge and if we get there early. . .' Her eyes had sparkled as she helped Wyn dress. Together they crossed the bridge unchallenged and stood at a little distance from the muddy riverbanks watching casks and baskets come ashore. To their dismay they saw that little groups of people were already clustering around the traders, haggling for their goods, and they hung back awaiting an opening. With only her woman accompanying her, Wyn preferred not to be noticed and she watched from the shadows as two men disembarked; they were richly but sombrely dressed, and were greeted by monks she recognised from the community that clustered close to the church of St Peter the Apostle. Guests, perhaps, of the archbishop or the abbot, or scholars drawn by the reputation of the library.

Or was their coming connected with the rumours that swirled like an evil miasma around Ælfwald's hall these days? She watched as they stood, their heads bowed in prayer, giving thanks, perhaps, for a journey safely concluded, and wondered a little. Even men of God, she had heard her father say, were not above treachery. She looked across to where house slaves were unloading wine to be served in the hall tonight, for her father had guests of his own; trusted allies, invited here to Eorforwic to hold council, as the swell of rumours grew.

Unnoticed by Wyn, one of those who clustered around the foreign traders had lifted his head to look across at her. He watched her for a moment, concluded his transaction and detached himself.

And came up behind her. 'The lady Ælfwyn.' Her heart lurched at the sound of his voice and she swung round, eyes wide. 'Has she not trinkets enough?'

She felt herself colouring. 'I didn't know that Modig had come—'

He squeezed her arm to silence her. 'Who said that he had?' he murmured, pulling her to one side. Her serving woman stepped forward but Heri motioned her to be easy. 'Is she your only attendant?' he asked, and frowned at Wyn's nod. 'Then Northumbria's king grows careless.' She made to retort, but bit her lip and Heri's eyes laughed at her. 'Unless, of course,' he remarked, 'he doesn't know that you are here.'

'My father has more pressing concerns, and I'm safe in Eoforwic.'

'Are you?' He reached out and, as he had done that other time, he lifted an escaping lock of her hair to his lips. Her woman stepped forward, protesting. 'Peace, girl,' he said, and flicked her a half coin, which fell at her feet. As she scrabbled for it in the mud, he grabbed Wyn's arm and pulled her behind a high upstanding wall, a hand over her mouth. He let her struggle for a moment, holding her effortlessly, and then removed his hand, laughing at her fury. 'Safe indeed! And now, away on a fast horse for a fat ransom. You should be more wary, Ælfwald's daughter.'

She tried to push past him. 'My woman will raise the alarm,' she told him, but he blocked her.

'She should be beaten for her neglect of you.' He had held

onto her arm. 'I'll release you presently and besides, I'll take better care of you than she. Won't you stay awhile?' She gave up the pretence of resistance and he led her to a low wall where he sat her down. 'So, you bought nothing from the traders,' he remarked, taking a place beside her.

'We came too late.'

'The price of sloth,' he mocked, and pulled something from the fabric of his tunic. He held a closed fist towards her, turned it and opened his palm to reveal a pin with a silver shaft, its flattened head decorated with a tiny design of two creatures, their serpentine bodies entwined, facing away from each other. It was too light to hold a man's clothing. 'I was earlier than you, sweet Wyn, and saw you before you saw me.'

She shook her head, thrilled by the rush of emotions coursing through her, not sure if she should refuse his gift, but he was already pulling aside the edge of the coif she wore and attaching the pin, frowning with concentration, his face so close she learned the smell of him. And then his hand slid to her upper arm and she saw his eyes blaze as he found what her sleeve was concealing. 'Did I not say that we would meet again?' he said, turning the arm ring, gently twisting it on her flesh.

'You cannot know it's yours.'

'It is though, isn't it?' Unskilled at flirtation, she made as if to rise but he gripped her arm, preventing her. 'Wait. Don't go. We might have no other chance to speak alone.'

She relented, for she wanted to remain. 'Why are you here?' she asked.

'I come in Modig's stead.'

'Is he unwell?'

His face darkened. 'No, maid, it's your father's kingdom that sickens. Modig stays to guard the marches. No man leaves his lands at times like these.' Then he smiled, that slow smile of his that lit his eyes. 'And I came also for reasons of my own.'

She pretended not to understand him. 'Does my father fear a rebellion in the north?'

He shrugged. 'The northern lands were ever restless.' He stared down towards the river where more were gathering as word of the ships' arrival spread. Fishing nets writhing with silver fish were being hauled ashore from boats drawn up beside them while men stood about in clusters, deep in conversation. He turned back to her, his expression softening, and he began walking his fingers up her arm to reach the ring again. 'I believe that Northumbria's king should seek a closer alliance with Modig.'

'But Modig is one of my father's most trusted—'

'Loyalty must be nurtured.' She looked up at him and saw that his eyes were dancing. 'Modig is old and I speak as his successor.'

'So it is *your* loyalty that is in question?' she remarked, raising her chin.

'It is not, but the king should take steps to strengthen it.'

She lowered her eyes again lest he read her response, for her face was burning. 'I leave such matters to him.'

'Do you?' The fingers walked back down her arm. 'Alliance can take many forms.'

Her breathing had quickened. 'I expect he knows that.'

'Should I remind him, do you think?'

'Perhaps,' she said, meeting the question in his eyes, and felt his hand close over hers.

Abruptly he changed the subject. 'But tell me about Earl Sicga. Does your father confide in him?'

She was conscious of disappointment, having no wish to speak of Sicga, who was a loud-mouthed, smooth-tongued man who frequently disconcerted her, and she shrugged. 'They've been friends since boyhood.'

'Has he ambition of his own?'

She frowned at him. 'He's my father's friend, I tell you.'

'And grows rich and powerful thereby.'

'You reach swift judgement, Oshere.'

He raised an eyebrow. 'My friends call me Heri.'

'And Sicga is my father's friend.'

His fingers began trespassing again. 'And yet the king grows careless.' She was getting out of her depth and made to rise again but he pulled her down. 'Tell me then of your kinsman, Osred. What sort of man is he?'

A weak one, a vain one, a threat to no one, but she would not say so. Perhaps she had already said too much. 'He is, as you say, my kinsman.'

'And sticks to your father like a cleg.'

'He is loyal, if that is what you ask. But without my father's support he is. . .' she struggled for a word.

'Nothing.'

'You judge again. He is kin and he is loyal, and that is enough.' Lately though her father had hinted at more, implying that he needed to bind his nephew closer. She had realised that he was considering a marriage between herself and Osred and wasted no time in telling him what she thought of the idea and he had listened, his face expressionless, and then simply flicked her cheek. Would he consider Heri as an alternative to secure the northern lands? The thought set her pulse racing. 'Why do you ask?' she said.

'Clegs drain blood from their hosts,' he replied. 'Then flit to a richer vein.'

'Have you dared say that to my father?'

'Do you think I lack the courage, sweetheart? I'm sent here to listen only, and observe.'

'And judge. And carry tales back to Modig.'

He shrugged. 'Why else would he send me? So do you love your loyal kinsman, Wyn?'

'No!' The question caught her off guard.

'And yet the man brags of his bond to your family, hinting that soon it might be closer.'

Had he? He had no right! 'I told my father that I—' She broke off, having again said more than she ought.

Heri looked away, and when he looked back at her there was a glint in his eye. 'Perhaps I should have brought that fast horse.'

She rose and this time he did not stop her, but fell into step beside her. Her woman spotted them and ran up, scolding in her relief, but Heri bid her be gone. Wyn's mind was in a whirl, alarmed by the treachery at which he hinted, but disturbed in another, quite delightful way. Words deserted her and they walked in silence until they reached the bridge, where he dropped respectfully behind her, her own tall, wild-mannered bodyguard. 'Walk beside me,' she said, and he did, giving her a slanting look that told her that he knew the effect he was having on her, and that it was the same for him, and they continued in step as if already bonded. He walked with a swagger and she lifted her chin proudly and they made their way, side by side, up the cobbled thoroughfare that led to the core of the fortress. Her woman, resentful, trailed behind. And as they went she saw that Heri was looking about him, taking in the crumbling remains of barracks that had once housed Rome's northern force but which had lain in ruins for centuries. Trees now grew through long-fallen roofs while blackthorn and brambles covered collapsed walls and debris. A more complete structure had been patched up and served as a dwelling while in another a smith had set up his workshop, but nettles and ferns had conquered the rest.

Heri stopped at the place where the two main thoroughfares crossed and looked along the route to the north, and he spoke almost to himself. 'The great northern Wall these Romans built divides us still,' he said, his face serious again. 'And between the wall and the Sea of Iuddew are Modig's lands, once of the Gododdin, of battle-loving men. They will remain loyal to Ælfwald but to the man himself not the kingdom. There is trouble brewing, Modig says.'

'But he stays true?' She was desperate that it be so.

He nodded. 'Aye. But there are rumours in the wind and they grow stronger. Æthelred, they say, has returned from exile.' She turned to him in horror and he returned her a grim look. 'He's been seen in lands to the west.' Æthelred, son of a usurper with no true lineage, had taken Northumbria's throne and ruled savagely for five years, exacting terrible revenge against those who had deposed his father, until Wyn's father had contested his position and gathered forces to remove him. Ælfwald had a right to rule, the blood of royal Ida flowed in his veins, and so he had wrested the throne away from Æthelred and banished him from the kingdom.

She kept stricken eyes on Heri. 'Does my father know this?' At the least sign of discord Northumbria's feuding dynasties would once again turn on each other, vying as they endlessly did for power and influence. No one could be trusted.

Heri nodded. 'Aye. And he knows that Æthelred still covets Northumbria's throne. He is a man bent on vengeance, Modig's spies have told him, especially against those who ousted him, and boasts of what he will do to any who would thwart his return. Many say that Ælfwald should have put him to the sword when he had the chance, and I believe they have the right of it.'

CHAPTER 8

'I've had the stones covered with an oiled cloth,' the vicar confided next morning before taking John through to the morning room, 'since you thought it best.' His wife greeted him frostily and his patient gave him only a tight little smile before looking away.

'How did you sleep, Miss Malkon?' he asked.

'Well, thank you.'

'If I may, I'll examine your head.' She nodded assent and suffered his examination with so clear a desire to distance herself that he could almost believe she knew. For last night he had dreamed again of Olwen Malkon, the sort of dream that no doctor should ever have of a patient. And it refused to leave him. . . Frowning with concentration, he removed the bandage. 'No need to replace this,' he said, with cool detachment, 'the air'll do it good.' A repetition of his questions from the day before received the same answers and so in less than half an hour he found himself back outside.

Case closed?

If so, then it was no bad thing. His dream had been sensual and passionate and he had awakened sweating and aroused; they had been laid together, she spent in his arms, beneath a clear blue sky, and she had raised her hand to his face as she had done in the vicarage garden, smiling up at him with that same look of tenderness in her eyes. But they were far from Yorkshire, transported north by the dream to where he had been raised, in the borderlands amongst his beloved hills. And he had smiled down at her, stroking a wiry sprig of heather across her cheek, teasing her with it, drawing it across the ridge of her nose, over her lips and down between her naked breasts, before throwing it aside and kissing her; he grew hot again at the memory. Dear God, he must be careful!

The dream stayed with him, fading slowly in the following days as he was kept occupied with the dreary round of fractures and sprains, childhood afflictions and the endless tribulations of the elderly. He was hardly busy though and none of this work challenged the skills he had been so long in acquiring. Perhaps it was the time of the year – everyone was out in the fields taken up with spring planting or were too poor to summon a doctor, or perhaps they preferred the quackery of his predecessor. Whatever it was, his mood was gloomy and, at the end of the long week, he returned home and was relieved to find no other patients awaiting him in the hall, so he let Mrs Crawford go and wandered into his consulting room. It was a bare, simple room with just a desk, a couple of chairs and a low couch, worn and old-fashioned, inherited from his predecessor. The sight of it compounded a growing sense of dissatisfaction. Was this what his life was to be?

He indulged that depressing thought for a moment and then straightened his shoulders, deciding that he at least owed it to his patients to impose some order on the place, and began sorting through the papers on his desk. In so doing he found articles on epilepsy he had brought south with him, and these returned his thoughts to Olwen Malkon. Quite apart from any personal feelings he might have (and was trying hard to suppress) her case intrigued him. It had just that element of mental disorder to take his interest and engage his intellect. He also found tucked inside a book the letters of introduction addressed to the medical superintendent at St Hilda's House, a mental institution in York known for its progressive approaches; these had been provided by one of his former tutors who was aware of John's interest in diseases of the mind and might yet come in useful.

He sat back, considering again what he determinedly called the Malkon case. Seeing the carved stones in the vicarage garden must have played a part in that last episode, but he could not know for sure unless he asked her, and it was unlikely that he would get the chance. What could it be about them that had triggered such an extreme reaction, he wondered, staring blankly ahead. While he felt a measure of professional satisfaction that he had managed to release her from her cataleptic state, he knew that he was well out of his depth in such matters. As a student he had taken every opportunity to sit in on visiting lecturers and had seen demonstrations of hypnosis and been fascinated. His tutors, however, had greeted his enthusiasm with scepticism and warnings, some maintaining that only those already emotionally disturbed would be susceptible to hypnosis, or mesmerism as they still called it, while others declared that patients placed in a state where commands would be blindly obeyed were open to all manner of risk. Outside the profession too, a spate of lurid novels and dramas, which took little account of scientific facts, had heightened a general wariness of hypnosis.

John had only ever attempted it himself that one time. 'It was a lovely sort of floating feeling, my dear,' the streetwalker had said, 'and your voice was so soothing.' Was that supposed to happen? He really had no idea. . . He had been startled by his apparent success and would have attempted it again while the girl was in a compliant mood, but she had risen, her palm raised for payment. Soon afterwards he had qualified as a physician and such horseplay was out of the question and so he had never tried it again. He sat a moment longer considering these wider issues, and tried to prevent his mind from returning to the softness of his patient's hair and those violet eyes that had looked up at him with such an expression. . .

He rose abruptly and took the epilepsy papers through to his private sitting room where a fire had been laid. He lit it, poured himself a drink and settled down to read. If there should be further episodes, there must be no more makeshift experiments, he would stick to what he knew.

When a knock came at the front door he was well immersed in the detail of the report and listened, waiting for Mrs Crawford to answer it, before remembering that she had gone. He went himself and was astonished to find Olwen Malkon stood on the doorstep, a shawl over her head and shoulders, her hand raised to knock again. He looked beyond her for her aunt but saw only the housemaid, hovering at the end of the path. 'Are you unwell?' he asked, taken aback by her sudden appearance.

'Is that not why people come to you?'

'What? Yes. . . Of course.' He beckoned to the housemaid, who came quickly down the path. 'But I'd have come to the vicarage, they had only to send.'

'I wish to consult with you myself. . . although not on the doorstep.' He stepped back hastily, apologising, and ushered them into the consulting room where he gestured to the chair in front of his desk and to another against the wall for the housemaid. He straightened his jacket and brought his mind to order.

'How can I help you?'

'Susan must wait in the hall,' she said. 'I need to speak to you privately.'

John glanced at the girl, who was looking aside, as if distancing herself from such an irregular suggestion. 'No. . . I don't think—'

'Have no fear, Dr Osbourne. Susan will swear that she never left my side, and I don't expect to detain you very long.'

He was horrified. 'No, really, Miss Malkon, you must consider—'

'If you won't see me alone then it was pointless me coming!' She lifted her eyes to him and he saw despair in them.

'Your aunt—'

'She, like you, believes I'm malingering. But—' she broke off, glancing at Susan, and bit her lip, ' – I'm not.'

Her accomplice was trying, unsuccessfully, to appear deaf and John rapidly assessed his options. He could not possibly see Miss Malkon without a chaperone but neither could he send her away. Glancing out of the window, he saw that it had stopped raining. 'What you suggest is out of the question,' he said, with professional firmness. 'But we could, a little unconventionally perhaps, have our consultation in the garden. There's a seat at the far end, under the trees, and your. . . Susan, is it, can sit up by the house and can, in all honesty, say that she never let you out of her sight.'

The girl looked relieved and Olwen nodded agreement and so he escorted them down the hall and out through the back door. Clouds were still racing across the sky but there were now widening patches of blue. He indicated a seat under the boughs of a venerable beech at the far end of the walled garden and fetched a chair for Susan, placing it against the side of the house, in clear sight but out of earshot. His patient looked unwell, he thought as he went back into the house, pale and peaky, heavy-eyed as if she had not slept. He carried another chair from the kitchen down the garden and placed it opposite her where he could see her face, and sat.

'Does the head still trouble you?' he asked.

'Not the bruising, but what's happening inside it.'

He searched her face. 'Can you explain a little?'

She raised her hands, then let them drop back to her lap. 'If only I could!' she said. 'Something is happening to me. In my mind. These turns I have. . . and dreams. . . or rather waking dreams, strange starts and. . . and always this sense of threat hanging over me.'

'Which began after your recent tragedies?'

She frowned at him. 'Don't dismiss it again as grief, Dr Osbourne! It's more than that.' She gulped. 'Ever since that episode in the church, it's grown worse. . . I think. . . I feel I'm no longer in control of my own mind. . .' Her face suddenly contorted with emotion and he had to stop himself from reaching out to take her hand. 'I know you consider me to be a silly girl, reading ghoulish books to frighten myself, but. . . it's real. . .'

Little flushed patches had appeared on her cheeks and her eyes had such a wildness about them. 'I'm sorry if I implied such a thing,' he said quietly. 'But explain if you can. . . *what* exactly is real?'

She turned away, fixing her gaze on a spread of daffodils, and was silent for a moment. 'I was reading Stevenson's book for a purpose, you see,' she said at last, with rather more composure. 'I'd read it once before and remembered the theme of duality, two natures within one consciousness – ' a lively mind, indeed, he thought ' – and I hoped to find something that might explain. . . But I was disappointed, Dr Jekyll brought about his own fractured state by using drugs. I find myself in the same position, except my *other* is not a worse version of me, but a. . . a troubled one.' He felt a chill creep over him, this was far beyond his experience. Her face had gone quite white. 'At first the dreams were like an imagined story in an idle mind, but now she surfaces into this world, insistent, as she did that time in the church, and again when I reacted so violently to those broken old stones. But it was not me, it was *her* – ' she broke off again ' – reacting *through* me. I feel what she feels, very deeply. And. . . and. . . she's frightened.'

The girl had begun shaking. She pulled her shawl tight and wrapped her arms around herself, her breathing coming fast and shallow. Unconsciously he gripped her shoulder and she gasped, her eyes flying to him, and he pulled back. 'Breathe, Miss Malkon, breathe. I'll count.'

She closed her eyes, taking deep breathes, and when he stopped counting, she opened them and looked directly at him. 'I believe I'm possessed.'

Good God. He shook his head. 'No. You aren't.'

Her face contorted again. 'You cannot know that.'

'I do.' He spoke firmly, hoping he conveyed more confidence than he felt. Where had this come from? Her uncle? Surely not. Had she been in contact with spiritualists or some other cranks? God help her if she fell into the clutches of table-tilters and rappers, with her mind in the state it was! 'Whatever your anxieties, they are of this world, I promise you.' He tried to look reassuring. 'We'll find you some help.' Serendipitous that he had found those letters. 'But tell me, Miss Malkon, was it coming across the carved stones beside the glasshouse that triggered that last episode?' She nodded, her eyes not leaving his. 'Do you recall what you felt when you saw them?'

'Fear, a terrible fear – ' she spoke quickly, and with passion

'– and while I lay there, unconscious, I *became* that other person, glimpsing fragments of a story. . . It haunts me, Dr Osbourne, it's. . . it's like a wildly distorted version of my own troubles, and she is so frightened.'

'Tell me.'

It was a confused story sure enough. She was being taken into the church by her cousin, she told him, feeling uncertain and terrified for her brothers, not knowing where they were. 'It was as if they were living still. . .' Her eyes filled and he nodded, then urged her gently to continue. 'I was beside a cross that was standing tall in the churchyard – those fragments, you see – and my aunt was there, others too, in the shadows but all was different and – ' she spoke faster and faster, her voice strained and thin ' – and then I heard a voice coming from far away. . . and I knew that my cousin was lying to me and that my brothers were *not* safe, and I felt that I too was in danger. . . and then it dissolved into confusion, and. . . and then the distant voice became *your* voice.'

He stared back at her. 'You remember all this from a state of unconsciousness?'

She nodded, still shaking. 'Like it was a dream. Except it wasn't. On one level it was clear and lucid. . . more like a memory. . . a splintered memory, and on another, such a turmoil that made no sense. And it keeps happening, little episodes come to me, without order, but I believe that they're part of a whole that I cannot see. And. . . and every night that I dream now, more and more of a story unfolds. . .'

He was stunned. He said nothing, torn between concern and professional fascination; but this was way beyond his experience. 'Have you told your uncle, or your aunt?' She gave him a withering look. 'Or have you a friend in whom you could confide? Your uncle spoke of a former companion.'

A forlorn look crossed her face. 'I should like nothing better than to confide in Celia, she would listen and help me, but I don't know how to contact her. I expect letters daily, but none have come.'

There was one other question he had to ask. 'Can I assume you've had no dealings with spiritualists or mediums since your recent tragedies?'

'You really *do* think me a fool!' She made as if to rise.

'Be seated, please.' He spoke firmly for she was looking daggers at him. 'You'd not be the first to do so, and it was necessary that I ask. Those who claim contact with the spirit world can do a great deal of harm, but tell me, last time we spoke, you seemed calm and untroubled and I left you thinking that all was well. Has something happened since, to further disturb your mind?'

She glanced over to where Susan was sat beside the house, well out of earshot, but even so she lowered her voice. 'Alfred, my cousin,' she said. 'First, he made ridiculous allegations and then he accused me of being. . . sly, of keeping secrets from him. . . he has been goading me, watching me. . .'

Here was tricky ground. 'Forgive me, but your uncle implied there's an understanding between you and Mr Malkon?'

Her response was crisp and unequivocal. 'He has misled you, as he misleads himself. My father wanted me to wed one of my cousins, either him or Edmond, but I never shall.' An obstinate girl, her uncle had said, but he was conscious of his spirits lifting. 'And yet they too are inhabiting my dreams, together with my aunt and uncle, I recognise them, although they are. . . altered. Alfred was there, but stronger somehow, more powerful and. . . and he frightens me.' So she was being pressured, was she, John thought angrily, persecuted even, and with her mind already distressed. 'Is it true that I cried out last week, when I lay there, in the garden?' she asked abruptly. 'Susan said that I did.'

John looked back to where the housemaid sat, remembering what she had told him. 'Not in my hearing, although I understand you had spoken before I arrived.'

'But did I also address you as I roused, in a familiar manner?' she persisted, and her face flooded with colour.

'Aye, but with another's name.' He smiled and tried for a light tone. 'Your wits were still a-wandering. . . although if Mr Malkon imagines he has some claim on you, I expect he's curious as to the identity of this Harry you mistook me for. Do you know someone of that name?'

The flush on her cheek deepened and she raised her eyes to his. 'I don't. . .' she said slowly. 'But she does.'

CHAPTER 9

Olwen walked rapidly down the road back to the vicarage already regretting her impulse to confide. But she had had to see him again, to know. Behind her Susan was walking fast to keep up, complaining that she would be in trouble when her mistress noted her absence. 'Say that I insisted on you going for a walk with me,' Olwen replied over her shoulder. 'Say whatever you like, Susan, everyone thinks I'm tiresome as it is.'

And what of the doctor, she wondered, what did he think of her now? He had listened well enough but what had she expected, for goodness sake? That he would somehow *know* that her unruly mind had ascribed him a role in her fantasised world, and would thereby have insights into her confusion? He would think her quite mad if she told him! And how could she begin to describe such foolishness, the crazy, wild imaginings in her mind that seemed bent on mirroring those around her, creating uncanny doubles, pulling her deeper and deeper into. . .

Madness indeed!

No, it had been impossible to explain the whole to him. And yet, he had been kind. Before she left, he had offered his hand and gripped her fingers tightly. 'I will help you, I promise.'

But what could he do?

If only she could discover where Celia had gone; never had she needed her more.

As they approached the vicarage, she saw a man outside the gate, about to mount a familiar mare and, with a cry of delight, she hastened forward. 'Percy! Mr Percy. Wait!' The old man turned, stepped down again and doffed his hat. 'Oh, how good it is to see you! How are things at Swindale?' she asked, searching every wrinkle of his dear face. 'I do so miss you all. Are you well? What brings you here?'

He gave her a wide beaming smile, clasping her proffered hand in both of his. 'I'd business out this way and thought I'd drop by. Bring the vicar up to date with doings.'

'Doings!' The word was one of his favourites and she felt absurdly reassured by it. 'And what doings are they?'

He flapped his hand in a vague sort of way. 'Nothing special, Miss, just reporting like I was asked to do, Vicar being custodian, and all that. . .'

'How dreadful if I'd missed you! Were you offered something to eat? Won't you come back inside and tell *me* all the doings as well?'

He smiled and shook his head. 'I've had all I wanted, thankee, and I need to be heading back.' She stood, stroking the mare's nose, reluctant to see him go. Six months, she whispered to the creature, and then she would return home; it was a steadying thought. 'Good health to you, Miss Olwen, and God bless.' He remounted, raising a finger to his forehead, and she stood waving for as long as he was in sight. It was only when he had gone that she thought of asking if they had had word of Celia, and by then it was too late.

Slowly she went into the vicarage, back into the stultifying sameness, but she entered to find an angry scene unfolding in the hall. 'You take your orders from *me*, girl, not from Miss High-and-Mighty.'

She stopped on the threshold. 'Do not berate Susan, Aunt. I gave her no choice.' All the frustrations of her position rose like bile to consume her.

The vicar's wife turned, astonished at her tone, but recovered fast. 'You went to see Dr Osbourne, I'm told. Unchaperoned! And consulted him in his *garden*.'

Susan, it appeared, had crumpled at the first assault, and was now avoiding her eyes. 'I wished to speak with him in private.'

'About what?'

'My odd episodes, these strange—'

Susan was swiftly sent about her duties and her aunt stepped closer. 'There's nothing wrong with you, young lady, that a plain diet and a worthwhile occupation won't cure.' Olwen made no reply but raised her chin. 'Such behaviour! You forget your uncle's position.'

'Then let me return to where I belong.' She turned away and began to mount the stairs, looking back at her aunt. 'I'm constrained here without my consent, however you choose to represent it. Give me leave to go to my father's hall, and I'll depart at once.'

Her aunt stood, mouth open, and watched as Olwen calmly continued upstairs to her room. She closed the door behind her and leaned against it, shocked at her own audacity as the room tilted in front of her. Never before had she spoken to her aunt like that, but just for a moment she had seen another face, a face with that same pointed nose, the same sharp expression. . .

She went to the window, shaking slightly, and stood there, gripping the window sill. The patches of blue had vanished and rain had begun to fall from leaden skies, thinly at first but then more sustained, and she watched giant raindrops bouncing off the broad green leaves of the shrubbery. The first rain for a while and she sensed in the garden a deep thirst, a quickening. . . But even as she watched, her newfound courage seeped away; they would never give her consent to leave, it had been a foolish thing to say, and her aunt would find a dozen ways to punish her outspokenness.

But then again, she realised, it had not been herself who had spoken. . .

Dinner that evening was a quiet, tense affair. The vicar must have been made aware of events and expanded the grace with a theme of gratitude, then spent the meal giving her reproachful looks, while her aunt appeared quietly smug. Her cousins, either indifferent to or unaware of the tensions, had eaten quickly and departed while Olwen played with her food, consuming little beyond the soup.

She retired as soon as the meal was finished and began pacing up and down her room, deeply unsettled by this new development, this sudden and evident convergence of her two worlds, the real and unreal. It had come upon her so subtly, without warning; in an instant she had become her other, responding to her aunt with a defiance she had so far managed to keep in check. She puzzled over it as she continued to pace, but the restlessness only grew. Seeing Mr Percy had served to remind her that one day this purgatory would end and she had only to hold out and not bend to her aunt's will – she would rather die than marry either of her cousins! And Celia was right. 'They can't force you, you goose,' she had said. 'You've read too many Gothic tales!'

And as she went up and down her room she felt an angry energy building in her. If they *tried* to force her she would run away and report them to. . . to. . . the authorities. Dr Osbourne would know what approaches to make, and he had promised to help her, he was sympathetic, she was sure of it, and had a way of looking at her that turned her bones to water. . . She halted beside the window, her brain running on, seeing again in her mind's eye the wondrous tattoos on his muscled arms and that mocking smile. A fast horse, he had said. . . and she laughed out loud, suddenly elated as an illustration in one of her books came to mind, a woodcut of fair Ellen on Lochinvar's charger and, laughing still, she tried to image Dr Osbourne in such a role. But he had come down from the north, he had said, not out of the west, from the land of reivers and battle-hungry men. . .

The room began to tilt alarmingly and she squeezed her eyes shut. No. . . no. . . what was she thinking! That was not the doctor, that had been Heri, in her dream, down by the wharf where the ships were tied up, where he had given her the pin with the two serpentine heads. . .

The pin!

She swung back to the room, clutching at the bedpost. The pin. Where was it? She began scrabbling through her drawers, tipping out her trinket boxes and raking through the contents.

Lost already? Had it fallen off in the road. . . She must go back at once and look – Or in the garden perhaps. . . But no! She wailed aloud, sinking onto her bed, wretched with confusion, despairing of it all, and put her head in her hands. The pin did not exist, and the doctor had never looked at her in that way. . .

She took in deep breaths as he had told her to do and calmed a little. Perhaps she was turning into one of those absurd females who fawn on their physician, fantasising about them, dreaming of them. Oh, how he would despise her if he knew.

But now the energy was draining away to be replaced by a strange languor, an irresistible urge to sleep. It was all she could do to undress and crawl, still half-clothed, between the sheets, pulling the blanket over her head to try to drown out the turbulence and the noise that was filling her head.

For Ælfwald's hall was full of men tonight, drinking and carousing loudly at table, occasionally turning aside to speak in low voices. Heri, she saw, was seated between Earl Sicga and another of her father's kinsmen, listening and watchful. His eyes were fixed on Sicga and his expression chilled her. . . She felt again that flutter of panic. What did he know that her father did not? Her cousin Osred had been placed beside her but was giving his attention to the man on his other side, a man she did not recognise. Did this positioning beside him give a signal, she wondered, glancing resentfully down the table at her father. Was he progressing a match between them despite her resistance?

And if Heri spoke to him, asking for her hand, would he entertain the idea? Or was it too late?

Perhaps he thought that this was not the moment to raise the matter, and perhaps he was right, for it seemed that her father was uneasy with the assembled company, speaking loudly, raising his cup to his guests and being cheered in return, then falling suddenly silent and brooding, or leaning across the table to talk guardedly with men she barely knew. Heri was watching him too and once he caught, and held, her eye. But he did not smile. At the far end of the table she recognised one of the soberly dressed men who had disembarked the boat from Frisia talking earnestly, his head turned away, to one of her father's earls – one with whom her father had once quarrelled, although quarrels, like alliances, were as inconstant as the moon. Tension hung heavy in the grey smoke that rose from the fire, and she sensed men's eyes swivelling around the hall, assessing their company, hands hovering close to seax sheaths. She could almost smell the discord. One of her father's wolfhounds rose and padded over to her, pushed its face into her hand, whining, but she had no comfort to give. She saw her brothers go over to speak to Heri and saw his face lighten as he ruffled the younger one's hair before turning back to attend to something Sicga said.

Then a hand fell on her leg, bringing her attention abruptly back to Osred. His face was still turned to his neighbour but he squeezed her thigh and his fingers slid higher. She said nothing but rose abruptly, seized the black jug from one of the serving girls and went to fill her father's cup. He smiled and pulled her down to him. 'Sweet Wyn,' he murmured, his beard scratching her cheek as he kissed her. 'Fill up their cups, my child,' he said, 'and smile upon them all.' She nodded and did as he bid, stretching between the men to reach their cups, suffering lusty stares and bold remarks, evading wandering hands. When she came to Sicga's place he too pulled her down and bestowed on her cheek a smacking kiss, demonstrating to those around him the privilege of his position. He touched the pin that secured her coif. 'A pretty thing,' he remarked.

'Aye, my lord.'

'A lover's token?' he asked, looking back to where Osred sat, scowling now. Beside Sicga, Heri sat, his expression very dark and watchful.

'A reward for sloth,' she replied, with a light smile. 'Will you have wine, my lord?' She moved on, leaving him to shrug and dismiss her, then leaned forward to fill Heri's cup. And as she did he jerked his knee against her, unbalancing her, and the wine spilled. She stepped back and he rose, as the red liquid dripped from the table to pool in the straw at his feet.

'Forgive me,' she said, looking up at him.

She expected to meet laughter in his eyes but saw only a strange glint. 'No matter, maid,' he said. ''Tis wine, after all, not spilt blood. But, for the future, have a care.'

CHAPTER 10

John stood, hat in hand, before the half-glazed door and looked out onto a sunlit garden. Figures were ambling up and down the paths in ones and twos, making for a tranquil scene, a slow-moving tableau or the backdrop for a painting, perhaps, and it was very pleasing on the eye.

I will help you, I promise, he had told her, and so he had come here, bearing his letters of introduction.

St Hilda's House was one of a number of private asylums established on the principles of kindness pioneered in the last century by The Retreat, a progressive and influential institution situated nearby. And John approved of what he saw. The place had a homely atmosphere, there were paintings on the walls, ferns spilling from planters, colourful rugs on wooden floors, wicker armchairs and low tables, all reassuringly domestic. Except for the uniformed attendants and the eccentric behaviour of some of its residents, it could have been mistaken for a large guesthouse. One woman, her slippers on the wrong feet, had approached him with a wide smile. 'Now I know *just* who this is,' she had said. 'Have you come to take me home, son?' An attendant had hurried forward, apologised, and led the woman away, bleating about a longed-for release. Poor soul. Then another attendant arrived to take him to the office of the medical superintendent and led him down a corridor where paintings of pastoral landscapes hung on papered walls and modern ceiling lights cast a brightness over all.

The room was occupied by an enormous mahogany desk behind which sat a youngish, harassed-looking man. He rose to his feet and came forward. 'Dr Osbourne. Welcome to St Hilda's,' he said. 'I'm Dr Linton, standing in for Dr Nicholson who is, I'm afraid, in London at present.' He gestured to John's letters of introduction, which lay open on his desk. 'I took the liberty of reading these. You're recently come from Edinburgh, I see, there's admirable work going on there, such fine doctors. . .' He trailed off, clearly distracted.

John apologised for arriving without prior warning and the man muttered something civil and ran a hand through already ruffled hair. 'Perhaps I could make an appointment to see Dr Nicholson upon his return?'

'To be frank I'm not entirely sure when to expect him back. A short teaching commitment. . .' John's consternation must have shown. 'But I can spare you a few moments myself, if you'd like.' He gestured to the letters. 'You've a practice close by, I see, and a troubling patient. If you would care to expand upon it? Delusional, you say.'

He indicated two armchairs beside the fire and they sat. Briefly John summarised the case as best he could, giving no names and omitting anything that would obscure the essential facts. 'I've an interest in afflictions of the mind,' he concluded, 'but I've no training in this area. I'm a general physician, not long qualified, and would value advice—'

'I believe we can offer you exactly that.' Dr Linton's face had lightened as he spoke. 'We've a colleague visiting from Zurich, a Professor Brandt, who arrived two days before Dr Nicholson left for London and, in truth, I've been hard-pressed to keep him occupied! His methods are most interesting, but rather different, you see. . .' He trailed off again. 'He came at rather short notice and it was impossible for Dr Nicholson to alter his commitments. A very energetic gentleman, is Herr Professor, but I believe he might be able to help you. He has a fascinating approach and his English is excellent.'

Dr Linton's hopeful expression suggested he saw the chance to pass one problem visitor on to another, but the mention of Zurich sharpened John's interest. 'I'd be delighted,' he said.

A bell was rung, and a servant sent with a message.

She returned a moment later confirming that the professor would meet Dr Osbourne in the summer house in the garden, and so John shook Dr Linton's hand and followed her through another door into the garden with its neat box hedges and gravel paths where he had watched the patients taking the air. A small wooden structure stood in a secluded corner, its doors flung open, and, on a little terrace in front of it, there sat a dapper man smoking a thin cigar and writing busily. Very European in appearance, John decided as he approached, with his panama hat, pale linen jacket and such extraordinary shoes. Books and papers were scattered across a table where he worked but, at the sight of John, the man put down both pen and cigar, raised his hat and stepped forward with a hand outstretched.

'Herr Doktor. How splendid! A new colleague.' He gave a little bow, looking past John at the departing attendant. 'I ordered refreshments. . . Ah yes! It comes. Here, if you will, *fraulein*.' Beloved of staff and supervisors, John thought, briefly amused as the maid gave a pert bob and rapidly retreated. 'You will have coffee?' the man asked, dispensing a thick dark liquid into china cups as he gestured for John to be seated. 'It is not as I would have made it myself, but it will suffice.' Handing a cup to John, he too sat. 'You wished to consult with me, I understand, and I am at your service, but first, please tell me a little about yourself.'

John briefly described his training at the Medical Faculty in Edinburgh and his work at the hospital there. 'I developed a personal interest in illnesses of the mind, and read with fascination the recent advances in thinking in Europe.'

'Yes! We progress. We stand on the shoulders of giants and from there we observe new horizons. We have reached a watershed, I truly believe it, a new enlightenment, the ascendancy of science. It is an exciting time! But, tell me now, how I can help you? A troubling patient, I understand.' John outlined the case again and the man listened, smoking, and occasionally scribbling a note, but he made no interruption other than nodding from time to time as if what was being described was familiar. When

John finished, he sat back, tapping his teeth with a teaspoon as he gazed across the gardens. 'Delusional, you said.'

'Yes.'

Abruptly he sat forward again. 'No nausea? No convulsions? No rigidity?'

'She went stiff at one point, rigid in fact. I'd overlooked the possibility of epilepsy—'

This was brushed aside. 'And you were right to do so, I believe. What you have described is interesting but perhaps not unusual, and the young lady is typical of such cases being young, bereaved, displaced from familiar surroundings and above all female.' He gave a short laugh. 'Invariably such cases involve youthful, unmarried females. But be assured, my friend, there are treatments. Will you bring the young lady to see me?'

John stalled. He had sought advice not annexation. 'I've not told her guardian of my intention to come here today. I'd letters of introduction brought from Edinburgh and sought simply to make contact. I must proceed slowly, and with caution.'

The professor nodded, watching him. 'Very wise, of course, but you are most fortunate that I am here visiting and have time at my disposal, and most assuredly I must see her! Have you tried any medication?'

'No.'

'Excellent. Too often it does more harm than good.' John began to like the man. 'No, no, we must reach into the mind itself, and explore, and the sufferer must lead the way. Who better, after all! And if she cannot articulate her anxieties then we must discover them together, through hypnosis.' John frowned, and a finger was wagged at him. 'Ah! You scowl, my friend, and I know from discussions with the excellent Dr Linton that his colleagues hold their disdainful noses at the word. But I am no Franz Mesmer with his purple cloak, things have moved on, and in Europe the treatment enjoys a renaissance.'

Hypnosis and the hysterical state make a risky pairing, especially in cases where epilepsy is suspected. . . John had read the night before. *Conditions which make patients susceptible to hypnosis carry considerable risk and such therapies – if hypnosis can be so described – can result in replacing one set of symptoms with other, potentially more harmful, ones.*

The professor was watching him, his elbows on the table, his fingertips bouncing off each other. 'You are dubious, my friend,' he remarked, apparently amused.

'Aye.'

His host continued to smile. 'I would, of course, need to see the young lady first.' He leaned forward again, his eyes keen. 'Only consider the excellent Braid, your fellow countryman – reservations about his work had no basis in clinical reasoning, none at all, but merely resulted from professional jealousy. Perhaps you did not know that? No, no, hypnosis offers a fast – and sure – route to understanding the vagaries of the mind. The curative possibilities, dear Doktor, far outweigh imagined dangers.'

He continued to expound his views and because there was something mesmeric in the way the man himself spoke, John found himself describing the method he had used to bring Olwen Malkon out of her trance-like state. The professor clapped his hands in approval. 'There you see! Instinctively you knew what to do, my friend. I congratulate you! But beware, if she slips into such a state again, it might be more difficult to rouse her. She was rigid you said?'

'For a short spell.'

'And her eyes had rolled back?' John nodded. 'Confused upon rousing?'

'Briefly.'

Again the man tapped his teeth, this time with the pen. 'Undoubtedly I ought to see her, my friend, as I believe I could help her – although not perhaps in the customary way.'

'I'll discuss the matter with her family,' John replied, deciding it was time to escape from this determined man.

'She told you she was possessed? She used that word?'

He nodded. 'But she is, as I said, delusional. These dreams she has—'

'Has she perhaps indulged herself with seances, or encountered mediums and their tawdry tricks?'

John smiled. 'I insulted her by asking that very question and had an emphatic denial; I believe her to be an intelligent young woman.'

'Is she of a religious persuasion? No! You said it was the church that disturbed her. Interesting. . . And yet she lives within a religious household. Hmmm.' He looked at John again and he saw that he had piqued the man's interest. 'Or I could come and see her, perhaps?' He touched John's sleeve and glanced across the garden, narrowing his eyes and lowering his voice. 'It might be better if I did. I have been surprised, my friend, and somewhat dismayed, by what I have discovered here. Behaviours which simply fail to conform to convention are considered lunacy, eccentricities seen as pathologies. The goal appears to go no further than establishing the outward semblance of normality, and much reliance is placed upon the bromide and the chloral to sedate and depress not only the more excitable patients, but all of them, as a matter of routine. Physical restraints have been replaced by chemical ones – far more dangerous, in my view. Few attempts are made to address the core of the problem, but merely to contain its excesses. They douse the flames and once medication is withdrawn, symptoms flare up again, as inevitably they will, and nothing has been achieved. . . I did not expect to find it so, not here, no, no. . .' His face darkened. 'This is why I work here, in this little house, from where I can observe them as they move around the garden. It is a pretty scene, is it not? Here in the spring sunshine with their parasols and their bonnets, the men with their straw hats. Visiting families are reassured. But only see how slowly they walk, their heads down, shoulders drooping – disciplined, drugged, submissive, the walking dead. . . it is a progression that I observe too often. Better that I see her in her home.' John watched a small group of patients, attended by uniformed staff, and saw that their wanderings were indeed aimless. Brandt's voice dropped further. 'And I believe there are those here whose families are content with this regime, they require nothing more than quietude, and pay well for their relatives to remain so, kept here in such a state.'

He sat back and gave John a slanting look. 'You would not wish it for this fair young patient of yours – ' he said, flashing white teeth in a very European sort of smile ' – for she is fair, I think,' and then, the smile lingering, he gave his attention to the extinguished cigar. 'I think we will meet again, Herr Doktor, in a very short time.'

CHAPTER 11

There was much for John to think about as he continued his routine rounds of the village's sick and needy upon his return from York. He was undecided whether or not to tell the vicar about his trip; he really ought to, even if only to reassure him that help was available, should it be needed. But given Miss Malkon's reluctance to discuss her concerns with her aunt and uncle, he held back. His duty, after all, was to her, not her family, although her uncle might reasonably expect to be told. He wondered whether Susan had proved a sound ally or if they had learned of Olwen's private consultation on his garden, and what they might have made of it. Perhaps the wiser course was to wait a while and see how things developed.

So, on Sunday, when he took his customary place at the back of the church where lapses in concentration went unobserved, he was surprised, but pleased, to see Olwen Malkon enter from the porch. She paused a moment then walked steadily, if a little stiffly, down the aisle on her cousin Alfred's arm, looking directly ahead, not noticing him. A little pale, he thought as she passed him, although perhaps the mourning black exaggerated her pallor, but from what he could tell from her profile, she seemed well enough. The fact that she had steeled herself to come at all was a very good sign indeed.

Time, the great healer.

Behind her came the vicar's wife on the arm of her younger son, nodding like royalty to parishioners on either side of her, keen no doubt to quash any lingering speculation about her niece's previous odd behaviour. The woman glanced in his direction, then swiftly away with only the briefest acknowledgement.

The vicar, John noticed, had already emerged from the vestry; he seemed a decent sort of man but, like so many of his kind, rather blinkered, and John sensed he had a keen eye to his standing in his parish. He waited now, under the chancel arch, watching his family making their way, slowly – very slowly, in fact – down the aisle to their pew at the front, his hands clasped in front of him, head on one side and a benign, if slightly smug, expression on his face. The family's progress slowed to a crawl and, as if to mask this fact, John saw the vicar's wife bend to speak to a woman seated at the end of a pew beside her. They reached the spot where the previous incident had occurred, and John found himself stiffening.

It was Miss Malkon, he suddenly realised, who was slowing the little procession.

Her cousin turned to her in enquiry, and he saw Edmond step forward and take her other arm. Then, with an appalling suddenness, it happened. He heard the girl's anguished cry and watched her twist away from her cousins' hold. John had already started to move when, to his horror, he saw her lash out at Edmond, seeing blood spurting from the lad's nose. A gasp went up from the congregation and John was out of the pew then, charging forward, pushing aside those who had stepped out for a better view. Miss Malkon was struggling to free herself from her cousin's grip, kicking him, her fists flying, repeatedly crying '*No!*' as he tried to restrain her.

'Let me pass!' John demanded, forcing his way through.

The vicar had come down the chancel steps, wringing his hands, and reached her before John did, by which time Alfred Malkon had her under control, her arms pinned to her sides, and John saw her eyes widen at the sight of her uncle. '*No, priest! I will not. . .*' she cried, her words ringing clear as she struggled in her cousin's grip. '*Murderer! Traitor!*' The wild words reached a crescendo as John arrived. '*Devil!*' and he was just in time to see her spit up into her cousin's face.

Alfred, taken by surprise, must have loosened his hold and it was then that Olwen Malkon saw John. '*Heri!*' she cried and reached out to him but Alfred appeared to grab at her and she gasped, her body went rigid, eyes wide, starting in their sockets as her arms still stretched towards John and then suddenly she convulsed, bent double and vomited noisily before collapsing onto the floor, a gurgling rattle in her throat.

An appalled silence fell.

John went down on his knees beside her, horrified. Dear God! She had stiffened into some strange contorted shape, quite rigid, her eyes wide open and staring. His own hand was shaking as he took hold of her wrist. Her pulse was slow, and getting slower and he knew that they must get her out of the church at once. He gestured to Alfred Malkon who stood, his face a mask of fury, indicating that he should help him lift her, but in her rigid state she defied their efforts. Damnation. More folk were leaving their pews, drawing close and, as he cast around desperately for a solution, his eye fell on a wheeled contraption beside the wall in the south aisle. 'Fetch that,' he ordered Edmond, who was standing by, eyes agog, mopping at his bloody nose.

'*That?*'

'Bring it here.' He turned then to the vicar, who stood whimpering at the foot of the steps. 'Get them back in their pews, for God's sake,' then added savagely, 'let them sing a hymn, or say a prayer, anything! And someone fetch a mop – ' The smell of vomit was spreading through the church like a sour miasma. '– a bucket and some water.'

His wife, for all her shortcomings, had more sense than her husband. 'Hymn One Hundred and Thirty-Five,' she hissed at him. 'Start them off.' A bucket of water was sent for and the organist, having caught her words, hit the solid opening chords of Nicaea's reassuring melody.

And as his sons helped the doctor lift and position Olwen's stiff frame onto the flat boards of the wheeled rig, the vicar, clearly badly shaken, waved his congregation to their feet. Like frightened sheep they returned to their pews and raised quavering voices while herd-like, their eyes followed the rigid body of Olwen

Malkon as she was borne on creaking, unoiled wheels, out into the churchyard.

'The girl is *possessed!* There can be no other explanation.'

The service had been curtailed and the vicar, having soothed his flock as best he could, had returned to the vicarage. He now stood on the threshold of the morning room goggling at the corpse-like form of his niece who had been laid out on the daybed, his face purple with indignation. 'You heard her, Doctor! *No, priest, I will not. . .*' His bottom lip trembled in petulant affront. 'That was a demon in her speaking!'

Here was another side to the man, thought John as he struggled to keep his temper in check. 'Her affliction is of the mind, vicar, it's not the devil's work.'

'You think not? I'll have you know that just yesterday she refused to go into the church and pray with me, saying she found no comfort there.' He came closer, staring down at her in abhorrence, little beads of spittle gathering at the corners of his mouth. Gone was the benign shepherd, this man was seething with a righteous anger. 'Who says *that* except a sinner, or one possessed of the devil?'

'A troubled young woman, sir.'

'And what if I tell you that she said she *feared* to enter the house of God!'

John looked back at him, repelled. 'She told you that, and yet you insisted she attend service today?'

The vicar ignored him. 'Has she roused at all since you brought her here?'

'No.'

Mrs Malkon appeared at the door and pushed her husband aside, her face a matching shade of pink. 'Where I was brought up, those who behaved in such a disgraceful manner were shown a firm hand to restore them to their senses,' and before John could stop her, the woman bent over her niece and gave her cheek a hard slap.

'For God's *sake*, woman!' Appalled, he pulled her away, and her face grew pinker still when the slap failed to achieve its expected result.

The girl had not moved a muscle.

'I shall contact the bishop,' said the vicar. 'He'll know what to do.'

God grant that he's a sensible man, John thought, for if the vicar believed in demonic possession, what horrors was he considering? Or was he about to discover that reason and science were still in conflict with belief, with Lucifer yet unvanquished?

The door opened and Alfred Malkon entered and he too glared at the doctor. Here was another but this one, John reckoned, had designs upon her person and her purse rather than her soul. 'Has she rallied?' he asked.

'No.'

Alfred stood, staring down at her still form. 'So what happens now?'

'We wait.' John glanced towards the vicar. 'But with your permission I'll send word to a colleague at St Hilda's House.' Briefly he explained to him about his visit to York and his discussion with Professor Brandt.

'You discussed Olwen with this man?' he asked, indignant. 'Without my knowledge!'

'I mentioned no names. And we spoke in the abstract only, colleague to colleague. I wanted advice, in case of further episodes.' Which was entirely reasonable and he disliked being put on the defensive.

'Then apply what you learned, sir,' the vicar demanded. 'Or walk her back up those steps, like you did before.'

John shook his head. 'I believe this is different,' he said, without being exactly sure why. 'Last time she had banged her head, but this time there has been no physical injury. She needs professional help.'

The vicar continued to stare sourly at his niece. 'Very well. If you think it wise, send for this professor and let's hear what he suggests. Meanwhile,' he turned to his wife, 'let us eat dinner, my dear, and restore a little normality. Will you join us, Doctor?'

It was a half-hearted invitation and John shook his head. 'I'll stay here. And if you'll bring me writing materials I'll write at once to Professor Brandt.' Before the wretched man, replete with Sunday dinner, saw fit to change his mind. Pen and paper were brought; the scribbled note was sealed and handed to the vicar. 'Is there someone who would take it now?' The stable boy would go at once, the vicar assured him and left the room with his wife.

But Alfred lingered. He came to stand on the other side of Olwen. The girl's slapped cheek was a shade pinker than the other, but otherwise she was as white as alabaster, her limbs still lay at odd angles, her eyes remained closed. 'Is she so deranged then,' he asked, his eyes not leaving her face, 'that you would go to St Hilda's?'

'Disturbed,' John replied. 'And we need to understand the nature of her affliction so that—'

'Her father was quite eccentric, you know, and her brothers allowed to run wild.' John made no comment. There was nothing lover-like in the way the young man looked down at her, then his gaze shifted to John. 'She called you that name again.'

'Aye, she did.' John sat back, giving him look for look.

'Why would that be?'

John held his glare. 'Do you suspect a dalliance, Mr Malkon?' The young man did not reply and went back to considering his cousin. 'She also cried devil, murderer, traitor,' he reminded him. 'How d'you account for that?' Alfred shrugged and John dismissed him. 'Go and eat your dinner, man, and close the door behind you.'

But Alfred was not done. 'Pa's not the only one talking of possession, you know. Everyone's a-buzz with it, saying the girl's cursed.' He gave a mirthless laugh. 'But then what do you expect, for God's sake, after that performance and then, on top of it, they see her taken out of church like a corpse, wheeled down the aisle on the coffin bier.'

He left John standing there, staring at the closed door. The coffin bier! Good God. In the heat of the moment he had not realised. What a macabre sight it must have been. . . But what else could he have done? He went and sat again beside Olwen, chastened and now even more deeply concerned.

Half an hour passed and she did not move. How still she was, and how pale. Her pulse had strengthened a little and steadied, but her breathing was still shallow. Brutal as her aunt's treatment had been, it had at least demonstrated that this was no performance. *If she slips into such a state again, it might be more difficult to rouse her*, Brandt had said, and John prayed the man would come, though he could hardly be expected before morning.

Would she lie like this until then?

He let his gaze dwell on her. No other patient had ever had this effect on him, never before had he had this strange feeling of being drawn in, of a very personal involvement. And a responsibility that went far beyond the professional. . .

He rose and went to the window, struggling to restore the physician in himself, and went on standing there, staring out at the garden. A little gust of wind blew in and he turned back to her, seeing it lift a tendril of hair on her forehead, giving the illusion of movement, and he went back to her and said her name. No response. He sat down again and continued to watch her and, as the sun moved round, the room grew warm, and his eyelids became heavy.

His chin sank onto his chest.

And suddenly he was away with her, and her brothers too, and they were fleeing in desperate haste. His heart was pumping hard as they hastened down overgrown streets, past long-ruined buildings, urging them forward, tense and furtive, checking over his shoulder, pausing at every corner. Veering off down a narrow alley, he crossed a patch of wasteland, before turning, beckoning them on. And then, bizarrely, he was lowering her brothers down a hole in the ground – into a well or some such – and he was telling her that she must go next, and she did and then he went down after them, pulling a slab over the hole, and they were in darkness, underground in some sort of dark enclosed tunnel, forced to crouch as they scrambled along—

He woke with a start, blinking and shaken, his pulse still pounding. He had slept! Good God. And dreamed again. . . He glanced at the clock, his mouth dry. Five minutes only. The dream had done what dreams so often do, distorted time, racing on.

And then he saw that Olwen had changed position, just a little and, even as he watched her, she began to straighten. He leaned close, watching her intently, hardly daring to believe, but saw a softening ripple through her body. It was like seeing a marble statue come to life and she shifted where she lay, realigning herself; her lips parted and she made a sound somewhere between a moan and a sigh.

'Wyn?' he said, keeping his voice low. 'Can you hear me?' He saw the tip of her tongue emerge to moisten her lips.

Her eyes opened, and became fixed, staring, onto his.

'You came,' she said.

But he barely heard the words for he was looking into her eyes, hardly able to credit what he saw, and she looked back at him, unfocused and confused.

And in seeing pupils that were pinprick small, he realised that a very different sort of devilry had been at play. *Damn them!* He felt his gorge rise and swore softly, leaning close, noting now that her breath smelled strong and cloying, that her skin was clammy. Opium – laudanum, most likely – the signs were very clear. He got to his feet and stared down at her, grim-faced and furious.

That was how they had got her into the church!

And it changed everything.

He turned, prepared to go into the dining room there and then and make an almighty scene, but he stopped halfway to the door. What if he was mistaken? What if these symptoms were associated with whatever else afflicted her, something outside his experience, something he did not understand?

And what if they denied it?

She had closed her eyes again and now appeared to be sleeping, no longer in a trance; her breathing had become more regular, her mouth slightly open. Her colour was returning too. No, he must wait, and consider. By tomorrow the effects would not be apparent but if Brandt came, he must tell him of his suspicions. They might dose her again in the meantime and then Brandt could judge for himself, but if he was correct, then much was explained. The physical symptoms fitted and if they had been feeding her laudanum this would account for a great deal - her strange dreams, her paranoia, her delusions. She had told him herself that her aunt had given her the wretched stuff to help her sleep and perhaps she continued to do so.

Mrs Malkon chose that moment to enter the room. 'No change?' she asked, glancing coldly at her niece.

'Quite the opposite,' he replied, with equal frigidity. 'She roused briefly, and now I believe she's sleeping, not exactly naturally, but if I'm right I imagine she'll remain asleep for several hours.' He watched the woman's face as he spoke but she showed no emotion. 'When she wakes, I suggest she's given very simple food, porridge, fruit, vegetables, nothing that is binding. It will help her to recover. And *nothing* else at all.' Still no response.

'Very well, Doctor.'

The vicar appeared and John repeated what he had said and saw only relief in the man's face. No, he thought, glancing again at Mrs Malkon, it was his wife who was the culprit here.

'I have written to the bishop,' the vicar said as John took his leave. 'He will know what we should do.'

CHAPTER 12

He had called her Wyn.
Wyn, he had said, *Can you hear me?* Knowing that he had come at last had given her a such profound relief that she had sunk into the deep cushion of sleep. But relief was soon shattered, for now it was not Heri whose voice awakened her, but her elder brother Ælf, scratching furtively at her chamber door. '*Wyn!*'

She rose, pressed her cheek to the wood and whispered back. 'What's wrong?'

'Open the door, Wyn, but *quietly*.' The fear in his voice had her fumbling for the bolt and she opened the door to find him stood there and had just enough time to see movement in the shadows before a hand closed over her mouth.

'Say not a word.' Instantly she recognised the soft northern burr.

Another figure stood in the doorway of the boys' chamber, his hand resting lightly on the shoulder of her younger brother, Ælfwinne, who stood, wide-eyed and trembling, a sack at his feet. 'Black treachery, lady,' Heri whispered in her ear. 'The king is dead and your brothers' lives hang by a thread.' Her eyes flew to his and he removed his hand. 'Make no sound, we must away.'

'*Dead!*' she breathed.

'Bring only what you must.' She stood frozen, incapable of thought. 'Swiftly now. Trust me, lady, we must fly!'

And so through the sleeping hall they crept, past the cold embers of the fire where last evening they had sat, she sewing, the boys playing a game. Osred had been there with them, lounging beside the hearth, watching her over the rim of his ale cup. As they passed through the hall now, one of her father's wolfhounds raised its head, its tail thumping a greeting, but Ælf bent to reassure it and it settled again. Nothing else stirred in the hall, and they slipped out through the door where a cold dawn was lightening cloud-heavy skies.

Heri led and his companion followed after, casting frequent glances behind him, a seax in his hand, and they weaved their way between the collection of buildings outside the hall heading, not as Wyn expected, towards the great west gate but in the opposite direction, into the heart of the old fortress, flattening themselves against walls at every corner. Wyn followed her brothers in a daze. *The king is dead. . .* But how could this be? He had been gone but a week, to a sudden council in the north. . . *and your brothers' lives hang by a thread.* The boys were following Heri as if in a trance, ashen-faced, numb but trusting, close on his heels. It was impossible to absorb and yet if what Heri said was true, he was right; without their father they were as defenceless as puppies, too young to have followers of their own, too weak to extract revenge. And once word spread that Northumbria's throne was empty even their staunchest allies might pause, reconsider their fealty, and realign themselves. She knew this all too well.

In a former side street, now little more than a rough path, Heri pulled them aside. They waited behind a spread of alder scrub and thistles that grew in what had once been the courtyard of a dwelling while the two men checked again that they had not been followed, then Heri led them down an alley. Between broken but upstanding walls an area had been cleared and turnips were ripening in a patch of cultivation beside a half-ruined building. He went across to a shadowed corner and, after glancing back one last time, he bent and prised up a large flat stone. 'Bri!' he called, and his companion went to him.

Together they slid the stone aside. It had been covering a hole. A well?

'We go to ground – ' Heri said, with a nod to the boys ' – like foxes. You first, Ælf, then your brother. Watch your footing, crouch low and move along a little way so there is space for the others.' Before Wyn could protest the men had seized her older brother and lowered him down. He vanished into the blackness and Heri turned to Ælfwinne. 'Ready, lad?' and the boy, wide-eyed but stoic, nodded. Wyn came alive then, pulling at Heri's sleeve. 'But what is it?'

'An old water system, from ancient times, leads to the river. Now you, Wyn.' He called softly down to Ælf to be ready, then lifted her and she too descended into the unknown.

It was not a long drop and Ælf steadied her until she found firm ground. She crouched beside him gripping onto his hand and, as her eyes adjusted, she saw that they were in a low tunnel that headed off into darkness. Something black scuttled past her legs as the two men leapt down and crouched beside them. 'I'll lead,' Heri said. 'Ælfwinne, follow me, then Ælf, you last, Wyn; Bri will be right behind you. Follow close, use your hands to guide you, crawl when you must.' He brought his face close to Ælfwinne's and gripped the boy's shoulders. 'We'll lead them, eh lad, you and I?' And as the stone was slid back into place, the darkness was absolute.

Half crouching, half crawling, they made their way along the tunnel and she breathed in the rank odour of rot and decay. In places they had to scramble past roof falls, and once she looked up and saw a screen of brambles above them, filtering in the early morning light. Heri allowed them to stand there for a moment, and stretch. He had been down here before, he explained, in happier days, brought by one of her father's men, outwitting friends who were searching for them above. 'There are others too,' he told them, 'leading down to the river.'

'Is that where we're going?' Ælf asked.

'Aye, lad. Press on.'

And so they continued. Wyn stumbled frequently but followed blindly, scraping her knees and snagging her clothing, too terrified to think, too distraught to consider where they were being taken. Once she caught her head on the low roof and cried out.

'Courage, lady,' Bri said from behind, his hand under her elbow, steadying her. Then she noticed that the floor was wetter than before and, at the same instant, Heri called back to them. 'The tide has turned. Make haste!' The tide! But of course, the tunnel would fill as the river rose; a drain flushed twice daily. Panicked at the thought, she hurried forward, all else forgotten, until she glimpsed daylight ahead.

They emerged, one by one, to find that the skies were lighter and that they were at the riverbank, a little way downstream from the bridge, and they hid, shivering, beside a boat on a rubbly slipway, catching their breath. On the opposite bank she saw the ramshackle timber buildings close to where the ships from Frisia had pulled up that day.

Heri caught her eye, and held it a moment, then turned away to confer with Bri.

'Wait here,' he said, and was gone before she could protest. Bri pulled the two shivering boys close, tucking one under each arm, holding them to his broad chest. He was a big man, sandy haired and bearded, and exuded comfort. 'Rest, lady,' he said to her. 'We've a journey ahead.'

'Where are we going?' Ælfwinne turned his head to look up at him, but the man just ruffled his hair. And so they sat and they waited and they watched as the tide edged higher, and as it did the boat against which they were leaning began to move, rocking slightly as the tide pushed upriver. Gently the stern began to lift.

Suddenly Heri was back, sliding down beside them, breathless, a pair of oars in his hands, his eyes very much alive. He spoke quickly to Bri before turning to where Wyn sat huddled beside her brothers. 'We take this boat. You first, lads, climb in and keep low. Now you, Wyn,' he said, and gave her his hand.

And so, in a stolen boat in an awakening day that was like no other, they set off upriver, the men pulling hard at the oars, keeping to the middle of the current with the three fugitives hunkered down at their feet. Last night's moon had been full so the tide was strong, conquering the current and thus easing their passage under the low arch of the bridge. And soon, she saw, they would pass in front of the great tower behind which lay their father's hall.

The king is dead. . .

The horror of it hit her at last and she closed her eyes in defence against the words. It could not be true! When she opened them again she found that Heri was looking down at her as he rowed, guessing, perhaps, where her thoughts had taken her. His expression was grim but he said nothing and resumed his scanning of the riverbank, his head swivelling from side to side as he pulled at his oar, in rhythm with Bri, harnessing the tide. Had their disappearance been discovered, she wondered, was the hunt already on?

'Osred!' she cried out suddenly, having given him no thought until now.

Heri looked down at her. 'What of him?'

She had no love for the man but he too was her father's kinsman. 'Will he not be in danger?' The two men kept rowing. 'He didn't go north with my father, he remained here, with us, in Eoforwic.'

'Aye.'

'But he'll not know what has happened,' she insisted, but the men rowed on, harsh faced, and their silence was eloquent. 'What are you not saying?' she asked, hardly daring to imagine.

'The cleg has a new host, lady.'

She stared at him. *'No!'*

And who did he mean? Not Æthelred surely? Heri scowled back. 'Do we return then, lady, and ask him?'

She slumped back in the boat, her heart pounding painfully. Conscious that her brothers, still in shock, were looking to her for guidance, she lay there staring up at the sky where clouds were thickening, and already there were spots of rain. The wind too was rising but it was blowing north, favouring them. Only last night Osred had sat across from her in the hall, watching the boys at their game. 'They'd be as brothers to me,' he had said, pressing his suit, which was now under negotiation. The boys

had looked up, exchanged glances and Ælf had muttered something that had made his brother laugh.

Had Osred truly known what news this day would bring? And
would he have had them slain?

A mile or so upriver, well away now from the sprawl of ancient
ruins and riverside shacks, the two men pulled into the bank and
rested a moment, drawing the boat under the drooping branches
of a willow. Heri reached into his jacket and pulled out a flat cob,
dividing it between them, giving the smallest piece to her. 'Osred
will be declared king in your father's place,' he said, with brutal
directness, 'but he'll be king in name only. There are stronger
forces at play.' She stared at him, speechless. He *must* mean
Æthelred, the banished one. 'Some say that Mercia was involved,'
he continued, 'others believe that the northern earls seek to forge
a new alliance. But whichever is true, Osred is a traitor and fool,
and will be king for only as long as it suits their purpose.'

'But *I* am my father's heir!' Ælf declared with all the bravado
of his thirteen years.

Heri looked grimly back. 'Aye, lad, and for that reason you'd
have been ravens' meat by sunset.' Ælf's face blanched and she
saw fear bloom in Ælfwinne's eyes. 'But your father has loyal
men too. We'll take you to a place of safety, and see what Modig
plans.'

'But Osred is our kin, he was to marry our sister,' Ælfwinne
protested. Three years his brother's junior, he was still trusting
of the world. 'He'd not have harmed her.'

Heri bit off a chunk of bread and chewed, considering her.
'Perhaps not. And wedding Ælfwald's daughter would strengthen
his position.'

'I'd see him burn first.'

He smiled a little and nodded at the bread, untouched, in
her hand. 'Eat, lady. Defiance requires strength.' Then he pushed
the boat back out into the current and the two men took up
the oars again.

'Where are we going?' Ælf asked again as they settled back
into the rhythm of rowing.

'We go north,' Heri answered and for the first time she saw a smile light his eyes. 'To Hen Ogledd, the old north, beyond the Wall, to the ancient realm of the Gododdin and the heroes of old.'

CHAPTER 13

John was down at the vicarage early next morning. Brandt had sent a message that he would arrive by ten o'clock and John hoped to catch him before they saw the vicar, explain the situation more fully and confide in him his suspicions. His own arrival, however, coincided with that of a large old-fashioned carriage that had drawn up outside the vicarage gate, and he saw the vicar scurrying across the gravel to greet the descending occupant. He spotted John, who then had no option but to go forward and join them.

'Bishop, dear me. And Doctor. Good morning! I didn't expect. . . so soon. A timely arrival. . .. Bishop, this is Dr Osbourne. Doctor, my bishop. Goodness. . . So quick. . . my letter to you can hardly have—'

The bishop nodded briefly at John before turning back to the vicar. 'I've received no letter,' he replied in stern tones. 'I am here in response to disturbing news brought by a parishioner last night, who came in great distress, and she spoke of an appalling business.' The vicar tried to interject. 'A hysterical outrage, in your church, by your *own* niece, no less! Screaming, cursing, spitting, vomiting—'

'Bishop, I—'

'And then, some parody of a funeral!'

'No, really, it was—'

'And not the first incident, I understand. Why was I not told?'

Any hope that John would be dealing with a rational individual evaporated. The bishop was elderly, he had a sculptured face with a hooked nose, thin lips, and an uncompromising eye under which the vicar was visibly quaking as he ushered him into the house, grovelling and incoherent. John hesitated a moment and then followed; he had planned to wait outside for Brandt but decided he must hear how the vicar would present matters.

The household was thrown into confusion by the prelate's unheralded arrival. There was no sign of Olwen Malkon but the vicar's wife emerged from the morning room and greeted the bishop, obsequiously offering refreshments, which were curtly refused; she managed only a tight smile for John.

They would go into the study, the vicar said, where they would not be disturbed. Once there, he embarked on a tortuous explanation whose main objective seemed to be to deflect blame from himself. John sat back and left him to it, interjecting only occasionally, or when appealed to by the bishop. 'Losing all her family,' he remarked as the vicar's garbled account drew to a stumbling close, 'makes her distress entirely understandable.'

'But *we* are her family,' the vicar wailed. 'We stand between her and the world. We've done all we could for her, Bishop, and it's no secret that it was her father's dying wish that she marries one of her cousins. Alfred, the elder, has the *most* affectionate feelings for Olwen and in time. . . The future holds no worries for her.'

The bishop was unmollified. 'And yet she behaves in this outrageous manner! Is the girl wilful or wicked?'

'Neither—' John began but was baulked by a splutter of indignation from the vicar.

'She is *afraid* to enter the church, she told me so herself.'

'It was unwise to have forced her,' John remarked, which earned him a quelling look from the bishop.

'Of what is she afraid?' he asked.

'She says she doesn't know, but it's my belief that she's—'

'In cases such as these,' John interjected, desperately wishing that Brandt would arrive, 'an irrational paranoid fear is not unusual and it's—'

The bishop put up his hand. 'You are a physician, I understand. So what is her physical state? Is there anything actually *wrong* with her?'

That he could ask such a question said a great deal about the man. 'The physical and the mental are inseparable.'

The answer failed to satisfy. 'But has she physical complaints, symptoms, a fever, no. . . no complications of a female nature?'

'These are not the only criteria—'

'Because if there's nothing actually wrong with her *person*, then logically her malady is of an emotional – a spiritual – nature and is therefore the concern of the Church rather than the medical profession.' The vicar nodded vigorously in support. 'You are a Scot,' he continued, ignoring his subordinate and continuing to address John, 'and as such, not of our Church?'

'I was brought up a Presbyterian,' John replied, disliking where the conversation was heading.

The bishop gave a thin smile. 'The authority of the Church is understood rather differently north of the border. But you will appreciate, I'm sure, that I have two matters to consider here. Two duties. To the girl herself, of course, but just as importantly, to the congregation. What happened yesterday in church was an abomination and will have upset a good many souls. It cannot continue.'

John kept onto his temper. 'Miss Malkon would be the first to agree with you.'

'She said some extraordinary things, I hear.' The bishop put on his spectacles and pulled a piece of paper from his pocket. 'I made a note of what I was told. She cursed one of her cousins in a most unseemly manner and then struck the other, and began brawling with them like a common. . . well, never mind. What concerns me more are the words *No, priest. . . I will not. . .* addressed to you, Vicar. And then *Murderer, Traitor* and – ' he paused weightily ' – *Devil.*'

John attempted to interject again but the bishop raised his hand and continued, still consulting his notes, his glasses on the end of his nose.

'She then proceeded to spit at her cousin, indulge herself in some sort of fit and vomit in the aisle before going into some sort of rigid trance-like state.' He removed the glasses and moistened his lips with a pale tongue. 'An appalling litany, sir! And while she has our profoundest sympathy regarding her recent bereavements, such a very public rejection of God, manifest in the person of her uncle, speaking these dreadful words before the altar, and her persistent refusal to attend church. . . Well, this troubles me deeply, Doctor, very deeply indeed. In short, I believe the devil has found a way into the wretched girl's soul.'

The vicar made an anguished yelping sound, and nodded vigorously.

Thoroughly disgusted with them both, John held hard to his temper. 'Demonomania, Bishop, is hardly a useful diagnosis—'

'You misunderstand me, Doctor. I am not suggesting that Miss Malkon *believes* herself to be possessed, but that she *is* possessed.' Again the lips were moistened.

John struggled to conceal his revulsion. 'Bishop, her symptoms quite clearly indicate—'

'But she *has* no symptoms, you said so yourself.'

It was perhaps fortunate that at that moment Susan tapped on the door to announce that Professor Brandt had arrived and was waiting in the hall. Never had John felt more in need of a colleague's support! The vicar had clearly forgotten the arrangement but hastily explained who their visitor was. The bishop frowned and looked on the point of refusing him when Brandt walked briskly through the door, handing his hat and coat to Susan.

'Good morning, gentlemen,' he said. 'I came, as requested, with all speed.'

John breathed again and made the required introductions. Brandt looked keenly at the two churchmen, making each a small bow, and then sat, looking from one to the other while John, as succinctly as possible, brought him up to date with developments. 'For some reason, which is unclear even to Miss Malkon, the church appears to be the trigger for these episodes,' he concluded. 'Although we—'

'Happily, we find ourselves in agreement on this point.' The bishop reasserted himself, speaking loudly in urbane tones. 'The young lady apparently remains more or less calm and normal until she is brought to the church, and once inside the demons writhe.'

Professor Brandt stared at him. 'Forgive me. . . I do not understand.'

'The girl is possessed, my good Professor! *No, priest, I will not.* Nothing could be more clear; demons speak through her! And for her to exhibit such a clear, and *violent*, rejection of her uncle and the Church this points in one direction only – ' Brandt exchanged a startled look with John. ' – I believe her to be suffering from demonic oppression, some evil force has gained control of her and—'

'No.' Brandt spoke firmly, and John could only hope that he would be a match for the man. 'A hundred times no, sir! We have moved far from such thinking in matters of the mind. What you suggest is preposterous!' The bishop bristled. 'And if you are considering subjecting this girl to some form of exorcism, or even if you compel her to go back into that church against her will, you will be responsible for doing her a very grievous harm—'

The bishop's expression hardened. 'While one can only admire the strides made by modern science, some ancient truths still hold. The devil remains at large in the world, make no mistake, and weakened vessels provide an easy target. Young women, by nature passive and fragile, all too frequently fall prey in this manner and the only remedy is for her to be made to confront her demons. They must be driven from her!'

'You reject decades of advances in medical science and understanding, Bishop,' Brandt stated sternly.

The bishop glared back. 'And you, sir, reject centuries of Christian teaching. You must forgive me if I remark that you are very sure of yourself for one who has yet to set eyes upon the girl!'

'Let that be instantly corrected. It is why I am here.'

A stubborn look had settled on the bishop's face and John thought rapidly. It would be a risk, but could perhaps be turned to their advantage, and might serve his purpose very well. 'Since you too, Bishop, have not yet seen her, why not let Miss Malkon come here now, and speak for herself.' Brandt shot John a worried look. 'Then we can all hear what she has to say.'

There was a moment's quick discussion between vicar and bishop and then the bell was rung and Susan despatched.

Miss Malkon appeared a few moments later, halting in the doorway, clearly taken aback at the sight of the four men gathered there, all eyes turned towards her. John wished he could have spared her this but her wretched aunt must be called to account. She looked across at him but he could only give her the briefest of nods by way of reassurance before the vicar beckoned her in. There was something doll-like in her obedience, he noted, and his suspicions were rekindled. He vacated his own chair for her and went to stand beside the window where he could see her face.

She looked pale, a little dazed, as well she might.

'My dear Miss Malkon,' the bishop began. 'We are all distressed by your circumstances and were just agreeing that mind and body are as one in many ways – ' Brandt raised an eyebrow '– and while ailments of the body are best treated by physicians, disorders such as yours are of a spiritual concern.' The girl looked blankly back at him, saying nothing. 'And so, to better understand what it is that troubles you and, at the same time, to seek the comfort of the Lord, I should like you to come now, with myself and your uncle, into the church, and we—'

Damn the man. 'Bishop—' John protested.

'No.' It was Miss Malkon who spoke, her voice somehow altered.

John stiffened.

'And why is that, young lady?' the bishop asked,

'Because. . . because of what will happen there.'

'What will—?'

'Wait!' John went across to her. 'Look up at me, if you will,' he said and she raised her eyes to his. At once his suspicions were confirmed. 'Have you taken laudanum this morning, Miss Malkon?'

'Laudanum. . . ?'

'Or rather, have you been *given* laudanum?'

Brandt too was on his feet, peering into her eyes.

John swung round on the vicar. 'Yesterday, you drugged your niece to get her to the church, didn't you? And that was why she—'

Brandt took a grip on his arm and squeezed it with surprising strength. 'My dear colleague,' he murmured, then turned to the vicar. 'But this is a fact we must establish, sir. Miss Malkon would certainly appear to have consumed opiates. The signs are very clear.'

The vicar stared back at him, goggle-eyed. 'I. . . I really have no idea.'

'Let's ask your wife.' John strode across the room and tugged at the bell. The vicar protested and the bishop straightened in his chair, frowning, but Susan appeared and they had little option but to summon her mistress.

Mrs Malkon, however, made no pretence of denial. 'A few drops in her tea at breakfast, to calm her. She has been distressed.'

John turned aside, not trusting himself to speak. The bishop, however, beamed at her. 'I occasionally find the tincture beneficial myself—'

'Are you aware, sir, of the strong hallucinatory properties of laudanum?' Brandt enquired, cutting him off. 'Especially for those unaccustomed to it, and more particularly for those already in a fractured mental state.' He paused but, eliciting no response, continued. 'It produces a short-lived euphoria or restlessness, an unnatural animation, followed by melancholia, which craves relief in larger doses for it is a highly addictive substance.' He looked severely from one to the other but still no one spoke. He glanced back at Olwen Malkon, who sat, staring at them in a bewildered, rather vacant, way. 'It can cause alarming behaviours, feeding the imagination with vivid, often hideous images, causing delusions, in some cases wild mood swings, and even suicidal impulses. More or less exactly those aspects that have been chronicled in this young woman's case.' Brandt spoke in a detached clinical manner but his contempt was obvious. 'Here be your demons, Bishop, conjured from a bottle, not the pit of Hell.'

Both bishop and vicar were silenced. It was unfortunate that a flame in the hearth chose that moment to leap and spurt in a display of iridescent colours as gas was released, hissing, from the coal. It seemed to give the bishop renewed confidence. 'You exaggerate, surely.'

Brandt turned to the vicar's wife. 'For how long have you been feeding her laudanum, madam?'

Mrs Malkon had taken a seat and was sat upright, hands folded on her lap, and was in no way discomforted. 'Since she's been having these silly fits, disturbing everyone with her hysterics.'

So two weeks at least, John calculated, time enough for damage to be done, but perhaps not irreparable harm. 'Increasing the number of drops each day, I imagine?'

She nodded. 'As required. Initially, it was just to help her to sleep, to cope with the grief of loss.'

The Bishop nodded. 'Very wise.'

But Brandt's eyebrows had shot up. '*Initially?* So ever since her father died, in fact? Which is almost a month ago, I understand.'

She bridled. 'Not every day.'

John swore under his breath and turned to the window, his hands thrust deep into his pockets; he would have cheerfully throttled the woman.

The bishop, however, was making soothing noises. 'I'm sure you acted with the very best of motives, Mrs Malkon.'

'Even so, unwittingly or not,' Brandt continued, 'the results will have been most injurious. It takes so little time to form a dependency, and in the meantime the experiences endured can be terrifying.'

The bishop gave him a long considering look. 'My understanding is that laudanum also reduces inhibition.'

'It does.'

'Allows a lowering of the defences, a moral recklessness?'

Brandt nodded. 'In some cases, a complete change of personality.'

'Which, in turn, leaves a person prey for evil forces—'

John swung back, revolted. 'For God's sake, man, will you cling to your demons?'

'I wish to leave.' Miss Malkon, who had said nothing throughout, now rose and stood, swaying slightly. 'I'll hear no more, I should like to return, with Heri, to my father's hall and I demand to see my brothers. You can no longer hold me here.'

All eyes went to her, and even the bishop was silenced. 'She harps on her brothers so,' the vicar whispered, 'and there is that name again.'

But Brandt was watching her intently, his eyes narrowed, and he too rose. 'Would you allow me to escort you instead?' he asked.

She looked at Brandt, puzzled, as if struggling to place him, then looked across at John. 'Shall I go with him?'

'Yes,' said John, holding his fury in check, his heart breaking for her. 'You can trust this man.'

'But later, *you* will come, won't you?' He saw that her eyelids were drooping and Brandt put a hand under her elbow to steady her. Beneath the pleading there was an intimacy clear for all to hear.

'Yes,' he said, gravely, no longer caring what they thought. 'I will come.'

CHAPTER 14

John's eyes remained fixed for a moment on the door through which Brandt had taken Olwen Malkon, trying to imagine where it was that her mind had gone, and when his gaze returned to the two churchmen, their scowls were as one. 'Tell me, Dr Osbourne, why does my niece repeatedly refer to you as Harry?' The vicar spoke coldly.

'Confused by the laudanum, I imagine, as Professor Brandt described.'

The bishop and the vicar exchanged looks. 'Indeed?' said the bishop. 'Or perhaps, something more. . . ?'

It was clear what they were thinking and the vicar became emboldened. 'It seems to me, Doctor, that much of Olwen's affliction, as you like to call it, can be traced to her first association with *you*.'

John snorted. 'In that I first rendered her assistance when she was first afflicted, yes. It's often so with doctors and their patients.'

His sarcasm was lost on the vicar but the bishop looked down his nose at him. 'And one must consider what else often transpires between doctors and youthful female patients,' he said, and turned to his subordinate. 'I think, Vicar, that a second opinion is to be sought.'

'Which Professor Brandt will be able to offer,' John replied, knowing he was losing ground.

'A foreign gentleman. . .' the bishop murmured, and continued to address the vicar. 'I shall ask my own physician to come and see her, as I believe there is more to this than what can reasonably be laid at laudanum's door.'

'That would be most kind.' They turned away, conferring in

low voices while John watched the door, waiting anxiously for Brandt's return.

He appeared a moment later. 'The young lady is sleeping,' he said, addressing the two churchmen, 'which is no surprise given, I understand, that some ten drops of laudanum were added to her morning tea.' John made an angry sound. 'Any hope of reaching a conclusion regarding her condition is lost for the moment.'

The bishop rose. 'You are very good to have come here at such short notice, Dr Brandt. And your services too have been appreciated, Dr Osbourne. I will, however, send my own physician, a very experienced man, to see Miss Malkon as soon as can be arranged, in the expectation that further light can be cast on this sorry situation. Once we have his view, the vicar and I will be better able to decide upon a course of action. Do you agree, Vicar?'

'Most assuredly.'

'A fresh set of eyes, I think, and a rather different approach, is needed here.' He reached for the bell and rang it. 'Good day to you both, gentlemen.'

John strode away from the vicarage more angry than he had ever been, grinding the gravel beneath his feet.

'Calm yourself, my friend,' the professor called after him. 'And let us repair to the churchyard, a fitting place for reflection, I think.' He went through the lychgate and John followed him to a seat beside the churchyard wall.

'Was she all right?' he asked. 'Wyn. . . Miss Malkon, when you left her, was she all right?'

Brandt inspected the seat, brushed aside a twig, and sat. Reaching into his pocket he brought out a silver cigar case, selected a cigar and proceeded to light it with great deliberation.

John, feeling anything but reflective, found his fury rapidly transferring to the man. 'Well, was she?' he demanded.

Brandt drew on the cigar, inspected it, and gestured for John to sit. 'As I said, she fell asleep almost at once, which was hardly surprising after ten drops, though the lady of the house was uncertain of the strength of the tincture.'

John put his head in his hands. 'We *have* to get her away from there.' Brandt continued to regard him, his eyes narrowed against the cigar smoke. 'The bishop'll not give up on his demons, you know, he's positively relishing the idea of ridding her of them!'

Brandt took another draw. 'A symptom often associated with the use of laudanum is of heightened sensuality,' he remarked, 'and increased sexual arousal.'

John looked up. 'Meaning what?'

Brandt considered the end of his cigar then gave John a dry smile. 'More frequently associated with the patient, however, than the physician.' John's brows snapped together and Brandt laughed, displaying his white teeth. 'I do not censure you, my friend, but your attraction for this young lady has deprived you of your ability to reason and, I fear, has robbed you of your patient.' John glared at him and Brandt continued smoking, allowing him time to absorb the rebuke. 'Although, I fear, the die was already cast; science was in retreat. And you are right, the churchmen want their demons, that much is clear, but how do we prevent them? Hers is an interesting case, and I believe that I could help her, although I doubt I'll be given the opportunity to do so.' They sat in silence for a while. 'And when you are calm again, you will, perhaps, tell me what it is you have so far kept from me.'

'What? Nothing. . .'

'Who is Harry?' Brandt arched his eyebrows in enquiry. 'As we went up to her chamber she was asking me why he had remained behind. It was perfectly clear to both myself and her aunt that she meant you, and there was something very tender in her tone.' John looked aside, thoroughly confused himself, and watched the bees flitting amongst meadow flowers growing against the wall. 'If I am to be of any assistance in this case, then you must tell me every detail of your encounters with this young woman.'

John stared across at the church, and took a moment to collect his thoughts, struggling to disentangle the facts from the dreams he had had, and to separate himself from the emotion the latter had engendered. Then he turned to Brandt and recounted as faithfully as he was able the events of the past weeks, and as he spoke the cigar between the professor's fingers went out and he did not relight it. Instead, as John concluded, the man sat back and closed his eyes.

'You called her Wyn, just now,' he said, his eyes still shut. 'You asked if Wyn was all right, changing it swiftly to Miss Malkon.'

'Did I?'

'You did. Why was that?'

'I didn't know I had.'

'When I was with her I asked her name, to see what she would say, and she said it was Olwen – which of course I knew – but she pronounced it oddly, and then she said that most people call her Wyn.' He straightened and looked closely at John. 'Had she said the same to you at some time?'

John thought back rapidly. 'No.'

'So why did you call her by that name?'

'I must have dreamed it.' He frowned, distracted momentarily from his anger.

The professor studied him. 'Tell me about these dreams.'

'They are just dreams, nonsense, a meaningless jumble.'

'No dreams are without meaning. They include this young woman?'

'Yes.'

'You've dreamed of her often?'

He thought back, it was hard to remember. 'Two or three times, I believe. Maybe more. . .'

'Are they of a sensual nature?'

John glowered at him. 'Sometimes.'

'Go on.'

There was a quality to Brandt's voice that once again induced disclosure. 'In the dreams I feel responsible, more than one might expect in the case of a patient. And protective. . . Yesterday, for example, while sat waiting for her to rouse, I fell asleep briefly, and dreamed that I was rescuing her from some threat, some danger – which, in reality, I am catastrophically failing to do.'

'Describe this dream.'

And so John told him what he could remember of it, how her brothers had been there, and the dark tunnel through which they had escaped. Brandt listened gravely and then chuckled. 'You cast yourself as a heroic figure, my friend.' John shrugged. 'And why not, eh? If not in dreams where can we live out such fantasies?' He began the business of relighting his cigar. 'It would appear that the young lady is exercising a very strong influence on you, Herr Doktor and, whether or not you will admit it, you are powerfully attracted to her. A tunnel is not only a common trope in dreams but has other metaphorical associations, which I can leave to your imagination.' John turned away, beginning to regret involving him, but Brandt continued to chuckle. 'Unless, of course, you are playing host to the same cast of demons. Shall we return to the vicarage and put that suggestion to the bishop? If I am not mistaken in the man, he would seek a common purge or might decide to place you side by side on a pile of faggots and set you both alight.'

John found himself smiling in return. 'That'd make those demons writhe,' he said, breaking the tension between them.

They parted soon afterwards, Brandt recommending that John stay away from the vicarage for a day or two and then try to mend his relationship with the vicar. 'I believe that your initial diagnosis of grief is correct, but there is perhaps something more, for the moment masked and complicated by the laudanum. We can only hope that the bishop's physician condemns its further use.'

John held out little hope. 'And if he doesn't? And if they proceed with whatever ghastly ritual they have in mind, what then?'

'Then things will not go well for Miss Malkon.' Brandt's face was grave. 'But without her guardian's consent there is nothing you can do to assist her, so you must try to win back his trust.' He took John's hand and gripped it, fixing him with a stern eye.

'Do not do anything foolish. If you let your passions ride you, young man, you'll become as dangerous to her as the dreaded tincture. Act upon reason else your dreams will not be of heroic rescue but tragic failure. I will think a little more on the case and will write to you.'

CHAPTER 15

Olwen roused. Her head was far from clear, and she looked around the room trying to place what had happened. She must have slept. . . The foreign man had gone, taking the sharp-featured woman with him. She was alone. And she lay a moment and then pulled herself up and sat, cudgelling her brain to reason. Vaguely she recalled four men staring at her – one she knew and another who must have been the archbishop's emissary, and the stranger with the accent of a foreigner. And Heri! He had been there, but held back, his eyes searching hers but distancing her. Why was that? She felt tears surfacing and was hopelessly confused. Or had it been the doctor who was there? He had said she could trust the foreigner so she had gone with him, but she had been puzzled, looking back over her shoulder at him. Why had he chosen to stay? And she wanted to know what they been saying, these men who had gathered and who had questioned her. The foreigner had spoken kindly, asking her name, and his voice had been gentle, but why had they come? She slid back down under the blankets, despairing of making sense of things. Heri had said that he would come to her, and so she must be patient, and wait.

She closed her eyes, and slept again.

And found herself standing beside her brothers on the chilly riverbank watching the little boat that had brought them out of Eoforwic drifting away, broadside to the current, catching on overhanging branches as it made its way downstream.

'A lucky find for someone,' said Bri.

'Come.' Heri glanced at her just once and then he led them

along a track leading away from the river into dense woodland, through a cavern of autumn shades. Rust and gold leaves carpeted the forest floor, and she smelled woodsmoke on the breeze. It grew stronger as they walked but she felt safer here, less exposed, hidden by the trees. Heri set a rapid pace and they followed him in single file, not speaking, until they came to a patch of cleared land where stood a low hut with a grassy roof – almost part of the woodland itself. This was the source of the smoke that was issuing from a hole in the roof and a stocky, unkempt man appeared at the doorway, gesturing them inside. They looked for guidance to Heri and he nodded.

'This is Wrogan,' he said, stooping under the low lintel as he followed them in. 'A trusted man. And these—'

The man raised a hand to check him. 'Tell me nothing, master, then it's nothing that I know. Eat, rest, then take your horses and be on your way. And may God speed you.'

He had been expecting them, it seemed, and a pot stood simmering on the edge of a hearth. The good smell drew the boys close and, at a nod from Heri, they ate hungrily, watching their grizzled host with wariness. In response he barely glanced at them but went silently about his business. Heri and Bri ate with them, taking just sufficient for their needs, but Wyn held back. 'Eat, lady,' the man called Wrogan said, seeing her hesitate, 'there's little enough flesh on your bones. Eat while you can.' She accepted a bowl from him and he disappeared.

They ate in tense silence. Heri avoided her eyes and, with her brothers there, her questions must remain unspoken but she felt his presence keenly and wished they could be alone and then she might understand. But Wrogan returned almost at once and gave a brief nod from the door. Heri rose. 'Finish now,' he said and followed the man outside. When the others joined them, a moment later, they found two sturdy cobs cropping at the grass in the clearing. Wyn went behind the hut to be private and when she returned the boys were mounted together on the larger one, Ælfwinne behind his brother. 'You ride also, Wyn,' Heri said and lifted her onto the other.

'And you?'

'We run.'

And so they departed on a journey to she knew not where.
Wrogan watched them go, lifting a hand in farewell – two mounted
horses with two men running beside them, taking long loping
strides as if this was nothing unusual. She turned once and looked
back at the old man and, in acknowledgement, he raised a hand
again before melting back into the woodland. She urged her horse
forward then to keep up with her brothers, stunned still by the
swiftness of the catastrophe that had befallen them, too dazed to
think, and wishing now that she had demanded to know more.

But the time would come soon enough, she told herself, and
her trust in Heri was absolute.

They travelled swiftly, following shaded field edges and the
margins of woodland, occasionally traversing open moorland but
keeping to the gullies and folds in the land, avoiding the main
route that led north; they crossed intersecting tracks with care,
ever watchful. All day they journeyed and that night they slept,
exhausted, packed close together in an abandoned farmhouse,
its walls and roof timbers charred from burning.

She fell asleep straight away, waking once in the night to see
that her brothers had found escape in slumber, curled up like
young creatures amidst the autumn leaf fall and she felt the
weight of a responsibility heavy on her shoulders.

She was the last to stir in the morning and woke to the smell
of food. She sat up and saw that two partridges, caught in snares
overnight, were roasting on a small fire. The boys were gathering
dry beech mast to feed the flames, and looked better for having
an occupation. Heri was at the horses but he came forward,
greeting her quietly, and dropped a handful of berries in her lap,
but still he avoided her eyes, and she saw that his face was grim
and drawn, the muscles in his cheek taut.

And so the questions still hung there, too dangerous to frame.

As soon as they had eaten, they were on their way again seeing
through the trees to where skeins of early morning mist rose
from the land, drifting across it like an army of departing

phantoms. The sun was too low to warm the riders, but the men running beside them had a heat of their own, their breath steaming in the chill air. They were still heading north, this much she could tell from the position of the sun. But to what purpose?

They pressed on until midday, when Heri stopped on the top of a rise from where they could see woodsmoke rising from a village or settlement below. 'We will rest now,' he declared, 'but draw back under the trees and don't move from here. We'll return within the hour.'

And they left.

Wyn suppressed her panic as they vanished over the brow. 'Where've they gone?' Ælfwinne asked, his young face pinched with fear. Both boys looked at her, their eyes wide and scared, but she had no answers for them and bid them rest. They had not yet mentioned their father's death, as if to do so would make it real.

An hour later, just as she had begun to despair, the two men reappeared. Bri flung himself on the ground beside the boys and opened a cloth to reveal bread and a curdy cheese. 'Stolen food always tastes best,' he said, grinning at their expression.

'Eat quickly,' said Heri.

They pressed on north. At any other time Wyn would have gloried in the soft autumn colours, the muted shades of a countryside set for winter slumber, but the men's urgency was infectious and fear clawed at her. Heri ran on ahead now, pausing at every rise in the land, scanning their surroundings, halting at the edge of clearings before beckoning them on. They were taking a wide sweep to the west, weaving a wandering path, fording a shallow river, then doubling back, moving along a line of hawthorn and beech trees until they saw earthworks in the distance.

Abruptly they halted.

'Catraeth,' Bri said quietly, looking across at Heri.

'Aye,' he replied, then tensed and shot out an arm, waving them urgently back under the cover of the trees. She glimpsed movement through the branches and, as she retreated, she saw what he had seen. Horses. Several of them, tethered on open pasture in front of the earthworks, and there were men gathered around a fire, some twenty or so, eating and laughing; the wind had blown the smoke from it the opposite way and had failed to give them warning. Heri drew them further back while he and Bri conferred in low tones. Heri's brow seemed to darken, and Wyn saw Bri put a hand on his arm but he shook it off, and a moment later she watched with dismay as he went forward, disappearing over a rise.

'Where's he gone?' she asked Bri, sick now with fear.

'He'll be back.'

'But who are they?'

He paused a moment. 'We think it's them.'

'*Who?*' But he would say no more, and led the horses deeper into the woods where he distributed the rest of the food, his face strained and his eyes watchful. 'Where has Heri gone?' she persisted. 'Tell me!'

'Wait, lady. He knows his business.'

But it was a long wait. Ælfwinne sat in the shadows, his knees hunched up, his head pressed down on folded arms, shaking with silent sobs. She laid a hand on his shoulder but he flung her away and she knew that she could not comfort him. Ælf's eyes remained fixed on the point where Heri had vanished as if by the sheer strength of his will, the man would return.

Then suddenly he was there, coming silently from the opposite direction, and he crouched beside them, panting slightly.

'Is it them?' Bri asked quickly, and Heri nodded, his eyes glittering.

'*Who?*' she asked again.

'Come now, and quickly,' he said, not answering, and they retraced their steps, leading the horses, taking a wide sweep away from the fort until they came back to the river they had crossed earlier but well downstream of the earthworks. And there, on its banks she saw two horses, rough-maned and much like their own, hobbled and grazing.

Bri's eyes flew to Heri. 'Theirs?' he asked.

Heri gave back the ghost of a smile. 'They were tethered at

the west gate with just one man guarding them; it was as close as I could get. But I saw the white stallion. . .' Bri held his look.

He turned and bid Ælf remount and then lifted her astride again before mounting the larger of the two stolen horses himself, pulling Ælfwinne up in front of him. 'And the guard?' she heard Bri ask as he mounted the other.

'They'll not find him.'

Wyn looked across at him, frowning. 'Who were those men?' she insisted. 'You must tell us.'

'They are your father's killers,' he replied, 'heading for Eoforwic.'

CHAPTER 16

It was not difficult to get directions to Swindale Hall.

John's decision to go there and discover Celia Goodfellow's address had come to him that morning after he was turned, unceremoniously, away from the vicarage by the lady of the house. Alfred had stood, arms folded, behind his mother, and John's request to speak to the vicar had been refused, leaving him with no option but to depart.

It was as he strode away that he remembered Olwen's former companion. If he could only discover where she had gone, perhaps she could help. And the thought returned later that afternoon when he received a letter from the vicar, delivered by Susan, thanking him for his services and informing him that the Bishop's physician, a Dr Kemp, would now be attending his niece. A derisory payment was included. He balled the note and threw it in the fire, then stood leaning against the mantelpiece and watched it burn. Brandt was right, without the vicar's consent, he could do nothing and so he *must* find Celia Goodfellow, the only other person he knew who might have Olwen's best interests at heart.

Having drafted a note for Mrs Crawford, with a manufactured excuse for his sudden absence, he had saddled up and set off for Swindale Hall. It was just over a ten-mile ride to the north of Kirkthorpe, along a loop in the river, and he arrived at the pillared entrance without incident. Trotting down the drive, he noted with admiration the dense woodland on one side, the open pasture on the other and, as the drive swept round to reveal the hall itself, he could understand the vicar's ardent desire that his son should marry Olwen Malkon. It was a lovely old building, not huge but welcoming, built of a yellowy sandstone mellowed by the passing years. An ancient wisteria was just coming into flower, twisting its way up the front and arching over the door. Symmetry, so beloved of Georgian architects, had created a place perfectly proportioned, and beyond the spread of pleasing parkland he saw the glint of water that must be the fateful lake.

The lower windows of the house were shuttered and he saw that the knocker had been removed from the front door in the old-fashioned manner; the hall was sleeping, its troubled mistress absent. He rode round to the back and, in the stable yard, he was greeted by a farmhand who directed him to a cottage standing close by. 'You'll find Mr Percy there now, sir, having 'is dinner.' John gave his reins to the lad and knocked on the door.

It was opened by a plump woman with a kindly face. 'Mrs Percy?' John enquired. 'Please forgive this intrusion, I'm Dr Osbourne from Kirkthorpe and I come in connection with Miss Olwen Malkon.'

'Is something wrong?' She opened the door wide, her face instantly concerned. 'I'll fetch Percy.' She showed him into a neat little parlour where a clock ticked quietly on a mantelpiece and had bent to light the fire before he could protest. A moment later an upright man, somewhat past middle age, arrived, wiping his mouth on a spotted handkerchief. 'Is owt amiss with Miss Olwen?' he asked, and from the anxiety on both their faces, John saw that he had come to the right place.

Briefly he explained, simplifying the situation, and gave his purpose in coming. 'If I could make contact with Miss Goodfellow, I think Miss Malkon might find it helpful.'

'Oh, the poor lass!' Mrs Percy's face puckered. 'I knew she was taking things hard, she went that quiet, you know. It wasn't natural, I said to Percy at the time, didn't I? And then catching that nasty cold.' Her husband nodded, his expression matching hers. 'As blithe as any sparrow she was before, but closed in on herself when the boys died. And then losing her father so soon after. . . But she *has* Miss Celia's address?'

John shook his head. 'She hasn't heard from her.'

Puzzled glances were exchanged. 'They have it at the vicarage.'

'Have they?' If he explained that he was *persona non grata* there would they send him away? The housekeeper considered him a moment then, with pursed lips, went to open a drawer in an ancient dresser, took out an envelope and handed it to him: 'Read that.'

He took it from her. *Dear Mrs P*, the writing was well formed and elegant. *I trust this finds you both well. . .* he skimmed the next bit then slowed. . .

> *I confess, though, that I'm worried about Miss Olwen. Do you know how she's getting on? I've written several times but had no response. Perhaps a clean break is best for now, but given how quiet she became, I'm concerned that she's slipped into melancholia. Have you had word? I'd go and see her but doubt I'd be welcome at the vicarage. I shall leave it a little longer but if you should see her, give her my love and tell her I was asking after her.*
>   *With all good wishes,*
>   *Celia Goodfellow.*

And at the top of the letter was an address in Knaresborough.

'Miss Malkon has had no letters,' he said, meeting the house-keeper's eyes.

She took the letter back. 'And it doesn't tek a genius to know the reason why.' She fired a look at her husband. 'I said we should've paid a call.'

'I saw Miss Olwen not a week past,' the old man replied, 'though in truth I forgot to pass on the message.'

John made a note of the address. 'How long will it take me to ride to Knaresborough?' he asked.

'You'll not be going tonight!'

'I believe I must.' A plan had begun to form in his mind as he rode over and there was not much time if he was to spare Olwen the ordeal of Sunday service, and whatever else might follow. But Mr Percy was shaking his head in a resolute manner. 'Weather's closing in. It'll be dark long before you get there, and then you've to find the place and hope Miss Goodfellow'll open the door to you. Ye'll not be talking to her until tomorrow any road so stop here tonight, young man, and let your horse rest. I can tell you a quicker route, but you'll not find it in the dark.'

His wife got to her feet. 'I'll mek up a bed.'

John began to protest but then recognised the sense in what was suggested and surrendered, thanking them. Pounding on Miss Goodfellow's door after dark would hardly receive an answer. The note he had left for Mrs Crawford had invented a sick aunt, an urgent need to catch a train to Scotland, as the plan he was formulating, if executed successfully, could take a day or two, so he would not be missed. It was a gross dereliction of duty, of course, but he had felt compelled to act. Brandt's arch expression flitted briefly across his mind, as did his warning about reckless action. But, damn the man, what was he to do?

At his hostess's insistence he joined them for their interrupted meal in the cottage kitchen, a warm, homely place that had that same comforting simplicity of his mother's farm, and he answered their questions as best he could while he ate and he, in turn, learned a little more about the recent tragedies. 'They were scamps, right enough, the two of them, and allowed to run wild by that tutor of theirs, but it was a terrible thing to happen. They were just lads, after all, up to all sorts, it's only natural.' The housekeeper's eyes had filled with tears.

'Aye, and not the tutor's fault, least ways not on this occasion.' He had been on a short vacation, Percy explained, when the accident happened. 'For all some say he was lax, the lads'd not have taken the boat out on their own if he'd been there. Aping about on the lake like that. . .' He shook his head. 'Eh, I'd do anything to wind back the clock.'

'Did Miss Malkon blame herself?' John asked. 'I wondered if there was an element of guilt preying on her mind?'

'We all feel that way, but we'd pipes frozen, see, and the boys sneaked off when we were busy, excited to see the lake frozen over.' The housekeeper tugged at her handkerchief. 'Not a day passes when I don't blame myself, even so, and their tutor said the same, though he was miles away.'

They ate in silence and then John was struck by a sudden thought. 'Did Miss Malkon have a friend called Harry, a suitor perhaps?'

Mrs Percy grunted and shook her head. 'She'd have been hard-pressed to meet any young men, stuck here and not allowed to go anywhere. There were dust-ups between Miss Goodfellow and her father over that, I'll tell you, but he was set on her marrying one of her cousins.' Her tone conveyed her views on that plan. 'They'd taken to hanging around the place after the boys drowned, especially Mr Alfred, fawning on the old gentleman and making himself agreeable. Saw an opportunity there, he did—'

'Mrs P. . .' her husband growled.

'I'm saying no more than what you've said! No sons could have done more, the old gentleman used to say, but he'd had fine sons of his own and let that happen to them. . .' She retrieved the handkerchief from her pocket and blew her nose. 'Him with his cronies and his old books, it was all he cared about.' She blinked away angry tears and sniffed. 'But he went down fast after the drowning, did the poor soul, like he'd lost heart. Which fitted Mr Alfred's ideas very nicely.'

Her husband growled at her again. 'Let's fill up that pot of yours, Doctor.'

But John refused; it would be an early start and he needed a clear head. 'I'll stretch my legs a little before I turn in, if I may, get the stiffness out of them.'

The light was failing as he stepped out of the cottage and the air was sharp; he had done well not to set off tonight, he decided, and these were good people who could be relied upon. He had made enquiries about seeing the lake while they ate and Mr Percy stepped outside with him to point out the path. 'Will you walk that way, then? I can't look at it now without thinking of them young lads.'

'Their bodies were recovered, I take it?'

'Oh aye.' He stood a moment, shaking his head. 'The lake's not looking its best at the moment, we're draining it, see, and so the water's low. Need to clear the sluices, they get clogged, filled with all sorts, and if it doesn't drain then lower fields flood after a heavy rain. Clay soils, you see. I told the vicar it had to be done, not knowing what we'd find was blocking 'em. . .' He stumbled to a halt and glanced at John. 'The boat sank, you see. I didn't like to tell Miss Olwen.'

John nodded in understanding and left the man, following his directions past the closed-up hall. Beyond it he saw the lake and when he reached the bank he stood on the grass above muddy slopes and tried to imagine the scene. In February, Mr Percy had said, when a sheet of ice had stretched across it – a sudden idea, a giggling plan, eyes dancing, then the boat cleaving through the glassy surface with heavy oars smashing through the ice, turning to laugh at the trail they left behind, a boyish lark, a misjudged moment. . . They would not have had a chance once they were in the icy water.

Was their poor sister endlessly recreating the scene in her mind, he wondered? In her drugged state it seemed she imagined they still lived, while her subconscious invented stories in which they could be saved.

And while he slept, his own dreams were doing the same. How strange. . .

He turned and looked back at the house. No lights shone from the shuttered windows, and the darkness was closing in. The scene had a timeless quality to it, the tops of the woodland trees made stark silhouettes against the heavy sky where, in the west, the light still lingered. The smell of woodsmoke reached him and with it, for no particular reason, a sense of deepening unease. Something startled a water bird out of the reeds, sending it scuttling over the mud towards the low water, and he watched it leave a v-shaped wake across the still surface.

He turned back. And it was then that he saw a figure, standing motionless at the edge of the woodland, looking directly across at him.

CHAPTER 17

A fire was burning in the tiny grate of the room in the eaves of the cottage where Percy took him. Before he left John mentioned the figure by the lake, thinking it might have been a poacher, but Percy smiled. 'That'd be Reagan. Don't you worry about him, he lives in the woods, watching who comes and goes. Quite harmless, but he'd be wondering who you were. Now, Doctor, if you've all you want, I'll say goodnight.'

John undressed and slipped in between the cool sheets, shivering a little, and lay awake until he grew warm, considering what he might say to Miss Goodfellow, constructing and rejecting any number of plans to get Miss Malkon away, until sleep overtook him.

And condemned him to dream again.

The weight of responsibility hung heavy round his neck and so he pushed the others hard, still thinking of the men at Catreath. It had been a near thing. . . If they had blundered into that group beside the fire it would have been the end; the blood of Angles and men of the north would once again have stained the soils of Catreath.

On the careless snapping of a twig had all their fates depended.

But those men had not been expecting trouble. They believed they had time aplenty to reach Eoforwic and snuff out the royal whelps before anyone learned the fate of their sire. He had silently slit the throat of the guard at the gate, a paltry revenge but he had not dared risk exacting more, one against so many, and he had tipped the man's body into a bramble-filled ditch before leading two of the horses away, leaving the band to conclude that their man had run off with them. Seeing the white stallion had unsettled him, though, and he could hazard a guess as to whom it belonged. Without a doubt it was same creature he had seen just a few days earlier, bending its noble neck to graze while vile regicide was done.

And it was that thought which made him drive them hard, back to the lands that he knew, back to where he could keep them safe, putting distance between themselves and that murderous band. And as they rode, he began to feel a little easier, and besides, he thought, lifting his head, the smell of home was in his nostrils.

They made much swifter progress now that they were all mounted, and pressed on until noon when he halted them. Bri distributed the rest of the food and Heri stretched his legs out and leaned back against a tree trunk, feeling the tension within him begin to uncoil. Ælf, he saw, was watching him, scowling, and doubtless wanting to know more about the men they had just evaded. 'Do they still tell of the battle of Catreath in your halls?' he asked, to forestall the lad.

'What battle?' Ælfwinne asked, looking up, more easily distracted than his older brother, and Heri smiled across at him.

'Tell them, Bri. You're the poet, not I.'

Bri bit a chunk of bread and chewed, then swallowed. 'The battle in which our forefathers fought.'

'Against who?

He grinned. 'Each other.'

'Who won?' the lad asked, and Heri smiled, but Bri leaned forward, his knife tip at Ælfwinne's chin, and the boy's eyes widened.

'Shall I tell you, then? Shall you hear the story? Of bones shattered and blood split?' He sheathed the knife with a smile, pulling Ælfwinne close. 'They say that three hundred chieftains came down from the north,' he began, his eyes alight, his voice lilting, 'bringing battle-hungry warriors. Fierce men. There were men from beyond Bannog, from beyond the sea of Iuddew, men from Rheged who joined with men from Aeron, and others came from Gwynedd and from Elfed. They had feasted long at Din Eidyn, in Mynyddog's hall, and then they rode south.'

'To fight who?'

'The pagan hordes.'

'But—?'

'Men of Deira and Bernicia, before Northumbria was a kingdom.'

Ælfwinne scowled. 'We're no *pagans*!'

'You were then.'

Heri smiled a little as the boys exchanged glances, diverted as he had hoped they would be. 'It was long, long ago. . .' And, with all his skill as a bard, Bri told them the story of the rout of the men of the Gododdin, of the mighty warriors whose deeds were still told and retold around the hearths of northern halls, and he watched their faces and saw that the poem put new spirit into them. They were fine lads, these young princes, already he had a fondness for them.

And then he glanced at their sister, and saw that she was listening too.

It was hard to keep her at arm's length, avoiding her eyes, evading the questions, when all he wanted to do was to take her in his arms and hold her, claim her for himself. . . But he must not weaken, he must focus on the one goal.

And get her to safety. Her brothers too.

'Our father is of the bloodline of Ida of Bernicia,' Ælfwinne was saying, perhaps forgetting for a moment that he had no father.

Bri ruffled his hair. 'I know, lad.'

'And *we* won!' Bri grabbed him with a roar and rolled him over.

'That day, aye,' Heri agreed when the horseplay was done. 'But alliances shift like the clouds above the fells, never forget that. Trust no one.'

'Not even you?' Wyn asked and Heri switched his gaze to her, and saw the questions shadowing her eyes, and so he tilted his head against the tree and looked up at the sky to avoid them.

'Ah, lady. That you must judge for yourself.'

'You gave us little choice.'

'A fast horse and a fat ransom, is that what you're thinking?' he said, not moving and hoping that she was answered. Later though, he would have to tell her what he had seen.

And it was a telling that he dreaded.

They crossed the quiet upper reaches of a wide river late the next evening and, as the shadows lengthened, he led them to a half-fallen stone building hidden amidst a stand of oak and hazel. It would not be the first time he had taken shelter there, close to the line of the Wall that they had glimpsed snaking its way over crags and ridges. Night clouds were rolling in from the west, uplit by the rays of the setting sun, and a sudden flash of lightning was followed, moments later, by a rumble of distant thunder.

'We'll not risk lighting a fire tonight, not so close to our goal,' Heri said, scanning the area. 'Who knows who might be here, watching the comings and goings.' He glanced up at the canopy of deep golden leaves that had yet to fall. 'We've at least a little shelter and if we huddle close in the lee of the building, we'll stay warm enough.' He distributed the last of the food and they ate in silence.

'So do you take us straight to Modig?' Wyn asked.

He cut off a piece of cheese and handed it to her on the blade of his knife. The questions would keep coming, piecemeal, until he told her. 'I'm taking you to a farm in the hills where you'll be safe. And then I'll go and confer with Modig.'

She nodded and said nothing more, and soon they bedded down for the night, Bri at one end of the row, himself at the other, and he smiled as he watched the boys squabbling over who should sleep beside Bri while his companion laughed heartily, amused to be fought over. The matter was settled but it left their sister to lie beside him and he thanked God for the darkness as he turned his back on those deep violet eyes. He would not touch her, not yet, not until he had told her how her father had come to die.

The forest grew silent, even the night creatures were still.

Somewhere in the distance an owl screeched but for the rest the only sound was the breeze sloughing through the trees. And yet sleep eluded him. Sometimes, in recent weeks, as he rode through the hills of home, he had almost convinced himself that Ælfwald would be glad of an alliance with him, securing the loyalty of the northern lands in these unsettled times. He had intended to seek Modig's blessing for his suit, although Modig too was aware that the king favoured the match with Osred, blind to his kinsman's treachery. But what might happen now? He turned over to look at her as she slept beside him in the pale moonlight. . . so lovely, she was! He had wanted her from the moment he had first set eyes on her but would Modig countenance a match or would he imagine it signalled that Heri harboured ambitions of his own? If he did, then he was wrong! He asked no more than to stay in his own lands, see his people prosper and watch his unborn children grow – with Wyn beside him.

He propped himself up on his elbow and looked across at the others. In sleep, the boys looked more like children than the men they longed to be, and until they were grown to manhood they would forever be in danger, the dead king's sons, a threat to any usurper, a rallying point for men with ambitions of their own. By bringing them into his own lands he wondered if he had brought trouble there, for these half-grown princelings would be key players in this new game of power.

Silently he rolled away and rose to his feet. Bri, ever alert, raised his head but Heri gestured to him that all was well and the man settled again. He walked soundlessly to the edge of the clearing and stood, leaning against an ancient oak, and looked out towards the ruins of Scythlescester fort where, short days ago, he had seen murder done.

A waning moon hung in the sky, as luminous as a pearl, a half-shadowed orb floating in a sea of stars. But then his wandering gaze was caught by something else and he stiffened; a light had appeared in the night sky! A light larger and more bright than any star, rising out of the west where smudges of colour bore witness to the vanished sun. An intense fiery ball of light, with a long tail streaming out behind it, traversing the night sky. A portent! He stood, transfixed and fearful, for it seemed to him that it slowed its passage to hang a moment over the ruins of Scythlescester.

A twig snapped and he spun round, his seax drawn, but then he saw who the trespasser was and returned the blade to its sheath. And he stood there, in the shadow of the oak, and waited for her to come.

CHAPTER 18

It was good to have a horse under him again, John thought as he cantered along beside the hedgerows, feeling his muscle and sinew in tune with the creature's rhythm. The cross-country route Percy had given him would cut a few miles of his journey, following old tracks and ancient hollow ways, and it was one of those bright spring mornings that sets the blood coursing through a man's veins, reminding him that it was good to be alive. How much he had missed days like this, days when he would ride out from his mother's farm into the wide open spaces of the Borders where the light was sharp and the wind blew fresh down from the hills. He had learned to ride on the hill ponies that his mother's people would drive across the border, some traded, some stolen, no one wanting to know. When she had married his father, her mother had at first disdained her Romany blood, and developed ambitions for her son that he had not always shared. Since his father's death, though, he felt that he must provide for her and so he had accepted the patronage offered him by his father's family and left her for his studies. But he had gone with a heavy heart and, on recent visits, had felt himself drawn back. His mother was strong-willed and independent and for now managed well on the hill farm but the day would come when it was too much for her, and he knew that then he would return. She was the one person with whom he might have discussed these strange dreams; she would have understood for she had insights, and the ancient wisdom of her nomadic race. And it would have been a comfort to talk to her. . . Perhaps that was what last night's extraordinary dream had been about? A subconscious yearning for his home. . . And, he thought wryly, a desire to take Olwen

Malkon there with him. He had woken, clutching at the departing fantasy, trying to make sense of it – and of the sense of danger it provoked. *No dreams are without meaning*, Brandt had said, and he pulled a face, remembering the man's mockery that his dreams cast him in a heroic role. Was that what it was? His rescue plan transformed by his subconscious into a daring escape?

And once again her brothers had found a way into his dream. He frowned. Did this spring from a hopeless desire to save them, and to thereby please their sister? How odd that they should be so persistently there, and how extraordinary too that his mind had dredged up those stories his grandfather used to tell him. 'Only one man returned from the battle of Catterick. Aneirin, the bard, who told the tale.' John, with the cynicism of youth, had remarked that it was just as well that it *was* the bard who survived, and had his ears boxed for his impudence. How unaccountable is the mind, he thought as his horse forded a shallow stream, but he was yet to be convinced that these random threads had meaning.

The track led out of the wood and, just as Percy had described, came to a junction with a metalled road, which he joined, crossing over a stone bridge to find himself on the outskirts of Knaresborough, and he brought his mind sternly back to the business of the moment. If a self-ascribed heroic role was to be sustained then he must act, and act quickly, before Sunday came around again and the poor lass was dragged along to some archaic ritual that would terrify her and could only make matters worse. His plan had been developing in his mind as he rode, but Celia Goodfellow's cooperation was crucial to its success.

Leaving his horse at the stables of a public house near the station, he asked for directions and found Pear Tree Cottage squeezed in between two larger houses in a lane off the High Street. Too late, he thought, as he stood outside, to wish that he had taken a moment to brush the mud from his trousers and make himself presentable.

His knock was answered by a maid who looked him up and down and took the note that Mrs Percy had written, leaving him standing on the doorstep. A moment later a tall, elegant woman of about his own age appeared, the note in her hand and curiosity in her eyes.

'Dr Osbourne? Come in,' she said, 'and welcome.' She led him down the hall to the back of the house into a chaotic room full of books and worn armchairs draped with fringed shawls. Footstools and tables were weighted down with more books and he saw a piano tucked into the far corner, with sheet music open on the rack. French windows gave onto a long thin garden and the sun, having not yet reached its zenith, came in at an angle, flooding the room with sunlight. She gestured to a chair beside the window.

'You've a charming spot here,' he remarked. At the far end of the garden, he could see a gardener at work, turning over a vegetable patch with a fork.

His hostess smiled. She had a pleasant intelligent face and his spirits rose. 'We're very lucky.' She despatched a maid to bring tea. 'But tell me about Olwen; I should have paid her a call when I received no reply to my letters. It was very lax of me, but I told myself I was letting her settle in. And what with moving in here and. . . and I was preoccupied, which is a very poor excuse.' She held up the note. 'You come warmly recommended, Doctor. Please tell me what is wrong.'

Her straightforward manner made things easy. 'Miss Malkon never received your letters, I'm afraid, and had no way of contacting you. I went to Swindale Hall and got your direction from the Percys.'

'Good Gracious! You've surely not ridden over from Swindale this morning? It must be ten miles or more.' The girl who entered with a tray of tea was appealed to. 'Joyce, cut some sandwiches, if you will, and some of that fruit cake, this poor man is starving. You must have left at dawn, Doctor!' Briefly she took in his mud-splattered trousers. 'So that dratted woman kept back my letters, did she, how very wicked of her – though I'm not surprised. She detests me. But it must be serious, whatever it is, for you to take such trouble to find me.'

She had clear calm eyes and listened without interruption or expression as he explained how Olwen Malkon had come to be his patient and how matters had worsened in recent days, and he could see that she had grasped the gravity of the situation.

'Oh dear Lord, the poor child. And *ten* drops of laudanum, how iniquitous!'

'I must confess at first I thought she was seeking to make herself interesting.'

Celia Goodfellow shook her head. 'No, no. She's not that sort of girl. A vivid imagination, yes, but she had become accustomed to being overlooked; she would never wilfully seek attention. I'd been in my post for a while before I realised what a bright and witty girl she was. Her father could never see that in her, or at least he refused to.'

'Her affliction, I believe, stems from grief.'

'I'm sure you're right, she adored Oliver and William but she was never very close to her father. He was a difficult man, you see, with no interest in his children except insofar as his sons secured the dynasty, silly man. We'd have been at odds much more frequently, he and I, had he not been such a negligent parent. Olwen was living in her own little world when I arrived there, and it took time to draw her out, and then instil in her the view that women need not always be obedient.' A little dimple appeared in her cheek and her eyes challenged his.

'I believe you served her well, although laudanum is undermining your efforts.'

She rose and paced the room. 'It's unforgivable! And speaking frankly, Doctor, they are a ghastly family, other than Olwen and those poor boys. She was devastated by their death and I gave what little comfort I could. But after her father died the rest of the family simply smothered her in crêpe and bombazine, presenting her to the world as a helpless thing, a picture of woe, flaunting their Christian virtue in offering her a home. But between them all there's not a scrap of real sympathy or love for the dear girl.' Angrily she blew her nose. 'I never found common ground with the vicar's wife as I ignored her strictures concerning

Olwen's upbringing and refused to know my place. I'd have had my marching orders years ago if it was up to her, but old Mr Malkon was far too indolent to consider making changes and Olwen, bless her, was always fierce in my defence.' She came and sat again. 'The vicar's a fool, obsessed by his status, terrified of his bishop and his wife in equal measure. Edmond has inherited his father's lack of brains, and Alfred his mother's nastiness, as well as being a hardened gambler.' She leaned forward to pour the tea from a very fine silver teapot. 'There, you see, I'm every bit the outspoken wretch they believe me to be. Please do eat something.'

John smiled as he reached for a sandwich. 'I believe I've come to the right place.'

'Yes you have, but what's to be done? Olwen has no independence until she's twenty-one and her aunt and uncle would never listen to anything I might say. I very much want to help but cannot imagine how I can!'

John chewed his sandwich, recognising the truth in what she said and wondering how to present the plan he had been formulating. Glancing out of the window he saw that the gardener was approaching the house, a lean figure in baggy trousers moving in a leisurely way towards them, occasionally stooping to pull out a weed, clearly indifferent to the fact that his mistress was observing his desultory toil. He saw that Celia Goodfellow was watching him, amusement twitching at her lips.

She lifted her head and called out through the open French doors. 'There's tea, Gus, and sandwiches if you're quick, and fruit cake when Joyce has sliced it. I'll tell her to bring another cup. Take your boots off and join us.'

'Right-o,' the gardener called back and stood a moment on the flagstones knocking the mud off filthy boots before removing them and entering on slim stockinged feet. An irregular life, he remembered the vicar saying, his interest piqued, but it was only when the flat cap was removed and long auburn hair fell from it that his suspicions were confirmed.

'Hello,' said the gardener.

'Go and get cleaned up,' Miss Goodfellow said, the dimple back in place. 'This is Dr John Osbourne. You're much dirtier than I thought, Gussie dear, so do go and change and then I'll introduce you properly. Joyce, another cup and plate if you will for Miss Augusta.'

'Pleased to meet you, Dr John Osbourne,' the young woman said, coolly appraising him. 'I'll return directly, transformed.' She blew a kiss towards his hostess and left the room.

'So you see the depths of my depravity,' Miss Goodfellow remarked with a dry smile. 'The vicar would no more listen to my views than to old Beelzebub himself.'

John was not shocked, and perhaps ought not to have been surprised, but this revelation could well have a bearing on his plan. His hostess misconstrued his thoughtful silence.

'I can assure you that my former charge is entirely unaware of my current situation, and was as chaste in my keeping as the driven snow, if snow is chaste. Indeed, I was in ignorance myself as to how delightful such an arrangement as this could be until I met Gussie,' adding, almost to herself, 'which explained to me a great deal that I had previously puzzled over.' She returned to the moment. 'You've not had cake, Doctor, and it's a particularly good one.'

Miss Goodfellow's friend reappeared, wearing trousers and a striking silk garment that appeared be modelled on a gentleman's smoking jacket, and was introduced as Miss Augusta Dudley. 'The dis-Honourable Miss Augusta Dudley, I'd have you know,' the lady herself added as she shook John's hand, 'busily disgracing the family name.'

They had met, Celia informed him, at a meeting of suffragists earlier that year and taken this house just a month ago when she had lost her position at Swindale Hall. 'I was looking for a new situation, and then we found ourselves in this one, which suits us very well.'

Miss Dudley sent an arch look in her friend's direction. 'It does, though I'm damned if I'd expected gentleman callers.'

Miss Goodfellow laughed and rapidly appraised her of the

situation, remarking first to John that they had no secrets from each other while Miss Dudley lit a cigarette and perched on the arm of a chair to listen. 'Poor little chick,' the smoker said, when the story had been retold, and looked across at John. 'And so what brings you to Celia?'

John was beginning to think this had been a wasted journey. 'I had hoped to enlist her help.'

'To do what? They'll not listen to Celia.' The plan did indeed now seem unworkable. 'My father's a friend of that ghastly bishop of yours who, by the by, would positively relish the task of driving demons from a young girl, right up his twisted little street. Papa knows Celia's living here with me – it's a phase, he tells me, and has disowned me until I grow out of it – and doubtless he'll have confided in the bishop, who'll have told the vicar.' The withholding of Miss Goodfellow's letters was now explained. 'Celia's That Dreadful Woman, you see, and so any special pleading by her is quite pointless. Counterproductive, in fact,' she went on, drawing on her cigarette, 'no, we must bring the gal here to live with us until she is of age. It's only a few months, after all. We'll kidnap her.' John's eyebrows shot up and Miss Dudley looked back at him. 'Have you a better plan, Dr John Osbourne?'

'I want her to get treatment, in York. Professor Brandt believes that she—'

'Take her for treatment first then, and bring her to live with us afterwards. We could manage that between us, couldn't we?'

'But we can't simply kidnap her,' Celia protested, 'they'd work out it was us and come and take her back, and we'd be no further forward.'

Gussie drew on her cigarette. 'They'd have to find her first. We'll take her to Italy.'

Celia ignored her. 'I agree she should see this doctor of yours. Could you take her to Swindale, do you think, and let him see her there?'

'It could land the Percys in trouble,' said John, with one eye on the Honourable Augusta, who was clearly a handful. 'My plan was simply to get her to St Hilda's House, and while her case was assessed I'd hoped to find protection for her in law. It would buy me a little time to find out whether—'

'What sort of treatment?' Gussie interrupted, narrowing her eyes against the smoke. 'From what I've heard of St Hilda's they simply sedate or confine vexatious women, women who aren't mad at all but simply rebellious—'

'Professor Brandt is—'

' – demanding more of life than what was offered them, daring to be awkward. And not so long ago medical men were carrying out a particularly nasty sort of surgery to ensure—'

'Gussie! This is a colleague Dr Osbourne knows. We're not still in the Dark Ages.'

'Are we not?'

'There's not a lot of time,' John said, deciding to let the question of treatment slide for the moment. 'And I can't get anywhere near her, not now they've brought in the bishop's physician, but I'd had a vague idea that you, Miss Goodfellow, might turn up and offer to take her out for a drive and then we could have taken her to York—'

'Kidnap her, in fact,' remarked the irrepressible Augusta.

Celia bit her lip. 'They'd never let her go with me.'

This, he now saw, was almost certainly true. 'My concern is that the bishop and the vicar will be planning something for this Sunday, even if only ensuring that she attends church, suitably subdued, in order to put local gossip to an end. God forbid that they are considering anything else. We have to move quickly.'

'Do you play chess?' the Honourable Augusta asked him.

'Occasionally.' The woman was beginning to irritate him. 'As I say—'

She slid off the arm onto the chair and sat forward, tapping her cigarette into an ashtray, her eyes on John, sharp and keen. 'Knights and bishops are of equal worth, as I recall, although a bishop is generally considered more valuable. A doctor is hardly a knight, although in your case. . .' She sat back, her cigarette held at an angle. 'You see I find myself wondering a little at your interest in this particular patient.' John felt his face colouring and her eyebrows arched. 'Ah, you blush, my good doctor, how very endearing.'

'Gussie, behave!'

Her companion smirked. 'Please don't misunderstand me. I reckon a doctor could, in certain circumstances, perform every bit as well as a knight and therefore equal a bishop, leaving us daughters of Sappho ranged against the vicar and his ghastly wife. Evenly matched, I'd say. No wait! We've your professor on our side of the board. How splendid! Our second knight.'

'You forget the equally ghastly cousins,' said Celia, filling John's cup.

'Mere pawns. Expendable.' Gussie sat back again, narrowing her eyes against the cigarette smoke, still watching John. 'So, Doctor John, let's take them on.'

CHAPTER 19

He had said that he would come – but he had not.

And she was losing all track of time. How many days was it since she had entered the study and seen those four men turn their heads towards her? Three, or was it four; impossible to know. On one of them she had seen him coming up the drive and her heart had leapt but her aunt had seen him too and swiftly left the room, and next moment she had watched him striding away again and had flown to the morning room door, pulling it open only to find her way blocked by her aunt.

'Go to your room, Olwen.'

'But I wish to speak to Dr Osbourne!'

The vicar had emerged from his study and they had stood side by side, resolutely refusing to let her pass. 'Dr Kemp is your physician now,' he said, 'and he will be coming to see you very shortly. Until then you will remain in the house where we can see you, my dear, and care for you.'

And now they never left her alone, watching her constantly, one or other of them always with her. No matter how much she protested and railed against this treatment it made no difference and she oscillated from a wild sort of fury to a lethargy that would overcome her, leaving her quite helpless and desperate. Vaguely she remembered that day in the study when Dr Osbourne had become impassioned about laudanum, accusing them of giving it to her, and the foreign man too, the one who had escorted her to her room and spoken so kindly, she had heard him questioning her aunt. Perhaps that was it. She was being given it still and so she, in turn, started watching them, eating little at mealtimes, taking helpings only from dishes already sampled by the others.

When challenged, her aunt denied it. 'Besides, it was only ever to calm your distress.'

'I should have been consulted.'

'Common practice, you know, not unusual at all,' her uncle had added, ignoring her. 'The bishop himself finds it helpful.'

'I should not have been given it without my knowledge.'

'Perhaps so, perhaps so.' He waved a hand in dismissal.

The bishop's physician came to see her, and she answered his questions in monosyllables, deeply distrustful of the man, while her aunt, standing beside him with her arms folded, had filled in the gaps in a way clearly designed to convince him that Olwyn was malingering, rebellious – and ungodly.

She was never told what he had reported to the vicar.

Perhaps it was that her aunt had ceased to lace her food with laudanum, or perhaps her abstemiousness meant that she consumed less of it but gradually her world sharpened a little. She slept badly and sometimes woke in the night, craving relief, so her head was never completely clear but she was lucid enough to recognise how desperate her situation had become and anxiety was making her wretched. Without Dr Osbourne she had no other champion and found herself longing for Celia. Her aunt consistently denied that any letters had arrived and made it clear that she should not expect any. It was very strange. . . Books alone provided little solace these days and the garden offered no escape, bounded as it was by brick walls, and even there her walks were accompanied by one or other of her cousins, or watched from the windows by her aunt.

Having eaten what she dared at breakfast, insisting on pouring her own tea, Olwen retired with her book to the morning room where, a moment later, she was joined by her aunt. They sat in silence, her aunt, her gaoler, mending linen beside the fire.

She tried to read.

It was only a little later that the front-door bell rang and she looked up thinking it was early for callers, then she heard a woman's light voice and a trilling laugh followed by Susan's protesting response and next moment the morning-room door was flung open and a young woman flew across the room to embrace her. '*Olwen!* Oh my dearest girl.' Crushed in a perfumed cinch, she felt her arm being pinched. 'How I've *missed* you,' the stranger said, kissing her cheek, and, in a quick whisper, 'Celia sent me.'

Olwen stared in astonishment at the intruder. She was a slim young woman with auburn hair topped by a straw bonnet and she wore a pale mantle, underneath which was a cornflower blue dimity dress. Having released Olwen she spun round with a smile to Olwen's aunt and gave a little bob, holding out a hand with a grace that could only charm.

'Oh, do forgive me, Mrs Malkon, but I simply could not pass so close without calling. I'm Lady Sarah Bentley, and I've been staying with the Cuthberts, you know them of course, and I was so close, but we return home tomorrow, you see, and so it had to be today. I should have written, I know I should, but I wanted to surprise my dearest Olwen. I've been abroad since last summer as I expect she's told you, but I persuaded Mama that I simply must come home because an English spring simply cannot be missed, even if an English winter is to be avoided at all costs.' She gave a gurgling laugh and flashed a smile at Olwen. 'Oh dear, I'm chattering on, for which you always scolded me.'

Somehow Olwen managed a smile.

'We spent the winter in Rome.' The visitor turned back to a stunned Mrs Malkon. 'Isn't Rome divine? All those marvellous churches! Did you get my letter, Olwen dear? The post takes forever so maybe it's not reached you yet, but while Rome's all very well in winter it's wretchedly hot in summer and so things sort of decided themselves.'

Susan had followed her in and was standing nonplussed in the doorway. The visitor gave her a careless glance.

'Please don't blame your girl for letting me in, I just *had* to have my surprise.' She turned back to Olwen and seized her hand. 'And oh, my dear! When I heard about Oliver and William, my dearest girl, and then your beloved Papa too, I was quite distraught, I really was, I cried and cried for days. . . How have you *borne* it?' She bestowed a dewy smile on her hostess, who had made two failed attempts to interject. 'But how lucky you are to have a home here, darling girl, although you could have come to us. You're a favourite with Mama, you know, but family is best in such sad circumstances.' Another trilling laugh. 'But we were away, of course. . . what am I saying!'

Mrs Malkon came back to life and made another effort to interrupt the flow.

'I won't have tea, thank you, Mrs Malkon,' though none had been offered 'my companion is waiting in a trap in the lane. I'll just stay a moment and then go, but I'll leave my card and Mama will write to you and invite Olwen to stay. You will let her come, won't you, *dear* Mrs Malkon? Please, please do! I shall insist that Mama comes and begs you.' As she spoke, she was fumbling through a little bag, pulling out a handkerchief, a folding mirror, a comb and a motley collection of papers and the like. 'Good grief, what a mess, and I can't find my card case! It must be in another bag. How stupid of me.' The contents were rapidly replaced, all except an envelope, which she managed to slip under a fold of her mantle. 'Mama will write, though, I promise.'

Olwen saw that her aunt was gathering herself, preparing to take a stand, but the visitor's eye had fallen upon the book Olwen had left open on the table and she picked it up.

'*The Woodlanders*! Now you must tell me how you like it.' Her tone had subtly changed. 'He's sympathetic, is Mr Hardy, though it can only ever be a man's view of our condition.' She placed the book down on top of the envelope and rose. 'Mrs Malkon, you've been most civil. Such—'

She broke off as Susan reappeared at the door. 'Excuse me, madam, but the bishop has arrived.'

Mrs Malkon rose abruptly. 'Show him into the study, and fetch the vicar from the garden. Lady Sarah, I must ask—'

'No, no. I am gone!' the visitor said, leaning over to kiss Olwen's cheek, squeezing her fingers hard. 'Goodbye, dearest. We'll meet again very soon, I promise. I'll see myself out, Mrs Malkon, so you may attend to your august visitor.' And with that she half-opened the door and paused a moment, looking through it. Olwen heard the study door close, and then their extraordinary visitor turned, gave her a blazing smile, and was gone.

Olwen sat down again, taking care to slip the envelope inside her book. 'What a delightful surprise,' she said, smiling at her aunt.

But the woman was still staring at the door. 'And who, pray, is Lady Sarah Bentley?'

'The performance of a lifetime,' Gussie announced, stripping off her lacy gloves and tugging at the strings of her bonnet before tossing both aside. 'A very satisfying morning.'

'She's been crowing all the way back,' Celia told John with a smile.

He had spent the night at the public house in Knaresborough where his horse was stabled and from where Celia and Gussie had hired a shabby trap that morning, determined to carry through their rather reckless plan. All morning he had chaffed at his own enforced inaction, and waiting for them to return had been torment. In an effort to walk off the restlessness he had gone down to the river and tramped beside it, sitting for a moment above the weir, tossing pebbles into the flow and wondering gloomily whether the scheme had any chance at all of success. He had arrived back at the house just moments before the two women returned triumphant.

'How did she look?' he asked, and Gussie gave him one of her arch glances. 'Did she seem dazed, or was she alert?'

'Pale and peaky, I'd say, but quick-witted enough to see what I was about – and frankly the appalling Lady Sarah didn't let her get a word in so it was difficult to judge. The old harridan just sat there and goggled.' She laughed as she dropped into the chair. 'Let's have some lunch and then John can take us boating on the river. We need a man, for once, if only for the oars.'

John grunted and Celia sent him an apologetic look. The Honourable Gussie had clearly enjoyed herself, but this was no game. 'So she has our letters,' he said, addressing Celia, 'that much has been achieved. Next question is whether we manage to spirit her away.'

'Oh, she'll manage her end all right. I could see it in her eyes,' said Gussie, 'they came alive.'

'No pinprick pupils?'

'Forgot to look. But, oh dear me, John, I haven't told you. I had the narrowest escape! The ghastly bishop arrived.' He swung back to her in alarm. 'Don't worry, he didn't see me. He was taken into the vicar's study as I was bringing the performance to a rousing finale in the morning room, and in fact his appearance provided the perfect excuse to sprint away. If he'd caught sight of me, mind you, we'd have been in trouble; Lady Sarah unmasked as wicked fraud!'

'Why had he come?'

'I could hardly ask, could I!'

John turned away and stared hard out of the window. So they *were* planning something, those men of God; the bishop had not given up on his demons. Would tomorrow be too late? 'I must go back.'

'Don't be ridiculous.'

'You're in Scotland,' Celia reminded him.

'Be sensible, lovelorn knight,' Gussie agreed, 'and have some lunch instead.'

'But they might try something before Sunday, why else would he come today?'

Gussie shrugged. 'To plan. . . discuss.'. . . decide what to do, or to do nothing, any number of reasons. And besides, I think Olwen's a good deal more robust than you imagine. We're not all vessels of frailty, you know.'

'Once she's read the letters, she'll revive,' Celia reassured him, 'and she has wit enough to deal with any hitches.'

Olwen followed her aunt out of the room and took her book upstairs, her spirits soaring. *Celia sent me.* The words were like music. Celia! And that meant that not only did Celia know that help was needed but had somehow guessed that a direct approach would be hopeless. The household would now be busy fawning over the bishop but nonetheless she took the precaution of jamming a chair under the door handle before removing Lady Sarah's envelope from the book.

It contained two single sheets. She recognised the handwriting of the first and felt a surge of joy.

Oh, my dear girl!

I have written many times, I promise you, but explanations can wait. Dr Osbourne came and found me, and thank goodness he did! Read what he suggests and, if you agree, then we will be waiting for you in a closed carriage beside the smith's pasture tomorrow morning. The doctor is a good man, I like him. Bring nothing with you, we can supply your needs and any baggage would arouse suspicion. You've already met my dear friend (masquerading as yours!) and we are all determined to get you out of this fix. We'll be in place by nine o'clock in the morning and will wait until you come, so simply slip away when you can. The rest will keep, but know that you can be sure of the constancy of,

Your loving friend,

Celia.

She clasped the letter to her chest. Celia! Tomorrow she would see her! With a shaking hand she took up the second sheet, written in a bold, clear script.

Dear Miss Malkon,

Given recent events, I am concerned for your welfare if you remain at the vicarage and have enlisted the help of Miss Goodfellow and her friend to get you away. If you agree to this plan, they will take you to York where Miss Goodfellow and I will escort you to St Hilda's House and to Dr Brandt, who you briefly met, hoping he will be able to see you. He has spoken to me about hypnosis as a means to investigate these troubling episodes but you are not obliged to agree to this treatment, or any part of this plan. I am concerned, however,

that repeated doses of laudanum and insistence on your
attendance at church will combine to worsen your difficulties
– as would any attempt to rid you of wholly fictitious demons.
If you will honour me with your trust, I will do what I can to
help you.

  Yours sincerely,
  John Osbourne, physician.

She read it again. There was a formality to the tone, a distancing. *John Osbourne, physician.* And yet he had taken the trouble to find Celia! She recognised too that what he was proposing was extraordinary, and potentially ruinous to his career. *If you will honour me with your trust. . .* She lowered the letter and closed her eyes, remembering a cold dawn and a desperate flight through a ruined town. *Trust me, lady, we must fly.*

A knock at the door brought her back to the moment and she slipped the letters back inside the book. 'Vicar says will you come down, Miss Olwen, to his study.'

The bishop, she had forgotten about the bishop, but there would be no evading this summons. 'I'll be down directly,' she replied as her pulse began to drum again, her breath quickening. What did they want of her now? She felt the familiar sense of imminent threat, but with the possibility of escape so close, she must do her best to placate them, give the appearance of acquiescence in whatever they had planned, for now she had defenders of her own.

As she turned to go she caught sight of herself in the mirror and saw how pale and pinched her face had become. She must stay strong enough to resist them, for all that mattered was that her brothers remained safe— She froze. And then, just for a moment, another face looked out at her from the mirror, gone so quickly she must have imagined it.

Her face, but not her face.

'You'd best come, miss,' Susan said from the door, 'else Vicar said they'll come up to you.' And Olwen stared into the mirror, searching in vain for the fleeting image, then went to the door.

This time the two men were not seated but were stood side by side with their backs to the study's cold hearth. Her aunt was there too, standing in the corner, beside the window.

'Olwen, my dear.' The vicar gave her a smile that she no longer liked. 'Come in!' He gestured to a seat and she sat, but the two men remained standing, looking down at her.

This made her angry.

The bishop spoke in the full rounded tones that she remembered from the other day. 'My physician tells me that he can find nothing physically wrong with you, my dear, which is a great comfort to us all.'

'Indeed it is, sir,' Olwen agreed, and her aunt fired her a suspicious glance.

'And it confirms what we thought, that your troubles, my child, are of a spiritual nature, brought on by your recent tragedies. And I fear that this weakening of spiritual strength has allowed elements of evil to insinuate themselves, like serpents, into your mind.' How ridiculous he was, the loose skin beneath his chin shaking as he spoke, but she dropped her eyes and kept them lowered. 'This horror you have of entering the church, your extraordinary behaviour there, and then your response to your uncle who, quite apart from being your blood relative, is your spiritual guide. . . all these things point inexorably in that one direction.' He paused, and she felt his eyes on her, anticipating a protest.

She remained silent.

'And so, with the authority vested in me by the Church,' he continued, in a tone suggesting he believed he had her cowed, 'I intend to rid you of these demonic elements and bring you back, like a lost sheep, into the fold of your loving family, and so restore you to God.'

A chill began to course through her, a sense of helplessness, for her newfound courage was a fragile thing and if they were to demand that she go with them now, into the church, she would be lost. Dizziness rippled through her and she kept her eyes fixed on the carpet. She must at all costs, stand firm.

'Miss Malkon?'

She lifted her head then and met his narrowed eyes, seeing another man standing there, his hair cut in a monkish tonsure. He must have been sent by the prelate to whom she had given a sacred trust, assured of his steadfast loyalty. The weaker man beside him, the abbot, failed to meet her eyes. 'I will need a little time to prepare myself,' she said.

Her cool composure seemed to take them aback. Swift glances were exchanged and she knew then that she could outwit them.

'So you accept what I am saying?' the man demanded, thrown off his stride.

'Would I gainsay a man of God?' she asked, and that response appeared to startle them. 'That which is most precious to me is entirely within your hands.'

The man blinked rapidly and the abbot beside him looked baffled and would have spoken, but a hand was raised to silence him. 'I am. . . I am delighted that you have come to see matters in this way.'

It seemed to her that while he was speaking the room had darkened and the walls had closed in, cold stone walls. She glanced at the abbess, who stood in the ill-lit corner, her hands tucked into the folds of a dark gown, her eyes as hate-filled as ever. Only because the woman could claim kinship with Osred had she been raised to this position, one for which she was, in every way, unsuited. A dangerous woman. . .

Olwen bestowed on her a smile. 'You have told me repeatedly that I am safe here with you.'

The abbot beamed at her, and she sensed relief in his voice. 'But, of course, you are, my dear child. . . and most welcome. The loss of your father was a terrible thing, but it serves to bring us together and your home is here now, with us and you know that—'

'And my brothers. What of them?' She heard the sharpness in her own voice.

The abbot's mouth fell open. 'My dear, as you well know, your brothers are also safe, safe in the Lord's—'

His superior interrupted him. 'We'll not dwell on such matters today, but on Sunday I shall conduct the service at the church and will take for my sermon Psalm Thirty-Four, and we will offer up prayers for your deliverance from these corrupt and melancholy thoughts.' He gave her a smile, which failed to reach his eyes. 'In the meantime, yes, my child, prepare yourself with prayer and contemplation, and so strengthen yourself. After the service the vicar and I will stay behind with you for special rites – ' the tip of his tongue emerged to moisten his lips in the way she remembered ' – which will release you from your present evil.'

She rose, taking his words for dismissal, gripping hard to the arm of the chair, feeling suddenly much less confident. She must leave at once before she said something that would betray her confusion. 'The realm is blessed by such devout men of God,' she said, and heard her aunt gasp. 'And so I bid you good day, sirs.'

CHAPTER 20

'*Insolence!*' Mrs Malkon followed Olwen out of the room, her eyes hot with anger. 'I've never heard the like! Will you shame us before the bishop, you wretched girl?'

'I said nothing shameful.' Had she? The hall was swaying in an alarming manner.

'Looking down your nose and speaking like that. Sarcasm is most unbecoming, young lady, especially where respect is due.' But respect is earned, not owed, Olwen thought vaguely; Ælfwald had taught her that. 'The bishop stays for luncheon and if I hear one further word of insolence, I promise you there'll be trouble.'

This Olwen managed to avoid by the simple expedient of saying almost nothing during the meal, answering questions in monosyllables and keeping her eyes cast down. In truth it was hard to do otherwise as the world had begun to oscillate again and those around the table were shape-shifting, their voices coming and going, hollow-sounding, without sense or meaning, fusing and blurred. And, as the meal progressed, her detachment from reality became more marked. Alfred was seated opposite her and several times she lifted her head to see him watching her in an odd, considering manner. Boldly she returned his look and he smiled a little. Twice his foot encountered hers under the table and she saw his lips twitch with amusement as she pulled hers away.

She grew restless. The soup was cleared away and meat was brought to table, but she played with it, having no appetite, and the gravy congealed on her plate. The bishop was holding forth, occupying all the vicar's attention and requiring only the occasional remark from him to sustain the flow. Edmond was pretending to listen but was focused on his dinner while Alfred's gaze kept returning to her. She smiled back at him a little, just enough to placate, and moved her foot again to avoid his.

'You've not eaten much, Olwen,' her aunt remarked, with a slanting look.

'I find I'm not hungry.'

'No, dear? But at least you managed the soup.' The soup. A good full-flavoured onion soup served at table from a lidded tureen by Mrs Malkon herself. Their guest's bowl had been filled first, and then a pause to mop up a spill, and then Olwen's plate had been passed to her. She met her aunt's eyes and saw a smugness there. The soup. . .

She had dropped her guard.

Olwen dug her nails into her palms below the table and Alfred's foot became more persistent, as if daring her to protest. The situation seemed suddenly absurd and she had to suppress a giggle as her own foot dodged to avoid Alfred's again and she caught his eye, which glinted in response and the laughter kept bubbling up. As soon as she could she excused herself and made her way, a little unsteadily, to the door. Alfred was there before her, opening it, a hand beneath her elbow.

'Steady now,' he said in a low voice as she passed him.

By sheer willpower she walked in a straight line to the foot of the stairs.

Alfred followed. 'I'm right behind you.'

'Are you?' she said, feeling giddy as she mounted the stairs, each step heavier than the last. 'I can't imagine why.' Reaching the landing, she paused, conscious of him two steps behind her, and felt a frisson of unease. Why was he following her? 'I intend to retire and read my book,' she said with what composure she could muster, and crossed to her bedroom door.

He came up close. 'Then I will read to you, my dear,' he said, and reached out in front of her to open the door.

And with a swiftness that took her quite by surprise he propelled her into the room and, in a single movement, he managed to kick the door shut and pull her to him, blocking her protest with his mouth hard on hers. She struggled, desperate to free herself but Alfred was strong and determined. One arm encircled her waist while the other pulled up her skirt. The more she struggled, the tighter he held her, his mouth locked onto hers until she could no longer breathe. He pulled back to look at her, his eyes glittering as she gasped, and she smelled drink on his breath. 'Come now, sweetheart, we don't need to await the formalities.'

'Let me go!'

'Hardly! You might spit.' He kissed her again until she ceased to struggle and then swept her up and carried her to the bed, laying her down. 'Good girl,' he said as he fumbled with his trouser buttons, breathing hard, his hair falling forward. She was terrified, wholly unprepared for this assault, but a wild rage replaced the fear and she saw there was only one way to win and so she pulled her skirts aside. Shrugging out of his jacket, his eyes blazed. 'I knew you'd be game.' He unhooked his braces and had bent over her, grinning, just as she brought her knees up and kicked out with her feet, striking him hard in the groin with her heels. He gave a high-pitched cry and fell back, doubled up in pain, and swiftly she rolled away, off the far side of the bed so that it was between the two of them, and picked up the ewer from the washstand.

'Come after me,' she gasped, 'and I'll throw this through the window.' She gripped the handle hard. 'And I'll scream so loudly they'll come running from the stables.'

'Bitch,' he spat through clenched teeth, still clutching himself.

'Get out.'

'You'll regret that.'

She lifted the ewer. 'Get out.'

He made to come around the base of the bed, his eyes murderous. '*Damn* you, Olwen. You can't resist for ever, you know.'

She raised the ewer above her head, crooking her arm in readiness to throw, but in truth she was at the limit of her strength. 'Tell your mother that laudanum, even in soup, has unpredictable consequences.'

Flinging a curse at her he grabbed his jacket and left the room and, with her last shred of energy, she dragged the washstand across the door, and slumped to the floor.

How long she lay there she could not know but she roused, stiff and cramped, sometime later and got slowly to her feet. Her head was pounding, her legs still trembling with the shock of his attack. It had come from nowhere, so fast, so unexpected. Had he known his mother would drug her during dinner? And had bargained on her being subdued enough to risk a rape? Or was he drunk to have chanced such a reckless move with the bishop still in the house? There had been no wine served with the meal, but he had tasted of drink. Drunk enough to lose control, drunk enough to imagine that she had invited a rough wooing? Or had he simply seen a way to force her hand?

She dragged herself to her bed, rubbing her bruised lips, and took a glass of water. Tomorrow. . . Tomorrow she would escape. She would follow the plan Celia and the doctor had put to her and slip away early, at first light, before the house was awake, and she would hide in the hedgerow beside the smith's pasture and wait until they came for her.

She slept restlessly that night, the washstand still pulled across the door, drifting in and out of a fretful sleep, jumping at every sound, fearful of Alfred returning, dreading that she might over-sleep. As soon as she saw dawn lightening the skies she rose and dressed and began inching the washstand away from the door. Soon the servants would be stirring, lighting the fires and preparing for the day. If she judged it right, she could slip away once the outside door had been unlocked, the bolts drawn back, and while the servants were occupied in the kitchen. The boy, Tim, would be at the stables collecting fuel and drawing water before beginning his rounds laying the fires. She would hide in her uncle's study. The vicarage had an unalterable routine and the fire would not be lit in there until after early prayers, and so was always the last to be laid. She could watch from the window and wait until her uncle left for the church and then take her chance.

Stepping lightly down the stairs, she reached the study without incident and glided over to the desk from where she could watch the path without herself being seen. The lack of food and sleep combined to make her light-headed but soon she heard movement above her in the room where her aunt and uncle slept. A few moments later there were the sounds of her uncle descending the stairs, of murmured exchanges with the servants and the noise of the front door bolts being drawn back. Then she saw him from the window, on the path, on his way to the church.

But as she prepared to go her eye was caught by the seal on an envelope lying on her uncle's desk. The bishop's seal. It was broken, the letter opened. . . She hesitated a moment then pulled out the sheets, skimming the contents, the words jumping before her eyes. She stopped, in disbelief, and then reread the central paragraph.

> *In these exceptional circumstances I agree that there is no objection to a marriage before the period of mourning is over, in fact I would recommend it as marriage will be steadying, providing much needed guidance and giving her a proper purpose, and all within the close bond of family. It was, after all, her father's dying wish.*

She lowered the letter, staring ahead in shock. Had Alfred known of this plan when he attacked her, and been emboldened by it? She read on, her hand shaking.

> *You will be comforted to know that Dr Kemp can see no cause for concern regarding the laudanum already given and, in fact, recommends it continues, in small but regular doses up to the marriage and beyond, to give the poor benighted girl some peace as she adjusts to her new state. He suggests it be administered in strongly flavoured food and then there will be no resistance to the remedy.*

Fury cleared her mind. Glancing at the date she saw that the letter had been written on the day of the physician's visit, presumably immediately after the man had reported to the bishop.

> *We can discuss the matter further when we meet on Friday,*
> *and as to the rites we agreed upon for Sunday, please ask*
> *your wife to ensure that the afflicted girl is brought to church*
> *in an appropriate frame of mind and so—*

She got no further and just had time to duck down behind the desk before Tim, the boy, entered with a scuttle laden with coal and began filling the box beside the fire and raking out the ashes from the hearth. She squeezed her eyes shut, willing him not to see her crouched there, cursing for having allowed herself to be distracted. She remained quite still, not daring to move a muscle, until he had finished and then went to the door, opened it a crack and, seeing that the hall was empty, crossed it, light-footed and swiftly, and was out of the front door, away down the path and had just turned the corner into the lane when she saw the vicar coming back through the churchyard. Pressing herself into the shadows and holding her breath she waited until, with his head bent in thought, or prayer, he disappeared into the vicarage. She ran fast down the lane then, unnoticed by any except for the crows who looked down, beady eyed and curious, from the treetops.

No one knew to whom the patch of pasture beside the black-smith's forge belonged; by custom it was considered common land. Gypsies occasionally grazed their animals there while their women went selling from door to door, and farmers waiting to have their horses shod would leave them, hobbled, feeding on the pasture's lush grasses. It was a secluded spot, bounded on all sides by unkempt hedgerows except for a gap where once there had been a gate. In the far corner, close up against the woodland, the sun had already dried the dew and was even now lighting the nodding heads of cowslips and meadow flowers that were scattered like spots of paint among the grasses. The land dipped away there, into a shallow ditch overhung by hawthorn already bedecked with the buds of early blossom, and Olwen crawled into it, still breathing fast, thankful to have made her escape. Soon they would discover that she was gone and would go looking for her but here she was hidden from the road, and who would think to look for her in the hedgerows?

It was warm in the patch of sunlight, and still, with the sweet smell of grass and astringent mayflowers, and lovely too, with only the bees for company. She sat with her legs curled under her and closed her eyes, feeling the tension begin to leave her, playing out like the tail of a kite rising to the sky, light and joyous. She would never go back to the vicarage, that much she swore, never see Alfred again. . . And, as the sun rose higher, there came from the woods the drumming of a woodpecker and from somewhere close the sweet trilling of a robin.

Drowsiness overcame her, and she lay down on her side, and slept.

CHAPTER 21

S he woke to find her right side grown chill and Heri gone. Sitting up sharply she saw that Bri was still there, with Ælfwinne curled up beside him like a puppy, asleep in the curve of his body, conceding in sleep a need that he would not admit to awake. Ælf had a protective arm flung across his brother but he too appeared to be reaching for Bri's reassuring presence.

But where was Heri?

Silently she rose. Bri lifted his head and looked across at her, then gestured to the edge of the woodland and gave a nod as if he expected her to go.

And so she went, moving silently towards the edge of the copse, and saw that the night sky was cloudless, lit by a waning moon and studded with the brightness of stars. As she came to the limit of the trees she looked out beyond, and froze in wonder, seeing in the sky a great ball of light, its fiery tail streaking the darkness, and the hairs lifted on the back of her neck.

She saw Heri then, standing in the leafy shadows, looking towards her.

'Whatever is it?' she breathed, her eyes fixed on the light.

'A portent, lady. A sign.' His voice was grim.

'Of what?'

'Perhaps,' he said slowly, 'it's best not to know.' She went to him and together they stood and watched it. 'It rose about an hour ago, out of the west.' He paused and looked down at her. 'What woke you?'

'I grew cold.' She had longed for the warmth of his touch in the night but he had shown her only his back, and she had not known why.

He said nothing more and his eyes returned to the skies. They stood in silence for a while and then he looked down at her again. 'Seemed to me it hung for a moment over Scythlescester, where Ælfwald was betrayed.'

She stared at him. 'Here! It was _here_?'

'That was why we came this way.' His voice was grave but gentle. 'I wanted you to know the place.'

She looked out into the darkness, stricken, pain clutching at her heart. 'How do you know?' she asked.

'I was there.' She stiffened, gripped by a sudden alarm, but he shook his head at her. 'I could have done nothing to save him.'

'Tell me, Heri. You cannot set me at a distance forever. Tell me now, while my brothers sleep.'

He raised his head and stared at the trail of light, dimming now as the sky began to lighten. 'I've no wish to distance you, my love, or do anything but hold you close.' He took her hand then and led her to a fallen tree, pulling her down beside him, and he kept hold of her hand, gripping it tight. 'It will be hard to hear, though better that you have it from me than from another.' He paused as if searching for the words, then began. 'We heard rumours, north of the Wall, vague at first, but they kept coming. Modig was sick, a wound from hunting wasn't healing, and he sent for me.' And so Heri had ridden up to Dun Eidyn, he told her, and listened to what Modig had learned. 'Chieftains were being called to council, drawn from far and wide, but Modig was told he need not come, his loyalty was well known. This made him suspicious.'

'Why?'

'He smelled a trap.'

A trap to catch a king.

So Modig had sent Heri south to see what he could discover. Not as an envoy but as a spy with just five men, using untravelled routes, alert for trouble. Ælfwald was coming to Scyth-lescester, Modig had heard, together with Earl Sicga, to meet those leaders called to council. 'Ælfwald would have sent word himself, Modig decided, he would have explained. . . but Modig had heard nothing from him. And so we came here, Bri and I and three others, and we found a small army encamped on that stretch of land between the river and the old fort, just a little way upstream from here; we could see the light from their campfires a mile away.' He paused. 'And who, we asked ourselves, brings an army to council.'

'And was my father there?'

He looked away. 'He had come—' She gripped tight to his hand, dreading what he would say. 'We spread out amongst the men, laughing and drinking with them, it was easy to pass unnoticed for these were men from many places who had come together as strangers. Then, when we could, Bri and I slipped through the gathering and made for the hall, believing that was where we would find the king.'

The wild call of a curlew reached them, presaging the dawn. 'And did you?'

He returned the pressure on her hand. 'I believe he was dead before we reached the place.'

'So you didn't see him!' She tried to pull away but he did not release her. 'Why are you so sure that he's dead?'

He pulled her to him then, and held her close, and his voice grew tight. 'I would spare you this if I could, sweet Wyn, for what I saw that night will always stay with me.' He paused again and then spoke quickly. 'I saw drunken men celebrating, strangers mostly, wild-eyed and murderous and, dear God, I saw Sicga, your father's friend, raise his king's bloodied head to the rafters, roaring in triumph.'

He held her close while she wept, silently stroking her hair, pressing her cheek against his chest. 'There were men from Rheged there,' he continued softly, 'and men from Strathclyde, and lawless men who will give allegiance to any man, and still betray. And there were men from Mercia too.' His hand rested a moment on her head. 'I sent two men back to report to Modig, and then Bri and I rode south. We had to reach you before they did.'

'Those men at Catreath. . . ?' she said and he nodded. How narrow had been their escape! She began to shake as the horror of it hit her. 'And my father's body? Was it left for the wolves and the ravens?'

He dropped a kiss on the top of her head. 'No, Wyn. I sent the last man to Hexham to tell the monks there that Northumbria's king had been foully murdered, and must be buried with all due honour. They will have him now.'

'Then I must go and see where he lies.' She tried again to pull away. 'Tomorrow, before we cross to the north.'

His arms tightened. 'And so light a beacon as bright as that ball of light? No, my love. They would come for you, and they would find you. You'll be safe for only as long as no one knows where you are.' He was looking over her head to where the tail of the comet was still visible. 'There's been talk before now, mead-driven, foolish talk of a new northern alliance, of taking back land ruled by Northumbria, land lost centuries ago at Catreath. Gowk talk by discontented men who lust for battle, flame-lit talk whipped up by those who care nothing for such boasting but would harness it for their own ambition.'

'Meaning who?'

The scowl deepened on his face. 'Æthelred has indeed returned from exile.' She stared at him. 'And they say that he moves with Mercia's blessing.'

She felt sick. This was what her father had most dreaded. 'And Modig, what will he do with us?'

'He will keep you safe.'

She turned her head to look at him. But Modig would surely serve his own interests first. And Heri was heir to his lands. . . She could guess how valuable her brothers would be in the power struggle that was to come. How far had that played into his thinking? 'Why did you come for us, Heri?'

He gave a twisted smile, his hand cupping the back of her head as he pulled her to him again. 'You ask me that? Your brothers would have been slain by sundown, and you, Wyn, would only have been spared to become Osred's bride.'

'That was to be my fate, anyway,' she said bitterly. 'You say that Osred betrayed Ælfwald, but he had remained in Eorforwic?'

'So he could appear in ignorance of the deed.' She felt him tense. 'Did you wish to wed him?'

'I despised him.'

'As others do. . . And if he imagines that he'll be king for very long then he's a fool; his reign is but a step towards a greater purpose. And you, Wyn, with Osred dead, could only hope that Ida's bloodline would tempt the next usurper into matrimony.' She looked aside, knowing that he was right. A woman of royal blood was a mere vessel, a link between forefathers and sons. Then he brought his face close to hers. 'Your brothers I took for love of your father. . . and you?' He touched his lips to hers. 'Ah Wyn, you know why I came for you.'

A little breeze swept over her, flattening the grasses on its way to the woodland, and the chill of it woke her. The dream faded, leaving her with an aching sorrow but still with the taste and touch of him upon her. . . Slowly she opened her eyes to find herself staring into those of a weather-beaten man in ragged clothes who sat hunkered down at the edge of the wood, resting his back against a tree, not a stone's throw from where she lay. She began scrambling away from him but he calmly raised a hand. 'No, maid, I offer you no harm, I watch over you. Do you not know me?'

She stared at him, wide-eyed and bewildered, and then came an improbable recognition, and she frowned. 'Are you. . . are you Reagan?' Reagan, the half-wild man who came and went in the woods at home, tolerated because he did no harm. He nodded and gave a wry smile. 'From Swindale?' He nodded again.

'But whatever brings you here?'

'It's spring,' he said, as if that explained everything. She would have questioned him further but he raised his head, listening. 'Horses,' he said, with another flash of the gap-toothed smile. She turned her head, and heard them too. 'Godspeed to you, lady.'

And when she looked back, he had gone.

CHAPTER 22

John turned and paced back up the platform at York station. He had been doing this for over an hour, in a state of mounting tension, and had already met two trains.

He had told the others he would come on ahead partly to maintain the proprieties by not travelling with his patient, but also to allow himself time to send a message to Brandt, warning him to expect them. If all went to plan, Celia and Gussie would collect Olwen from the smith's pasture in Kirkthorpe, and then drive to the little branch line station, leaving the hired carriage there, and catch the train into York. The village was a mere fifteen miles from York but they were coming by a circuitous route, dictated by the small branch line, which necessitated a change of trains. But if something had gone wrong, he would have no way of knowing, and it seemed to him, as he paced, that any number of things could have happened. She might have been caught slipping out of the vicarage and brought back, or been seen getting into the carriage, or been recognised and challenged at the branch line halt. Perhaps they should, after all, have arranged to travel together.

He walked back down the platform but, as he turned, he saw that another train was coming in and moments later the vaulted ceiling of the station was filled with noise and steam as, with the screeching of brakes, the engine came to a halt.

Passengers began to disgorge onto the platform and, to his relief, he spotted Celia Goodfellow descending from a carriage at the far end and hurried towards her. 'A crossing gate was stuck,' she said, coming forward to greet him, 'but we're here now and everything else went to plan. Olwen did splendidly.' Olwen then emerged from the compartment and he stepped forward to offer her his hand. He had not seen her since that interview in the vicar's study and was shocked by her appearance; she looked almost fey. . . Her clothes were crumpled and her hair, though pinned in place, was dishevelled. 'She fell asleep under a hedge, waiting for us,' Celia explained with a bright, unconvincing laugh, and shot him a speaking glance, 'having lain awake half the night fretting that she would oversleep.' There were dark rings under the girl's eyes and, when he greeted her, she looked away.

But there was no time to consider this now if they were to reach St Hilda's House by the time that he had told Brandt to expect them. John shepherded them quickly out of the station to where a long line of cabs stood waiting and they crowded into one at the head of the line. He sat opposite Olwen, covertly studying her – how pale and drawn she was – while Celia took the place beside her. Gussie, having given instructions to the cabby, sat on the remaining seat. Her job, while he and Celia took Olwen to St Hilda's, was to find rooms for the night and, as they pulled out of the station, the two women discussed which hotels she might try. Olwen sat looking out of the window, saying nothing. 'I'll find my own place,' John said; better that he slept in a different hotel to maintain a distance.

'Don't fret, Doctor John, I'll find you somewhere close by.'

The station area was alive with wagons and carts delivering their loads, their drivers shouting out, vying for space as cabs and carriages collected and deposited passengers, but soon they were passing under the arch that pierced the city walls and onto the bridge, where they slowed to a crawl. Halfway across they came to a halt when a laden wagon in front of them stopped and the driver got down to secure his boxes, ignoring the curses rained down on him from every cabby and carter now stalled on the middle of the bridge.

John fumed at the delay but then he saw that Olwen, who had been sat listlessly in the corner, had stiffened and was leaning forward, staring down through the window. He looked down as well, trying to see what had taken her interest.

'The tide!' Her anguished cry made his heart leap and her eyes flew to his. 'Heri, the *tide!* It's out, how will we get away!'

'My dear?' Celia leaned across to take her hand. 'What is it?' Gussie too was staring at her so neither of them noticed that John had sat back, stunned, plunged in utter confusion. Whatever did she mean? Then he sat forward and looked down again and saw that the river, which usually flowed strongly under the full span of the bridge, had, for some reason, shrunk to less than half its normal size.

The tide, the *tide*. . .

And it came to him then with vivid clarity, a chill dawn, a flight from the city and, as his eyes met Olwen's, he knew exactly what it was that she was seeing.

A stolen boat on a rising tide.

'What is it, my dear?' Celia asked again, but Olwen had turned away from them, breathing fast, her gaze fixed again on the shrunken river. Celia kept hold of her hand and looked across at John as he struggled to master his confusion. It was his dream. Dear God. . . she was seeing *his* dream! He swallowed hard and gave Celia a quick nod of reassurance that he was far from feeling, and at that moment the carter jumped back onto his cart and their cab lurched forward.

They dropped Gussie, together with the bags, at The Black Swan on Coney Street and, a few minutes later, pulled up on the circular drive of St Hilda's House. John, his head still roaring with confusion, forced himself to focus as they went up the steps and through the front door where he gave his name to an attendant who appeared primed to expect them.

'The professor asked that your companions wait in the garden; there's a seat just beside the door,' she said and gave a tight little smile. 'And he requested that they speak to no one, but simply wait. Please follow me, Doctor.'

He exchanged a puzzled look with Celia as he left them and followed the woman down the same corridor as before with its colourful rugs and landscape paintings to an office at the far end.

They entered to find Professor Brandt standing at the window with his back to the door. He swung around as John was shown in, and abruptly dismissed the woman.

'Dr Osbourne,' he said, contemplating him.

'We made it,' John said, as soon as the door was closed. 'She has her companion with her—'

'Do you come with her guardian's blessing?'

John shook his head. 'That'll not—'

'Then you are quite *mad*, my friend, and while I do not think you are unprincipled, this is recklessness to the point of folly!'

Brandt was glaring at him and the muscles in John's jaw tightened. 'She needs treatment. She needs protection—'

'And you think this escapade will serve either of those purposes! My God, but the attraction must be strong to drive you to this.' He sat abruptly behind the desk, gesturing John to a chair opposite, and continued to glower at him. 'Whatever are you thinking?'

'You said that you could help her.'

'I did not offer to flout the law! Beside I can do nothing for you so this wild scheme achieves nothing.'

John stared at him. 'But—'

'Since we spoke, Dr Osbourne,' Brandt continued, grimly, 'two things have happened. Firstly, I received a letter from Miss Malkon's uncle declining my future services on behalf of his niece, and secondly Dr Nicholson has returned from London. It transpires that we agree on very little in matters of our profession and he too has received a letter with the same message, from the bishop in his case. I, in consequence of this, have been reprimanded for seeing patients outside the institution, without Dr Nicholson's knowledge or consent. In short my visit here has been terminated with immediate effect and had you arrived this afternoon you would have found me gone.'

'Oh God, Brandt, this is my doing! I am so—'

Brandt held up his hand. 'I do not accuse. I do not seek an apology. I could have refused to come when you asked, and I could not, in any case, have remained here under Dr Nicholson's regime, such is the gulf in our understanding. I have been deeply dismayed by what I have observed here, and am at the point in my career where this incident will in no way harm me. But for you, my friend—!' He made a gesture of despair. 'Despite my warning you have allowed your passion for this patient to destroy your ability to reason. The authorities will catch up with you, you will be arrested. You must know this, yes? It was for that reason I suggested the garden for your patient. Better that you were never here, I think, and my advice to you, Dr Osbourne, is to return the young lady to her guardian at once and plead insanity yourself—'

John shook his head. 'I can't do that.'

Professor Brandt threw up his hands. 'But you *must*. And at once!'

John straightened his shoulders and looked back at Brandt. 'On every level she is vulnerable. If it wrecks my career then so be it but I cannot give her back into their hands.' The professor made a scornful sound, and John felt an intensity of emotion building in him, such as he had never known. It threatened to overwhelm him. 'I will not let her down again.' Brandt narrowed his eyes, staring at him, and John felt as if his head would burst. 'Last time it ended in bloody murder and in grief. That will not happen again.'

A strange drumming sound was beating in his head, and as it grew louder, his fury became focused on the man before him who rose slowly from behind the desk.

'Dr Osbourne? John—'

John rose too, squaring up to him, he would strike him if he must, an action that would once have been unthinkable. 'You commanded me once before to take her back, against my judgement, against every instinct, even though I begged you to let her stay. And if you will not help me now, then I must act alone. Conflict with you, Modig, is the last thing I desire, but if you stand in my way—'

The man before him was changing form in an alarming fashion and John put out a hand to steady himself. Then a sudden loud sound in his ear made him jump and blink and things steadied.

He heard another clap and went weak at the knees. A strong hand came swiftly under his elbow and lowered him to the chair. He sat, nauseous and giddy, then groaned and put his head in his hands, and began to shake uncontrollably. Someone was speaking to him, words that did not penetrate, words that had no meaning but which calmed him, and he lifted his head.

'Brandt,' he said, overwhelmingly relieved. 'Good God.'

Brandt looked back at him, exploring his face with a sort of wonder. 'Good God, indeed, Doktor! Where did you go, my friend? Do you know?'

'No. . .'

Gradually the room steadied and the nausea retreated. Brandt went over to a table and poured water into a glass, watching John where he sat, drained and bewildered, and brought it to him. 'Drink,' he said, 'and take a moment, then tell me what you can.' He sat down behind the desk again, his fingers locked together, keenly contemplating him. Presently he asked, 'Who is Modig?'

'My grandfather,' he replied, with a weak laugh as Brandt raised his eyebrows. 'At least. . . in another world, which is, I believe, the world that Wyn inhabits.' And, in broken, incoherent sentences, he told Brandt about that moment on the bridge.

'She knew of your dream, you conclude?' Brandt asked when John had no more to say and he nodded. 'And yet you have never told her of it. . . and, just now, for a moment, I think you became that heroic figure from your dreams. Harry, is it?'

'Heri.'

God, what madness was this? He lifted desperate eyes to Brandt, who gave him a wry smile in return. 'And it appears I would do well not to anger this hero.' They sat in silence, John still struggling to regain control as Brandt continued to consider him, bouncing his fingertips lightly off each other. And John felt a growing conviction that his own sanity depended on the outcome of that consideration.

'What had you planned to do, had I agreed to see Miss Malkon?' Brandt asked at last.

John hauled his mind back to the moment. 'To stay in York

tonight and see what transpired here for her while I made contact with the authorities, and raised my concerns. Beyond that we thought of taking her back to Knaresborough, where her companion now lives. There was talk of going abroad from there—'

Brandt shook his head at him. 'A scheme with so little to recommend it.' John scowled at him but Brandt held up a hand, his brow furrowed in thought. 'My strong advice to you is that which you have already rejected – take Miss Malkon home and hope that the vicar is truly a Christian and will overlook this moment of madness.' He took in John's mulish look and shrugged. 'No? You favour the heroic role. Then do as you planned, Doktor. Take her back to Knaresborough in the morning, and I will come to you there.' He came from around the desk and laid a hand on John's shoulder. 'As a professional man I cannot treat this young lady, but as a private citizen I can speak to her, explore a little the mysteries of her subconscious. I do not promise to be able to help, mind you, and I will leave directly afterwards for Zurich and then you must do what you can to set matters right with the law. Your position is already compromised but, for myself, I would prefer not to be arrested.'

'Brandt, this is—'

The professor cut him off. 'Nicholson has angered me with his narrow-mindedness and they would have nothing to offer her here, but this case intrigues me, and I believe that there is something important to be learned. But I only do this on one condition.'

'Which is?'

'I also examine the young woman's enslaved physician.'

CHAPTER 23

This was what Olwen Malkon had meant about possession, John thought as he gathered the two women from the garden, explaining curtly that they must leave, taking in Celia's startled look as he ushered them back through the hall. The bishop's demons had no part in it, this was something else entirely, and the experience had been terrifying. He nodded briefly at the attendant, who watched them with some curiosity as they went rapidly back down the steps onto the drive. It had been the most outlandish sensation and completely defied understanding. He hailed a cab that had just unloaded visitors and the three of them squeezed into it.

'Dr Brandt is leaving St Hilda's, some disagreement with Dr Nicholson, I gather,' he said, though Celia seemed to recognise this was only half the story. 'But he'll see Olwen privately.'

'When? And where? Where will he see her?'

'I suggested your cottage,' he said, uncertain of her reaction.

She agreed readily enough but the implications would have to be made clear to her and Gussie. He found himself unable to look at Olwen, who had shrunk into the corner of the cab, looking much younger than her years, her own eyes turned resolutely away. He had no idea now what he would say to her.

Back at the hotel where they had left Gussie less than a hour earlier, they found her reading in a small sitting room. She looked up, astonished to see them back. 'Gosh, that was—' Celia's expression stalled her.

'Gussie dear, I wonder if you would take Olwen up to her room while I order some lunch for us?' she said, brightly. 'Go with Gussie, my love, you were up awfully early and might like to lie down for a little while. We'll keep some food for you.'

Gussie took the hint, leading Olwen away, and Celia turned in enquiry to John who had, by now, regained some measure of control. He was able to describe what Brandt had said, though omitted any reference to the uncanny episode that had persuaded the man to agree to see her. For how could he possibly explain?

'But he *will* see her. What a relief! Oh, John, she's in a dreadful way.' Celia bit her lip. 'I've never known her like this. She simply fell on me when we picked her up this morning, but has hardly said a coherent word. She had run away at dawn, she said, and hidden under a hedgerow! Whatever have they been doing to frighten her so? She's not ready to speak of her troubles, poor child, so I do hope Professor Brandt can help her.'

Celia's concern for her former charge meant that his own emotional turbulence passed unnoticed. 'I'm sure he'll do whatever he can but he was very damning of our scheme, said it was reckless. Doubtless he's right. . . But you must recognise, you and Gussie, that taking her to your house in Knaresborough will implicate you in all this and could land you in serious trouble.'

'As it will you, John,' she said, with that clear direct look of hers.

'I know.'

She looked at him a moment. 'I'll speak to Gussie, but I know what she'll say. We're determined women, you know, especially when it comes to looking after our own.'

Gussie returned a moment later and said that she had left Olwen falling asleep. 'Curled up like a child, she was, but still silent. She's been ill-treated, I'm sure of it.' When the proposed course of action was put to her, Gussie did not hesitate. 'Of course she must come to us!' she said, dropping into a chair and tucking her legs up under her. 'Once he's seen her we can whisk her away where they will never find her, and if we get arrested before then, all to the good, we'll trumpet her case from the rooftops and revel in the notoriety.' She grinned at John. 'Send a message to your professor telling him we'll expect him and will arrange lodgings – and for you as well, as I imagine you'll be coming. I've secured rooms for you at The Mail Coach for tonight, it's close by. But you'll have lunch first, won't you?'

John shook his head. 'I need to walk, clear my head. And if Olwen wakes she will confide more readily without me being here. When shall I suggest Brandt comes?'

'As soon as possible. Tomorrow if he can. Before they catch up with us.' A messenger was despatched with a note to this effect.

Leaving the hotel, John stood a moment on the threshold, gathering himself and then set off to wander down one of the narrow water lanes, drawn, inevitably, to the river, and he reached a stone wharf and stood there looking down at the incongruous sight of a river drained of its life blood, at sloping banks where boats lay askew on mud exposed for the first time for centuries. A young man was trying to entice holidaymakers onto his rowing boats, urging them to step onto a ramp he had laid across the sludge and silts, but they laughed at him, more taken with the extraordinary sight before them than the prospect of splashing about in the murky residue of the vanished river. Sections of massive pipes lay on the mud beside the scorned boats and John listened to the conversation between two gentlemen who had also come down to look. The river, once tidal but now controlled by locks downstream, had apparently been drained as part of an ambitious project to lay the pipes beneath it, designed to take away the city's effluence and secure a clean water supply. To achieve this, the river had been temporarily dammed upstream and part of its flow diverted.

As he listened, John lifted his eyes and looked across to the other bank where instead of the brick warehouses and stores he could, in his mind's eye, see low timber structures lying haphazardly amidst ancient ruins. And he could see three small ocean-going vessels, their masts lowered, pulled up on the banks with people clustering around, and a silver pin with an animal motif securing the coif of a girl with violet eyes. . . Images came and went, his mind leaping uncontrollably between then and now, no single moment stable enough to grasp. Possession indeed. . . He dropped his gaze to one of the man's rowing boats which lay, half afloat and rocking gently in the sluggish current, and he saw again that other boat, and that other time.

He arrived, some hours later, at his hotel where he found that his overnight bag had been sent across from The Black Swan and with it had come a message.

> *We must speak, John. Urgently. I'll come to your hotel at*
> *seven o'clock. Gussie will stay with Olwen.*

One of Celia Goodfellow's strongest attributes in John's eyes was her ability to come directly to the point, but that evening her blunt reporting of the reason behind Olwen's silent withdrawal was devastating. He rose and went to stand at the fireplace, holding onto the mantelpiece to steady himself.

'In her own room!'

'With the bishop still in the house.'

He swore. 'And had we not laid the plans we have—'

'We're entirely vindicated, John, she's simply not safe there. Thank goodness she was able to fight off the wretch. She was very brave but she took a risk; he's a strong, athletic young man.'

John's knuckles whitened as he gripped the mantelpiece, wishing he had Alfred Malkon's throat within reach. 'He'll need to be,' he said, then looked across at Celia. 'How is she?'

'Tearful when she finally told us, but perhaps relieved when she found that she could. More angry now than anything but – ' she paused and her brow puckered. ' – but dreadfully confused, hardly making sense. She told us that when she woke in the smith's pasture, there was a man there looking at her. She said it was Reagan.'

'Reagan?'

'He's a sort of vagrant who lives in the woods at Swindale – ' Fleetingly John remembered the ragged figure he had seen at the edge of the woods by the lake, and what Percy had told him. ' – but I find it hard to believe it was him. She claims he was watching over her. Guarding her.' Her frown deepened. 'It's nonsense, of course, she can only have been dreaming. But that's not all, by any means.' She pulled a crumpled paper from her pocket. 'She gave me this.'

It was a letter, badly creased, but it had been smoothed and refolded, and he read quickly: *I can see no objection to a marriage, even before the period of mourning is over.* . . He looked up sharply.

'Read on,' Celia said, tight-lipped.

. . . *no cause for concern regarding the laudanum already given, in fact it is something that he would recommend continue.* . . 'Good God!'. . . *in small but regular doses up to the marriage and beyond.* . . He read through to the end, then scrunched the letter in his hand.

'No! Don't. This is evidence, John. We might yet need it.' She took it from his fist and smoothed it again. 'I'll keep it safe, I promise you. Gussie was fighting mad when she saw it and wanted to expose that beastly bishop and his physician at once, but we must be cannier than that.'

'How did Gussie come by it?'

'Olwen had it. It was on her uncle's desk, she said, and she saw it while she was hiding in the study. She didn't remember taking it, but woke in the pasture to find that she had it in her pocket.'

'They'll be squirming once they realise that she took it.'

Celia nodded. 'And they might think that's why she ran away, so it'll buy us a little more time while they hunt for her.'

There was a tap on the door and one of the hotel servants asked if they were ready to eat.

'I ordered dinner,' John said, 'hoping you might stay and eat with me.'

She gave him her clear, calm smile. 'I'd like that.'

John nodded to the servant, who came in and began laying the table. He asked to see the letter again and read it through more slowly. . . *given with strongly flavoured food and then there will be no resistance to the remedy.* . . Remedy! My God, they were conspiring to poison the girl into compliance. He sat and glared into the fire, rehearsing what he would say to the accursed bishop, and her uncle, and that nest of vipers that had her—

'John?' Celia was addressing him. He apologised. 'I simply asked how you spent the afternoon.' She smiled, with a slight nod in the direction of the servant. And so, while the man arranged the cutlery and began to bring the dishes through, he told her about his trip down to the riverside and what the lowering of the river signified. 'That's a great step forward,' she remarked. 'As a girl I remember hearing about the cholera epidemic of 'thirty-two and the city's grown so rapidly since then another such outbreak would be devastating.'

With the covers now laid the man withdrew, suggesting that they rang the bell should they require anything further, otherwise he would leave them in peace, in private. This last was said with an insolent inflection and John lifted his head, ready to be angry, but Celia simply waved the man away. 'It happens all the time. Two men can meet and dine privately,' she said, 'and two women can usually do the same, but when an unrelated man and a woman meet in the same circumstances how tongues do wag and eyebrows lift.'

'You care little for convention, Miss Goodfellow,' John remarked, passing her the gravy and thinking again what an excellent ally she was.

'Are we to be formal again, Dr Osbourne? I was Celia earlier.'

He smiled and poured her a glass of wine. 'Forgive me. I'm not used to such openness, and such uncomplicated good sense.'

She raised her glass and considered him. 'And yet I believe you to be a man of good sense yourself.' He shrugged. 'Which makes this current escapade all the more remarkable. Are you in love with Olwen? Gussie says you are.'

He ceased to smile and sat, twisting the stem of his wine glass between his fingers as he considered his reply. Openness, after all, cuts both ways and he was becoming aware that whatever it was between himself and Olwen Malkon, a girl he barely knew, it went to the heart of the issue; she had, it would appear, an extraordinary hold over him. Celia did not press him but sat, eating quietly, allowing him the space to decide how to answer. And so he found himself telling her about the strange connection between them, describing his dreams, and from there it was a short step to recounting, as best he could, what had occurred in Brandt's office earlier that day. And he found release in the telling.

Celia was a good listener, hearing him out without comment, continuing to eat as if it was commonplace to have her dinner listening to a man tell her that he believed that he was dreaming the same dreams as someone else and that he had, for a moment, become quite another person. 'Brandt now sees me as a "case" and insists on examining me as well,' he concluded wryly, refilling both their glasses and sitting back, feeling haggard and exhausted.

'How fortunate it happened while you were there with him so he could observe you, as I see it would be difficult to describe.' Her matter-of-fact response was hugely comforting. 'I must confess, though, I don't begin to understand.'

'Nor do I, and Brandt seemed dumbfounded.'

'Does Olwen know that you share her dreams, her story?'

'I didn't know myself until today. . . though, this morning, when we crossed the bridge—'

Celia nodded. 'Yes, I wondered what happened there and I'm pleased I understand that now. Or, at least, to have it explained.' What had she thought, he wondered. 'Perhaps better not to say anything to her, it would only confuse her more, unless the professor advises otherwise.' She sipped at her wine, looking across at him with concern. 'And you say that down by the river, just now, you experienced something similar?'

He nodded, staring in front of him. 'Like a memory from a distant time, becoming clearer as I stood there. The low water, the exposed mud and the river's current against which we rowed. . .' He gave an unsteady laugh at the 'we' but Bri was as real in his mind as Celia was. 'And, most weirdly, her brothers were also there, to be protected, shielded and I knew, viscerally, that the threat to them was very real—'

She looked baffled. 'But you never met Oliver and William, did you?'

'No. I didn't even know their names until you told me, and yet I can see their doubles so clearly, I know how they spoke, how they laughed and how hard Ælf tries to be brave and how Ælfwinne looks like a child when he sleeps—' He broke off again, his jaw tightening as he struggled for control, feeling again that awful certainty that he had failed them.

Celia stretched a hand across the table to him. 'John, my dear man, these are dreams.'

'Are they?'

She stared at him, and he lifted a hand to his brow, squeezing his eyes shut. 'I know, I know. . . I keep telling myself that. All afternoon I've been reasoning with myself, telling myself that they are inventions, the result of sympathetic imagining on my part, born of what Olwen has told me, and of my concern and. . . and yes, I admit to a strong attraction, but it is much deeper than that. . .' He paused again. 'Olwen told me once that she was possessed and I dismissed what she said, but that was exactly how it felt this morning. Not possessed by demons, not by something evil but I was, for a moment, another man. . .' Celia looked back at him, troubled and clearly mystified. 'You know, I've always considered myself to be a rational, enlightened individual, cynical even, and yet. . . and yet I was deranged enough to spend the rest of the afternoon trying to trace the route we'd taken from the king's residence to the entrance of the tunnel down which we escaped that morning.'

'And did you?'

It had taken him a while to get his bearings but, as he walked towards them, the modern buildings seemed to retreat and some sort of awareness, deep in his subconscious, guided him down streets imprinted on the line of former *viae* of the Roman fortress, seeing before him the ruins of buildings cleared centuries ago, crumbling away beside piles of rubble overgrown with nettles and briars. 'Some sort of sixth sense took me first to one corner of the old fortress where there are now stables and a livery, and from there I retraced my steps, as far as I was able, and came to an area that was blocked off where men were working. Digging. . .' He swallowed hard, still barely able to credit what he had seen. 'Part of the pipe-laying project, I was told. There'd been problems with recurrent flooding in that particular area, water surging up and filling the gutters after heavy rain, and so men had dug down—' He stopped, his throat drying up.

'And found?' she prompted.

He took a drink. 'Part of the old Roman sewer system. A tunnel, in fact, large enough for a man to crawl along.'

CHAPTER 24

Olwen followed Gussie into the sitting room of the little house in Knaresborough, finding it hard to reconcile the giddy Lady Sarah with the stylish young woman now wearing a broad leather belt cinching in a neat waist and a skirt, of mid-calf length, which swished as she walked. She was intrigued by Celia's friend who had been so kind to her last night, and then so angry on her behalf. How confident she was, and Celia too, how redoubtable and how wonderfully comforting they both were. It must be delightful, she thought as she looked around the untidy sitting room, living here together, just the two of them, pleasing themselves entirely. Last night in York she had woken in the night, and listened to the gentle rhythm of their breathing and had sat up in her truckle bed and looked at them, sleeping in each other's arms, an abandoned chaos of limbs and linen and unpinned hair.

But there had been an air of tension this morning as they waited at York station. Dr Osbourne's eyes were constantly skimming the crowds and he had frowned when it was announced that their train was running late. 'Sunday trains never keep to schedule,' she heard Gussie say. 'But don't fret, Doctor John, the vicar'll be too busy saving souls today to search for lost lambs.' Celia too had sought to reassure him. 'And no one will be looking for three women and a man, travelling together.' Olwen had felt a moment of alarm at the thought of being hunted, and shared in the general relief when, at last, their train pulled out of the station. No one said much during the journey and she had fixed her gaze out of the window. The dream she had had in the smith's pasture had not been forgotten during the frenzied day, nor had that moment on the bridge when she had seen the vanished river and called out. Dr Osbourne had seemed stunned, and had been altered in his manner ever since. She sensed a new tension in him, and occasionally, reflected in the glass of the railway compartment window, she had caught him watching her, and found it impossible now not to see, on his features, the imprint of another.

He had left them at the station to go to the hotel where he was staying in order to arrange a room for Dr Brandt, who would arrive later in the evening. 'But you'll come back and eat with us, won't you?' Gussie had called after him and he had raised a hand in acknowledgement.

Arriving at Celia's house and hearing the front door click behind them had been such a profound relief. Celia had hugged her in the hall, holding her close. 'How delightful to have you here,' she said. 'Go with Gussie, my love, while I pop into the kitchen.'

'Come on, chick.' And Gussie had brought her upstairs and shown her the spare bedroom, which had a dormer window looking out over the garden, and was small, and quite perfect. Just enough space for a bed, a washstand and a bookcase, all arranged and decorated with simple, pleasing taste. 'Oh! Celia's books,' she cried, recognising beloved titles that had once been brought to Swindale Hall. 'Old friends. . .' Gussie had smiled and left her immersed in them until she heard a gong being sounded and Celia calling up to her. She was laughing as Olwen descended the stairs. 'Absurd, I know, but Gussie said we must have a gong to give us consequence. We never use it, of course, but tonight is by way of an occasion, having you here with us,' she gave Olwen another of those spontaneous hugs that she had missed so much, 'and Dr Osbourne too.'

Olwen turned and looked through the open door into the tiny dining room. She had not heard him arrive but there he was, seated at the table, looking back at her. He half rose as she entered, sitting again when she did and, for a moment, they were alone. 'Did you find a room for Professor Brandt at your hotel?' she asked politely, not quite able to meet his eyes. Whatever should she say to him?

'I did. Thank you, yes.' He was searching her face in that intense way of his.

'It's handy for the station.'

'Yes, indeed. Very.'

He seemed as awkward as she was and conversation faltered and it was fortunate that Celia arrived a moment later, carrying a plate of cold meat. 'We'd given Joyce the day off as we weren't sure what time we'd be back but we've raided the pantry – it'll earn us a scolding tomorrow, throwing her plans in disorder – and Gussie's made some soup, which will be sustaining, and there's bread and cheese and some of last year's apples. Will it do?'

'Of course, it will,' Gussie declared, following her in bearing a soup tureen balanced on a tray. 'We all eat far too much as it is.'

Perhaps Celia and Gussie had agreed in the kitchen that conversation would stay away from the central reason that they were gathered here as they made a great fuss of distributing the food. Perhaps it was to set her at her ease, to distract her from tomorrow's appointment with Dr Brandt, that they went on to describe in some detail which vegetables they had grown themselves and what they were planting for the coming year. Quite what would happen tomorrow was not entirely clear; it had been explained to her last night, but everything yesterday had been a blur, a rolling turmoil of emotions from the moment she escaped from the vicar's study until she had crawled, spent and exhausted, into the truckle bed at the hotel in York.

She glanced across at Dr Osbourne and saw that the tension had left his face and he was smiling at something Gussie said, his face transformed, his eyes glinting in a way that was so oddly familiar. It was quite impossible now to look at him without seeing Heri, in the same way that she had glimpsed that other woman's face in her mirror, two faces overlain but as one. For herself the distinction between herself and her *alter ego* was now hopelessly blurred; she came and went without warning, putting words into Olwen's mouth, implanting memories, and seemed to have a relentless grip upon Olwen's emotions. It was terrifying to lose so much control.

But could she ever explain this to him now? For her, the dream in the smith's pasture had changed things between them, although he might never know it, and that thought brought her dismay. . . She watched him now as Celia encouraged him to take another slice of the ham while Gussie interrogated him about his life before he came to Kirkthorpe. The soft cadences of his voice were familiar too. '. . . from the Borders, not far from Kelso.' And she knew that he was now central to her confusion.

'I've never been there,' Gussie replied.

'Then you're the poorer for it. They might not have the grandeur of the Highlands nor the romance of the islands, but the Borders have their own appeal.' He saw that she was watching him, and smiled. 'Beloved of Scott and Stevenson, as Miss Malkon once remarked, and they have a wildness of their own, their red soils seeped in the blood of ancient feuds.' It was the day they had met, she remembered, when he had eaten at the vicarage, little knowing what lay ahead. 'The Cheviots might appear benign,' he went on, 'but they've a granite heart; even the Romans could not hold the land for long.' She found her breathing quickening, it could be Heri speaking. . .

'Reiver country,' Celia remarked, glancing at Olwen with a smile, she too perhaps remembering days out on the lawns at Swindale House devouring Walter Scott's ballads.

'Aye, a lawless, disputed land.'

'Were you raised there, Sir Knight?' Gussie asked.

'I was. At the end of a long open valley above Yetholm, a gathering point for wandering gypsies; my mother is descended from one such but she married my father, a local farmer, and settled there.' In her mind's eye Olwen could see the great sweep of the valley rising to the uplands. 'She's run the place since he died, and she runs it still. Sheep mainly but a few cattle too, some for milk, some for slaughter.'

'How splendid of her.'

'Aye, but it's not an easy life, especially in the winter when the snow comes. She was determined that I'd not stay there though, but would go off and better myself.' He gave a laugh that was almost bitter. 'More or less threw me out, in fact, but I'm not sure she had the right of it.'

'Meaning what?' Gussie asked.

He shrugged. 'Meaning a part of me hankers for the place, for the life there. It's home and that's a strong thing. Perhaps I'll end up going back. . .' He paused, his eyes staring off beyond the little room, and Olwen found herself hanging on his every word. 'There's something about it, a special quality to the light, especially in the evening when the low sun rakes across the landscape – ' and her other self went with him, seeing the low stone farmstead so clearly ' – the clouds hang low in the folds of the land, casting shadows that race over the hills, for there's always a wind – ' and she saw again the stream that ran through the valley, the burn where brown trout hid in the shady shallows, where the water tumbled over the rocks casting diamonds into the sunshine, where they had watched the dipper plunge to walk on the pebbles beneath the surface, defying nature's laws ' – and if you climb up above Halterburn the wind's so strong you can lean into it and it—'

'– can tear the washing off the gorse and send it flying across the heather!' The room had vanished and she laughed across at him, assailed suddenly with the sparkling memory of that day. 'We chased after it, do you remember, the four of us, and you let Ælfwinne get ahead, pretending to trip and you wrestled Ælf to the ground so that he wouldn't get there first – ' she became breathless in her laughter as the images flooded her mind ' – and somehow I overtook you all but Ælfwinne pushed me over and then threw himself onto the clothing, battling it as if it was a live thing – ' Then Heri had pulled her to her feet and there had been that moment that hung there, and when the boys had stopped laughing he had bid them go back with the rescued garments and they had looked up, surprised by the hoarseness in his voice, and when they had gone, disappearing below the brow of the hill, he had taken her in his arms and kissed her in a way she had longed for him to do—

She broke off and looked around, suddenly at a loss, and saw staring faces and a room that rippled and surged, and had fallen silent.

'Wen, darling.' Celia slid a hand across the table to her but she was seized by a strange choking sensation and she pulled her hand away, gasping, as grief – no, something more than grief – hit her, taking her breath away and she cried out, doubling over, wrapping her arms around her body in defence against the confusion, and then Celia was on her feet, pulling her chair back, saying that it was all right when it wasn't, telling her to rise. 'Come with me, my dear.' But she looked instead across to where he sat, the man who had become her lover that day, masked in a stranger's guise.

'Wait!' John rose abruptly. 'Celia, wait.' This must now be acknowledged; there was no longer any doubt. Everything that Olwen had just described he recognised, it had flashed across his mind as she spoke as clear as day; he had been there, with the boys on the fellside, he could see every detail. And he had to tell her. 'Let me go with her. Better that we confront this now.'

Celia stepped back, uncertain, but Olwen rose, with such a look on her face, half fear, half wonder, and he led her into the little sitting room and to a chair beside the window, and crouched down beside her.

'Olwen,' he said. 'I begin to understand.' Though never was a word less adequate.

'You *know*?' she asked, her eyes wide.

He nodded. 'I'm not sure what I know, and what I understand is even less, but I know that day and that hillside.' And what later transpired.

'So it is the same for you?'

He nodded and smiled a little shakily. 'I think perhaps it is.'

'Thank goodness.' She closed her eyes. 'I truly believed I was going mad.'

'If you are, then I'm there beside you.' He took her hands, palms together, and held them between his. 'That moment on the bridge—'

'The day we fled?' She looked back at him, eagerly now, her eyes no longer evading his.

'Aye.' And it was enough. Enough for now, at any rate. They understood each other. Her eyes had deepened to that violet hue he had seen them do before and he longed to take her in his arms but knew that he must not. Not yet. . . 'I knew then, for certain, and later with Brandt. . . But don't let's try to understand the whole of it. Better that we leave the matter until tomorrow, he knows of this strange connection between us, I've told him, and I'll see him this evening, talk to him. You know that you're safe here with Celia and Gussie, and tomorrow perhaps we'll begin to understand a little more.' She nodded, her eyes gleaming. 'Shall I fetch Celia?'

'Yes.' He released her hands but immediately she grasped his again. 'You will be here too, won't you? Tomorrow? You will come?'

'Be in no doubt. I promise.'

CHAPTER 25

They spoke long into the night, he and Brandt. They began, sitting in a smoky corner of the hotel taproom, drinking ale at a stained table, while John unburdened himself, keeping nothing back, the compulsion to talk now so strong that his words fell over each other. He was incoherent, he knew he was, as he tried to describe what had happened that evening – that, on top of what had occurred on the bridge and later in Brandt's office. Brandt leaned forward, listening intently, but, when John had run out of words, he simply put up a hand.

'Let us walk, my friend. Our brains need fresh air, not this tobacco smoke. Go and fetch your coat, the air is chill. Go! I will wait at the door.'

They took an erratic route skirting the old churchyard then headed up through the narrow winding streets, the wet cobbles slick in the light from street lamps. The deluge of words had at last run dry and John now found it hard to speak, impossible to cudgel his brain to reason, but this too Brandt took in his stride.

'Wait. Be calm. We will take stock, my friend. We are physicians, after all, men of science with cool rational minds and so we consider first and foremost the facts, before we turn to conjecture.' A black cat ran across their path, chasing a shadow, and disappeared up an alley. 'Miss Malkon is a young woman who has, by her own admission, a vivid imagination and a love of stories and she has suffered great losses, one after the other, and her mind has been unbalanced by it all. Add to that the hallucinogenic and frightening effects of the laudanum she has been given, the threat of having demons expunged from an already brittle mind by men with authority over her and now, you tell me, an attempt at rape by her cousin – Dear God! – the very man she is being pressured to marry!' He threw up his hands. 'Ach! Is this not enough to drive anyone mad, let alone a young woman on whom society and circumstance already impose so many limitations?'

'Aye, but none of that explains why *I*—'

'I'm coming to you, sir. Wait!' Ahead of them the ruins of the castle keep stood large and solid above the Nidd gorge, silhouetted against the darkening sky. 'You, my esteemed colleague, are a physician with an interest in the mind, trained to care for your patients, and you are puzzled by this case, drawn in, understandably more intrigued by it than by the sprain of some fat farmer's ankle. And you are a young man, a *passionate* young man, I think, and so interest leads swiftly to attraction and your physician's reason and common sense desert you.' John made a sound in his throat that the professor ignored. 'Both man and physician are rightly appalled by the treatment this young woman has endured at the hands of her family—' He broke off, drawing John over to a bench beside the wall of the keep and pulling him down beside him. 'You have heard of thought transference, my friend?'

'Of course.' Vexed, he brushed the question aside. Was that all the man had to offer? 'But there are the physical aspects, the proof, if you will, that there's more to it than that. The low river and the connection we both made upon seeing it. The tunnel—'

'Have you spoken to her about any of this?'

'No, except to—'

'Then you do not know what is in her thoughts. These things might mean nothing to her.'

He was wrong. They did. 'The story of the blown washing then. I *knew* that story, it was as clear to me as if. . . as if I'd lived it.'

'Had you ever thought of it until today?' John paused. Had he? Perhaps not. 'No? So that too can be explained by thought transference, from her imagination to yours, it can be instantaneous. Telepathy, if you prefer that word, although we understand very little of what—'

John began to lose patience. 'You're wrong, Brandt. I don't

accept your reasoning. Why, for pity's sake, did my instincts take me to the exact spot where an ancient drain was being exposed, a tunnel I can remember leading her down?'

Brandt shook his head. 'You made a connection between what you saw and your dream but there need be none.' John sucked in his breath, exasperated, but Brandt raised a hand. 'I do not claim to have all the answers, my friend, and there are those on the margins of our profession who regularly remind us that there are many things beyond our understanding. Things we cannot explain. We've all had the experience of entering a place we've never been before and finding it familiar, or we are introduced to someone and know that it's not for the first time. Some call it a magnetic rapport, drawing on Mesmer's theory of animal magnetism, Boirac would have us call it the transposition of the senses, and Hamlet tells Horatio that there are more things in heaven and earth than are dreamed of in his philosophy. . .' He smiled a little. 'I could go on, but for myself, I look first for simple explanations before I surrender to the psychic. And I believe seeing the low water, yes and the tunnel too, simply reminded you of your dreams, and the rest, my friend, could well be your own construction.'

John turned away, biting back his disappointment; he had hoped for more from this man. Olwen would draw little comfort from being told that all her woes were creations of her own imagination! He began to wish they had not embarked upon this crazy venture. . .

'And yet, and yet. . .' Brandt looked up at the ruined keep towering above them and gave a sigh. 'Perhaps Hamlet spoke the simple truth of it. We sit here with this great castle behind us, once the seat of power that dominated the region, and now but a broken shell, a husk. Centuries have passed since it was abandoned and yet here it remains. Does an echo of those times still rebound off its walls, audible to those who will but take the time to listen? Are there conversations embedded in the plasterwork, or do emotions still leach from the ancient stones? I'm not sure, these are romantic notions but perhaps they should not be scornfully dismissed. Sitting here, in the darkness, it takes only a little imagination to hear the whisper of long-dead voices.' John turned back to look at him, the yellow light of the gas lamp reflected in his wise old eyes. 'We are only just beginning to understand the workings of the mind, we are at a watershed, and approach the matter from many angles. Are we so arrogant that we claim that we will ever understand the whole? The church has long believed in demons – still does, it would appear – while spiritualists conjure up the dead through their outrageous mediums, taking the gullible and the grieving with them. And yet reincarnation is something to which both, in their different ways, give credence. Prophets and those credited with second sight foretell the future, so must the idea of a spiritual *memory* be dismissed? The physical manifestations of the past are all around us, yes? So must it be impossible that an emotional imprint of those times survives? Or does it comes down, in the end, to individual persuasion and what one chooses to believe?'

'And yet—'

'And yet,' Brandt continued, raising a figure, 'as men of science we are taught to disregard that which has no basis in science and search for certainty.'

'Exactly.'

'But that too is a fallacy; science, as it progresses, is dogged by uncertainty. In medicine a new treatment is tried in a spirit of hope that it will be efficacious but there is always doubt at the outset, not certainty. Science advances at the pace of a snail, and then at the leap of a lion, but it can also lose its way and falter, and must retrace its steps and begin again. As man learns, he believes he is evolving, leaving behind the barbarism of the past, secure in the belief of ongoing progress. But here too there is an ambivalence, this certainty also begins to stumble. We stutter, we stall. . . And we observe things that no existing body of evidence can explain, at least not yet. Maxwell was derided as well as acclaimed when he predicted the existence of radio waves, but I have seen it demonstrated conclusively that they exist, and the significance of this discovery is even now being investigated by men of science with feverish excitement. Who could have thought that likely when you were born?' He paused a moment. 'Already we find ways of communicating over distances that could not have been imagined. So must thought transference and dream telepathy be dismissed as impossible? Are forces of the past truly extinguished, drained of all their energy?' He shook his head. 'I do not repudiate what you tell me, John, I simply explore first that which we *can* understand before entertaining those aspects we cannot. If a telegraph can carry a thought across a physical distance, perhaps a memory too can be distilled and survive, latent somewhere until some spark reawakens it, centuries later, and gives it form and shape and meaning, and the unreal becomes, once more, a part of reality. Our understanding is, perhaps, bounded only by the limits of our imagination.'

John sat there, staring into the darkness.

'You say she mentioned the names of her brothers today,' Brandt went on. 'Were these familiar to you?

'Yes, I knew their names from my dreams.' And the boys themselves, he could see them clearly.

'But she hadn't previously told you those names?'

He shook his head. 'No. And I didn't know the Malkon boys' names until Celia told me. But when Olwen spoke of Ælf and Ælfwinne, I knew who she meant. I knew *them*.'

'Or believe that you did,' Brandt murmured. 'And in my office yesterday your mind confused me with your grandfather – which was not a flattering moment. What was his name?'

'Modig.'

'And does she know this name?'

John went back through the conversations they had had. Had she ever said it? He thought not and began to see where Brandt's thoughts were leading. 'She will know it, I imagine, but she has never spoken it in my hearing. Do you plan to put it to the test?'

Brandt nodded. 'And are there other names that you have dreamt or absorbed from her thoughts which she has never spoken of?'

It was hard to remember for the dreams had faded. It was as

if it required her presence to reignite or refresh their story, as if she was some sort of battery that stored and then released fragments of it, whether real or imagined. 'In her world, or at least in what my dreams reveal of her world, she is the daughter of Ælfwald, an ancient king, but she has never said so, and she has a cousin, Osred, who she doesn't trust.'

'And has she ever said these names in your hearing?' John shook his head. 'Good, then tomorrow, my friend, we will see if she produces them and we might learn something, and better understand if she is somehow transferring these thoughts, this imagined world, to you.'

CHAPTER 26

'No purple cloak!' Olwen was on the landing, about to descend the stairs, when she heard the doorbell ring and Gussie go to answer it and invite their visitors in. 'It was the very least that I expected,' she heard her say, and listened as Dr Osbourne made introductions.

'Already I disappoint!' She recognised Professor Brandt's accent.

And then Celia's voice. 'Ignore her, Professor, you are very welcome. Let me take your hat and coat. Were you comfortable at The Wheatsheaf? It's homely rather than splendid, I think.' The voices faded as they crossed the hall and went towards the sitting room at the back.

Olwen retreated to her room and sat on the edge of the bed. Her breakfast tray was where she had left it, the food hardly touched as her stomach was nervously churning. Celia had brought it and had sat with her awhile, watching her as she nibbled at the toast, asking how she had slept, how she felt. . . In point of fact, she had slept well but had woken with a confused memory of having embarrassed everyone at supper, and then of an extraordinary conversation with Dr Osbourne. She sat staring out of the window, considering what had been said.

There was a tap at the door and Celia put her head round again. 'They've arrived, my dear, and he seems very nice indeed. Very dapper, very European, and he's busy sparring with Gussie at the moment, quite unoffendable it would appear. But you've met him already, of course, I keep forgetting.'

'And Dr Osbourne. . .'

'Yes, he's here too. Shall we join them?'

Olwen followed her down the stairs. 'You confuse science with theatre, dear lady,' she heard the professor's voice through the open door of the sitting room. 'What demonstrations of hypnosis show—'

'What they *show*, dear man, is a deliberate exposition of the frailty of women to a collection of men, half of them voyeurs, who seek thereby to reaffirm their power and authority over them. Tell me, are there women doctors in Germany?'

'Of course! Women attend medical school—'

'I meant mind doctors, like you.'

'Not so many, perhaps.'

'No? So even though the majority of those so-called afflicted souls are women, it is the men who—' She broke off as Olwen entered and Professor Brandt rose with a smile and came forward.

'Miss Malkon! How delightful to renew our acquaintance!' He gave a little bow and held out his hand. 'And you are amongst good friends here, I think.'

'I am.' She smiled a little in return and glanced towards Dr Osbourne, bidding him a quiet good morning.

'Can I get you some refreshment?' Celia asked but the professor shook his head.

'Thank you, no. But let us sit a moment, all of us, and become better acquainted. Your hostess already considers me a fraud.' He nodded towards Gussie, but addressed Olwen with a twinkle in his eye. 'She anticipated the purple cloak of Franz Mesmer, and perhaps some occult symbols, some candles, incense perhaps.' Olwen smiled. 'But these I think would be alarming so I left them at the hotel. Today I am neither magician nor physician but a well-wisher and so we will just talk, you and I, if you are content to do so. And then I will try to direct your thoughts a little to see if we can reach into your mind, into your subconscious, and together we will explore. Yes?'

Nervousness grew, for where might this exploration take her? She wondered for a moment exactly what this man had been told, how much he knew. 'When we met before, at the vicarage, I was confused. . .'

'You had been given opiates, your aunt told me, which would account for that.'

'But not wholly. My uncle claims I'm possessed, and I believe he may be right.'

Brandt considered her, then gently said, 'Perhaps it is more a question of finding the right word, *fraulein*. You are not possessed in the way that your uncle means.'

'No, but I can think of no other word that fits. . . consumed, perhaps, inhabited.'

'These are matters we will explore, if you permit. And I promise I will not lead you into danger.' She considered, and then nodded. His calm manner was reassuring, and surely the need to understand was paramount. 'Good. And Dr Osbourne will remain with us, unless you prefer that he does not?'

She looked across at him and he looked steadily back, allowing her to decide. 'I should very much like him to stay if he will, for I believe. . . I believe him to be afflicted too.'

John nodded, and warmed her with his smile. 'I will stay.'

Brandt looked from one to the other. 'Also good! And your friends tell me there is a great deal of gardening to be done so they will be out there amongst the plants, but very close by. You need have no fears, Miss Malkon, you are quite safe here and you can relax entirely while we see what, between us all, we can discover.' He sat back, which Celia and Gussie took as a signal; they rose. Celia gave her a swift kiss and they withdrew and she watched them set off down the path towards the potting shed.

The professor then began rearranging the furnishings, speaking with a soothing fluidity as he did. 'Dr Osbourne, you will go and sit over there by the piano and you, Miss Malkon, will make yourself comfortable here on the daybed. Stretch yourself out, if you will.' He pulled the curtains slightly to darken the room, and smiled at her. 'It is more restful, yes?' he remarked. 'Sometimes we do not want the stimulation of the sun.' He pulled a chair up beside her and continued speaking in a low tone, bidding her close her eyes, to relax '. . . every part of your body, starting from the toes.' He worked his way up her body, naming each part in turn. 'And now your fingers, good, wiggle then a little and then let them go, and let your shoulders droop, very good, breathe in through your nose and out through your mouth, excellent. . .' And as he spoke, she felt a great languor creep over her followed by a lightness, and she was floating, hearing his voice coming from a great distance. 'You were happy that day the washing was blown off the bushes, I think.' He knew about that. . . someone must have told him. . . 'Describe it for me. Who was there with you?'

'Heri, and my brothers.'

'And your brothers are?'

She paused a moment. 'Ælf and Ælfwinne.'

'Where were you, that blustery day?'

'With Heri. At the farm, with Heri's mother's people, north of the Wall.' Where life had been so very sweet. . .

'And why had you gone there?' A little frisson of fear went through her and must have shown on her face. 'It is quite safe to tell me,' he reassured.

She hesitated. But by now everybody must know. 'Because Ælfwald is dead.'

'And who is Ælfwald?'

Was he mocking her? She frowned a little. 'Ælfwald was my father, the king. He was murdered. . . and Heri brought us away from Eoforwic. . . he hid us with his mother's people because my brothers were not safe – ' A great anguish grew in her. ' – and oh how I wish we had never gone from there!'

'Be calm, my dear. Let us leave that for a moment, and return to it later. Tell me more about this place where you were happy.' And so she told him about the farm, seeing it as she remembered it, nestling within the circle of more ancient walls, one of a group of squat stone buildings with turf roofs, a small community of farmers. And she told him how they lived simply but well, how she had helped the women with their tasks, enjoying their company, and how the boys had thrived there. And how Heri—

'Who is Heri?' the distant voice asked.

She hesitated for just a moment and then with a blaze of pride.

'Heri's father was Modig's son, and he is heir to the ancient line of Gododdin's kings.'

John squeezed his eyes shut, the pain in his heart so great it must burst. He would have leapt up then and gone to her but Brandt sensed this and, without looking at him, raised his hand to forbid it for Olwen was continuing. 'My father trusted Modig, and Modig trusted Heri.'

'And you, did you trust Modig?'

Her eyes remained closed but John saw that her face was working, her brow creased with strain. 'He said that we must go.'

'And you wanted to remain?'

'I would have stayed there forever! For the boys it would have been different, in time, when they were grown, but Modig said they must go back, and so I could not let them go and stay myself.'

'Back where?'

'To Eoforwic.'

York's ancient name rang a strong chord in the back of John's mind. And he knew then that Brandt was wrong to doubt him last night. Olwen *had* seen what he had seen, the low water, the boat being rowed upstream on a rising tide. . . But she was speaking again.

'They would be a rallying point, Modig said, young as they were, because of *who* they were and because they had Ida's blood in their veins! They would be a unifying force, he said, a force for peace in the kingdom. He told Heri that Osred had sent out an appeal for them to be found and brought back, insisting that his reign was no more than a regency, keeping the throne for Ælfwald's sons until they were grown.' She was talking quickly now, breathlessly. 'I *never* trusted Osred, nor did Heri, but Modig said that Osred had pledged his word, before God, that if the boys were brought back they would be safe, they would be given into the care of Eanbald, the archbishop, educated and schooled. I begged for them to be allowed to stay in the north until they were older, but Modig said that soon someone would discover where they were and this would bring trouble to his people and. . .'

And John relived the furious exchanges he'd had with Modig, pleading her case in Dun Eidyn, for he knew that she was right: Osred's word was worthless. But Modig was resolute and refused to listen and, knowing Modig as he did, knowing that he would never sway him, he had then begged that Wyn be allowed to stay, safe with his mother at the farm but Modig had shaken his head, his eyes narrowing as he contemplated his grandson, asking why he had made such a request. And so he had told him that they had become lovers, were handfast, he and Wyn, and Modig's eyes had opened wide and he had roared his fury. 'So do *you* think to sit on Northumbria's throne?' he had demanded, jabbing a finger in his face. 'Do you see yourself wedding the dead king's daughter and so making a claim? Is the land I leave to you, the land of your forefathers, not enough? You will bring ruin upon us, our foes will rally against us in common cause and the bards will lament another Catreath! No. I forbid it! Better that you had left Ælfwald's spawn for the ravens than take this course!'

John sank his head in his hands, his mind in uproar. 'Ah Wyn, *nothing* I said would convince him that I cared only for you!' he cried. 'I begged him and he cursed me and would have had me constrained had I not given him my word to obey him. He'd have sent you south anyway, without my escort; it was the choice he gave me, stay in chains or go with you and keep you safe. But I should have defied him, and fled north to Pictland with the three of you, while I could.'

The room fell silent.

He raised his head, the room steadied, and he saw that Brandt was staring at him. Oh God, it had happened again. . .

'Dr Osbourne,' Brandt spoke in a low authoritative tone. 'Go, very quietly, into the garden, and remain there. Go now.'

John rose unsteadily and his legs shook as he walked across the room.

'Why must Heri go?' he heard her ask, plaintively, as he stepped through the French windows but Brandt's response was inaudible.

He slipped into a leafy corner beside the house so that Celia and Gussie should not see him, and sat on a bench beside the wall, beneath an entangled mass of honeysuckle and climbing roses, his mind in utter confusion.

How long he remained there, bent forward, his elbows on his knees, staring at the flagstones, he was not sure, but eventually he saw Brandt step out of the door, looking from side to side to find him. He came across and stood, looking down at him. 'How are you, John?' he asked quietly.

'More to the point, how is Olwen?'

'She is sleeping now.' He sat down beside him, examining him. 'You're a little pale, perhaps, and distressed?' John shrugged and Brandt nodded. 'It was harrowing, I observed.' He was silent for a moment. 'And, my friend, before we say anything more, I must tell you that I have never, in all my years and experiences, encountered such a case as this.'

From somewhere close by, as if in mockery, there came the cooing of a dove.

They sat a while longer, in silence, but were soon spotted by Celia and Gussie, who downed their tools and came over. Brandt succinctly explained what had happened and Celia left to go to Olwen, while Gussie perched on the edge of a stone trough and contemplated John.

'And you've no explanation, either of you?' she asked, looking from one to the other.

John shook his head but Brandt raised a finger. 'You are too hasty, Miss Augusta, we have only just begun. This matter will not be concluded so soon. Miss Malkon will sleep for perhaps a couple of hours, and should be left to wake naturally. Perhaps this evening we might have another session, but we will see, it might be better to wait until the morning.' He turned to John. 'And now you and I will walk a little, and discuss.' John nodded and got to his feet. Fleetingly he thought of his deserted practice and felt a pang of guilt. It was unconscionable, he ought to return but this must now play out. . .

Leaving the house, they retraced their steps from the evening before and found themselves once again in the inner ward of the castle. Brandt led them to the same bench and they sat. 'I am humbled today, my friend, and confess that I am a very long way from understanding what just occurred.'

'Everything she described I recognised,' John said and he told him of Modig's fury, of the choice he had been given. But while he sat beneath the honeysuckle in Celia's garden another extraordinary realisation had come to him. 'What she described, the farm where I – where Heri took her – it is my mother's home. Now. Today. There are earthworks on the fells above us, hut circles, within an ancient enclosure.' Brandt turned to look at him. 'And as I sat in the garden just now, trying to understand, trying to describe. . . it came to me that it is like looking through one of those stereoscopes where two separate images converge into one to give a depth of perspective. Except that one or other of the images is always blurred, out of focus. The same but not the same.'

Brandt digested this. 'And the boys, her brothers? This I do not at all understand. You never knew them, her real brothers?'

John shook his head. 'But the same thing applies, they merge into one.'

'Yet you feel this sense of responsibility for only these other-world boys.'

He nodded. 'And such a weight of. . . of guilt.'

'And for their sister too?'

John's brain slammed closed. 'I don't know, I cannot go there.'

Brandt frowned but said nothing for a moment. 'At some point we must decide what it is that we believe. Either this story, incomplete as it is, is the product of Miss Malkon's imagination, a complex delusion that somehow she is transmitting to you, or—'

John completed the thought. 'Or these things actually happened.'

Brandt nodded slowly. 'In which case they are an imprint, some form of energy that has survived the centuries. Like memories, but not *your* memories, you have simply become encumbered: Miss Malkon with a dread fear of what is to

come, and you with remorse for what you failed to prevent.'
They sat in silence while above them the crows circled the
untidy nests of twigs they had built high up in the ruined
tower. 'I cannot imagine why you have become so afflicted,
either of you. . . and I sense, I fear, that there is a greater
anguish still to come.' He turned on the seat to look at John.
'Do you, as my colleague, not as my patient, believe that it is
safe to proceed?'

John did not hesitate. 'We must! Things can't be left as they
are.'

'No. But we must proceed slowly.' He got to his feet. 'And
now, my friend. I shall return to the hotel and rest and consider,
and I think that you should do the same. Such unburdening,
even of another's woes, will have taken its toll on you.'

CHAPTER 27

John continued to walk. Too agitated to rest, he left the castle enclosure and descended the steep steps down the side of the crag to the River Nidd below, and from there he wandered downstream to the weir, past the linen mill with its clacking looms, to where the river was braided with small islands and shingle bars. He stood for a while and thought again how Olwen had described, with astonishing clarity, the valley where his mother lived, and was overcome with a sense of longing for home, for the hills and racing clouds. When all this was over and resolved, he must consider more honestly what it was he wanted from life.

So distracted had he been when they left the house, he had come out with only his jacket, leaving his topcoat behind, and a cold wind had got up, driving spots of rain. He decided he would return to the house, collect his coat, and then take Brandt's advice and retire to the hotel for the rest of the afternoon. He felt drained, his brain no longer capable of thought, and he made his way slowly back up through the town and turned into the bottom of the street.

And stopped.

A small crowd had gathered halfway up. It took only a moment to register that both the attention of the crowd, and the presence of a carriage drawn up on the opposite side of the street, were focused on Pear Tree Cottage. There was an air of suppressed excitement amongst those gathered there, and with a sinking dread he knew what this must mean.

They had been discovered.

So soon?

A man in police uniform was standing, self-conscious but aloof, outside the door of the cottage, ignoring questions flung at him by the onlookers. John withdrew behind the carriage, thrown off balance, and then remembered Brandt, at the hotel, in ignorance. He, at least could be saved! John beckoned urgently to a delivery boy who was standing on the edge of the group. 'Go to The Wheatsheaf, will you, and give a message to the foreign gentleman staying there, a Professor Brandt.' He dug a sixpence from his pocket together with a piece of paper and pencil and scribbled rapidly. 'Give him this. It's important. Understand?' The boy seemed inclined to linger, half his attention still on the constable as if weighing up what he might miss against the prospect of a sixpence. 'If you're quick he might give you another. Off you go now, run!'

Brandt must be protected from what was bound to be a messy business, but for himself he had only one option so he crossed the road and approached the cottage.

'No one's to go in, sir,' the constable informed him.

'No?' John replied and was up the steps before the man grasped what he was about.

'Oi!' A ripple of appreciation came from the onlookers; action at last in this promising drama. 'I said. . .' But John was inside before the man caught up with him.

Another man, in plain clothes, stepped out of the sitting room and into the hall to confront him. 'He barged straight past me, sir!' the constable complained from the doorway.

'Very good, Jones, go back to your post.' The man looked John up and down. 'And who, sir, are you?'

'Dr John Osbourne.'

His eyebrows shot up. 'Are you indeed! How very obliging of you. . . Well, I'm Inspector Redman, charged with finding Miss Malkon, which has just been accomplished. My next goal was to find you. Constable!' Through the open door he could see Celia and Gussie, their faces flushed and furious; Olwen was clutching tight to Celia's arm. A second constable stepped into view. 'Secure this man, will you.'

'Wait,' John said. 'First let me speak to you—'

'I'm not inclined to wait, Dr Osbourne, and you'll have every opportunity to speak to me tomorrow.' He addressed the constable. 'You and Jones take Dr Osbourne back to York while I deliver Miss Malkon to her family.'

'No!' A chorus of protests broke from the three women, the loudest from Olwen herself. 'I won't go back.'

The inspector's face was uncompromising. 'The law says you will, young lady, and I'm here to uphold the law.'

John tried again. 'Inspector, I must speak—'

'Have you even *asked* why she ran away?' This from a furious Gussie.

The man was unmoved. 'More of an abduction than a runaway, I'm told. And since you're implicated yourself, Miss, I'd be careful what you say. I'll be questioning both of you ladies in due course and I'm ordering you here and now to keep me informed of your movements.'

'Ask your questions, damn you! The answers might surprise you. Or arrest us as well, why don't you?' Gussie was defiant, her chin thrust forward.

'No, don't,' John said, quickly. 'The responsibility for this is mine.'

'And the decision who to arrest is mine, Doctor,' the inspector remarked mildly. 'But right now my priority is to get Miss Malkon home, and you, sir, locked up back in York. Fetch Jones.' The second constable disappeared.

'I won't go with you.' Olwen had gone white.

The inspector sighed. 'I have the authority to compel you, Miss. Why make it difficult?'

'Listen, Inspector—' The man must be made to hear him out.

The inspector, however, was no more inclined to listen than he was to wait. 'Cuff him, Jones.' Steel handcuffs were produced, and to a chorus of renewed protests, John's wrists were secured. Poker-faced he submitted, there being nothing to gain in resisting.

'Inspector, I must beg you—'

'Save your breath, Doctor.' Redman turned back to Olwen.

'And now, Miss, must I do the same to you? I'm perfectly prepared to do so, you know, and, if you resist, Jones here will carry you over his shoulder like a sack of potatoes, out into the street and deposit you in the carriage. And there's quite a crowd gathered now. Is that what you want?'

'Let me come with her.' Celia spoke suddenly, moving in front of Olwen. 'She'll be terrified if you force her. Let me come with you in the carriage; you can ask your questions as we go, and I can explain.'

John rejoiced again at Celia's good sense; Redman had a determined look to him and would doubtless carry out his threat. Olwen, he saw, was now gasping for breath, well on the way to another, potentially disastrous episode. 'Having treated Miss Malkon, Inspector,' he said, in a low voice, 'I can tell you she's about to go into convulsions.'

Redman was watching her sourly. 'A handy trick, I daresay, but very well,' he said, nodding to Celia. 'If you come, Miss, you'll be coming on with me to York.'

Celia agreed. John took a step towards Olwen, awkwardly taking her hand with both of his, which were now locked together. 'Go with them, Olwen, you must. But this isn't the end of it, I promise you.'

'Last time—' she began, chokingly, looking up at him and gripping tight to his hands.

'I know, but it'll be different. Trust me.'

The inspector was following this exchange with interest. 'All done, Doctor? Right then, Jones, carry on to the station and get on your way.'

John extracted his hands from her grip and one of the constables took his arm, pulling him towards the door, and it was all he could do not to shake him off. Celia held Olwen back, an arm around her shoulders, but as they crossed the hall, Gussie, who had remained strangely silent after her outburst, slipped past them and was at the front door before them. 'We're still on the board, John, and this knight plays the bishop.' Her eyes were very alive and he nodded at her, only half understanding.

Then, on a sudden thought, he said. 'And the other knight knows not to make a move. Tell Celia.'

She took his meaning and laughed. 'Excellent. Play on, Doctor John.'

CHAPTER 28

Olwen felt sick. It was not simply that the carriage was badly sprung nor the jolting over the cobbles as they pulled up the hill but the shock of a sudden awakening from deep oblivion, and then the confusion of uniformed men, and now this hard-faced man sitting opposite her, intent on returning her to the one place from which she thought she had escaped forever.

The thought terrified her.

And to see Dr Osbourne arrested, led away in handcuffs. . .

She glared furiously at the inspector. 'I was not abducted. I escaped and came willingly, by choice.' The man merely nodded, uninterested, and Celia, beside her, squeezed her hand. 'So why must I return to where I am mistreated?'

'I've explained why, Miss,' he replied, looking out of the window. 'It's the law.'

'Laws exist to protect people, don't they? Not to put them in the way of danger.'

'I don't make the laws,' he said, not shifting his gaze. 'I'm paid to uphold them.'

'And you do so blindly? Without consideration. And are there not laws against poisoning? Against rape?' Anger was building in her. How dare this man take custody of her!

He looked coolly back at her, then switched his gaze to Celia. 'You were this young lady's governess, I understand.'

'I did my job rather well, don't you think?' she replied.

'No lessons on abiding by the law, then?'

'Oh, she gave me plenty,' Olwen retorted. 'On natural justice too, and taught me that women must resist persecution, for this is what I have endured.'

Celia gave her hand another squeeze and leaned forward. 'She's quite right, Inspector, she's not safe at the vicarage. They have been treating her in a shocking manner. Everything she says is true!'

'Rape?' he enquired, eyes narrowing.

'He tried it. My cousin, but I fought him off.'

'Ah. No rape.' He went back to his contemplation of the scenery.

'There are other forms of abuse, Inspector. Is there not some form of protection under which Miss Malkon could be placed, at least until our concerns are heard? They are very real ones and this is a. . . a complex situation. Surely you must see that Dr Osbourne wouldn't have acted as he did without good reason.'

'I'm told he'd a very *good* reason, the oldest in the book,' the inspector replied. 'Miss Malkon is a wealthy young lady, I understand. And that was a rather intimate little scene just now, don't you think, hardly a professional exchange? Called you Olwen, I noticed, and what was it he said? *This isn't the end of it. I promise you.* I must make a note while I remember.' He pulled a notebook from his pocket and scribbled in it. 'And what *did* happen last time, Miss Malkon?'

Olwen bit her lip and looked out of the carriage window, hating him. 'You couldn't begin to understand.'

He gave her a dry look and put away his notebook. 'I think I can.'

'You're quite mistaken, you know,' said Celia. 'It's not the doctor who has designs upon Olwen's property, I assure you, but the Malkons themselves. I'll answer any questions you choose to ask and I'll answer you honestly, and then perhaps you'll understand.'

'I intend to question you *after* we have left Miss Malkon with her legally appointed guardian.' And with that he closed his eyes and they continued on their journey in silence.

Celia held tight to her hand but even she, it seemed, was powerless to prevent this new catastrophe. Could she pretend she was about to be sick, demand that the carriage stop and then flee across the fields? But she would never outrun the man, he looked fit as well as determined, and besides where would she go? Very little of what had happened that morning with Professor Brandt was clear in her mind but Celia had whispered to her to say nothing of his visit. Being a foreigner, she supposed, he would be anxious to stay clear of the law. But where had they taken Dr Osbourne, in handcuffs, like some criminal? Never had she felt so desperate – even when Gussie had squeezed her arm as they left and said, 'Chin up, chick, we'll not let you down.' The thought of confronting the vicar and her aunt was appalling – she would be right back where she had been – but it was the prospect of seeing Alfred that she feared the most. He had sworn at her so horribly, his face red with pain and fury, promising her that she would regret what she had done.

All too soon she recognised the outskirts of the village. She looked longingly out of the window as they passed the smith's pasture and, as they pulled into the drive of the vicarage, she felt panic rising in her. The carriage came to a halt and the inspector opened his eyes. 'Right then,' he said.

'I beg you, Inspector—' Celia leaned forward again, but he unlatched the door and let down the step without so much as a glance at her.

Olwen saw the vicarage front door was opening and watched her uncle emerge. 'Olwen, my dear child, you are found!' he called as he came towards them, his arms outspread. 'Welcome home. Inspector, I cannot thank you enough for—' Celia leaned forward and his face froze. 'Miss Goodfellow!'

'Vicar.'

Inspector Redman looked from one to the other. 'Miss Goodfellow was good enough to offer us her company on the journey,' he said, mildly, watching the vicar's face.

He sniffed. 'I'm sure we're obliged to her.'

'The only obligation I place you under, Vicar,' said Celia, 'is to treat Olwen with kindness and respect, to keep your sons well away from her and to cease dosing her food with laudanum. I intend—'

The vicar turned his back on her and addressed Redman. 'Has this. . . this person been arrested? Will you lock her up?'

The inspector answered him evenly. 'Miss Goodfellow is returning to York with me, but she is not under arrest.'

'And the other. . . the wretch who tricked her way—'

'Miss Dudley is not under arrest either. But Dr Osbourne came forward and has been taken in for questioning.'

'Excellent! That at least is something. He is a disgrace to his profession. An abomination! And mark my words, Inspector, the bishop and I expect to see him charged, and in court, held accountable for his crimes.'

The inspector said nothing, but a frown had appeared on his brow. He held out his hand, nevertheless, and commanded Olwen to descend. 'Now, Miss Malkon, if you will.'

Was it worth one last appeal? '*Please* don't leave me here,' she said, earnestly, taking his hand and gripping it. 'Let me stay with Celia. Let her explain—'

'Olwen, my dear niece, if you knew how worried we have been. You can have no idea, my child, of the danger—'

Perhaps if her uncle had remained silent, or perhaps if her aunt had not chosen that moment to appear, things might have gone differently. Mrs Malkon had come up behind the vicar and seen Celia in the carriage. '*You!* How dare you come here!' she hissed, a viper's venom in her voice. 'You. . . you unnatural creature—'

Redman swung round to look at her aunt as Olwen's world began to undulate. She grabbed at the frame of the carriage as the figures on the drive wavered and the scene in front of her shifted. Transfixed by the woman's eyes, she let go of the man's hand and descended from the carriage, straightening as she did. 'You will not speak to her in that way, she, of all people has remained faithful.' She turned back to the man who was now staring at her oddly and addressed him. 'I stay because you compel me, but for no other reason, and yet I ask you again to consider my position, and that of my brothers.' His eyes narrowed and the abbot backed off, wringing his hands and making a woeful sound. 'While you,' she said, turning and eyeing him with contempt, 'you hide, craven, behind your cloth, and let this woman pursue her treachery. . .'

Somewhere she heard a distant voice, 'Wen, my dear girl,' but she steeled herself against it. They might like to pretend otherwise but she would be a prisoner here, and yet they would not see her cowed. 'When Modig learns how I've been treated, and when Heri comes, there will be a reckoning. See to it that you've nothing to regret.' She had silenced them for now, she thought, lifting her chin. 'And if a single hair of my brothers' heads is harmed, then I promise you, I will set your worlds aflame.' She felt her legs begin to tremble and turned while she still had the strength and walked, head held high, towards the monastery gate.

CHAPTER 29

As the train trundled along the seventeen-mile track between Knaresborough and York, John looked out across flooded fields, cursing himself at the turn events had taken. The River Nidd, swollen by recent rains, had overspilled its banks, driving cattle to ridges of higher ground where they stood, marooned, surrounded by water. A fitting metaphor. . . They should have seized the opportunity while they had it and got Olwen away, right away, abroad, or to Scotland even. But how had they been discovered so quickly? How had Redman made the connection and concluded she was in Knaresborough? He ground his teeth, in despair at the thought of Olwen being returned, friendless, to the vicarage, and at the promise he had made that he saw no way of keeping. Would Celia be able to convince the granite-faced inspector that there was more to this case than he would ever learn from the Malkons? He was not hopeful, the man had an inflexible look. But what sort of state would Olwen be in when Celia had to leave her? It did not bear thinking about. . .

Troubling too, he thought, staring at the flooded land, that it appeared laudanum was not needed to tip her into a state where her delusions – her *alter ego* – took over but that this could apparently happen at any time when she was in a state of heightened emotion even when, thinking back to supper last night, those emotions were memories of good times. And just for a moment, in his mind's eye, he saw again that fold in the land, the sweet grass-scented dip where, hidden from sight, he had lain with her and other promises had been made.

They too had been broken.

He clenched his fist with rage that he should now be so

powerless. Then, remembering how two days ago at St Hilda's House, enraged by Brandt, he too had slipped into another's skin, and he forced himself to stay calm. Any loss of control at this point would completely undermine him. But where was Olwen's mind now, he wondered desperately. Brandt had left her sleeping, caught somewhere between her two worlds, and her sudden awakening might well have left her in some liminal place. And, dear God, he thought, his knuckles whitening as he strained against the steel, if they began to feed her laudanum again. . .

He stared out of the window. The floods had completely transformed the landscape. Hedgerows no longer delineated fields but crisscrossed stretches of water, and in places all separation had vanished, fields merged with pasture, and the water meadows had become shallow lakes. Gates and fences had disappeared, all familiar landmarks were gone, the course of the river itself could no longer be traced and its floodwaters had drowned every dip and fold, reducing hillocks to islands, creating a new world for the gulls and waterfowl.

The same, but not the same.

But when the waters receded the cattle would come down from the ridges and a familiar world would reassert itself; normality would resume. But it would not be so for him. His position here, his livelihood, was gone, that much was certain. He had failed Olwen, and wrecked his own career, all to no avail.

It made for bitter contemplation.

Soon the train reached the outskirts of the city and the fields gave way to rows of houses, and the engine let out a mournful wail before pulling into York station. John, still manacled, ignored the gaze of the curious and was marched briskly towards a cab that took them across the river, picking its way through the old town until it reached the sweep of a wide new street on which stood an imposing red-brick building. They drew up at a door to the side of it, above which hung a police lantern.

Once inside the police station the humiliation resumed; the cuffs were removed and so were his braces and his necktie, his watch was taken, his pockets emptied, and the contents placed in an envelope. He was led along a bleak tiled corridor to one of the cells and the door clanged shut, bringing home to him the gravity of his situation. And he stood and listened despairingly to the constable's retreating footsteps.

It was a cold, comfortless night that he spent, shivering beneath a thin unholy blanket. The food he had been offered the evening before had been inedible and so he had lain there all night, hungry and thirsty, unable to sleep. Through the slit of a high window, he could see the yellow glow of a street light but, as the night wore on, that too was extinguished. The smell of stale urine was inescapable and the only furnishing, other than the cot, was a rank bucket in the corner to which, perforce, he added his own befouling when he rose next morning. He had just buttoned up when a hatch slid open and a piece of bread floating in a dish of greasy porridge appeared beside an enamel cup of cloudy water. He looked at it and decided to continue with abstinence; the prospect of perching over the bucket with loosened bowels was too ghastly a prospect, and he was not yet desperate for food. But, by God he could do with a wash.

Some hours later – he lost track of time – he was allowed out and, having been required to empty his bucket, he waited in line with his fellows for a brief sluicing. When he returned to his cell he found the constable called Jones awaiting him. He was taken upstairs and into a bleak bare room furnished with a scratched wooden table and two chairs; a third chair was positioned by the door. He was left there, and heard the key turn in the lock.

This room too was lit by a high barred window, its corners black with cobwebs, the cracked glass fly-blown and opaque with dirt. Leaving him to stew there seemed to be part of the procedure but it was a relief to be out of the fetid cell and he paced up and down the room, glad to stretch his legs. He had been there for perhaps an hour before Jones returned and silently sat on the chair by the door. Inspector Redman appeared a moment later and bid John a cold good morning.

'Take a seat, Doctor.' He placed an official-looking notebook on the table and briefly glanced at him as he pulled out the seat opposite. 'How's your aunt?' he asked.

'My *aunt*?'

'Or was it a cousin? I forget.' He gave John a dry look, which he returned evenly, already wrong-footed. First point to Redman. The man opened his notebook and sat back.

'You never went to Scotland, did you, Dr Osbourne, but I'll waste no more time on that little diversion as the charges against you are about as straightforward as they come.' He consulted his notes. 'It has been reported to me that Miss Olwen Malkon disappeared from her home last Saturday morning, having been last seen by her family the previous evening. Later the same day she was observed, in your company and that of a woman we now know to be Miss Celia Goodfellow, at St Hilda's House here in York.' He looked up but John remained silent. 'You left the two women in the grounds there and were taken by an attendant to the office of a visiting doctor, a Professor Brandt, and stayed with him for around half an hour and then returned, collected the two women and left.' He raised his head again. 'Do you dispute any of these statements?'

'No.'

He recalled then the curious look the woman attendant had given them when they departed so abruptly; she would certainly have remembered them.

'Excellent. Neither does Miss Goodfellow.'

John looked up sharply. 'Is she here? Are you holding her as well? Look, Inspector, she isn't—'

Redman put up his hand. 'I'm conducting this interview, Dr Osbourne, but to set your conscience at rest, no, I am not holding her. I questioned her on the journey into York and she declared her intention to stay here overnight, and has been asked to keep me informed of her movements. As has Miss Dudley who, I understand, is joining her here. Where did you take Miss Malkon after this?'

There was no reason to lie and, given what he knew of Celia Goodfellow, she would have decided the same, and so he told the inspector about the night in York and the train to Knaresborough next morning. Thank goodness he had insisted on staying at a different hotel.

'You dined alone with Miss Goodfellow that night in York at The Mail Coach, in a private room, I understand.'

'That's right.'

'Leaving Miss Malkon with Miss Dudley at The Black Swan on Coney Street.'

'Yes.'

'The waiter at The Mail Coach has been questioned this morning and said that you were very keen to be private with Miss Goodfellow.' John thought wryly of Celia's remarks about the perils of dining alone with a man, and wondered where the inspector's thoughts were heading. 'Why was that?'

Had he cast Celia as some sort of procuress, enabling a seduction, or as his lover, feeding a rapacious appetite? 'She had just learned from Miss Malkon that Mr Alfred Malkon, her cousin, had attempted to rape her the night before. Understandably she wanted to tell me this in private.' He glared at the man but the inspector's face remained impassive. 'Fear of Mr Malkon and of his family was the reason behind her flight.'

'But she did not flee, Dr Osbourne.' Redman sat back, tapping his pen on the table. 'She was lured away by Miss Augusta Dudley who had gained access to the vicarage by a deception, using an assumed name, during which visit she presumably conveyed to her a message. Miss Dudley, it would appear, plotted the abduction together with yourself and Miss Goodfellow.' This man was no fool, but how the devil did he know all this? The inspector continued to contemplate him, registering his surprise. 'Miss Goodfellow too was impressed with our powers of penetration,' he remarked, drily. 'It was a very successful ruse but for the fact that the bishop, who arrived at the vicarage as Miss Dudley was leaving, saw her from the vicar's study window. He thought that he recognised her although, at the time, he was told he must be mistaken. It was only when he learned of Miss Malkon's disappearance that he thought of it again and that, you see, led us very swiftly to the connection with Miss Goodfellow, and then to Knaresborough.' Damn the man, with his smug expression, and damn the bishop. 'He has known Miss Dudley since childhood, you see, and had been appraised of her new. . . friendship with Miss Goodfellow, a former governess-companion of Miss Malkon. It all hung together very neatly.'

– and this knight plays the bishop, Gussie had said as he was being led away. Had she a plan, then?

He could only hope so and he dropped his eyes so that Redman would not see them gleam, lifting them again a moment later and saying: 'My understanding is that abduction involves the forcible taking of a person against their will. That was not the case here, Inspector. Miss Malkon was given a choice and came willingly.'

'Miss Malkon is a minor, under legal guardianship of her uncle, and this escapade was entirely contrary to *his* will, as you very well knew. It is he who is pressing charges.' John said nothing. 'If your sole aim was to rescue this young woman from perceived dangers and to deliver her to her former companion, then why were you still in Knaresborough yesterday, other than for reasons of your own? You saved us the trouble of finding you by coming forward, but what was your purpose there?'

Here was a new dilemma. No further mention had been made of Professor Brandt and John was determined, if he could, to protect the man. But what had Celia told Redman? 'I was hoping to be able to treat Miss Malkon for the mental afflictions from which she suffers.'

The inspector considered him through narrowed eyes. 'Hoping. . . So having been turned away from St Hilda's House by Professor Brandt who, I'm told, had received a letter from her guardian declining any further treatment, and has been required to cut short his visit to the institution, you then decided to treat the young woman yourself. Am I understanding you correctly?'

'Yes.'

The man continued to regard him. 'Are you trained in such treatment, Dr Osbourne?'

'Miss Malkon is my patient.'

The inspector shook his head. 'That ceased to be true earlier this week when you were told, by a letter delivered into your hand, that your services were no longer required.' John clenched his jaw shut, loathing the man. 'You had no authority whatsoever to treat this young woman.' He paused again but John had nothing to say. 'Can you describe the treatment you were able to offer?'

Deeper and deeper into trouble. 'A form of hypnosis, during which—'

'A patient is placed into an altered state of consciousness that allows their actions to be controlled by another, I'm told.'

By whom, John wondered. 'There's rather more to it than—'

But the inspector was consulting his notes again. 'And you undertook this treatment?'

'We had made a start.'

'And were you alone with Miss Malkon, in her altered state of consciousness?'

Oh God. He was sunk. 'Miss Goodfellow was formerly Miss Malkon's governess and companion, and she—'

'I asked whether you were alone with Miss Malkon during the treatment.'

'Miss Goodfellow was within earshot in the garden, as was Miss Dudley.'

'But not in the room?'

'No.'

Again the inspector referred to the notebook. 'How interesting. Miss Goodfellow stated that at no stage were you alone with Miss Malkon.'

Damnation, and God bless her. It was true, of course. 'I expect she meant that they were within call.'

'Do you?' Redman's voice was smoothly cynical and he sat back again and examined John in that same unnerving way. 'And would you consider your treatment of Miss Malkon to have been successful, Dr Osbourne?'

'Too early to say.'

'So you would persist with it, given the opportunity?'

John struggled to hold his anger at bay. 'Look, Inspector, she needs professional help. What I was able to offer was simply a beginning.'

'I saw for myself that she is in an emotional and unstable state. When I left her at the vicarage yesterday she was talking a strange sort of nonsense—'

John swore. 'And yet you still left her there, damn you!'

Redman's face hardened. 'As I was bound by the law to do. But tell me, who is Mudik, or Modik? She spoke of him.' John's heart lurched. Dear God, she *had* slipped back into her other-world. . . Had he and Brandt, with the best of intentions, left her in a worse state than before? 'And she was clearly expecting someone called Harry to come to her assistance. What do you know of him?'

John looked aside, his mind churning; somehow, he *had* to convince this man to get help for her. He leaned forward. 'Inspector, Miss Malkon is delusional, it is part of—'

'According to what I've been told, she has referred to *you*, quite specifically, as Harry on at least two occasions.'

How much worse could this get? 'Yes, but that's not my name, is it! When emerging from a coma-like state she has been momentarily confused and she—'

'Mistook you for someone else? On each occasion?'

'No, no, what I mean is—'

'Putting names aside, Doctor Osbourne, it's the family's belief that you have been meeting her, seeking to gain her trust and conducting yourself in an inappropriate and unprofessional manner.'

'No—'

'She is, I understand,' he continued, 'now in a very bad way after her experiences and required a strong sedative to calm—'

John slammed his hand on the table and stood abruptly. '*Damn* them!' The chair fell to the ground with a clatter. 'What have they given her?' At a signal from Redman, the constable picked it up and pressed John back into his seat.

'You could do with something similar, it would appear,' the inspector remarked, eyeing him curiously. 'Calm yourself,

Dr Osbourne. I've more than enough to charge you with, don't make matters worse. There is a range of offences to consider including kidnap, wrongful treatment of a minor no longer under your medical care and no doubt several other infringements of the law, some of which carry lengthy prison sentences. And your accomplices likewise. But before I charge you – and trust me, I intend to – I am interested to hear why you, a trusted, well-qualified physician, have acted in this wholly reckless and unlawful manner, spectacularly ruining your career.'

John sat with his head in his hands, barely taking in the words. He should have thought things through more carefully, planned for this to happen. . .

'Dr Osbourne?' The inspector leaned forward. 'If you have nothing to say then I have no alternative but to formally charge you with—'

'Wait.' John swallowed hard and raised a hand. 'Wait.'

And so he told the inspector how he had come to treat Olwen Malkon, the episodes in the church, in the vicarage garden, the laudanum, the violence offered her, omitting only the strange inexplicable connection between the two of them and adding nothing to what had already been said with regard to Brandt's involvement. 'She was drugged, without her knowledge or consent, in order to be brought to the church, the very place that had so disturbed her mind,' he concluded, 'and she has, with the full knowledge of the likely harmful effect, been given further opiates without her knowledge or consent. The vicar and the bishop believe her to be possessed by demons and plan some hideous ordeal by which to rid her of them. It will be disastrous for her! After I learned that was planned, I had no option but to act, and that was *before* I learned her cousin had attempted to rape her. I swear that I've never met her other than in a professional capacity, and never alone.'

'Until yesterday.' The inspector jotted down a few notes, which in no way could have encapsulated what John had just said, and then looked up again. 'Why not simply inform the authorities?'

'Her guardian is a clergyman, supported by his bishop, and it was his son who attacked her, in the vicarage, no less! They would simply have denied it.'

'But you made no attempt?'

John looked back at him. 'I'm reporting it now, to you. So what will you do?' Redman gave a half smile and John leaned forward again. 'She needs protection, Inspector. I'm not the villain here. She's vulnerable and in danger from the very people entrusted with her safety, and if my intentions were malign or dishonourable then I've behaved in an extraordinary way, wouldn't you say, ensuring that she was chaperoned and not compromised in any way, and why, for God's sake, if I was intent on seduction, would I take her to a mental institution!'

Was it his imagination or had the inspector's expression altered a little?

'Believe me, Inspector, this was no abduction.'

CHAPTER 30

Somehow Olwen reached her bedroom, shut the door and leaned against it. Her legs had turned to jelly and without its support she would have slid to the ground. She closed her eyes and swallowed hard.

After a moment she opened them again and looked around her. Everything was exactly as she had left it; it was as if she had never been away. She frowned, trying to remember how long she had been gone. Two nights only – one in York and one in Knaresborough. It felt so much longer. . . She went across to her bed and sat on the edge of it. And when had she last eaten? She had hardly touched her breakfast so it must have been last night, at Celia's, and even then she had not eaten much, abandoning the meal halfway through. Lack of food must explain the light-headedness, the strange floating feeling that brought with it a sense of hopelessness. She had tasted freedom, for two days she had escaped and now. . . A knock came at the door and she froze.

'Vicar says you've to come down.' It was Susan. 'You'd better come, Miss. Mistress is in a rage.'

Her aunt and uncle were waiting for her in the study, standing side by side with their backs to the fireplace in a show of solidarity that would have been comical had it not been for the expressions on their faces. Gone was the smiling, open-armed welcome from the vicar and his wife's eyes were those of a serpent.

It was she who fired the first salvo. 'You are a wicked, ungrateful girl.'

The vicar followed through. 'The inspector spoke to us before he left and told us the dreadful things you've said about your treatment here.' She had never noticed before how mobile her uncle's face was, like clay or putty that could be moulded to any form he cared to project. And all artifice was dropped now.

'I told him nothing but the truth.'

'You said Alfred *attacked* you!'

'He did.'

'A wicked lie!' Alfred's mother spat the words. 'And you said we mistreated you. Nothing could be further from the truth.'

'You drugged me to make me obedient.'

'You were distraught, a danger to yourself—'

'We gave you a home!

'And for whose benefit was that disgraceful performance just now?' Her aunt stepped closer. 'For the inspector or that depraved creature to whom you fled?'

Olwen held her ground and said nothing. Everything depended upon keeping hold of her errant mind, for if she allowed it to escape into another world now, she had no one to rescue her from it.

'And what a sordid little episode it was,' her aunt continued, 'but at least the doctor is where he should be, his ambitions exposed.'

Still Olwen said nothing, and she began to feel strangely detached from the scene.

'And what you said about your poor brothers? The purest nonsense! What did you mean by it?'

At the mention of the boys the room seemed to sway and she gripped the back of the chair. But still she said nothing.

The vicar's tone was less shrill than his wife's but the words were no more kind. 'We all grieve their loss, Olwen, but to use that tragedy to gain sympathy was a callow, shameful act.'

That remark strengthened her. 'If you've said all you wish, I should like to return to my room.'

'Some papers have gone missing from my desk. A letter. Did you take it?'

The letter, she had forgotten about that. It had been left in

Celia's safe keeping. She looked directly back into his narrowed eyes. 'What letter?'

'A personal letter, addressed to me. Did you take it?'

'Search me by all means. You'll find no papers of yours.'

He looked aside, unable to sustain her gaze. 'You will return to your room and remain there, contemplating your behaviour and asking the Lord for forgiveness. Aided by a fast to sharpen the senses.' Olwen gave a twisted little smile, at least she would be free of opiates. 'And in the morning, we'll put all this behind us. Start with a clean slate. Your accusations regarding Alfred are especially hurtful as you know of his fondness for you, but you may be sure that he will never learn of them from us.'

'He knows perfectly well what he did,' she remarked, turning to leave, 'and will perhaps find a pretence of fondness now rather difficult to sustain. Tell him to save himself the trouble and pursue another route to fortune, as he'll never have mine.'

CHAPTER 31

Back in his cell, John was feeling far from satisfied with the interview, but at least he had not been formally charged. Did this offer a glimmer of hope, or was Redman simply delaying while he considered other offences?

Pacing his tiny cell only added to his frustration so he sat on the edge of the cot and tried to calm himself. Looking around he saw that someone had chipped away at the nauseous yellow-glazed tiles, scoring an obscenity there, and the walls had been liberally marked in other ways by his predecessors. The whole cell reeked of despair. He stretched out on his back, balling the thin blanket into a pillow until the smell of it became too much and he tossed it aside, resting his head on the crook of his arm instead, and he stared up at the fly-blown ceiling. His situation was bad, he had dynamited his own future to no avail, but how much worse was it for Olwen. Lost in a place of shadows, in limbo between this world and another, in a house where she could expect neither sympathy nor understanding. Could he have made a more complete mess of things?

Covering his eyes with his other arm, drained now and exhausted, he lay there, and after a while, he slept.

An hour or so later he was woken by the rattle of keys outside and the door swung open to reveal an elegant stranger on the threshold. 'Dr Osbourne,' the man said, stepping into the cell under the watchful eye of the constable. 'I'm Toby Farquharson.' He put out a hand as the door clanged shut behind him. He was about John's age, maybe a little younger, immaculately dressed and his appearance, in sharp counterpoint to his own, piqued an unreasonable resentment in John.

He blinked, still sour with sleep, and looked down at the man's beautifully manicured fingers. 'I wouldn't, if I were you,' he said.

The man wrinkled his nose and dropped his hand. 'I take your point. Must get you out of here, Doctor. Not even a chair to sit on!' He strode back to the door and banged his fist on it, demanding a chair from the constable. A chair was brought. 'And one for my client.'

This one was refused and so John remained sat on the cot, leaning back against the wall, eyeing his visitor. 'Am I your client?'

'You most certainly are, sir. Gussie sent me. A clarion call to arms, threatened to reveal all my guilty secrets if I let her down. Not sure what she meant, but Gussie has a nasty way of knowing things she shouldn't. Couldn't risk it. And she told me to bring you this, said you'd be hungry.'

He handed John an oiled paper package that he found to his joy contained bread, some cold meat and a slab of cheese, and from his pocket he produced a bottle of beer. John fell on it, and began to like the man. 'God bless her! Are they all right, she and Celia?' he asked, tearing off a corner of the bread and devouring it. 'Have you news of Ol— of Miss Malkon?'

'Of her, no. Of them, yes, and they are well, send their love and all that. Celia wasn't held and Gussie's arrived in York and now they're busy plotting. Don't waste time worrying about them. All this is right up their street, you know, Gussie's an old hand at it, likes nothing better than a bit of conflict with the patriarchy. It's you that's in the mire, my friend, but she says to tell you she's paying my fee and since she's filthy rich we can both be comfortable with that arrangement.' He gave a boyish grin.

'You're a lawyer?'

'Didn't I say? And I'm a rather good one, so tell me all. Gussie's brief was simply to get you off, and out of here, so I'm all ears.'

At the end of half an hour, during which time the man said nothing but listened with a focus that John found reassuring, his visitor nodded in an incisive fashion. 'Put bluntly, you've not a leg to stand on.' Reassurance vanished. 'But since you've not been charged yet, Gussie's plan's the best.'

'Which is what?'

'Get 'em to drop the whole business.'

'They won't.'

The man laughed. 'Fancy a wager? Gussie intends to make a stink regarding the bishop and his penchant for little girls – claims she fought him off some years ago, and that he has the scars to prove it – ' John's eyebrows shot up ' – back of his hand, prongs of a dinner fork, drew blood, so she says, scars still visible. He tried groping her during dinner on some occasion, apparently, slipped his hand under the tablecloth, and she wasn't having it. Feisty even then, God bless her. It was hushed up by her Pa, but she'll threaten to make it public, very public. And she will, you know – '

. . . *this knight plays the bishop*. . .

' – says she'll write to the bishop and tell him that the vicar must withdraw all charges or else she'll do her worst. I'm to go and explain all this to him.' He pulled a face. 'It'll ruin his evening, of course, but he sounds a gruesome sort so I'm happy to oblige. If we play fair, on the other hand, and it gets into the courts you could be charged under the Offences Against the Person Act 1861. Bang on, in fact, textbook case. Miss Malkon's an heiress, under age, and that'd be enough even without any evidence that you took her to "carnally know" her, as the Act would have it.' John protested indignantly, but his visitor batted him aside. 'You told Redman you were alone with her at Gussie's, so you *could* have dishonoured her, that'll be enough on its own, I'd imagine. And Celia stating that you *weren't* alone with her looks suspicious – contradictory statements, you see, not good, especially if during that time you've admitted deliberately putting her in a trance-like state. And it's no good fibbing. I know you want to keep your professor out of it but you'll not do it, it'll get out somehow. Bound to. And since you've already lied to Redman, concealing Brandt's part in this, that'll count against you too. Any way you look at it, it's bad news in the courts. What with Brandt's services being declined by the vicar, him being thrown out of St Hilda's for dubious practices and then you both conspiring to hypnotise the girl.' He shook his head. 'Hard to see how it could be worse, really. Hypnosis has a bad reputation, you know, so you'll be cast as an evil predator, abusing your position, a disgrace to your profession and a guilty verdict—'

'You're good, you said?' John snapped.

' – carries a maximum sentence of fourteen years. Yes, I am good, and I'd make sure you didn't get that, but Gussie's way is surest. Old-fashioned blackmail, judiciously applied, should do the trick. Does me out of a fat fee, of course, but she says you're entirely innocent and a warrior for the cause, whatever that means.' He grinned again. 'I've known the wretch from childhood when she'd regularly reduce me to tears. Terrifying harpy.' He got to his feet. 'I'll go and see this inspector of yours and drop hints that there's more to this case than meets the eye, scandalous implications at a high level et cetera, needs careful handling, that sort of thing. I'll enjoy doing that. . . And it buys me time to see the bishop and put the wind up his cassock.' He made as if to offer his hand again, but withdrew it with another grimace. 'Another time. In more salubrious surroundings. Soon, I promise you. Good day, Doctor.'

CHAPTER 32

Life at the vicarage was unaltered except that now Olwen was treated as a pariah by all except Edmond, who seemed quite oblivious to the dark undercurrents. She ate her meals silently and with great circumspection, taking only what others had sampled first, and spent most of her time in her room with the washstand pulled across the door. Alfred regarded her with hooded eyes that seemed to follow her everywhere. He made no further attempts to pursue her, but she remained on guard, taking care never to be alone with him.

Even the garden, she decided, was too great a risk.

It was all too easy to give way to despair.

They were just finishing their meal on the second evening after her return when Susan brought a message through. 'From the bishop,' she said, 'and I was told it was urgent. His man's waiting for a reply.'

The vicar and his wife exchanged glances as the vicar broke the seal, and Olwen tensed; the bishop was her enemy. . . and she watched as her uncle's face suffused with colour, his eyes bulging as he read. 'But. . . but this is *preposterous*! Whatever is he thinking. . .'

He thrust the letter at his wife and she hissed as she read it, then looked across at Olwen. 'This is your doing!'

Olwen said nothing, but her heart gave a leap of hope. Something unexpected had occurred, something they did not like.

Alfred was watching her carefully. 'What is it, Ma?' Edmond asked, but was ignored as his mother read the letter again.

'He says that he'll explain—' she said.

'I should hope he will!' the vicar expostulated, taking it back from her. 'He owes us that at the very least!' He skimmed it again. 'And I am to write this. . . this letter, am I, couched in terms that—' He broke off and glared at Olwen.

'You must do as he asks,' Mrs Malkon said, thoughtfully. 'Although I believe—' She bit her lip. 'We must talk, Vicar.'

They left the room and a moment later Olwen heard the study door close.

'Scheming again, coz?' Alfred asked, sitting back to consider her. 'We must keep an eye on you.' She rose and went to the door but he was there before her, opening it with exaggerated courtesy.

'Don't you dare to follow me.'

He laughed as she passed before him. 'All in good time, my dear, all in good time.'

It was hardly a surprise to hear the key turn in the lock of her bedroom door that evening and she lay awake wondering what the bishop's letter had contained to so upset them. Had Celia somehow managed to persuade the inspector that she had been mistreated? Or had Dr Osbourne been released, but if he had the bishop would hardly have been informed of this before the vicar. And this letter that the vicar must write. . . what was that? She could only hope that whatever had happened might play to her advantage.

Next morning, however, brought a new development. When Susan came into her room with a jug of warm water she was followed in by her aunt, who seemed to have recovered her confidence. 'Dress quickly and come down,' she said, in icy tones. 'We've visitors arriving immediately after breakfast.'

She left and Olwen looked enquiringly at Susan but the girl simply shrugged and hurried away, as if fraternising with Olwen would bring only trouble. Unsettled now and on her guard, Olwen dressed and went downstairs. Alfred and Edmond were still at the breakfast table but the vicar's place had been cleared away. Her aunt came and sat, tight-lipped, at the foot of the table.

No one spoke. Olwen watched Edmond pour himself tea from the pot and then filled her own cup. Her aunt reached for a piece of toast, Olwen took the adjacent slice. Her aunt buttered hers, and so did Olwen, and was rewarded with a dark look.

Alfred was watching her again, but she refused to look at him. Breakfast eaten, her aunt rose, crisply bidding Olwen to be quick and finish so that the table could be cleared.

'What did Pa say?' Edmond turned to his brother as soon as she had gone. 'Was he livid?'

'Never mind that now,' Alfred replied, his eyes still on Olwen.

'Alfred's won a horse, at cards,' he explained to Olwen. 'You remember Tommy Thompson, out Boroughbridge way? It was his, a lovely creature.' Edmond appeared uninterested in anything other than his brother's extraordinary good fortune. 'Pa's not going to be happy, though, gambling, playing for high stakes, bad example and all that—'

'Shut up, Edmond.'

' – quite apart from the cost of feeding the beast. Is he in the paddock now?'

'Why not go and see?' Alfred suggested and Edmond said that he would, directly he had finished eating.

'Who are the visitors?' she asked him, ignoring Alfred.

'I heard Pa mention the bishop again, seems to haunt the place,' he replied, between mouthfuls. 'And someone else. A doctor, I think.'

She paused, the cup half-raised to her lips.

'Not that doctor, Olwen dear,' Alfred said, lazily rolling his silver napkin ring backwards and forwards on the table, regarding her. 'The other one, the one who said you weren't so much mad, as bad.' Edmond gave his awkward guffaw. 'Putting on a show.' She ate on in silence, feeling the menace of his presence.

A moment later there was a commotion in the hall and she lifted her head, hearing male voices, recognising the bishop's booming tones. 'Why are they come?' she asked, again addressing Edmond, but he shrugged, got to his feet, swallowed the last of his tea, and left.

It was Alfred who answered. 'They've your best interests at heart, you know, we all do.' He leaned towards her. 'And we want to keep you. . . absolutely. . . safe.' She got to her feet, and was about to follow Edmond out of the door when her aunt reappeared and bid her go to the morning room.

'Why? Who is there?'

'Or shall Alfred bring you through?' she asked and her cousin rose.

Olwen cast them both a furious look and crossed the hall, entering to find the bishop, her uncle and Dr Kemp in a huddle in the centre of the room. They turned as she entered; it felt like a reprise of the last time, except that now she was friendless.

'Olwen, my dear, you remember Dr Kemp, and the bishop. Come in and sit down.' Her uncle gave a genial smile, which made her wary. 'We'll all sit, shall we, as we would like to. . . ah. . . to ascertain how. . . in what way, we can help you now that you are back with us.' They sat in a semicircle like judges or predators assessing cornered prey, and she felt a wave of alarm. Was this gathering connected with last night's upset over the bishop's message? 'In a moment Dr Kemp will examine you again—'

She looked at the doctor and then back at her uncle. 'But I feel completely well.'

The vicar ignored her and turned to the others. 'Twice since her return her mind has wandered,' he said, 'her words make no sense and she tells quite outlandish stories, making baseless accusations. . .'

So she *was* to be judged here 'It was confusing, to return here so suddenly,' she said.

The three men exchanged glances and the bishop spoke, fixing her with a frowning look. 'If you are now completely well, Miss Malkon, will you attend church on Sunday with the rest of the family and cause no more unpleasantness?' She paused. Was it best to try to buy herself some time or admit that nothing would persuade her into the church? But she hesitated too long. 'Your silence is eloquent,' he remarked drily, a little gleam in his eye.

'I will, of course, consider whether—' she began.

'You see!' The vicar was almost bouncing in his seat. 'She prevaricates! It is as I said, we're very far from out of trouble. That rogue of a doctor has encouraged her wickedness, and those benighted women have incited her to rebellion. How can I possibly maintain my position in the parish if—'

The bishop raised a hand to silence him. '*Why* will you not go to church, Miss Malkon?'

Unanswerable. She was indeed cornered. 'I've not said that I won't, I simply need time to consider—'

'There! See!' Her uncle was like a bottle from which the cork had been drawn, his outrage frothing over. Her aunt entered the room and he addressed her like petulant child. 'She *still* refuses to go to church.'

'Of course she must go. And if she becomes hysterical again, she will be disciplined,' the woman replied, taking a seat beside her husband.

The doctor cleared his throat. 'If I may. . . while hysteria amongst young females is no longer thought to result from a malfunction of the reproductive system, it is amongst such individuals that such displays most frequently manifest themselves.'

Had she somehow become invisible? Hysteria? Was that his diagnosis? How she longed for the quick wit and ready tongue of Augusta Dudley.

'Go on,' prompted the bishop.

'Nevertheless, it is possible that the preparation of the female body for reproduction depletes the brain, leaving it in a weakened state, which is why this modern idea of educating young women beyond what is useful to them can be harmful.' Olwen stared at him; he was a monster! Celia and Gussie would tear the man to shreds. 'The quickening of the womb leads to unwarranted fervour, so some means of calming, some form of balm to suppress. . .'

The vicar and the bishop were leaning forward listening intently, and she felt a hotness behind her eyes from unshed tears of fury.

'She was away from home for two nights, in very questionable company,' her aunt remarked. 'Staying in an hotel, if you will, and then in the home of those creatures. One hardly likes to imagine what ideas they put into her head—'

Something in Olwen snapped. 'Shall I tell you, Aunt, then you need not imagine?'

' – or indeed what might have taken place there.'

The ground was being cut from beneath her but she raised her chin and surveyed them. 'I received from Celia and her friend only kindness and concern.'

'An examination would ascertain—' the doctor began but broke off as Olwen stood.

Beside her there was an arched recess where a set of shelves displayed Mrs Malkon's prized collection of porcelain, which she reverently washed herself once a month. On the lowest shelf stood a pair of Derby figurines – a shepherd wearing a brimmed hat holding a basket of fruit and offering an apple to the demure shepherdess. At his feet was a dog, at hers a lamb. It was a sugary portrayal of enticement and submission that had always annoyed her. She took one figure in each hand, and her aunt gasped in horror.

'You have more affection for these lumps of clay than for me, Aunt, and you, Uncle, are only concerned for your standing in the parish. If you try and force me to go into your church or to marry your son or if you poison me or starve me into compliance or if these men offer to examine me or rid me of demons, I will resist you all, and unless you assure me that none of these things will happen, I'll throw these simpering figures into the hearth.' The bishop gave a little smile, which should have warned her, and the doctor turned aside, reaching into his bag. 'I know full well that I'm only here because of what my aunt and uncle hope to gain through me – which, I promise, they never will. I wish to return to my home at once.'

The vicar's face had turned as red as the proffered china apple, his wife's as pale as the porcelain. '*Outrageous!*'

The bishop, however, looked down his long nose at her, unmoved. 'Doctor, I do believe. . .'

But the doctor had already risen. 'Now, now, my dear girl. Your distress is quite unnecessary, you know, your charges imaginary! Let me have the ornaments.' He put out a hand, keeping the other behind his back, and approached her with a little chuckle. 'Why take it out on the poor shepherds, after all?' And then with a sudden movement, for which she was quite unprepared, he seized her arm and jabbed into it the needle of a syringe he had kept hidden behind him. She struck out at him, too late, and her aunt leapt to her feet in time to catch the china shepherd that Olwen had dropped in her surprise. She could not, however, save the shepherdess, which slipped from Olwen's fingers and rolled down her skirt, striking the chair leg with a crack to lay, in pieces, at her feet.

CHAPTER 33

'Be careful of her head as you bring her out!'
Darkness had descended upon her. She must have fallen asleep, that would explain it, but she was waking now, in some confined, unfamiliar place, and her head was thumping and thick. Where was she? There was a man sitting beside her, a man she recognised. . . he had been at the vicarage, and she realised then that they were in a closed airless carriage with the blinds pulled down. It had come to a halt, the door had been opened and she saw that they were outside a large imposing building, and that too was familiar. People were converging on her, strangers clustering around, peering through the open door; she sensed they came with some common purpose, their faces dispassionate and determined. 'No!' she cried as one of them took her arm and tried to pull her from the carriage, and she lashed out wildly, suddenly terrified. Nausea rose up from her stomach, souring her mouth with bile, and she leaned back, resisting them with all her strength. But then the man at her side began coaxing her to descend as if she was a child, pushing her while the others pulled. She jabbed her elbow in his gut and had the satisfaction of hearing him give a whoof of pain.

'Fetch the chair,' someone called. 'We've a flighty one here.'

But it was no good, there were too many of them and she was dragged, spitting and biting, out of the carriage and onto the driveway, her arms almost pulled from their sockets.

'Do *not* twist her arm, nurse, you know the correct methods of restraint!' It was the same voice that had cautioned care with her head.

A woman answered, hotly. 'She lashed out, Dr Linton, you saw her. She *hit* me!'

'She is ill, Mrs Whitely, not vicious, and may well be hallucinating.'

Her last shreds of control were slipping away, and her breath was coming fast and shallow. 'I've done nothing wrong! Do you not know who I am?'

'You're a troublesome wench, that's who,' the woman muttered.

'No, nurse. She's frightened and you're making things worse.' The same steady voice. She saw someone else approaching, pushing a chair on wheels. 'Now then, gently, lift her in. Take care, I said. A little kindness, if you will. . .'

'My father might be dead,' Olwen cried as the woman, a brawny soul, wrestled her into the chair, 'but you owe me some respect, you treacherous slut!'

'*Slut* is it. . . ?'

'You'll have to sedate her again, Linton.' Another man was speaking now, in a detached authoritative tone.

'. . . we'll come to see who's owed respect.'

'There are visitors arriving and this is *not* what we want them to see.'

'It could be dangerous to sedate her, sir.' The first voice again. 'Do we know what drugs she was given earlier?' They continued their discussion as she struggled, resisting the woman who was hurting her, holding her down while straps were wound around her.

But she was tiring. . .

'A small dose, nurse, just to get her upstairs,' the detached voice said. 'You, sir, you're her physician?'

'I'm Kemp. The bishop's physician. He sent a message ahead to expect us.'

'Yes, yes. I have it. I'm Nicholson, medical superintendent. How d'you do. Follow us in if you will, sir. Yes, Mrs Whitely, in her upper arm.'

Olwen, now held down by the straps, could no longer move. A man was looking down at her, his brow furrowed. 'Really, Dr Nicholson, it's not necessary, she's calming. . . no, really—'

Olwen felt a sharp pain in her arm and then, vaguely and quickly fading, a jolting sensation as she was wheeled over the cobblestones.

It was some time later that she surfaced and found herself lying on a bed with an iron frame. Voices were speaking close by but she closed her eyes again, trying to focus on what they were saying. It was the man who had been with her in the carriage: '. . . a perverse disposition. . . quite wilful. . . no moral discipline as a child, I understand, and an inflated sense of pride. . . frequently delusional. . . violent. You saw for yourselves. . .'

Then the cold voice that ordered her to be subdued. 'What treatment has she been receiving?'

Something was said that she could not hear but then the first man spoke again. 'An adventurer, it seems, a Scot. . . some form of hypnosis. . . quite unconscionable. . .'

But then the voice that had seemed kinder than the others. 'Surely we need to hear the whole history. And we need two signatures to hold her here. One is not enough.'

'The bishop's observations will suffice for the moment.'

'With respect, sir, the bishop is not a physician—'

'Thank you, Linton.'

Try as she might she could not catch everything that was being said, but some conclusion must have been reached.

'Until then, gentlemen, and thank you, Dr Kemp, that would be most helpful.'

She opened her eyes, determined to speak before they left her, and tried to raise her arm to get their attention but it had stiffened. She tried to sit up but she found she could not and turned her head to see that her wrists were bound, not with steel, but with linen cuffs and tapes that were tied to the bed head, her elbows angled beside her head. Panicked, she moved her legs and found that they too were constrained, held slightly apart, each ankle cuffed and taped. She struggled furiously as the world around her began to oscillate and shift.

'Ah, she's coming to,' and she looked up to see three be-whiskered men peering down at her.

'Release me!' she demanded.

'It is for your own safety, my dear. You were likely to harm yourself.'

'You have no right to hold me!' She fixed her eyes upon one with a worried expression. '*Please* help me. . .'

But it was the other man who spoke, ignoring her and addressing the man who had been with her in the carriage instead. 'This is where we excel here, managing unfortunate cases such as this,' he said. 'A firm hand is needed, though self-discipline can, you know, be instilled over time.'

The eyes of the other man had not left her and she looked beseechingly up at him. 'Let me but speak to my cousin Osred! He sent for us, for my brothers too, and the archbishop has them in his keeping. Do you not know me? I am Ælfwyn, daughter of the late king. For pity's sake, sir, will you not get a message to Osred?'

The man put out a hand and laid it on her shoulder, and she saw compassion in his eyes and the other man gave a dry chuckle. 'We will, of course, your highness,' he said. 'And in the meantime, nurse, a dose of the usual night-time sedative, I think, and we'll review the case in the morning. By mouth if she will have it, through a tube if she resists.'

CHAPTER 34

Three days after his arrest John was brought back up to the room where he had been questioned before. He had spent his time in pointless fuming, trying to persuade his gaolers to take a message to Celia but without success, having nothing with which to bribe them. In desperation he had eaten some of the prison fare, with the anticipated results, and had never felt more wretched in all his life. He placed little confidence in the exquisite Toby Farquharson and none at all in the stony-faced Redman. But, dear God, *someone* must be made to listen! It could be weeks before he got a formal hearing. His only comfort was in knowing that Brandt would, by now, be safely on his way back to Switzerland and could not be charged. That would have added greatly to the load his conscience had to bear. But this left only Celia and Gussie to act on Olwen's behalf and the authorities would doubtless dismiss them as mere viragos, an outrage to society, and they would struggle to make themselves heard.

The sound of the door unlocking had brought a spark of hope that he might speak to someone with a grain of intelligence and compassion. 'Where am I going?' he asked the constable who led him away.

'The inspector has further questions.'

The spark extinguished. This time he was not held for long before Redman appeared. He gestured for John to be seated, sending the constable away, and came quickly to the point. 'I've been told that all charges against you are to be dropped.'

John stared at him in disbelief. He had underestimated the combined force of Gussie and Toby Farquharson. God bless them both!

'I've a letter from the vicar to that effect. He has decided upon Christian clemency.' Briefly he met John's eyes. 'I could, nonetheless, hold you on other charges as something untoward is obviously going on and a breach of the law has clearly been committed.' John said nothing and Redman contemplated him a moment. 'Your counsel came to see me, implying that the case was not as it appeared; he didn't elaborate beyond saying that august individuals could be implicated in it. And then shortly afterwards I received the vicar's letter.' He paused and John kept his face impassive. 'Instinct and experience tells me that pressure has been brought to bear on Miss Malkon's family in order to secure your release. Enlighten me if you will?'

This man was too sharp by half. 'I've no idea.'

'Forgive me, Dr Osbourne, if I say I don't believe you. This is a strange case and I'm reluctant to close it completely until I understand it rather more. Somewhat against my better judgement, I *will* release you, but I require you to keep me informed of your movements, *all* your movements, and if I discover that arms have been twisted to get you released, or blackmail threatened, I'll not hesitate to bring you in again. You're holding something back, and this would be a good moment to tell me what it is.'

John looked back at him. 'I've nothing to add to what's already been said.'

'My concern is for Miss Malkon's safety and well-being—'

'As is mine.'

The inspector's face was unreadable. 'Then you must take very seriously the condition I am placing on your release. You must make no further attempt to contact Miss Malkon or her family, or in any way try to influence the course of her treatment.' John stiffened. 'Understood?'

'*What* treatment?'

'I'm informed that she was admitted as a patient to St Hilda's House yesterday, having had some sort of fit. Since that was where you took her yourself hoping to secure her some treatment, you cannot fail to be delighted by this news.' He paused, subjecting

John to further scrutiny. 'Good day to you, Doctor, and do as I say or I shall come after you.'

John was escorted back downstairs. He pocketed his loose change and his watch, his mind working furiously as he scribbled his signature on the voucher, then went up the steps to the wet street, squinting at the unaccustomed daylight. St Hilda's House! A patient there. . . God only knew what that meant. He must get home, get clean and think.

'John!' He had only taken two steps when he heard the cry and turned to see Celia Goodfellow, her head stuck out of a cab parked across the road. The driver was crouched, smoking, against the wall. Celia beckoned to him. 'We've been waiting for you.'

'How very good of you. But for how long?'

'Since Toby tipped us off.' Gussie leaned forward to reply, wrinkling her nose. 'You're not very savoury, John dear.'

'We've taken a room for you at The Black Swan,' said Celia. 'You can sweeten up there. Step up, driver, if you will.' The man knocked out his pipe, pocketed it and swung into his seat.

But John was shaking his head. 'I need to get home and get changed. Olwen's been taken to St Hilda's House. I must see what I can do for her.'

'We know. But there's everything you require at the hotel,' Celia said, 'and you'll be wanting a decent meal. We need cool heads now. Things are moving fast.'

With some reluctance he stepped into the carriage and allowed himself to be conveyed the short distance to the old coaching inn. Avoiding the curious gaze of the landlord, he took the key that Celia handed to him. 'We requested a bath for you, John. Dinner in an hour or so? We'll be down here when you're ready.'

He let himself into the room, shut the door and stood a moment with his eyes shut and allowed the image of the vile cell to recede. He opened them again to see that his own clothes, brought from home, had been laid out on the bed, and smiled. What efficient allies these women were! And he saw too that a tin tub had been placed in front of the fire.

How little we value freedom until it is denied us, he thought as he sat in it, a few moments later once the maids had filled it and gone, and he closed his eyes again, letting the travails of the past few days recede into steam. And at least Olwen was away from her family, but what had Redman meant about a fit?

Having bathed and dressed in clean clothes he was surprised to discover that his own hairbrush and other toiletries had been set out on the dressing table, and noticed for the first time that his large leather valise was in one corner of the room. These masterful women must have instructed Mrs Crawford to pack for him, but how long did she expect him to be away?

He went downstairs where he was shown into a private parlour, panelled with blackened oak, where Celia and Gussie were waiting for him. Gussie gestured to a jug of ale, which he seized upon. 'So you threatened a bishop,' he said, eyeing her over the rim.

She grinned back at him. 'Worked like a charm, my boy. Toby's joining us for lunch.' The door opened. 'This'll be him now. . . Ah no! Excellent. The chessmen assemble.'

John swung round and saw Brandt standing in the doorway, looking across at him with a wry smile. He sprang to his feet. 'Brandt! I thought you'd be safely back in Zurich!'

'Then you've a poor opinion of me, young man,' he replied, shaking John's hand and examining him. 'And you have paid a price for your passion, I think.'

'But we cannot allow you to be drawn into this, Brandt. It's much more than we should ask of you, consider your reputation—'

Brandt put up his hand. 'You do not ask it of me, my friend. And my reputation, as you remark, is mine to consider.'

Conversation was paused by the arrival of the meal and the aroma of roast lamb sent John's stomach churning; it was all he could do not to set upon the food like a barbarian. As it was being served the door opened again and Toby Farquharson arrived, apologising that he had been delayed. He was introduced to Brandt and pulled out a chair beside John.

'You're looking rather more the thing, Doctor,' he said, forking a piece of meat onto his plate. 'And Gussie's plan worked. Should have insisted on that wager.'

John smiled. 'The inspector suspects blackmail and arm-twisting.'

'Shrewd man, that. I thought so at the time.' A potato was speared and put beside the meat. 'But what a business! Has Gussie told you?'

Gussie shook her head. 'I said you'd fill us in.'

He loaded his fork. 'Right. Well, I went to the bishop's residence, bearing Gussie's letter, and watched the man's liver curdle while he read it. Went a very pretty shade of green.' He raised the fork to his mouth and chewed. 'He was just beginning to bluster when I mentioned that a certain other letter had come into my hands which would be embarrassment to both him and the vicar, and that doctor of theirs, pointing out that clergymen drugging and forcing a girl into marriage, even with the sanction of a medical man, would provoke considerable interest in the courts, and sell a great many newspapers. Only by dropping all charges against you did I think that could be avoided.' He loaded another forkful, his triumph apparently having whetted his appetite. 'Putty in my hand after that, he was, once he'd made it clear that my soul would roast in Hell. On the cards, already, I told him. Anyway, I suggested that he instruct the vicar to write to Redman telling him that they had decided upon Christian clemency. He was livid, of course, but in the end he agreed.' He looked up with a smile. 'And there the matter stands.'

'Except that Miss Malkon is now incarcerated, and beyond our reach.'

'I know. One thing at a time, my dear fellow. They need the signature of two physicians to hold her, so we can soon challenge that. It would be in Kemp's interest to provide one, but my understanding is that those employed by an asylum cannot be used to get her put away. Once she's been formally admitted, however, it gets more tricky, there are precedents. . .' He trailed off, looking less confident.

'I've already presented letters of introduction at St Hilda's,' said John. 'I'll go and see Nicholson and make the man listen.'

Toby raised an eyebrow. 'Did Redman explain about the condition of your release?'

'He did.'

'That would break it.'

'Yes.'

'Then my fee looks promising again.'

John scowled at him. 'What else do you suggest? Shall I just go home, carry on as before, forget the whole thing?'

Toby glanced across the table at the two women. 'You've not told him, have you?'

Celia and Gussie exchanged looks and Celia took a drink. 'I'm afraid you can't go home, John. As you must know, the occupation of the doctor's house is at the discretion of the estate, and as control of the estate is currently in the vicar's hands. . .' John lowered his knife and fork. 'Pure spite, of course. We went there yesterday to collect some clothes for you, and Mrs Crawford told us then. It's all round the village as you'd expect, the vicar's telling everyone that you've been evicted for malpractice and she was all of a dither.'

'But it gave us free rein to pack up your things,' Gussie remarked. The valise was explained. 'Didn't take us long. You travel light.'

'We've arranged for the rest of your things to be sent to Knaresborough.'

'The job's gone too, I expect.'

'Yes, I'm afraid it has.' Celia gave him a look of concern.

John dropped his eyes to his plate. It was one thing to consider the possibility of losing everything, quite another to face the reality. 'Keeps things simple, I suppose,' he said.

'Don't worry. Olwen'll reinstate you when she comes of age. Bound to.' Gussie, born to wealth, seemed oblivious as to what this meant to him. And a reputation, once lost, was not easily regained. 'And we'll not let you starve in the meantime.'

'Come back to Zurich with me, John,' said Brandt. 'There is interesting work there to be done.'

John gave a tight smile and a nod of thanks, and directed his attention back to his food while he absorbed these blows. 'So I've nothing to lose by going to St Hilda's House,' he said, after a moment, 'and trying to reason with Dr Nicholson.'

'And everything to gain by way of accommodation, which Redman will happily provide,' Toby Farquharson replied. 'He meant what he said, you know. He's a tough one.'

John's sharp riposte was interrupted by Brandt. 'Here I believe I can be useful. There is one, on the staff of St Hilda's – you met him, I think – he was gracious enough to defend my methods against Nicholson and the reactionaries, and came to me after-wards to commiserate upon their decision. I believe he could be persuaded to help us. From him we can at least learn a little of the state of Miss Malkon's mind, and of plans for her treatment.'

John remembered the harassed young man he had met that first time – Dr Linton. 'Would he do that?'

'I believe he would. He is a man much dissatisfied with the workings of the institution and is, I believe, gathering material in order to present a case to the Trustees.' He nodded towards Toby Farquharson. 'This is something, sir, you did not hear me say, and which I would deny.'

'Understood.'

'How soon could you contact him?'

'I'll send a message at once, asking him to meet me.'

'I'll come with you,' said John.

Brandt put up a hand. 'No, no. You'll be too passionate, my friend, too blunt. It requires a subtle touch or he'll refuse.'

'And then what?' asked Gussie. 'Would he treat her?'

Brandt shook his head. 'If she comes to St Hilda's with the patronage of the bishop then she'll be Nicholson's patient, it was always the case with those that are well-connected, but he will doubtless sit in on her clinical assessment and the patient's notes are kept in a place where all the medical staff can see them. He would not be breaking any rules if he looked at them.'

'If he appraises you of their content, he would,' Toby retorted. He wiped his mouth, discarded his napkin and got to his feet. 'You'll be able to speak more freely without me here, and what

I don't hear I won't know when I come to prepare your defence. You seemed determined, between the lot of you, to end up in court but at least I'll get a decent fee out of this so I thank you for that, and for the meal. You know where to find me, Gussie.'

CHAPTER 35

At the insistence of the two women, John spent the remainder of the afternoon in the hotel. In truth he was in no state to resist and fell into a deep and dreamless sleep, stretched out on his bed, fully dressed. He woke a couple of hours later to see that a note had been slipped under his door. It was from Celia. Brandt had been true to his word, she wrote, and reported that Dr Linton had agreed to meet him that evening. He would return in the morning and report.

John went back downstairs to find the women sat in the small parlour, reading beside the fire. 'Did you sleep in your clothes then, John?' Gussie asked, looking him up and down. 'You're barely respectable, after all our hard work to redeem you.' He apologised meekly. 'Are men born uncivilised, I've often wondered. Shall I order tea?'

Darkness was closing in and the curtains had been drawn. 'Where was Brandt was meeting Dr Linton?' he asked.

'Wouldn't tell you if we knew. You'd scare the poor man off with that storm cloud expression.' John grunted and pulled up a chair to the fire, relishing the simple pleasure of a soft chair, a fireside and human contact. 'He'll tell us in the morning.'

He caught Celia's eye and she gave him a sympathetic smile. 'There's really nothing you can do, John. At least she's in the safe hands of professionals and not with that ghastly family of hers.'

The report that Brandt brought next morning, however, dispelled any such complacency. It was evident as soon as he arrived that the news he brought was not good.

'Linton was very familiar with the case,' Brandt said, pulling up a chair. 'He was there when Miss Malkon arrived, and is already concerned about her.' He paused. 'Where to begin. . . It is a sorry story, my friends, but you must hear it. . . It appears she was given something to subdue her at the vicarage and was just regaining consciousness when she arrived at St Hilda's. Kemp had come with her in the carriage but Linton said that she was bewildered and frightened, resisting efforts to get her into the wheeled chair, and had to be physically constrained.' John swore under his breath. 'They took her to the upper floor where the more wealthy patients are housed, but into one of the more secure rooms there. Linton went with her and he heard Kemp report that she'd been given an injection of a very powerful sedative, not a drug I know but Linton tells me it involves chloral hydrate and an opiate. As a result, he said, she was experiencing violent hallucinations.' He gave John a look from under his brows. 'Lashing out at the attendants, claiming that she was owed obedience as a king's daughter, declaring them to be traitorous, speaking of her brothers and demanding audience with someone called Osred, her cousin, she claimed. Quite wild, Linton said. . .'

John rose and went to stand at the window looking out into the courtyard. 'Go on,' he said.

'They calmed her down with medication, and some physical restraint so that she would not harm herself if she woke. They have since met in Nicholson's office, together with the senior female attendant. Linton was there and heard Kemp's full report.'

He paused again.

'And?' John had remained staring out of the window, his hands thrust deep into his pockets.

'Come back to the table, my friend, and sit.' Brandt gave a little smile as John turned to him. 'It is easier to address a face rather than a back, and more difficult for you to become impassioned if you are seated.' John glanced quickly at him and did as he was bid. Brandt nodded. 'I would ask you to listen to *all* that I have to say, if you will, without interruption, and then we will consider it with cool heads. Yes? Choler only impairs the reasoning.' Gussie urged him to get to the point and his eye glinted at her. 'Very well. Facts have been twisted, my friends, and presented in a light that is far from helpful. According to Kemp's account, Miss Malkon's troubles began with deliberate manipulation by her physician, a villain by the name of Osbourne, who frequently contrived to be alone with her, even luring her to his own home on one occasion for some dubious consultation. He undermined the loving care offered by her family, sowing seeds of distrust in her mind, with the clear goal of seduction.' John said nothing, clamping his jaw shut. 'This charlatan then enlisted the assistance of a controversial and later discredited foreign doctor – myself, of course – but their conspiracy was thwarted by her uncle (a man of the cloth, her legal guardian and so forth) and so Osbourne turned instead to two degenerate women of his acquaintance, one a former governess who had been removed from her position, the other the scandalous daughter of a peer, cast off by her family. Between them they plotted to lure her away from her family, bringing her to York for immoral purposes—' It was Gussie's turn to swear, but Brandt patted her hand and continued. 'The poor girl was finally tracked down at the home of these irregular women, and rescued before further debauchery could take place.'

'Did we suck her blood while corrupting her,' Celia enquired, with arched eyebrows, 'or had we already drained her of it?'

Brandt raised a hand. 'I continue: these experiences, it would appear, have so far unbalanced the harmony of Miss Malkon's mind that, upon her return to the vicarage, she became violent, confusing what she had undergone at the hands of this vile trio with the benign actions of her own family, accusing them of confining her, poisoning her, starving her, and threatening violence against her person. She allegedly argued with the bishop, made various outrageous accusations and began breaking valuable items, until she was sedated and brought to St Hilda's.' He stopped, and looked around the table. 'And so, to conclude, a diagnosis was made, one which in Europe we believe belongs to another era and which, Dr Linton informs me, is rarely now given. A diagnosis of moral insanity.'

'Good God.' John stared at him.

'On this one man's word!' Celia exclaimed.

'Linton made that very point but his remark had only the effect of them agreeing that it would be a working diagnosis, to be confirmed by observation, but for the moment she would be treated as morally insane.'

'Oh, my poor girl.' Celia pressed a hand to her mouth and Gussie reached out to her. 'Whatever can we do?'

John sat silent, aware of Brandt's eyes fixed upon him.

'This was planned,' he said at last, and Brandt nodded. 'This has been thought through.'

Brandt continued to nod. 'I share this view. And, when I put that opinion to Linton, he agreed that Kemp's report was well rehearsed.'

'They've twisted every fact, defused every charge that might be made against them!'

'And, I fear, the reason is obvious,' said Brandt.

John had reached the same conclusion. 'They're planning to keep her there.'

'*No!*'

'She's wealthy,' John said, turning to Celia, 'and if she's declared insane by professionals, her uncle will have no trouble in establishing in the courts that she's incapable—'

'– and so he'll argue he must continue to administer the estate on her behalf,' Gussie concluded. 'And no need for a marriage at all!'

'And the attempted rape is put aside as delusional.'

'Exactly. And if the estate will pay the institution to keep her there indefinitely, there's no incentive to try to help her. If she's not mad now she soon will be.'

Celia looked back at him. 'With all of us discredited, she has no one to defend her—'

They sat in stunned silence.

'But surely,' Gussie said, 'Toby told us they need the written testament of two independent physicians to legally hold her, and they only have one. On that basis he said he can get her released!'

Brandt looked at John from under his eyebrows again. 'Linton raised this but they claim that two, or even three physicians *have* seen her, and that taken together with the independent and personal observation of the bishop, they believe this will satisfy the law, should anyone challenge them.'

'Who are these others?' John demanded.

'You are one, my friend, and I the other.'

'*What!*'

'The note you wrote, when you brought your letters of introduction, supports their case as in it you state your concern about a patient who was delusional.'

John looked back at him in horror. 'But I never mentioned her by name.'

'From subsequent events, however – you brought her to see me at St Hilda's, my attendance at the vicarage – it is clear that Miss Malkon is the patient in question.'

John rose. Were any of those involved within reach, then murder would be done. 'We need Toby. Gussie, get him to come.'

But Toby, when summoned, was sobered by what he heard. 'Christ, what a coil. I need to give it some thought.' He remained silent for a while, chewing his bottom lip, then looked at John. 'Sounds like we were lucky to get you away. Keep your nose very clean, Doctor, or you'll be inside again and we've enough to consider here. If they're feeling more confident then they might decide to press charges after all. We need to devise a strategy.'

John snorted. 'We need to get Olwen out of there before they destroy her mind!'

'Of course, but by legal means—'

'By any means! And fast.'

'The place is not easy to escape from,' said Brandt, his eyes following John as he paced. 'This much I know.'

Toby rose. 'Let me think on it,' he said. 'I need to be at another appointment, but I'll return this evening and we'll discuss matters again.' He started towards the door, and then stopped, turning back to John. 'But be very sure, Doctor, if you do something stupid, I wash my hands of you.'

CHAPTER 36

Remaining at The Black Swan was now insufferable. John vacillated between fury and despair, knowing that he was closely watched by the two women in case he did anything rash. Though what that might be, he could not imagine as he could see no way of doing anything that might help the situation.

Brandt had gone to meet Linton again, but still refused to allow John to join him. He was going, he told him, not only to keep abreast of how Miss Malkon was faring but to help his erstwhile colleague prepare a case to bring before the Trustees of St Hilda's House. 'There are things happening there that should not be happening,' he said grimly, as he put on his coat and hat. 'Miss Malkon's case is only one of several where the therapeutic value of what is offered is very questionable. I observed others myself. It has become a matter of widespread concern, I understand, this confining of patients, especially women, against their will, flouting all ethical considerations, so perhaps some wider good will come of all this.' John watched him go and then flung himself into one of the armchairs beside the fire and stared at the smouldering coals.

Celia too was deep in thought. 'Dr Linton's account is worrying. She still keeps harping on about her brothers, poor thing, which is so very odd, as she would hardly speak of what happened at the time. We were all in shock, I think, and her wretched father was demanding all the attention as if the loss was his alone. But now. . . it keeps resurging, in this oddly distorted manner. It cannot have been good for her to bottle it up as she did.' She pulled out a handkerchief and blew her nose. 'And she blames herself, you know, for not watching over them, but if anyone was neglectful it was me. A thousand times I've berated myself for not knowing where they were that day, with their tutor being away. We'd had a keen frost and the pipes were frozen and I was helping Mrs Percy with kettles and boiling water and we'd no idea what they were up to. But it runs on my mind, and it must do so in Olwen's. . .'

'Perhaps in her deluded state she imagines she can still save them,' Gussie said and John looked across at her; for once her impish face was serious. 'We had some interesting discussions with your professor while you were locked up,' she went on, 'and wondered how far guilt lay at the root of this delusion. As Celia says, it must play a large part, and somehow she's managed to transfer the guilt to you, even though you never even met the boys.'

'She's never spoken to me about her *real* brothers,' John remarked. 'And it's her. . . her others who stalk my dreams.'

'How strange. . . Perhaps it's how her mind is trying to come to terms with their deaths,' Celia suggested, 'creating an imaginary world in which their loss can be explained, and she's somehow conveying this fantasy to you.'

'Or. . .' Gussie moved to sit opposite him, her eyes sharp. 'It's something else entirely.'

'Meaning what?'

'Meaning that she's tapping into something from the past, something that actually happened.' John raised an eyebrow. 'I know what you're thinking. . . Table-tilters. Psychic nonsense. And yes, the whole matter of psychic research *is* populated by cranks and the credulous, but I've read papers written by men of science with open minds who will still explore these taboo areas.' He grunted; he had read them too. 'And I've attended exhibitions and seances where phenomena have supposedly appeared, although frankly I was never convinced. Spirit writing is an obvious sham, but there are some uncanny occurrences that defy explanation. Brandt himself has a flexible attitude.'

'On the manifestation of spirits? Hardly!'

Gussie shrugged. 'Nevertheless he firmly believes that Olwen is, unwittingly, communicating her other world to you by thought transference—' She broke off and laughed. 'I should love the bishop to hear his suggestion that prayer is really thought transference, a deliberate effort to communicate with God, supported by faith, not science. But what happened to you both at Pear Tree Cottage *could* mean that you were somehow tapping into a shared experience.'

'Maybe. . .' John had thought a great deal about that evening but it still baffled him.

'So if we go a step further and accept that it was a *real* experience, of something that *did* happen, then perhaps Olwen, in her fragile state, has become a bridge or a conduit to another time, unlocking an archive of emotions connected to past events, events that run parallel to her own experience.'

John raised an eyebrow. 'Or perhaps, Augusta Dudley, you have attended one too many seances.'

'You're hardly one to scoff, Dr John. Who was it went searching for their dreams and found a tunnel?'

She was right, but if he was indeed a scientist and a man of reason, which he had always thought himself to be, he ought to resist such an outlandish suggestion. 'Brandt explained that away as coincidence,' he replied, ignoring the fact that he had resented this at the time. 'So you're suggesting that Olwen's *alter ego* is not a delusion but is a woman who once existed?' Gussie nodded. 'The daughter of a king? Ha! Have *you* heard of a King Ælfwald? I haven't.'

'But that means nothing. There's a very great deal I don't know.'

John shook his head, still resisting such an outlandish explanation, and yet. . . and yet, in his dreams he had seen the man, seen so vividly his careworn countenance and troubled eyes, felt his hand on his shoulder, bidding him to rise. And the memory of the man's severed head, held aloft in triumph, still had the power to shock.

'It can't be too difficult to discover—' Celia broke off as a knock came at the door and one of the hotel maids entered with a message on a salver for John.

He took it and read it. '*Damn him!*' He got to his feet, balled the note and hurled it into the fire. 'Redman,' he said grimly, abandoning the psychic world for a more immediate threat. 'I've got to report to the police station to answer further questions.'

'Oh, *John*! When?'

'This afternoon.'

'Take Toby with you,' Gussie said. 'I'll send him a note.'

'Wait. Let me think.' He went to stare out of the window, his mind racing. Curse the man! What could he possibly want now? He had seen enough of Redman to know that taking Toby with him would make no difference to his intentions. Had he discovered the rather blatant blackmail? He had said he'd not tolerate it. . . But to be rearrested now would scupper him, and the thought of returning to that sordid cell was intolerable. He must remain free to act.

'I'll go to ground.'

'John—'

He swung back to them. 'If Redman decides to hold me, I can do nothing, I'm useless!'

'Wait for Toby's advice.'

He shook his head. 'He'd tell me to go as instructed, he could do nothing else. And I doubt he could help.' Toby, after all, was tainted by the blackmail too. But John's brain had begun sparking again, because it had suddenly become clear what he must do. But first. . . 'I need somewhere to hole up where Redman won't find me.'

Gussie continued to insist that he should at least speak to Toby, but Celia had gone silent.

'Swindale,' she said, after a moment. 'You must go to Swindale.'

'I can't involve the Percys. And it's too far away.'

But Celia was shaking her head. 'Ten miles, twelve at the most, and the Percys would want to help. There's a keeper's cottage, it's been empty since the vicar decided he didn't need to pay the keeper's wage. Redman'll look for you in York or Knaresborough, and might try Swindale, but he'd never find you in the woods.'

'*Celia!* Don't encourage the man!'

But Celia ignored her. 'You can catch a train to Felton, and then get a lift on a cart, they come and go to the station all the time, and they'd drop you at the end of the drive.'

Gussie was on her feet. 'Honestly, Celia! It's usually me who throws caution to the wind.'

The dimple appeared on Celia's cheek. 'Then my turn is overdue. I'll write a letter to the Percys for you to take. They're very loyal and will keep you safe while we think of a plan.'

John gave her hand a squeeze. 'But I *have* a plan. Somehow we'll get her out of St Hilda's and then I'll take her north, to my mother's farm.'

From where, in another world and at another time, he should never have removed her.

CHAPTER 37

The path to the keeper's cottage was overgrown. It was part of a longer, more ancient trackway that once led up from the river and passed behind the hall before disappearing into the woodland beyond and then out across the vale. With not even a gamekeeper's boots on it in recent weeks, nettles and the fiddle-heads of ferns had encroached upon the edges. Percy led the way, insisting on carrying John's holdall as well as a basket that his wife had hastily packed with provisions when John had appeared, unannounced, at the door of their cottage that evening. They had read Celia's letter, exchanged looks and turned at once to the practicalities. The cottage had been closed up, Mrs Percy had said, with an anxious look, and was certainly damp. 'It doesn't matter, really it doesn't,' John had assured her, refusing her offer of a room in the house, and she had pursed her lips and said they would see about that.

Between them they had packed essentials to make the place habitable and he and Percy had set off, Mrs Percy calling after them that she would send hot food daily. They walked in single file along the narrowing path and it grew darker as they penetrated the forest. Great pine and cedar sentinels soared above them, filtering the sunlight. 'Planted by Miss Olwen's grandfather,' Percy said in answer to John remarking on them. 'Brought back from the Americas, I'm told.' The tall trees seemed to create a stillness and a quietude beneath them while the shafts of low evening light filtering through had an almost theatrical effect.

Redman would be hard-pressed indeed to find him here.

They emerged eventually into a little clearing beside a copse of a more ancient woodland of chestnut and ash, gnarled oak and spreading beech trees beside which stood the keeper's cottage. It was a squat building, with a low-pitched roof of untidy slates. Percy pulled a key from his pocket and opened the door to reveal a single room with a sleeping loft above, reached by a fixed ladder. 'Soon get the fire lit,' he said, going across to the hearth where he began clearing away debris that had fallen down the chimney. 'It'll smoke a bit 'til it starts to draw.' The only furniture was a table and two wooden chairs, one with a broken back. 'It'll not suit you for long, Doctor,' Percy said.

John decided it would suit him very well, pared to the bone.

He went up the ladder and confirmed that the straw mattress was, as Mrs Percy had predicted, damp. 'Throw it down, sir,' Percy called from below, 'and I'll set it in front of the fire. It'll do for tonight and I'll find you summat better for tomorrow.' Anything was better than a cold cell stinking of urine, with a locked door between him and the world. 'There's a wood pile outside and you'll not go hungry, we'll see to that.' John slid the mattress down the ladder and descended after it. He found a lantern on a shelf and began to clean the wick. 'Lamp oil's in the basket,' Percy said and, having got the fire blazing, he set the mattress in front of it. John filled the lantern and placed it on the table and Percy left, promising to return at once with food and blankets.

A sense of peace descended and John sat on the unbroken wooden chair staring into the flames, soothed by the crackle of burning wood while outside in the silent forest, the light continued to fall. Being reduced to nothing was strangely liberating. And he now had but one purpose. . . He allowed his brain to freewheel as he sat there, forming and dismissing plans to get Olwen away from St Hilda's House. Once that was achieved it would be easy; they would head over the border where he would be on his own territory and he could keep her safe in the hills above Halterburn where countless others had hidden from the law, and an unkind world. Beyond that he would not think.

He stretched out his legs and felt the tension in him unwind and he became drowsy, letting the fire warm him. . .

Too late to help her brothers, poor lads, and he felt again a pain deep within him at the thought of them. They had come to feel like his own kin and, in his mind's eye, he could see them so clearly down by the burn, or out on the hills with Bri, stalking the hinds, joyful lads with their quick minds alert and bright eyes shining. If only he had had the strength to have resisted Modig and kept them there.

With Wyn.

A log shifted in the hearth and he jolted upright, blinking and disoriented. And the dream hung a moment in the smoke, leaving behind it a profound sense of sorrow. Was Olwen's pain now so strong, he thought, so focused, that it could even reach him here? He rose and put more wood on the fire, comforted by the simplicity of the place – bare stone walls, ancient beams supporting the loft. Ageless.

And outside, only the forest.

He glanced towards the window, and froze.

A face was pressed against the glass. A man, an old man, was out there in the darkness, staring back at him. He vanished and John went at once to the door, raising the lantern above his head, and called out into emptiness. And then he saw another light, coming towards him out of the darkness, swaying through the trees.

'Doctor?' It was Percy. 'Is owt amiss?'

'There was a man here just now, a face at the window,' he said, holding up his own lantern, still surveying the copse.

Percy chuckled as he reached him. 'Should have warned you, sir. That'd be old Reagan, he sometimes sleeps in the wood shed – '

Reagan. The figure he had seen by the lake.

' – not quite all there, if you take my meaning and he's not usually around this late in the year. Once spring comes and the nights get warmer, he heads off somewhere north, he told me, then turns up again when the leaves start to fall. He's used to having the woods to himself, you see, and he'd be curious. Turn the key in the lock tonight, else he'll be moving in, and he'd make a strange bedfellow.' He continued to chuckle as he closed the shutters, building up the fire, and gestured to a pot of food in the hearth. 'It's only stew but it's a good one.'

John still stood by the door. 'I saw him before, down by the lake, that other time.'

'Aye. Been living in these woods as long as anyone can remember, knows every inch of them. A scavenger, he is, half-wild, lives off the land, steals food sometimes, eggs and the like, only what he needs so no one much minds. Gypsy blood in him they say. . . The boys used to run off to find him when they heard he was about and he'd be good with them, harmless as a butterfly, showed them where the badgers had their sett, and how to set snares and all sorts.'

The boys. Oliver and William, not the other boys. . .

'Guardian of the forest, he calls himself,' Percy went on. 'He tells me about poachers if he doesn't like the look of them, but he has his own views on who has need and who's just thieving. Helps himself mind, as if by right.'

Between them they lifted the mattress back up the loft ladder and arranged the blankets Percy had brought and, having been assured that there was nothing else he could do, Percy bid him eat up and departed, promising to return in the morning.

John ate half the stew, leaving the rest for breakfast, and then sat there, running through the only idea he had for getting Olwen away that had any chance of success. Somehow Brandt must persuade Dr Linton to assist in her escape. Everything depended on that. Briefly, as he was flinging what he needed into his smaller valise, he had discussed this with Celia and Gussie, urging them to raise it with Brandt. All Linton would have to do was leave a door unlocked at some predetermined time, but would he do it? John had not spent long enough with the man to get his measure. Once Olwen was out of there it would be a matter of quick action; they would need to get on a northbound train before anyone started watching the station. Alternatively, he mused, they could travel by road, in stages, following the route that Heri and Wyn had taken, though not by field tracks and forest trails. And once they reached Halterburn he could leave Olwen at his mother's farm and take refuge himself with her Romany kin who knew many ways to make folk disappear. . .

He was not sure what disturbed him. He had gone up to the loft and fallen asleep almost at once but woke, dry mouthed and coughing, something catching in his throat. Burning, he could smell burning. . . He came sharply awake, hearing crackling, and saw the shadow of flames leaping on the walls. He was up then, and half fell down the ladder.

Reaching the ground he stopped and stared in astonishment. There was a fire sure enough, a great roaring one, but it was in the hearth where a fire ought to be, its flames fanned by a breeze from the open door. And there, sitting on the chair was the old man he had seen at the window, staring into the fire, apparently deaf to the clatter of John tumbling down from the loft.

'What the—!' He went to shut the door and the flames subsided.

The figure in the chair turned to look at him. 'You've come back.' He spoke as if John were the intruder, not he. 'I wondered, when I saw you before, if you would.'

Reagan.

'I saw you too,' John replied, taking a slow step forward. 'Earlier, looking through the—'

But the old man was continuing as if John had not spoken. ' – and before that on a black gelding breathing fire. Four times, you've come, and now the fifth.' A flame leapt again in the fire and the shadows shifted. 'First time, you and that other one, with two rough-maned mounts that you left in my care.' John went still. 'And later you came back.'

A chill crept up his spine and, keeping his eyes fixed on the old man, he pulled up the broken chair and sat. 'When?' he asked softly. 'When did I come?'

'You came back later that day,' the old man went on, 'and you had the boys with you – and their sister. Frightened they were, but trusting.' He turned back to the fire. 'They were good boys, always were. Good lads.'

John felt the space closing in around him, shrinking down to that arc of light before the fire holding the two of them within its thrall. And he saw again the boat adrift on the current, a lucky find, Bri had said. And Wyn. . . Wyn watching him, understanding the danger as her brothers did not.

And a man – this man – leading the horses forward.

Wrogan.

He pulled the chair closer, hardly daring to breathe, desperate not to break the spell. The remaining stew, he saw, had vanished and they sat in silence together in the half circle of light. A hundred questions jostled in his mind, but he sensed he must stay silent.

'I set you on your way that day, I did. The boys on one nag, the girl on the other and wished you Godspeed.'

He looked at the old man's ageless profile in wonder. 'Wrogan,' he said, and the old man nodded. 'The trusted one.' He had sworn to mind the horses and then forget who had come and gone so swiftly that day.

It was as if time no longer had meaning, folding in on itself like pleated linen.

'And I saw their sister again, asleep in a hedgerow with the sun on her face and I wished her Godspeed then as well.' John frowned. That was surely what Olwen had told Celia, and she had dismissed it as a dream. 'That other one came once too, the dark one, late one evening. . . Thought I didn't see him, thought I didn't know. . .'

John frowned. Had they been followed? No! He was certain they were not. They had got clean away north of the Wall. 'Who came?'

But the old man sheered off again, telling things his own way. 'I saw them pass on the northern road, a murderous band, their leader on a white stallion, and I knew you'd slipped past them and I rejoiced. And then later I saw him at the lake, thought he was a poacher, or a thief, but he was well shod – '

'Who came?'

' – and when he came out of the boathouse, he'd nothing in

his hands, except what he went in with. Dropped it in the bushes, he did, and I'd no use for it.'

John's brain tried to grapple with these wayward thoughts but he dared not question too closely, the stories were too fragile. . . But the boathouse would not have been there, in that other time, the lake itself was an artificial creation. Time had flowed forward again.

He risked another question. 'What was it, the thing that he dropped?'

Reagan continued to stare into the fire. 'It'll be there still, I daresay.'

'Will you show me?'

'You'll find it. Beside the old track, the way you came when you left the horses.' Then he turned his head and looked directly at John. 'Why have you come?'

'I needed somewhere to stay.'

The old man shook his head; the answer had not satisfied. 'You've come as you did before, to save them. But you've come too late, remorseful and distraught again, no doubt, like you were before – ' John's head was spinning. The man's tone was scathing, but what was he being told? ' – half dead, you were, all bloodied, carried by that other one. And you wept then and wanted to die, but the other one wouldn't let you go. Tricked, you were, he told me, lured with false promises. . .' The old man sighed. 'But the boys' fate was decided when their father died, you must have realised that—'

The man made no sense at all. 'But their father died *after* their drowning.'

Reagan shook his head. 'He was dying long before the drowning, he was dying from the moment someone wanted him dead.' He sighed again, a weary sigh, and lifted red-rimmed eyes to John's. 'Greed for power. King or pauper. It never changes. But the matter should be closed now.' He held John's gaze, apparently amused by his confusion. 'That's why you've come, that's why you're here. Did you not realise? They say Sicga fell on his sword.' Sicga? The name stirred a distant memory but could not be retrieved, and the old man was getting to his feet. 'I saw you ride off on that black gelding like the devil was on your tail the day you learned where *he* was.'

He was making for the door and John rose too. 'Wait, stay! Explain—'

'Explain? You know already if you will but harken. She knows too, in her heart, poor lady. The dark one has no sword to fall upon, no honour to preserve, but he must still be brought to account.'

John shook his head, desperate that he should stay and say more. 'You speak in riddles, Reagan.'

The old man leaned towards John, his breath rank and sour, but his eyes gleamed in the firelight. 'You saw murder done at the Wall, you told me, and now, if you'll but listen, I'm saying what *I* saw. Sicga sheltered amongst the holy ones, craving sanctuary, wailing remorse, fearful for his soul, but you found him that day and damned that blackened soul to hell. But who now will avenge the innocents? He stood on the lake edge that day, the other one did, and he watched, as still as a heron he was, aye, and as cruel, but who'll listen to what a half-mad wodewose says?'

He turned to go. John put out a hand to delay him but, with a strength he could not have imagined, Reagan pushed him aside and John lost his balance, tripped on the chair and fell his length. By the time he was back on his feet the room was empty, the door stood open and the fire, fanned once more by the wind from the woodland, flared into flame.

CHAPTER 38

Next morning John was pounding on the door of Percy's cottage as soon as it was daylight. Last night he had lain awake long after Reagan had left, desperately trying to understand what the old man had been telling him.

If there was any sense in it at all, then only one conclusion could be drawn. Someone had tampered with the rowing boat. And had stood and watched the boys drown.

He had been half tempted to go and find Percy last night but decided there was nothing to be gained by it, and had woken half convinced that Reagan's visit had been another curious dream, but the sight of the empty stew pot and the ash-filled hearth told its own story.

He had hurried along the path, his head swivelling from left to right, anxious to avoid fieldhands on their way to work, but encountered no one. Once he reached the stable yard he waited until a man with a scythe over his shoulder disappeared down the lane, then he went round to the back of the Percys' cottage, vaulted over the fence into their yard, and pounded on the back door.

Percy opened it, his shirt half unbuttoned, his eyes wide, but seeing who it was, he pulled John inside. 'Eh, Doctor! You didn't ought to have come—'

'I had to,' John said, and told him the story while Percy finished buttoning his shirt. Then Mrs Percy appeared and the story was retold. 'A great deal of it made no sense at all, but I know he was trying to tell me something.' The Percys stood staring back at him as if he too was crazy. 'I think he saw something that day.'

'But there was *no one* there. No one saw what happened.'

John shook his head. 'He said he saw someone standing there, in the cover of the trees, a still as a heron, and as cruel, was how he put it.' And the phrase had played through his head as he lay in the keeper's cottage last night, staring up at the cobwebbed rafters.

'He said that? About a heron.' John nodded, watching him exchange a look with his wife, and there was horror on his face. 'He said something to me. . . something about a heron, weeks back. Said he'd seen a heron in the reed beds the day the boys died. And I just sent him off, thinking he was cracked to tell me that on such a day.' He turned frowning back to John. 'But you know, sir, he's not right in his head. He could have just seen a heron.'

John shook his head again. 'Perhaps he wasn't sure what he had seen, or was scared to say more. And he said he'd seen someone at the boathouse, a well-shod man, but it wasn't clear to me whether he meant that day or another.' He looked from one to the other, at their bewildered expressions, and repeated what Reagan had said. 'A man went into the boathouse with something in his hand and later came out with it, dropping it beside the path, the old path from the river. He was precise on that, if on nothing else.'

'Did he say what it was?' Mrs Percy asked.

'Only said that he'd no use for it.' Percy began pulling on his jacket. 'And that it would be there still.'

It took them only a little while, searching both sides of the path, before they found what the man had dropped. John had reasoned that the occasion must have been after the leaves had fallen and before the shoots of spring had grown high, so they had every chance of finding it.

After just ten minutes Percy bent and pulled something from beside a patch of bluebells. 'Well now. I've been seeking this.'

It was a screwdriver, a large one. 'That's it, that's what was dropped!' John exclaimed, his heart racing, certain that it was. 'And you recognise it?'

'Aye, it's mine. It vanished from my shed—'

'When?'

Percy was shaking his head. 'Only knew it was missing when I went to get it, a week or so back. I use a smaller one for most jobs.'

John weighed it in his hand. The wooden haft was black with damp and the metal showed patches of rust. He glanced towards the boatshed. 'Was the rowing boat kept in there?'

'Aye, always.'

There was no boat there now, of course, and the empty boathouse had nothing to tell them. When John had come to Swindale that other time the water level had been low, the lake in the process of being drained to clear the sluices, but now it was full again, the water gently lapping at the edge of the mooring. 'The sluices,' he said, turning to Percy, 'did you find what was blocking the sluices?'

Percy's face had grown pale. 'Aye. We did.'

'It was the rowing boat, wasn't it?' Mutely, the man nodded. 'Did you bring it ashore?'

Percy left the boathouse without another word, walking quickly round the curve of the lake, and John followed him to a patch of scrub a few yards back from the lakeside where a boat lay on its side, a sad and forlorn sight, shrouded in dried weed and caked in mud.

Between them they rolled it over, turning it hull up, and pulled away the weeds. Percy grabbed a handful of grass to clear away the mud. The planking seemed sound, a few gouges and scratches, nothing more. Transom and bow were intact, as was the port side, but on the starboard side. . .

John looked up at Percy and the old man gave a low sort of moan. 'Oh no, no, no. . .' and he crouched down beside John. Together they examined a misaligned plank low on the starboard side.

Once they had cleaned away the sludge, the reason it had sprung became clear. Three of the four screws that attached it to the rib were screwed in to less than half the length of their shafts, and there were scratches scored through the layers of varnish that sealed in the caulking; the caulking itself was missing. The plank would have stayed in place only until someone boarded the vessel, and then their weight would have taken it below water level, and the play of weight and water would have dislodged the plank and the boat, unseen beneath the decking boards, would have started to fill.

Percy lifted a stricken face to John. 'Oh, Doctor. . . I never thought, I never looked. We just dragged it ashore and dumped it here, I couldn't bear the sight of it. I'd have burnt it once summer came so that Miss Olwen would never come across it. . .'

John sat back on his haunches. This was what Reagan had wanted him to uncover. 'Who was there, at the house, the day the boys drowned?'

Percy shook his head. 'No one, only the family. I'm certain of it, it's not a day I'd forget.'

'Had there been visitors in the days before?'

Percy took a moment, his head bowed in thought. Then he looked up and shook his head. 'No one except family again.'

John knew he had to press him. 'Just the immediate family?'

'Aye. Just Miss Olwen and the boys, and old Mr Malkon. And his nephews, they came regularly as the old man grew ill.'

'The vicar's sons? Mr Edmond Malkon and—'

'Aye, and Mr Alfred. They came often.'

CHAPTER 39

'What is it for?' Olwen backed away from the woman who held out a small beaker of fluid. 'I don't need it. I feel quite well.'

'It's just to help you sleep, dear.' The attendant had a fixed smile that failed to reassure. 'We do the rounds every evening, and settle patients down.'

'I've been sleeping all day, on account of what I was given last night. I don't wish to do the same tomorrow.'

The woman looked over her shoulder at the door, and spoke coaxingly. 'You have to take it, miss, they'll check with me. If I say you've refused, they'll force you again.'

Last night there had been an appalling, humiliating episode when Olwen had refused to swallow whatever it was that had been brought round on the trolley now standing outside the open door. The burly attendant who had been so ungentle upon her arrival had pushed her into a chair, her eyes gleaming, and had held her arms while one of her acolytes forced something like a tiny wooden paddle between her teeth, turning it to force her mouth open, then held Olwen's head back while the liquid was poured between her lips, pinching her nose until she swallowed.

That same woman now appeared at the door. 'Has she had it?' she asked, her face as hard as granite. Olwen quickly took the beaker and raised it to her lips, making a pretence of swallowing, but the woman gave a crow of laughter and crossed the room, grabbed Olwen's chin and tipped her head back, tweaking her nose again. 'We'll have to put you on the awkward list.' The attendant left the room, but the older woman lingered. 'What was it you said about respect, dearie?' she asked, smirking. 'I'd get into bed if I were you before you fall.'

Olwen watched her go, hating the woman, feeling a great lassitude coming over her.

She had woken that morning to find the linen cuffs had been removed from her ankles and wrists but her head was in such a state of muddled confusion that no other restraint was necessary. She had felt giddy and nauseous all day and could no more have formed a plan of what to do than she could fly out of the window.

And now she was being drugged again! Slowly, with her eyelids already heavy, she climbed into bed and lay on her side, drawing her knees up high, and pulled the blankets over her. Did Celia know where she was, she wondered. Did Dr Osbourne? But no, he had been taken away by the inspector and imprisoned because of her. Whatever would become of her now? Tears of vexation trickled down her cheeks but sleep was fast becoming irresistible and she was floating, floundering. . .

She woke next morning to the clatter of the breakfast trolley, and her head again was thick and heavy. An attendant came in, pulled back the curtains, and set a tray down beside her and was followed in by a man. He wore a dark suit and looked like a physician, and Olwen's stomach tightened; she had learned to mistrust such men.

'Miss Malkon,' he said, and she recognised him then, the man with the worried eyes. 'Don't let me disturb your breakfast.' He nodded dismissal to the attendant. 'My name is Dr Linton. How are you feeling?'

She eyed him warily. 'Well enough.'

'Did you sleep?'

'I'd little option.'

He gave a slight smile. 'No. Though I see from your notes that you've been put down as awkward, twice refusing your nightly dose.' He walked over to the window, looked out a moment and then turned back to stand there, contemplating her in a detached manner.

Had she only been here two days? It felt like an eternity. 'Am I to be drugged every night?'

'It is the policy at St Hilda's to assist patients to sleep.' She lifted the cover off her plate and saw two boiled eggs and two pieces of unbuttered toast, and replaced it. 'Food,' he remarked, 'tends to counteract the after-effect of the drugs, and will help to remove them from the system. I advise you to eat.'

'Why am I here?' she asked, making no move to do so.

'Your family is concerned about you, and want us to assess you for treatment. We will do so this morning.'

'Are you now my physician?'

'Dr Nicholson is in charge of your case. I am his assistant.' He gestured to the tray again. She removed the cover and picked up her spoon. Could she trust this man, she wondered.

'I should like to contact a friend of mine,' she said.

'That's something to discuss with Dr Nicholson.'

'So that she can come and take me away from here.'

'I'm not sure that will be possible.'

'Am I a prisoner then?'

He made a deprecating sound. 'Dear me, no. A patient, yes, but not a prisoner. We want to help you, and address your family's concerns, and keep you safe.'

She cracked open one of the eggs. It was boiled to bullet hardness but she filled her spoon and raised it to her mouth. 'If I'm not a prisoner, then I should like to leave. I'll be perfectly safe and happy with my friend. I never want to see my family again.'

He raised his eyebrows. 'I imagine they'd be sorry to hear you say this.'

'They drugged me to get me here, and now you drug me to make me stay. And yet you say I'm not a prisoner.'

He regarded her for a moment longer and then moved away from the window and came closer to the bed, speaking in a low voice. 'When Dr Nicholson carries out his assessment, you'd do well not to express your resentment in such terms; I say this as one who has your interests at heart.' She paused, the spoon half raised, and looked back at him. 'The best chance you have of leaving here is to come across as calm and rational. I'll be at your assessment myself but only to make notes, although you can be certain of my engagement with your situation, and it will make things easier if I can report you as being cooperative.' With that he abruptly left the room.

She stared after him. An ally? Or had he some purpose of his own? But the thought that here was someone who might listen to her lightened her spirits and she ate the remaining food quickly. The attendant returned, her tray was removed and she was told to wash and dress and be ready to go downstairs.

She dressed with care, taking time to ensure that her hair was neat and tidy, bearing in mind what he had said, and followed the attendant down the stairs, noting the layout of the building as she went. They descended two staircases, which meant her room must be on the second floor. It was at the front, overlooking the road; she had stood at the window earlier and watched people and vehicles going up and down the street, carters making deliveries, carriages and cabs coming and going, and attendants wearing large dark blue capes over their uniforms walking up the drive to start the day.

They crossed the hall where she remembered waiting with Celia and Dr Osbourne that day and she glanced towards the front door where an attendant stood, greeting, and no doubt monitoring, who came and went. Off the hall, down one of the corridors, she was taken into a large room mostly taken up by a highly polished table with chairs arranged around it. Wickerwork furniture had been placed in the bow of the window, overlooking the garden, and the attendant gestured to it and she sat, grasping the opportunity to further study her surroundings. They were at the back of the building and she saw that the grounds were bounded by a high brick wall through which she could see no opening.

If an escape was to be attempted, it must be through the front.

A slightly stooped, grey-haired man entered the room and bid her good morning. He was followed by the burly female attendant and Dr Linton, who did not meet her eyes. 'Come and join us at the table here, if you will.' She sat where he indicated and the three of them settled themselves opposite her, the grey-haired man taking the middle seat. The attendant retired to sit beside the door.

Another interrogation, she thought.

'I am Dr Nicholson,' the man continued, 'and this is Dr Linton my assistant, who will keep a record of our conversation today. Mrs Whitely, you've already met; she and her staff will be attending you on a daily basis.' He gave a smile devoid of warmth. 'Now, tell me, Miss Malkon, how have you settled in?'

'Very comfortably, thank you.'

He was watching her carefully. 'You were, I recall, a little distressed upon arrival here.'

'I hardly remember, I'd been given a drug that made me rather frightened and confused.'

The man looked down at some notes he had brought with him. 'Your physician, Dr Kemp, has given us a report outlining your difficulties, and the rather alarming events of recent days. All most unfortunate. . .' He studied the notes again. 'He and your family are concerned for you, Miss Malkon, and have placed you in our care so that we can ascertain how best to treat your condition.'

'I see,' she said, and if he expected more then he would be disappointed. She was conscious of Dr Linton writing assiduously beside him.

'Tell me a little about yourself, so that we might get to know you better.'

She hesitated. They must surely know about her father and her brothers' deaths, and if Dr Kemp had given a report, then they would have her family's account of the recent weeks. There seemed little point in describing any of this to them, and there was an air of aloof complacency about Dr Nicholson that did not encourage her to confide.

'Grief, I believe, is at the root of my upset, following the loss of my brothers and my father,' she replied, and he nodded. 'That and the distress of having to leave my home and my friends. I discovered recently that my aunt has, for her own reasons, been dosing me with laudanum, so I've been having vivid hallucinations that left me in a state of confusion.' Dr Nicholson frowned a little and peered over his glasses at her. 'Delusion and distress are frequently associated with the use of laudanum, are they not, Dr Nicholson?'

He had not expected to be questioned himself. 'In some cases, yes—'

'And its effect can be unpredictable, especially for those not accustomed to taking it?'

'That too is true —'

'Whatever was injected into me to get me here was, I believe, something different as the confusion and fear I experienced was much more alarming.'

His frown had deepened as she spoke and so she fell silent, noting, however, that Dr Linton was writing rapidly. She saw Dr Nicholson glance irritably in his direction.

He changed tack. 'I understand from Mrs Whitely that you have, on two occasions, refused to take your nightly dose of medication. Why is that, Miss Malkon?'

'I normally sleep well and I dislike having medication forced upon me. I believe my mind would be clearer without drugs. And you would then be better able to assess my condition, don't you think?'

She softened this little homily with a smile, but it annoyed him nonetheless. 'You may safely leave the matter of medication to us, Miss Malkon. You became violent, you know, on the day you arrived, and struck out at Mrs Whitely.'

'Did I? I expect that it was the medication at fault, and the fact I was brought here without my consent.' Dr Linton looked up and gave a tiny shake of his head and she switched her gaze to Mrs Whitely. 'I hope I didn't hurt you.'

The woman, stony-faced, said nothing and Dr Nicholson looked nonplussed. He tried another angle. 'You had been violent in the vicarage too, I read, smashing valuable china and making wild accusations.'

'How distressing that must have been for them. I wonder how much of the opiates I had been given that day.' She saw Dr Linton's lips twitch but Dr Nicholson's expression grew more severe.

'You experienced acute distress in your uncle's church, I'm told, and are frightened to go there. Can you tell us why that was?'

That was easy. 'I had another unfortunate reaction to a heavy dose of laudanum while in the church, causing embarrassment to my aunt and uncle.' She felt her confidence growing. 'Drugging me seems to result in rather extreme behaviour and I imagine I'd be better off without it.' The man consulted his notes again, perhaps to buy himself a little time, and she decided to drive her point home. 'Dr Kemp has only been my physician for a matter of days, you see. Previously I was attended by Dr Osbourne who understood me rather better.'

Dr Nicholson chose to ignore her. 'Would you feel uneasy about entering our little chapel here?'

How long would this ridiculous interview continue? 'Not at all. I should like to see it.'

He digested that. 'You have, on a number of occasions, spoken as if you believe yourself to be quite another person.' He consulted his notes again. 'The daughter of a king, no less, held under constraint.'

She raised her chin and gave another little smile. 'The stronger the drug, then the more lurid the delusions, I imagine. Dr Osbourne had warned me of the dangers associated with laudanum and was quite unaware that I was being given it. When he discovered what had been happening, he strongly urged my aunt and uncle to desist. Dr Brandt too was clear in his condemnation, believing my hallucinations to result from its use. I imagine that—'

'We need not consider the views of either Dr Osbourne or Dr Brandt as both have behaved in a way that has invited censure. Dr Brandt's association with this institution was regrettable, and Dr Osbourne, I understand, has been arrested.'

'Which is outrageous,' she cried out, unable to restrain herself. 'He is the only one who has ever listened to me!' Dr Linton looked up again and frowned, but anger was building in her. 'There is no reason for me to be here, I have friends who care for me, and I should like to leave and go to them.'

Dr Nicholson also frowned. 'Calm yourself, Miss Malkon.' He glanced again at his notes. 'We are here to help you and to keep you safe. I see that you refer very frequently to your brothers, whose loss is, of course, a tragedy, but you speak of them as if they are alive, and in danger.' At the mention of her brothers, a tremor went through her, an internal rumble like distant thunder and she clenched her hands below the table, clamping her mouth shut. Better to say nothing. 'This is, I believe, a key aspect of your current difficulties and something we can, over time, help you to come to terms with. Your grief is understandable, but they died some months ago, and your preoccupation with that sad event is troubling, and doubtless distressing for the rest of your family. You dwell upon it, I am told.'

The faces in front of her began to blur and something that had been lurking in the back of her mind bloomed suddenly like a black smoke. She leaned forward, her eyes glittering at the man. 'Yes, I dwell upon it, Dr Nicholson. I think of it a very great deal, I dream of it too, and lately I have come to wonder how it was that it happened.' She took a deep breath and spoke in a tight, strained voice. 'There was ice on the lake that day, and no wind. They were handy with the boat, my brothers were, so how came they to drown?'

CHAPTER 40

John and Percy returned to the Percys' cottage.

'Their father – old Mr Malkon – how quickly did he fail?' John asked. Mrs Percy had sunk onto a chair when they had told her about the damaged plank, and she sat, gripping the edge of the table, her mouth working. 'After the boys' death, I mean?'

She looked up at him. 'Why do you ask that, Doctor?'

'Describe his illness to me, if you will,' he said, as gently as he could. 'His decline. Did he eat, did he drink?' The Percys exchanged looks. 'Had he pain, physical symptoms?' John pulled out a chair and sat opposite the housekeeper, his eyes fixed on her, his stomach churning. 'Tell me anything you can remember, any detail.'

'He'd been ailing for months, Doctor, and was never a well man.' It was Percy who answered; he stood behind his wife, a hand on her shoulder.

'Or so he'd have us think,' she muttered.

'He'd poor digestion, pains in his stomach, cramps and the like. . . but that's nothing uncommon for an old gentleman.'

'Anything else?'

He shook his head, still pondering. 'He. . . he sometimes spoke of numbness in his fingers and his legs, but it was a cold winter.'

'He were always sat swathed in rugs and a fire burning.'

Did they see, perhaps, where his mind was going? He sensed some resistance, some denial. 'Was he taking anything, any medicines?'

'Oh aye, Dr Thomas was a regular here. He favoured purging the system so gave Master summat to mek him vomit, aye and it loosened his bowels and all. Never saw the sense it in it, myself, just seemed to weaken him.' On the other hand, John thought, grimly, it might have considerably extended the man's life. 'Forever dosing himself he was, then his appetite started to go, and he began sleeping badly, tossing and turning through the night, and then he'd drowse all day by the fire.'

'And his complexion, what did he look like?'

'His *complexion*?' Mrs Percy sat back and stared at him.

Mr Percy considered his answer. 'Well, he had been looking well. There was good colour in his cheeks but as the winter went on he turned sallow. Unhealthy like. But, we all do, I reckon, if we stay indoors.'

John looked down at the table, tracing scars in the wood with his forefinger. Where he was going was into dangerous territory, he was upsetting these good folk, and might be getting ahead of himself. 'I wonder what it was he was taking. Do you know?' Heads were shaken. 'His room's been cleared out, I assume, the medicine bottles all thrown away?'

'I couldn't bring myself to do it for weeks after the funeral,' Mrs Percy said. 'I just stripped the bed and left the room, but it's done now. His clothes are gone, his drawers turned out, the room closed up.'

Damn. 'And the medicine bottles, where did they go?'

'Onto the dump, wi' the rest of the rubbish.'

So it might not be too late. 'And after the boys' death, he declined quickly, you say?'

'Seemed to shrink in on himself, dried up like a wizened old apple. He hardly ate and the flesh seemed to drop off him, his hair thinned, like he was ageing twice as fast as what was natural in a man. Dr Thomas could do nowt for him and he kept to his bed, said he'd no interest left in the world.'

And Olwen, John thought bitterly, when her need for comfort must have been as great as his, would have sensed how little she was valued. He took a breath and steeled himself to ask the question that would make it very clear where his thoughts were leading him. 'But his brother's family visited frequently?'

Mrs Percy shook her head. 'Not the vicar, he'd his duties in the parish and the two of them were never close, and *she* never came for which we gave thanks, but they sent their sons. Very dutiful they were.' A sour note had crept into her voice. 'They'd come and read to him, Mr Edmond would play draughts and the like, and Mr Alfred would go seeking Miss Olwen—'

'But towards the end, having company seemed to tire him,' Percy interjected, 'and he'd be bad for days afterwards.'

Oh God. It was all painting a picture. . . 'But they still kept coming?'

Mrs Percy's eyes had never left his face. 'Oh aye. Miss Celia tried to hint them away but Mr Alfred was brusque with her, told her it wasn't her place to tell him what to do. Clear as day what he was up to, and poor Miss Olwen in such a state over the boys, and what with her father pressing her, she wouldn't have known how to keep on refusing him if it hadn't been for Miss Celia.'

But even Celia, John thought as he sat back absorbing it all, could not have suspected what was happening, that this might have been part of a plan that had been long in hatching. He needed to talk to her. 'Show me this dump of bottles,' he said.

Afterwards John went back to the keeper's cottage, built up the fire and slumped down in front of it. He had suggested that Percy tried to find Reagan to see if they could learn a little more and then returned to the cottage in case Reagan turned up there. Once or twice he thought he heard a sound and went to the door, calling Reagan's name into the silent forest, but there had been no response. He built up the fire several more times and, as evening fell, announced to the indifferent trees that there was hot food in the pot and a jug of ale. But Reagan, if he was out there, was not tempted in. Percy came by as evening fell but reported failure. The man, who knew the forest better than anyone, had either left it or chosen not to be found.

Eventually John gave up, covered the fire and climbed the ladder to the loft, and he lay there, an ear half-cocked, his mind churning over what he had learned. Before he returned to the cottage Percy had taken him to where the bottles from his late master's room had been dumped together with other household rubbish. The distinctive green and cobalt glass of medicine and household poison bottles had been easy to spot but he had stopped Percy from pulling them out. 'If the police become involved with this,' he had said, 'better that they excavate them themselves.' And he had told the bewildered servant to keep his master's hairbrushes safe, and not to clean them.

He badly needed to speak to Celia, to see what she remembered and present his suspicions to the scrutiny of her good sense. Convincing the authorities would be another matter entirely.

That night the dreams came swiftly upon him, fragmented and confused like Reagan's strange recital, and his subconscious seemed to flit between two worlds. One moment he was running desperately towards the lake, shouting and waving his arms, trying to drive away a black heron that was lurking in the reed bed, watching it lift on lazy wings and fly off into the night, while out on the lake a small rowing boat rocked alarmingly then sank through thin ice, the boys' pitiful cries reaching him across the water. This scene faded into another scene, one that had not come to him before, and he was with the other boys again, and their sister, and they were outside a gate into a walled enclosure within the city, announcing themselves to a tonsured man who stared at them in astonishment.

And the story came vividly into focus.

They had ridden hard, down from the north, escorted by five armed men, uneasy for every mile. A larger company would have been safer, but this way they had travelled fast and largely unnoticed, and reached the outskirts of Eoforwic without incident. Wyn rode silently beside him, her anxiety a visceral thing between them. Despite Modig's orders Heri had used every argument he had to persuade her to stay safe in the hills, but he had failed.

'If my brothers are returning then so must I.' She had raised her chin defiantly and nothing he could say altered her position.

'We seek audience with Eanbald,' he told the gatekeeper.

At Wyn's insistence they had gone directly to the archbishop's quarters, not the royal residence. 'I don't trust Osred, and neither, I think, do you?' she had said, looking up at him. 'They must be given into Eanbald's safe keeping.' But even so Osred would know that they had come. His men had accosted them on the road some five miles outside the gates and demanded to know their business, and then escorted them into the former fortress.

The gatekeeper scurried off, leaving them outside the enclosure, and Heri watched the boys' faces as they looked around them. They were tense. Ælf was oddly quiet, his brother excited, unable to stand still, and their eyes were darting about, alive with memories. For himself, he had a growing sense of dread, already regretting their coming, it was too great a gamble, too much was at stake.

But it was now too late to turn back.

The gatekeeper returned. 'You are welcome,' he said, keeping his eyes lowered. He had been instructed to offer hospitality to Heri's followers and to bring the royal orphans to Eanbald, who awaited them in St Peter's Church. Heri relayed this to his men, advising them in their own tongue to stay wary, and gestured to Bri to remain with him.

They followed the monk into the venerable building.

Eanbald was awaiting them beside a lavish altar. Heri strode forward shepherding the boys before him and his sense of unease grew; here were riches beyond belief! Above the altar hung a great lamp that held aloft three many-tiered vessels and the altar itself was covered with beaten gold and silver, studded with precious stones. Upon it stood a great silver cross, and it too encrusted with jewels; a golden flask stood beside it, together with a silver chalice, ensuring that whoever took the sacrament would be awed not only by the moment but by the might of those who could command such riches. And Heri found himself wondering which, if trouble arose, Eanbald would guard more closely: the sons of a dead king or the riches acquired during that peaceful rule.

Heri studied the benign smile on the face of the man who

stood before him and decided that expediency would weigh heavily in the balance for this man of God, and he cursed again that he had brought the boys south. They, however, looked relieved to recognise a familiar face and greeted Eanbald with bright-eyed confidence. Here was a link with a more stable past, a man their father had trusted, a man who had frequently eaten in the royal hall and sat beside the king at council.

Eanbald in turn welcomed them with open arms, holding them close to him, offering thanks to God that they were restored to the kingdom, looking over their heads to greet their sister, who bent a respectful knee. Then his appraising eye turned to Heri. 'You are Modig's grandson, I'm told.'

'Aye, my lord,'

'I do remember you,' Eanbald said, though Heri doubted him. 'And you have kept these orphans safe through these wretched times, for which all of Northumbria is grateful.' He doubted that too; there were those who would have snuffed them out like the candles on the altar. 'Although, in truth,' he added earnestly, not quite meeting Heri's eye, 'Osred would have protected them, you know, even as he now shall do.' The archbishop had survived the transition of kings and it was in his interest to remain loyal. 'He will be relieved to have them returned to us, and we will, he and I between us, school them and keep them safe until they are grown and ready to come into their father's kingdom.' The words were smoothly spoken but behind the man's smile Heri glimpsed something else, something swiftly hidden. 'Osred is as good a man as his uncle was, and a Christian king, and has been deeply concerned for their well-being.'

'But you must keep them here with *you*, my lord.' Wyn stepped forward and spoke for the first time. 'I plead sanctuary on their behalf. I will go now and tell Osred that they will remain with you, and seek his assurance for their safety. Keep them close, Eanbald, I entreat you.'

The archbishop smiled a little at her words and placed a hand on each boy's shoulder. 'Lady, there is no need for such concern. Osred and I are as one in being committed to their safety.'

Heri had continued to watch his face as he spoke and recognised then what it was he saw lurking in the prelate's eye.

It was neither ambition nor avarice.

It was fear.

John woke abruptly, and he lay there a moment trying to tease apart the threads of the dream. Where, for God's sake, did these stories come from, and why was it *those* boys he always saw, never the ones lost in the lake? He grew cold and rose, dressing quickly, and descended to find the pot of food he had left in the hearth untouched and congealed, evidence that Reagan had not paid a stealthy visit in the night.

He set about clearing ash from the hearth, determined to have it done before Percy arrived as he had another task for the man today. He had brought back writing materials from their cottage yesterday and last night had begun writing to Celia, summarising what Reagan had said and describing his suspicions. If he could finish it before Percy arrived, the man could take it to the station and catch the morning post.

But reading over what he had written, it sounded like a crazy story and so he began again; it seemed such an improbable tale that he was half-tempted to throw it in the fire but he persevered. So engrossed was he in the task that he had failed to notice that Percy had not arrived with breakfast as promised and, glancing out of the window, he saw that the sun had risen above the tops of the trees, filling the copse with light, and he felt a stirring of unease. Why had he not come, he was usually so prompt. . . John's stomach was growling with hunger and he was just deciding that he would set off, bringing his letter with him, and meet him halfway when he heard a tap at the door. 'It's open, come in,' he called, and bent to the fire to soften the stick of wax.

The door swung open.

'Aha. The outlaw in his lair.' He swung round in disbelief to confront the wry countenance of Inspector Redman. 'Are you alone, Dr Osbourne, or is there a band of merry men ready to pounce?'

He straightened slowly. 'You'd better hope not.'

Redman stepped inside and looked around, raising his eyes at once to the sleeping loft. 'I'll take the risk, although your accomplices have already assured me that you're alone.' He mounted the lower rungs of the ladder, satisfied himself that this was so, and descended again, raising a quizzical eyebrow. 'Oh, they withstood interrogation very well and denied any knowledge of your whereabouts until I produced Miss Goodfellow's letter.' Redman was carrying a small food pail, which he set on the table. 'I'm sent with breakfast, Dr Osbourne, so eat up, you've a journey to make and there's a carriage waiting.' John glanced at the door and Redman smiled a little. 'If you're considering throwing hot porridge in my face and making a run for it, I counsel against it. Unwise and unnecessary, I assure you, as was your earlier flight from justice. Sit, man, and eat.'

'Why are you here?'

Redman dragged the chair with the broken seat close to the fire and sat. 'Eat, I said!' Warily John pulled the pail towards him. 'Your disappearance was irritating but, as my note made clear, I have further questions to put to you.' He leaned forward, warming his hands on the fire, and glanced back at John. 'I'd no plans to re-arrest you.'

John grunted and began to eat. 'Must be important questions, for you to trouble to find me.'

'Very little trouble, actually. I simply asked Miss Goodfellow where you were, explained the circumstances and she told me. Hurry if you will, I'm keen to get back. Mr Percy said to leave your belongings, he'll send them on.'

John ate, watching him, thinking rapidly and wondering what could have prompted Celia to reveal his whereabouts. Had something else happened. . .? His eye fell on the letter he had written that lay, unsealed, on the table and, on a sudden impulse, he pushed it towards Redman. 'Read that, then, while I eat.'

Redman gave him a narrow look and picked up the letter. John watched his face as he read; his expression did not change but once or twice he raised his eyes to John, as if weighing up whether his quarry had departed from his senses. When he had finished, he lowered it. 'You make serious allegations, Doctor,' he said, 'with precious little evidence to support them.'

John continued to eat. 'I know. But I can show you the boat before we return and the bottles from old Mr Malkon's room are in a heap behind the stables. I've not touched them and instructed Percy to make sure they aren't covered with further rubbish until you've seen them.'

The inspector's face was unreadable. 'What do you expect to find in them?'

'Poison. Traces of arsenic, I imagine.' Redman's expression remained unchanged. 'Everything Percy told me about his master's decline is consistent with a slow arsenic poisoning. I've asked him to make sure his hairbrushes are not touched as hair begins to take up arsenic as soon as it is administered and it's my belief it'll show that old Mr Malkon was being poisoned for weeks if not months, long before the boys' drowning.'

Redman continued to contemplate him and John could see that sharp mind considering what he had been told. 'Who is this Reagan you speak of?' he asked.

John scraped the last of the porridge from the pail. A weak link in the chain, damn him. 'A man who lives in these woods.'

'A gamekeeper?'

'Self-styled, according to Percy.'

'And where is this self-styled keeper now?'

'I don't know. But I believe he saw something. That screwdriver—' The inspector waved a dismissive hand but John pushed the empty pail aside and leaned across the table, demanding the man's attention. 'It all hangs together, Inspector; once you've seen the boat, you'll see what I mean. Deep down I think Miss Malkon has her own suspicions and it is this, at least in part, that has so upset her mind. She senses something wrong, hence her preoccupation with her brothers' death, and her fear of her cousin. I lay awake last night, thinking I was going crazy, but I believe that there's a connection. Alfred Malkon gambles recklessly, Celia Goodfellow told me so, and he might have decided to take one huge risk, clear his debts and secure his future. His uncle was ill already, or considered himself to be, and if the boys' death could be made to look like an accident, he had only to pressure the old man, marry his cousin and all—'

'Put your coat on, Dr Osbourne.'

John sat back, then rose and lifted it off the peg on the back of the door, biting back his exasperation; he must keep the man's attention. 'If I'm proved wrong, then you can arrest me again for wasting your time, or for defamation of character, or stick me in St Hilda's House along with Miss Malkon—' He stopped dead; Redman was looking at him oddly.

The inspector had got to his feet. 'I'm inclined to do the latter, Dr Osbourne, except that Miss Malkon is no longer at St Hilda's.'

Circumstances. . . he had spoken of circumstances. John's arm was half in his sleeve and his guts turned to water. 'Where is she?'

'I expected to find that she was with you. That was why I came.'

Following Olwen's assessment she had been escorted to an airy workroom and offered a range of activities. 'We must find you an occupation, Miss Malkon,' Dr Nicholson had said in a falsely bright voice as he brought matters to a close. 'Occupation is calming for an unquiet mind.' Occupation apparently included work in the kitchens but these tasks, she understood, were offered to the lower-class patients while those housed on the upper floor were deserving of more refined amusements.

She would, in fact, have much preferred being in the kitchens where she could have established the position of back and side entrances, but perhaps one as reputedly violent as herself needed to be kept away from knives and things that could be thrown.

'Having something on which the mind can focus is wonderfully beneficial.' A bright-eyed woman, who introduced herself as Miss Green, echoed her superior's words. She, it transpired, presided over the workroom. 'Now you look to me like a needlewoman.'

'I'm not.'

'An artist, then, do you paint?' The smile seemed pinned to her face.

'When I choose to.'

'Splendid. Then let's find you a smock to keep that lovely dress clean. We have easels, paints and boards over there and paper in those drawers. Set yourself up in the window if you'd like to, dear, the wisteria would be a lovely subject, don't you think? Such a colour! Is it blue or purple, would you say? I can never decide.'

Olwen considered remarking that she did *not* choose to paint just now, but remembering Dr Linton's advice to appear co-operative, she dragged an easel over to the window, and resigned herself to an afternoon of floral painting, unsettled by the vacant stares of the other patients. Poor souls, how long had they been here?

As she was leaving the assessment room, Dr Linton had held the door open for her. She had risked a glance up at him and taken his fleeting smile as reassurance, and was already regretting her outburst. It had not been clever to have said those things, she decided as she held the paintbrush still for a moment, but whenever she thought of her brothers the world seemed to tilt and slide away from her. The recognition, the realisation of the fact that they should have been safe on the lake that day had been growing in her mind but this had been the first time she had articulated the thought. And she had chosen the wrong recipient.

Her mind continued to dwell on that day as she painted. The lake had been a favourite place for Olly and Will and they would spend hours there, catching tadpoles and minnows from its banks in the spring, fishing from the boat in the summer, their tutor cunningly combining learning with pleasure. He had been heart-broken by their deaths and her eyes glazed mistily as images, long banished, flooded her mind, seeing them playing cricket on the south lawn until, driven to despair by their noise, her father sent out orders that they desist. And then they would run off to the woods, Mr Philips in hot pursuit, determined to engage their attention in worthwhile activities, but sometimes they would elude him, going in search of Reagan instead, and would return as the light fell, bright-eyed and filthy, unrepentant and exhausted, to fall onto their pillows and sleep with all the innocent beauty of half-fledged Apollos. A pain swelled in her heart as she allowed them back into the place from where she had banished them. And then, insistent that they too be remembered, she glimpsed, behind their faces, those other boys. . .

She dashed a sleeve across her eyes and forced herself to concentrate on the delicate curl of a petal; grieving must wait until she was out of here, until her mind was clear and at peace.

The wisteria would be in flower at Swindale now, great swathes of blossom festooning the front of the house, hanging down like bunches of grapes, and the sparrows would be building their nests in the tangle of last year's growth, hidden from sight. It was tempting, she thought, to paint the blossom in tiger stripes to provoke the tediously cheerful Miss Green, but it would hardly help her cause, so she dabbed a conformist lavender on the paper, unaware that Dr Linton had come up behind her.

'You are an artist, Miss Malkon,' he remarked, and she turned her head.

Miss Green bustled straight across to join him. 'Indeed she is, Doctor, and she's been sitting there as good as gold since she came in, so quiet and composed, taking such pleasure in her work.' Not nearly so great a pleasure as tipping a paint pot over the woman would be, she mused, and caught an appreciative glint in Dr Linton's eye.

'A very competent performance altogether, I would say, Miss Malkon, even though you let yourself down in one or two places.' He pointed vaguely to the blossom she had just completed.

'No, no!' Miss Green protested hotly. 'Really, I cannot agree, Doctor. I think Miss Malkon's painting is altogether fine.' She dropped her voice as if, absurdly, Olwen would not hear. 'We encourage, Doctor, we always encourage,' and Olwen bit her lip to prevent a smile.

One of the other patients seated at the central table chose that moment to raise his voice in frustration, thumping the table with his fists, which caused the model his neighbour was building to collapse in pieces. There was an immediate furore.

'I believe Mr Tucker would benefit from a little encouragement at this very moment, Miss Green,' Dr Linton remarked and, as the woman hurried away, he turned back to Olwen, dropping his voice. 'You did well, for the most part, Miss Malkon. And take your medication this evening without protest.'

'Must I?'

'Of course, everyone must.' He looked round to check that Miss Green was fully occupied. 'You'd be astonished the lengths to which patients will go to avoid it. Spitting it out only results in another dose being given, but the more guileful place small pieces of wadding or absorbent scraps in their cheeks or under their tongue to soak it up and thereby reduce the dose consumed. A handkerchief dabbed to the lips can absorb a little more if deftly done.' He checked again with a quick glance. 'Self-induced vomiting is noisy, and can be painful.' Miss Green, she observed, was returning, and Dr Linton gave her a nod and raised his voice. 'I'll leave you to your painting, Miss Malkon, as I have reports to transcribe. I wish you a good day and a restful night.' She watched him go with her spirits lifting. Definitely an ally.

As the afternoon wore on Miss Green's watchfulness slackened a little and Olwen continued to paint, focusing with grim resolve upon the brickwork of the wall; painting brick by tedious brick, walling herself in like a reluctant novice resigned to her enclosed future. 'How patient you are, my dear,' Miss Green remarked, as she came to stand beside her. 'This is one we must hang on the walls for visitors to see.' On one occasion Dr Nicholson appeared at the door and looked in her direction and once again she heard the words 'good as gold' from her warder, and she smiled, having, in the course of the afternoon, managed to secrete away several cleanish scraps of rag and blotting paper.

Later she was told, begrudgingly, by Mrs Whitely that if her good behaviour continued then she would be allowed to eat in the dining room downstairs and Olwen murmured her gratitude, thinking that the sooner she gained a better understanding of the layout of the building the better. Dr Linton might be making a case for her being too sane to be here but she had no intention of meekly awaiting committal.

Dr Linton's ruse was at least partially successful and perhaps because she had consumed only a small amount of the deadening medication her dreams returned that night, sharp and vivid. She found herself standing beside Heri in what had once been her father's hall, paying her respects to Northumbria's new ruler. Bri stood close behind them.

Osred stood before her and she was shocked by his appearance. He was thinner, gaunt almost, and in every way diminished. Wary too, his eyes darting quickly towards Heri and Bri, avoiding hers. He might have gained the throne but she saw that he sat uneasily upon it.

He did, however, made a pretence of welcome. 'Wyn, dear cousin! You are returned at last, but in such wretched circumstances!' His eyes were dark-rimmed and shadowed. 'We grieve your father's loss, we offer prayers for his soul and we did the same for your safety, we sent out emissaries to find you, you know, to assure ourselves that you and your brothers had survived.' He looked around in an unconvincing manner. 'But where are they?'

'The archbishop has given them sanctuary.'

He had known this, of course, but feigned surprise. 'Sanctuary? My dear cousin, they have no need of *sanctuary!* Their safety was our paramount concern and their return will be a matter of rejoicing.' Heri stood beside her and she sensed him bristling with mistrust. Perhaps Osred picked up on this too, for he turned to him. 'And you, Oshere, I must thank, although, in truth, I wonder that you thought that my royal cousins would be in danger! I remained here, in Eoforwic, and would have ensured their safety.' Heri remained silent and Osred's eyes narrowed. 'And you removed them so speedily. . . how came you to be so well-informed?'

'Little happens north of the Wall that doesn't come to Modig's ears.'

Osred smiled a little, his eyes darting away again. 'I shall remember that.' He gestured to food and drink that had been brought. 'Refresh yourselves! Your men have been made comfortable, I hope, and can rest a little before you return north?'

'I thank you, sire.'

Sire. Aye, Wyn thought bitterly, Osred was king now, and would be keen to see the back of these unpredictable northern men. 'Why has my father's body not been brought to Eoforwic for burial?' she demanded. They had stopped briefly in Hexham on their journey south and she had wept beside Ælfwald's grave. 'Why does he not lie in St Peter's Church with Northumbria's kings?'

'He is venerated in Hexham, Ælwyn. His body was brought there by a great company of monks and clergy,' he laid a hand on her arm 'and he was buried with all honour in St Andrew's Church.'

She resisted the urge to shake it off. 'But not here, in Eoforwic, to lie in St Peter's Church, beside his ancestors.'

Osred was over-hasty to reassure. 'Already it has become a place of pilgrimage! Since his death a light has often appeared in the skies above the spot where he died.' She felt Heri stiffen beside her. A portent he had called it, that night they had stood beneath the stars. 'The monks took it as a sign that that was where he must lie.' Looking into Osred's shifty eyes, she remembered why she had so little love for her cousin. He had wed since she had been in the north and so she no longer feared his advances, but she must be careful what she said if she wanted him to entertain Heri's suit.

Even so her father must be commemorated. 'And how will *you* honour him, Osred?'

He took up a cup and drank. 'I have commanded that a church be built on the place where he was killed, where prayers will daily be said.' A poor liar, she thought, he had always been so. But now that the promise had been made, she would see that it was carried out. 'And I will honour him by caring for his sons as if they were my own. You too, I shall provide for – ' she sensed Heri stiffening again beside her ' – for now we must look to the future.'

The future. . . That thought lingered as Olwen woke, flooded by a sick uncertainty about what would happen now, and she lay for a moment suppressing a sense of deep foreboding. *Her* future, unless she could retake control of it, would be determined by others.

For who would help her now?

After breakfast it transpired that she was expected to return to the activity room, where she was greeted enthusiastically by Miss Green. 'Your painting has been much admired, Miss Malkon. Will you finish it or start another, do you think? A still life perhaps? We might borrow some fruit from the kitchen?'

'I'll go down and ask for some,' she offered, getting to her feet.

A firm hand pressed her back down. 'No, no. I'll ring and it'll be brought.'

But that would not achieve her end. 'Perhaps I will paint out of doors instead, in the fresh air.' If there was an opening anywhere along the brick wall the only way to discover it was to explore the gardens.

But Miss Green shook her head. 'Not today, dear. Dr Nicholson says that if the good behaviour keeps up, then one of the attendants will go out for a walk with you tomorrow, which will be a lovely treat, won't it? Everyone is terribly pleased with you and good behaviour is rewarded here, just as poor conduct is corrected.'

Much more time spent in this woman's company would have her behaving very badly indeed, Olwen thought as she set her painting back on the easel and picked up her brush. Brick after brick, she painted on through the morning. Since the world was behaving so strangely, perhaps could she paint in a door through the wall and it would become real. She could leave it open a tiny crack, awaiting only a push to freedom. . . Vaguely she became aware that a junior attendant had come into the room and was speaking to Miss Green.

Next moment the woman bustled across to her. 'You've a visitor, my dear. How lovely!' A visitor? 'Take off your smock and tidy your hair, we always look our best for visitors.' Celia! Olwen stood and tore at the strings of the smock. Oh, please God, let it be Celia. Miss Green beamed at her. 'How excited you are, my dear! But go calmly, now, *calmly*. Walk, never run. And please be aware that all visits are supervised; an attendant will remain in the room at all times—' Olwen brushed her aside; as if the presence of another would stop her speaking her mind ' – and conduct is recorded.'

She was taken across the hall and down the corridor to a room at the end of it. The attendant paused outside the door, glancing both ways, and then leaned close and spoke to Olwen in a low, hurried voice. 'I'm supposed to stay with you, but what if I were to wait in the hall, and leave you alone for a little while? Would you like that? A moment or two can't hurt and I know *I'd* want to be alone.' The girl gave a conspiratorial giggle and Olwen nodded and promised she would say nothing.

The girl opened the door, ushered Olwen in, and shut it quickly behind her.

The room was empty—

Then Alfred Malkon stepped out from behind the door and had his foot against it before she could think, and had closed a hand over her mouth. 'Don't squawk,' he said. She bit him hard and he swore, but held on. 'I'm here to help, damn you! If I let go will you behave?'

She hesitated, considered, then nodded and he removed his hand. Instantly she sprang away, getting a chair between them. 'Get out.'

'Hear me first, you fool.'

She was breathing fast, panicked at the sight of him. A quick glance showed her a bell pull beside the fireplace. 'Why have you come?' She could reach it before he could strike.

But he remained where he was with his back to the door, leaning against it, inspecting his palm where, she was pleased to see, she had drawn blood. 'To see how you were, of course, m'dear,' he drawled, 'and to keep you informed. Things move on, you see and, being incarcerated in here, you've no way of knowing.' He shot her a wry glance. 'You needn't look at me like that, I shan't touch you, you know. But I thought you should know that your precious Celia and her flirt are about to be arrested. Dudley threatened the bishop, it seems, accusing him of gross behaviour, but he's called her bluff. Blatant blackmail. Unwisely she wrote a letter, which he's taken to the police. Osbourne's implicated, of course, and will be brought back in.'

She stared at him. 'He's been released?'

A look of surprise, followed by one of annoyance, crossed his face. He thought she knew! 'Not for long.'

'Where is he?'

Alfred gave a half smile. 'No idea. Pa's evicted him from his house so he's nowhere to go. Could get fourteen years inside, though, once he's found.'

She swallowed hard, desperate to conceal how much his words shocked her. 'Why are you telling me this?'

His eyes gleamed. 'To make your position clear, coz. Help you decide on your best course of action.' He levered himself off the door and took a step towards her. 'With your associates all in trouble with the law on account of you, I'm the only friend you've got left.'

'You were never my friend, Alfred.' She gripped the back of the chair. 'You'd have raped me that day.'

'What a dreadful thing to say!' He took another step. 'And what utter nonsense. You're delusional, of course, I forgot, and besides, my dear, we're as good as betrothed! Why would I attempt something as energetic as rape when you're about to become my wife? Osbourne, on the other hand, I saw him mauling you myself, as did others.'

'That's a lie!'

He smiled, shaking his head. 'No, my dear, you're forgetting. Right at the start, I saw him, in the churchyard, off in that shady corner, and you can't deny he had you in his arms. Thought it odd at the time. Taking advantage of your affliction, he was, and he'd his hand up your skirt when you were unconscious that time, outside the greenhouse. Ma'll attest to that.' Another step. 'Abused his position, he did, and he lured you into his garden that time too. Are you forgetting? He laid his hands on you there too, Susan told me, she saw him do it. All those little endearments between you, little pet names, we all heard them. He had you under some sort of spell, Pa says.' As he spoke, he kept moving slowly forward, forcing her to step back, away from the bell pull. 'Quite a story for the court, even without the drama of the kidnap. He'll not do well in the dock, I fear.'

It was all she could do not to rake her nails across that smug face. 'And yet you tell me he's been released.'

The smile broadened. 'Ah, but when I show Redman those little bookmarks of yours, I think you'll find they bring him in again. Pretty damning stuff.' She stared at him. Bookmarks? Oh God, *the letters*, she had left them in her book! Celia's was there too. . . 'Got 'em safe, don't you worry.' He patted his breast pocket. 'So far no one else has seen them but it's clear evidence of conspiracy, wouldn't you say? Although. . .' He paused. 'I could be persuaded to destroy them, once we agree on terms.'

'Get out.' Her throat was dry.

'Take a moment to consider, Olwen. I'll go if you like, but I'll go straight to Redman.'

She felt sick. He was playing with her. 'What do you want of me?'

He opened his arms in a wide expansive gesture. 'What I've always wanted, sweetheart. The bishop thinks I'll have a stabilising effect on you and, trust me, I will. Otherwise. . .' He looked around with a wry smile. 'It's all very homely, of course, but—'

Was he mad enough to think she would even consider marrying him? 'Get out,' she said again.

'I understand from Pa that you're about to be formally admitted here. You'll be a damned sight more comfortable than your two friends, of course, as I imagine their sort have a rough time in gaol. Same goes for Osbourne.' He patted his pocket again. 'It's hardly a professional letter, is it?'

If she screamed it would cause a scene but if she could get to the bell pull. . .

'It needn't happen, you know, no further action, no further charges. It's in your hands entirely, m'dear. The bishop's all for a wedding, and Pa too – doesn't want a niece in an asylum, after all! How d'you think that looks? And I'd not be a demanding husband, you know, we can forget all about our previous little encounter, start afresh. I frightened you, that's all. . . There's a very nice little chapel here, I'm told; it need only be a small affair, and then you could go home. To Swindale, with a doting husband to guide you.'

She made a lunge to reach the bell pull but he caught her easily, pulling her to him, and kissed her roughly. She kicked at his shin, got an arm free and struck him, and had the satisfaction of seeing his nose spurt with blood. To her surprise he laughed and smeared the blood across his face. 'Perfect,' he said, holding her with one hand and reaching for the bell pull with the other.

After that, all was confusion. The attendant who had been waiting outside flung open the door and stared in horror at the scene. Mrs Whitely must have been nearby as she too appeared. Alfred had let go of Olwen as the bell rang and she had fallen to the floor, where she listened to him playing the shocked relation, telling them how she had attacked him, showing them the teeth marks on his hand. Mrs Whitely turned in fury to the attendant. 'You left them *alone?*'

'Please, don't scold her, ma'am,' Alfred said, dabbing at his bloody nose. 'I begged her to let me see Olwen alone. But I'd no idea she was so. . . so. . . that she would turn on me as she did.' Over the handkerchief his eyes glinted at Olwen and she realised, far too late, that this had been planned and that she had played straight into his hands. The girl, meanwhile, was made to turn out her pockets and, sobbing, produced a crown coin. Alfred hung his head. 'Unforgivable of me,' he said, 'I shouldn't have tempted her.' A lock of his hair fell forward with boyish charm. 'I just wanted Olwen to know that, despite everything, my feelings for her are unchanged.'

Mrs Whitely pursed her lips. 'I must ask you to leave, Mr Malkon. The matter will have to be reported.'

'Olwen, my love. . .' he began, and then left, in fine tragic manner, brushing past a figure who had appeared in the doorway.

Dr Linton came into the room.

'What has occurred here?' he asked, and reaching down he helped Olwen to her feet, his expression very grave. Mrs Whitely pointed a finger at the sobbing attendant but Dr Linton cut short her excuses: 'Dr Nicholson will deal with her while I escort Miss Malkon to her room.'

'She should be sedated, sir. She's quite wild! She bit Mr Malkon, and then struck him! Bloodied his nose, she did.' The woman, with one of her staff reprimanded, was looking to deflect attention.

'Thank you. Mrs Whitely, I am warned.'

CHAPTER 42

'He provoked me, Dr Linton. He *deliberately* provoked me,' Olwen whispered, fighting back tears of vexation as he escorted her across the hall and up the stairs. 'It was why he came, I see that now, and I played straight into his hands.' She was trembling, her legs weak.

Her escort was silent as they walked through the corridors and up the stairs and she sensed his withdrawal. 'You must believe me,' she insisted, but still he said nothing. Once they reached her room he turned to her. 'Why would he do that, Miss Malkon?'

'To demonstrate that I'm unstable. He came to give me a choice, to marry him or remain here—' she broke off. 'And he threatened to testify against my friends.'

'You bit him, and you struck him.'

'I was going for the bell pull and he grabbed me, kissed me, I was struggling and I hit him to get away. I bit him because he'd put his hand over my mouth.'

'He had his hand over your mouth *and* was kissing you? How is that possible?'

'No, no, that was before!' She was making a mess of this, and saw his confidence in her evaporating. 'When I went into the room, he was behind the door and jumped out at me. Please, you must believe—'

'Sit down, Miss Malkon, and calm yourself.' He moved over to the window, from where he contemplated her in an aloof, dispassionate manner. 'I know a little of your circumstances and I take an interest because of. . . well never mind.' He paused. 'But I've yet to be persuaded that there aren't good reasons for your being here, and such episodes do little to convince me.'

'He purposefully provoked me!' she wailed. 'To show me the weakness of my position.'

'It is not the act of a stable person to reply with violence.'

'But he *wanted* me to strike him—'

'Miss Malkon, you must surely see—' He was cut short as the door opened and Dr Nicholson strode in, followed by Mrs Whitely.

'Linton!' His eyes swept over Olwen and rested with a frown on his colleague. 'What have you given her?'

'It has not been necessary—'

The medical superintendent regarded Olwen as if she was a fairground creature that had performed badly, turning on its keeper and letting the ringmaster down. 'Attacking visitors is outrageous behaviour, to be avoided at all costs. Word gets out, you know, does us no good at all.' Was he addressing her, or his colleague?

'He deliberately provoked me,' Olwen repeated, but had little hope of being listened to.

'I'm told that you and Mr Malkon have an understanding, and yet—'

'No! We have *not*.' She clutched at the bedpost, feeling a sense of helplessness as her world began to fall out of kilter.

'Be that as it may, showing violence demonstrates a moral failing and is consistent with—'

'But can't you see! I *hate* him! He's driven only by his own ambitions.' The figures before her were no longer distinct and she redoubled her efforts to make them understand. 'He plotted vengeance while he was in exile and now. . . now he has returned and Osred would do well to be wary of such an ally.' They were staring at her and she reached out, grasping the sleeve of the man who had been kind. 'And, don't you see, if he is to achieve his goal, my brothers' lives are forfeit—'

'Mrs Whitely,' the other man said, 'the syringe, I think.'

'Please, *please*, send for Heri,' she clung onto him, desperate to be heard, 'or let me go to him.'

'Now, Mrs Whitely. If you will.'

★

Sometime later, she had no idea how long, she heard voices through the web of chaos in her head.

'. . . still out, I see. . .' The words came from a great distance and she kept her eyes closed, lying perfectly still. '. . . no trouble for a while yet. . . restraint later, perhaps. . . excitable. . .' The voices faded, moving away '. . . management, as I said, rather than treatment. . .' She opened her eyes a slit. The curtains at the window were drawn but she could see light in the gap between them. Restraint? Would they now chain her to keep her here? She closed her eyes again and slid helplessly back into a troubled sleep, rousing occasionally to see faces peering down at her, goggle-eyed and leering. Once it was Mrs Whitely, another time she thought it was Alfred, that little smile playing on his thin lips, and once it was Celia, who reached a hand out to her then pulled it away '. . . management, rather than treatment. . .' she said in a cold voice, and Olwen tried to call her back for if Celia deserted her she was surely lost! Then, suddenly it was Heri, as clear as she had ever seen him, smiling down at her and she was overcome with relief, but then she heard Mrs Whitely's voice and he vanished. '. . . *still* out. . .' she heard her say.

But even as the woman spoke the air was split by a piercing scream and the sound of breaking glass, followed by shouts and the sound of running feet. Mrs Whitely vanished and Olwen raised herself on her elbows, listening as the commotion down the hall continued with further shouts and cries. She swung her legs off the bed, feeling dizzy, and saw that she was still dressed; only her shoes had been removed.

And then she saw something else.

The door, so assiduously locked on every occasion, had been left ajar. Her head spun. This was Heri's doing! He had left it open, intending that she should follow. . . and he would not have gone far. She stood swaying slightly, gripping onto the bedpost, flushing as her heart started pumping. Slowly she crept barefoot across the room, nudged the door open a little wider, and pressed an eye to the crack. She could still hear voices down the corridor, but there was no one in sight, and so silently, without further thought, she slipped out and across the corridor, stepping into a window recess to hide before peering out again. The corridor appeared oddly aslant as if the building had slipped on its foundation, but it remained empty. The tumult was coming from towards the main stairs so she would go the other way. . . She tiptoed along the corridor and found herself at the back stairs and stood a moment, looking giddily down three narrow flights, which were undulating in an alarming fashion.

But if she was to escape it must be now. . .

And suddenly she was floating, as light as a feather, twirling round at every half landing, soundless, her bare feet hardly touching the treads, and she arrived, exhilarated, at the bottom, panting and wanting to laugh out loud. How clever she had been! From somewhere she could hear noises, the banging of saucepans in some strange kitchen medley and she was drawn towards the sound, laughing still, and wanting to be part of the weird and joyful din. But then she heard footsteps and excitement turned to panic and she pulled open a nearby door and shot inside only to discover that it was not a room at all, but a large cupboard with blue capes hung in rows on pegs with boots beneath, and she had to suppress another fit of giggles that she should be hidden here and no one knowing. It reminded her of home when she and the boys had played hide and seek in the house.

The boys.

The thought sobered her. She must get to Osred and plead for them, or find Heri and beg him to get them away, take them back to the north where they could hide in the hills. There was no time to waste. . . She opened the door a crack and looked out. The hall was empty and from somewhere there came a cold draught. The outside world! She slipped her feet into the nearest pair of boots. They pinched a little but would do and, pulling a cape from its hook, she wrapped it around herself, and went in search of that cool breath of freedom.

No one challenged her as she pulled back the spring-lock bolt on the side door, nor was she stopped as she headed down the drive, muffled in her cape, with the hood covering her face, the too-small boots viciously rubbing her feet. An attendant arriving for duty called out a greeting but Olwen did not reply, keeping her head down as she turned into the street. Any urge to laugh had left her now but she felt invincible, exultant in her sudden liberty. She would make for the river; she could see a glint of it at the bottom of the street, and from there she would get her bearings and make her way to the royal residence and demand to see Osred. He would hardly refuse her. Or should she go to St Peter's Church and find Eanbald; the boys had been left in his keeping. But where was Heri? He could not be very far ahead of her.

An angry shout brought her up short as she crossed the track, head down, not seeing the horse until it was upon her. She heard its hooves clattering past and the rider's curse rang in her ears. She pressed on, shaken, for the day was passing and soon the light would fail and then no one would care that she was Ælfwald's daughter alone, in a stolen cloak, in the darkening streets. But who could she trust in this town of strangers? She ducked down an alley to avoid a group of roistering men coming down the street, and flattened herself, wide-eyed, against the wall until they were past. Shops were closing, shutters were being put up and she found herself moving against the flow of people coming away from the centre. The street facades were oscillating in front of her eyes, disappearing to reveal a wasteland of ruins before coming abruptly back into focus as she stepped aside to avoid a cart. Excitement curdled to be replaced by a dread fear and she suppressed a wave of panic as she pushed on towards the core of the ancient city, her feet sore in the stolen boots. One minute all was familiar and next she was lost in a kaleidoscope of gaslights and people jostling her, pushing past as they made their way home, in a strange cacophony of sound. She lost all sense of where she was as darkness began to deepen, no longer knowing how to find her father's hall. This was madness indeed! Then, looming ahead of her she saw the Minster with the pinnacles on its great square towers piercing the leaden sky, occupying the place where St Peter's Church should be, and she stood and stared up at it. She would not find Eanbald there, for this was not of Eanbald's time.

She stood, hopeless and lost, at the junction of time where two great thoroughfares met and she turned slowly in a full circle, trying desperately to think. And then suddenly two men appeared, reeking of ale. They linked arms with her, laughing and spinning her round and round and round until someone called out, and they ran off, leaving her, dizzy and swaying.

'You all right, miss?' a voice asked 'Get along home, now.'

And then another voice. 'Come away, Bill, she's as tipsy herself.' And Olwen laughed then. Tipsy. . . Aye, she was tipsy; the woman was right, her whole world was tipsy, topsy-turvy, tipsy-turvy. . .

Then she found herself weeping, sliding down the side of a building to collapse in a huddle on the cold pavement, her head in her hands. A cat streaked away into the shadows, chasing a black shape that scuttled along the wall, and she heard other voices, outraged, scandalised, cruel. 'Right in the middle of town. . . her'll get picked up.' Then a laugh. 'Nah, nah, by t'constables, I meant. . . thrupenny upright. . . decent folk. . .' And then another laugh. 'Not so upright now!' One man came and bent over her, goggle-eyed, and pulled away with a grimace: 'Blubbing. . . can't do with a blubbing tart.' And as the darkness deepened and the townsfolk headed home, fewer and fewer remarked her presence until eventually she was alone and found the strength to stand.

No longer invincible.

Slowly, keeping close to the shadows between the pools of gaslight, she made her way back down towards the river; that at least would be familiar, unchanging, and perhaps when she reached it, she would know what to do. She passed the closed-up shops, the windows above them shuttered now or with curtains drawn, others unlit and empty. Was she going round in circles? A stray dog squatted in front of her and she swerved to avoid the steaming pile, pulling the cape close. Eventually she found an alley that led down to the river with tall buildings on either side of it creating a dark tunnel. . . and she remembered another tunnel that Heri had taken them along and through her weariness she felt a spark of hope.

Of course! He had told them to wait for him at the river, she had forgotten that, they were to wait beside the boat pulled up on the riverbank, he had *told* them to wait there and promised that he would come, and that was what she must do. Stumbling down the stinking alley, past broken barrels and piles of reeking rubbish she hastened and reached the water at last, and found the tide was still out and she saw a boat on its own, lying at an angle pulled up high. Was it that one? In the darkness she could not be sure. But she would wait there, as he had told her to do, and he would come, she knew that he would. She wrapped the cloak around her and sank to her knees on the mud, then curled up under the curve of the vessel's hull, making a pillow with the hood of the cape, and closed her eyes. He would come and her brothers would be with him, all she had to do was wait. . .

CHAPTER 43

'She disappeared sometime yesterday afternoon,' Redman told John as they left the keeper's cottage. 'And naturally I suspected you.'

'Was she *taken* from St Hilda's?' John asked as he absorbed this shocking new twist.

Redman raised an ironic eyebrow. 'Who would do that, if not you? No, it appears she left of her own accord, although no one is quite sure when. It wasn't reported to us until after seven yesterday.'

John was appalled. 'After sunset!'

'Quite. They did a thorough search at St Hilda's before reporting her disappearance, then a cloak and boots were found to be missing, and they decided that she'd fled. Last seen just after four.'

They climbed into the carriage waiting on the drive and John raised a hand in reassurance to Mr Percy who had come to the door of his cottage. Whatever had they done to her to make her flee? 'Do you know what sort of state was she in?'

'Confused, I gather.' John swore and stared grimly out of the window as the carriage moved forward. 'Miss Goodfellow and Miss Dudley have heard nothing from her, but as they pointed out, she wouldn't know they were in York. She'd no money to get to Knaresborough, and they could offer no other suggestions. Can you?'

John shook his head. 'Unless she tries to make her way here.' But with no money, no food. Confused? What did that mean? Celia would have known if Olwen had contacts in the city, friends she might turn to, but perhaps she had none. And, he thought with a growing sense of alarm, if she was confused, or drugged and hallucinating, which city did her mind inhabit? Was she wandering through the York that Redman's men patrolled or the Eoforwic that Heri and Wyn knew? He frowned, trying to imagine where, in that case, she might go. To the royal residence seeking her father? Or had she turned for help to the monks at St Peter's Church, seeking succour from an archbishop who had been dead for a thousand years?

Redman was watching him. 'You've had an idea?'

He shook his head again. 'Just trying to piece things together and consider where, in a state of delusion, she might have gone.' Redman went on looking at him but it was impossible to explain. 'She has a persistent set of delusions, you see, and I'm trying to remember what she'd told me.' This explanation seemed to satisfy but, dear God, if she had been out, alone, all night. . .

'Since we've a little time before we reach York, Doctor, I will ask you my questions now.' John's mind went swiftly on the alert as he tried to recall what he had told this man, and what withheld. 'Augusta Dudley has so far managed, by a very narrow margin, to avoid being charged with blackmail.' John schooled his face to blankness, and was rewarded with a sour look. 'Don't waste my time by pretending you know nothing of this; I've seen the letter she wrote to the bishop and on that basis alone she could certainly be charged. On a whim, however, I decided to go and ask her father if her allegations regarding the bishop's behaviour were true.'

'And he denied it.'

Redman nodded. 'Emphatically. But as I was leaving his wife came after me and told me a different tale. It had happened exactly as Miss Dudley described, she said, and it was only after she insisted that both her husband and the bishop gave large contributions to a home for fallen women that she was prepared to let the matter drop. She expressed herself willing to testify to that effect, if required. Not a harmonious household, I gather.' John nodded; Gussie was her mother's child. 'Lady Dudley has little time for the bishop, it would appear, and I doubt that he will press charges once he knows her position on the matter.'

John glanced curiously at him, seeing another side to this man.

Redman sat back in the carriage and returned his look evenly. 'Believe me or not, Dr Osbourne, but I was pleased when the charges against you were dropped – and I'm irritated that the vicar and bishop are considering rekindling them.' Were they? John felt a momentary alarm. 'As I've said repeatedly, my job is to uphold the law, but I believe that you, and your accomplices, for all your maverick ways, do indeed have Miss Malkon's best interests at heart; I'm less sure about her family.'

'Is that by way of an apology?'

'No, no, not at all. The law is quite clear on the matter, and you acted illegally – although Miss Malkon herself challenged me for upholding a law that did the opposite of what it purported to do.' John smiled a little at the thought. 'But I'd like you to explain to me Professor Brandt's role in all this?'

His smile swiftly vanished; Redman had tripped him up again, just when he had begun to like the man. 'I consulted him about her case at an early stage,' he replied, 'and he came, briefly, to the vicarage to discuss treatment. As you know, when I took Miss Malkon to St Hilda's, he refused to treat her.'

'And then?' Redman urged but John stayed silent. 'We'll save time, Doctor, if I tell you that I know that you and Brandt both stayed at The Wheatsheaf in Knaresborough and that a man fitting his description accompanied you to Pear Tree Cottage on the morning of your arrest, leaving with you later that same morning. And, later still, about the time we were putting handcuffs on you, the landlord of The Wheatsheaf was handed a note for the professor urging him to remain there.'

'He read it?'

'Landlords do, you know. So let us go from there.'

'I valued Brandt's opinion; he's more experienced than I.'

'So was it he who examined Miss Malkon?'

'He did not examine her, he simply encouraged her to talk. At my request.'

Redman shook his head. 'You're a very provoking young man, and I see you'll continue to split hairs all the way to York, which we will both find tiresome. Explain, if you will, with rather more honesty than before, exactly what lies behind all this.'

And so for the remainder of the journey John described to a more receptive ear, although in a modified form, the events of the previous weeks. At the end of it Redman said nothing, digesting what he had been told. 'But I'm now strongly of the view,' John concluded, 'that it is all connected to the circumstances of the boys' death, and that of their father, and I urge you to consider seriously what I told you this morning.'

'You've not a shred of evidence.'

'What if arsenic is found in those bottles, or in his hair?'

Redman shook his head. 'Anyone could be implicated.'

'But it's worth checking, surely!'

'Perhaps.'

'The loosened screws then, the sprung plank?'

'Poor maintenance? Or if you prefer deliberate malice, there are other possible candidates.'

'But few who would stand to gain. And a man was seen going into the boathouse – '

'Was he identified?'

' – and later stood and watched the boys drown.' The thought of it chilled him anew.

'Produce your witness, Dr Osbourne.'

John sat back, frustrated but knowing in his heart that the man was right. 'Will you pursue it?' he asked, after a moment.

Redman shrugged. 'Right now, my concern is to find Miss Malkon and to that end I'd like you to come with me to St Hilda's House and hear what is said there.'

Privately run asylums such as St Hilda's were currently coming under heavy scrutiny, Redman told him on the journey back to York, and there was a move afoot to involve justices of the peace in their governance, overseeing the admission of contentious cases and providing independent oversight. John nodded; he was aware of this and a number of recent high-profile cases came to mind where women had been wrongly held in institutions as the result of collusion between family members and medical practitioners. This was, according to Brandt, one of a number of concerns being expressed by Dr Linton with regards to St Hilda's House, but he saw no reason to tell Redman of their deliberations.

Upon reaching the asylum they were taken to Dr Nicholson's office, where they found the medical superintendent very much on the defensive. 'Her assessment correctly identified an unstable and paranoid condition, and a tendency to become excitable and delusional.'

Dr Linton was there too and had given John a brief nod of recognition before taking his seat beside his superior, remarking as he did, 'She was angry at being brought here, and questioned why she was constrained to stay.' His comments were rewarded with a scowl from Nicholson. 'She has, I believe, a naturally assertive spirit.'

Redman transferred his attention to Linton. 'And was it in that spirit that she left?'

'Who knows. She would still be under the effects of the drugs she'd been given an hour or so earlier.'

'Which were what?' John asked.

Dr Linton looked pointedly at Dr Nicholson. 'A combination of sedatives,' the man replied coolly, obviously resenting John's presence. When pressed for specifics he revealed what had been a powerful cocktail.

'Dear God!' John exclaimed. 'She could hardly avoid hallucinating after that lot! Why had she been sedated?'

'She had become agitated by a visitor with whom she had been left unattended—' Linton seemed determined to speak out.

'*Agitated!*' Nicholson cut across him. 'She went berserk, biting and hitting him, her own cousin—'

John's eyebrows snapped together. 'Which cousin?'

'Mr Alfred Malkon.'

'And she was left alone with *him*! The man who had tried to rape her?'

Nicholson's face flushed. 'That allegation is apparently without substance, a paranoid delusion. The lapse in adherence to regulations was, nonetheless, unfortunate and the attendant responsible has been reprimanded.'

Linton addressed John directly. 'Her cousin, she told me, deliberately goaded her into striking him. And, as a result of the agitation caused by his appearance, combined with the lingering effects of previous medication, she tipped into what appears to be a familiar delusion that she's the daughter of a king, and that her brothers are still living.'

'Linton!' Nicholson growled but John's fist came down on the table.

'And so, agitated and deluded, she was given some *other* powerful hallucinogenic drug, left unsupervised, and allowed to escape, to wander off alone into the city?'

'Correct,' said Dr Linton.

John put his head in his hands. 'She'll be lucky if we find her alive—'

Redman rose and dropped a hand on his shoulder. 'I think we've little more to learn here, gentlemen, so we'll take our leave and continue the search. Questions of negligence will be addressed in due course.'

They were halfway down the corridor when John heard his name called. 'Dr Osbourne!' Linton had come after them. 'Your contempt is richly deserved, and enquiries into procedures here are long overdue, but I might add that in her confused state Miss Malkon was asking to be taken to Osred, and for someone to find Harry. From the little I've been told of her case, it might mean something.'

'*Linton!*' Dr Nicholson had appeared in the corridor.

'Whatever help I can give. . .'

John nodded his thanks. He and Redman left the building and climbed back into the carriage. 'And does it?' Redman asked. 'Mean something?'

John was thinking hard. If Olwen had headed for her father's hall, she would find there only stabling and the livery behind the

Exhibition Hall; and God forbid that she had fallen into the arms of stable hands after dark. And if she had sought Archbishop Eanbald's help then the great Gothic pile that was York Minster would only have perplexed her and he wondered whether, in her dishevelled state, she would have been driven away from there rather than taken in.

'It might,' he replied.

They split up, agreeing to meet later, back at the police station. Three hours later, however, John had nothing to report. No one had noticed a young woman behaving oddly around the livery stables last night, and the official at York Minster pointed out that the cathedral and the close were secured after dark. Anxiety was now consuming him; almost a whole day had passed since she had left St Hilda's! A pretty woman, confused and wandering, falling friendless into the wrong hands, was as good as dead and probably grateful for oblivion when it came.

'We've not had a body reported,' Redman reminded him.

Earlier he had sent a message to Celia and one had come back telling him that his room had been kept for him at The Black Swan. He told Redman he would walk the streets a little longer and then make his way there. 'Have you heard from her family?' he asked, turning at the door. 'Are they out there, searching the streets for her?'

'Concern has been expressed,' the inspector replied.

CHAPTER 44

Olwen stirred on her muddy bed, half rousing. 'Why does he not come?' she asked the emptiness. Somewhere a dog barked but otherwise the city was silent. She opened her eyes and saw that it was still dark, and at her feet the shrunken river flowed silently by; the tide had yet to turn. Soon, if she waited, he would surely come. . . Shuffling further under the curve of the boat's hull she pulled the damp cloak close, and once again sleep overcame her.

'A double house,' Osred said, that day they returned from the north. 'The nuns will make you welcome, they will honour you. The abbess is kin to my mother, kin to me. . . the abbot too. . .'

And there had only been time for a snatched exchange with Heri before she was taken there. 'I *will* come,' he said, in a low voice, looking deep into her eyes. 'I promise it. As soon as I can. And, when the moment is right, I will speak to Osred, an alliance with the north can only strengthen his position, he must surely agree. He will want us with him, not as foes.'

'And if he refuses?'

He took her hand and smiled. 'Then it is that fast horse, my love, speeding north and let the devil take the consequences.'

And then she had had to go. Osred's men stood ready to take her and Osred was watching closely, having bid Heri stay behind and drink with him, tell him how matters were with Modig. 'I will not fail you, I promise.' He squeezed her fingers hard then released her, and Osred's men had taken her.

The monastery lay a few miles east of Eoforwic, and the abbot had greeted her respectfully upon her arrival while the abbess, a sharp-featured woman with cold eyes, simply inclined her head. 'We've prepared a room for you, lady, though in truth, word reached us but an hour ago. How happy must be your cousin, our kinsman, the king, that you are returned to us – and your brothers also.'

And since that day she had neither seen nor heard from them, nor had Heri come. She had grown increasingly desperate but her repeated requests to see them, to speak to Osred, had elicited no response and she had found herself all but a prisoner, watched and spied upon.

But today, as the light was falling, Osred had come and one look at his face told her that he was here, not at her request, but for reasons of his own.

She moaned and opened her eyes, seeing that the skies were lighter, and that Osred no longer stood before her. She lay under the boat, blinking and trying to remember how she came to be beside the dark water. Her legs were stiff with cold, and not only cold, they were wet too. She raised herself up on her elbow and saw that the river was flowing closer than it had been, and more strongly. The tide had turned! And still he had not come. Something must have prevented him. . . She tried to call out his name but could only croak. And she saw then that the stern of the little boat had begun to lift, it was moving, bumping against her legs where she lay, terrified now but unable to move. Her limbs were frozen and refused to obey her. He had surely not meant for her to die here, beside the river, to drown as her brothers had drowned! Summoning all her strength, she drew a deep breath and called out again.

CHAPTER 45

John arrived at The Black Swan to find Brandt sat, grave-faced, beside the fire, speaking earnestly to Gussie and Celia. They turned expectantly as John entered. 'No news,' he said. 'But no body either,' and he flung himself into an empty chair.

'Linton has informed me what happened at St Hilda's,' Brandt said, as they shared what information they had, 'and I have explained it to our friends here. The incident has caused an uproar, he says.'

John nodded. 'I saw him earlier, together with Redman, and he's clearly mortified.'

'To leave her alone with Alfred Malkon was unforgivable,' said Celia. 'But whatever had the man hoped to gain by goading her?'

'She told Linton that he was making clear to her how narrow were her options,' Brandt remarked. 'Marry him or remain there seems to have been the message, though it surely wouldn't suit his plans if she was forced to stay.'

'No, but it would suit his family very well,' Celia said. 'Control of her estate would remain with his father.'

'Which wouldn't please Alfred. It's very much to his advantage to marry her.' Gussie, John saw, was smoking one of Brandt's thin cigars though perhaps not enjoying it very much. 'And for all that the law protects the property rights of married women, the law doesn't see what goes on behind the doors. A man like Alfred Malkon could make her life hell.'

And, if what John suspected was true, he had already gone to desperate lengths to achieve his objective. 'Unless she's found soon, it's all irrelevant.'

Brandt was watching him with concern. 'Do not despair of her survival. The human spirit has strong instincts—'

'Unless it meets a rogue.'

Brandt clasped his arm. 'It is equally possible that she has encountered kindness, my friend. Or, like some wild creature, she has found herself a place to shelter and has yet to be discovered.'

Celia's face was pale and drawn and John saw that she took as little comfort from these words as he did. 'At least last night was not so cold,' she said.

'Forgive me. I must change.' Abruptly he left the room. It was impossible to remain there with them, feeding off each other's anxiety, clinging to a fading hope. He wanted to rid himself of the smell of woodsmoke, and he needed space in which to think. He washed and changed into clothes from the valise he had left behind, catching sight of himself in the mirror. His face was haggard. It was the price of failure. . . He pulled on his jacket and in doing so discovered that the letter he had written for Celia was still in his pocket but its content seemed unimportant now. He went to stand at the window, watching the ostlers leading carriage horses into the stabling, shouting out to each other, oblivious to a tragedy he feared was unfolding somewhere in the city. He could only pray that Brandt was right and that Olwen had found sanctuary somewhere. But how would they learn what had befallen her? If she was lucid she would hardly contact the police for fear of being returned to St Hilda's, so where would she go? Would she try to reach his old lodgings at Kirkthorpe, not knowing of his eviction, or might she attempt to get a message to Knaresborough, not realising that Gussie and Celia were here in York? Perhaps one of them should return in case she tried? If she set out to reach Swindale at least the Percys were there. And what if she was found, rambling and incoherent, by a good Samaritan, where would she be taken? Redman had assured him that the various hospitals had been alerted. But God help her if she was found by anyone who would do her harm!

That left only the river. . . dark and constant through time.

That thought ballooned in his mind; he had not thought to go there, there had seemed to be no point and the water levels were still low. In the darkness, though, in confusion, if she slipped from the muddy banks no one would ever know. . . Or worse, the drugs they had given her were known to produce a short-lived euphoria that was often followed by despair, a sense of hopelessness, and could lead to suicidal urges. . . After that thought, the image of her body floating in the river would not leave him and he knew he would not rest until he went down there.

He was at the door when he heard rapid footsteps approaching down the corridor and there came a sharp knock. 'John!' It was Celia and he opened the door to find her waving a note, her eyes alight. 'She's found!' He pulled her into the room and seized the note. It was from Redman. *Alive, but in a poor way. . .* he had written. . . *found down by the river* – the river! – *carried to the Ouse Bridge Tavern. Come as soon as you get this.* 'Brandt says he'll go with you,' Celia said. 'We'll follow.'

The Ouse Bridge Tavern stood on the cobbled King's Staithe a few yards back from the river. It was a small building, timber framed and centuries old, and they were shown up a narrow stairway that wound its way up to reach a small room at the back. A fire had been lit in the grate and there they found Redman, sat beside a narrow bed. He rose as they entered, making space for John to get to Olwen who lay, apparently sleeping, on the thin mattress. 'She was found just after dawn,' he told them. 'A boatman, nephew of the landlady here, found her lying on the mud beside one of his boats. Seems she'd been there all night.'

'Good God,' said John, looking down at her still form. Brandt went to the other side of the bed and felt her pulse.

'She's a good soul is Mrs Puckitt,' Redman continued, 'so she put her to bed with a hot brick and sent word to the parish priest.' He pulled a wry face at John's expression. 'Seems he was attending a deathbed in Hungate and only got the message when he returned; he came straight here, thinking he'd the job to do again here, and then sent word to the station.'

John looked down at Olwen. Her face bloodless, and so still. . . she could as well be dead. Dark rings encircled her eyes and there were smears of mud on her face and it was matted through her lank hair. Brandt's face was grave as he continued to examine her, lifting a closed eyelid and peering into her eye.

John, for his part, could hardly bear to look.

'Will she do?' Redman asked Brandt, who gave a half shrug by way of reply. 'She was very lucky,' he went on, 'they'd released water upstream into the river today, and it was only because the lad went down to check his boats were secured that he found her. Stiff with cold, he said. . . and raving.'

'Raving?' John looked up. Even if the water had not risen enough to drown her, she would not have survived another day. 'What do you think, Brandt?' he asked.

'Her pulse is weak and her breathing shallow. But this is not a natural sleep, I think.' He looked across at John. 'There is an irony, my friend, but whatever drugs she was given might prove to have been her salvation, slowing her system down, conserving her energy.'

'She'd a thick cloak wrapped around her, the lad said,' Redman added. 'The one she took from St Hilda's. It was soaked through, but provided some insulation, I suppose.' He looked from one to the other. 'Do we send her to the County Hospital, gentlemen?'

Both doctors shook their heads. 'She shouldn't be moved.'

The inspector took a step towards the door. 'Then I'll leave her in your hands and let you arrange things with Mrs Puckitt.' He paused at the threshold and turned. 'We've not met, Dr Brandt, though I feel as though we have. Perhaps, for form's sake, you'll call into the station before you leave the country, and answer a few questions.' He glanced drily at John. 'I trust that request doesn't have you heading for woods. You too, Dr Osbourne, in due course must correct your own statement, with a more liberal dash of the truth.' John nodded, no longer caring about anything other than the still form that lay in the narrow bed. The inspector's next words, however, brought him sharply to attention.

'And tomorrow, if Miss Malkon is in a state to be left with Dr Brandt, you and I, sir, will return to Swindale Hall.'

John descended some time later to find that Celia had arrived and arranged matters with the landlady. The tavern rarely took guests, she had explained, being more of a drinking establishment than an inn, but, by the liberal dispensing of money and charm, Celia had secured the woman's goodwill and arranged for two rooms to be made available, and for their use of a small snug.

'We can take it in shifts, sitting with her. Gussie stayed behind to pack our things and will bring them here. What about the professor, do you think? Will he stay where he is?'

Brandt, when asked, said that he would. 'And I will leave you now and meet Linton and relieve his mind. Herr Redman can inform Nicholson when he sees fit.'

John took his place beside Olwen and sat watching her. This was the third time, he thought, the third time he had sat beside this young woman as she disappeared into herself, absenting herself for a place he now knew a little, but where he could not follow.

Was she dreaming now, he wondered.

After a little while Celia tapped on the door and came to stand at the foot of the bed, looking down at her erstwhile charge. 'Will she pull through, John?' she asked, her face strained, and he could only answer with a shrug. She sat on the edge of the bed and took Olwen's limp hand in hers. 'Mrs Puckitt said she was quite wild when they brought her in, poor darling,' she said, looking across at him. 'Struggling with her nephew, crying out that Harry would come for her and that she must stay, claiming that her brothers had been waiting with her, and if she left them, they would drown.' Their eyes met briefly. 'She had them in such a tizz that Jo, that's her nephew, went running back to the river to see if there was any sense in what she was saying. There wasn't, of course, and by the time he got back, she'd fallen into this state.

That was when they sent for the priest, they really thought that she would die.' She leaned forward and gently caressed the curve of Olwen's cheek.

John looked at the girl's marble face and came to a decision. Reaching into his pocket, he pulled out the crumpled letter he had written to Celia in the keeper's cottage and handed it to her.

CHAPTER 46

Household rubbish, which could not be fed to the pigs, was dumped out of sight behind the stables at Swindale Hall, and when the pile grew too large and unsightly a pit was dug and it was buried. With the house being empty, little had accumulated in recent weeks and the last clearout was still there, in a heap, awaiting the next pit digging. Mr Percy had been startled when John returned with Inspector Redman in tow, and he now stood and watched anxiously as they pulled out a selection of jars and bottles and placed them in a wooden box he had provided for them. Some of the labels were still legible and served to confirm John's misgivings about both his predecessor's skills, and the personality of his patient. An assortment of powders, pills, ointments, salves, emetics and a variety of dubious cordials and tinctures all pointed to a hypochondriac who had been pandered to and indulged by a physician with about as much medical knowledge as a village folk healer. 'Dear God,' he remarked, reading the label on one bottle, 'it's a wonder the old man survived as long as he did.'

Yesterday, when she had read his letter Celia had lifted shocked eyes to meet his. 'No, John, *surely* not!' But, on questioning, she had admitted that it would have been the easiest thing in the world to have adulterated the old man's medicines; they occupied the entire top of a table in the drawing room beside his chair for everyone to see. 'He was ridiculously proud of his collection. As if it gave him consequence!' And she described a man entirely focused on his own comfort, querulous and demanding, easily flattered and obsessed by his health. 'Anyone wanting to poison him would have had ample

justification. No, no, I mustn't say that. . . But *surely*, John—'
Her eyes had filled at the suggestion that the rowing boat had
been deliberately damaged. 'I simply can't believe in such
wickedness, not even from Alfred.'

But, he had noted, she had not dismissed the suggestion.

At the rubbish dump Redman straightened, bringing John back
into the moment. 'That'll do,' he said, brushing the dirt off his
hand and placing the base of a blue glass bottle beside the others.
'I'll see these get looked at.' Percy picked up the box and took
it back to the house while John went with Redman to take a look
at the rowing boat. He examined the sprung plank and ran his
fingers over the scored lines in the varnish. 'As I said before, the
loose screws could be the result of poor maintenance but these
look deliberate.'

'Aye. They do.'

They then rolled the boat over, the right way up, and examined
how the decking planks would have sat. 'A good deal of water
could have accumulated underneath these and destabilised the
boat before anyone was aware,' John said, and Redman grunted.
'If the sluices hadn't got blocked, the boat would have sat on the
bottom of the lake and eventually rotted away, and no one would
have been the wiser.'

'How did it become known that they'd drowned?' Redman
asked.

'Percy saw a broken trail through the ice, he told me, and the
oars. And then later, the bodies were found.'

Redman nodded, but said nothing more and went to stand
beside the lake, looking out across the water. After a moment he
turned back. 'If it does transpire that we find arsenic, or some
other poison, in those bottles, then we are no wiser as to the
culprit. You do see that? Any member of the household could
have put it there – including Olwen Malkon or Celia Goodfellow,
or the Percys for that matter. Arguably his own physician could
have decided he'd had enough of him.'

'I know.'

Redman gestured to the boat. 'And this evidence amounts to

very little. Misadventure could be argued as convincingly as malign intent.' John knew that too. 'This witness you spoke of, would he convince a judge or jury?'

'I doubt it.' And Reagan, according to Percy, had not reappeared.

Redman pulled a wry face. 'And so, Dr Osbourne, I see little profit in pursuing this, however much you might want me to. I'll have the bottles looked at, as much to satisfy my own curiosity as yours, but beyond that. . . we'd be hard-pressed to convict anyone.'

He made as if to move off but John remained standing where he was. Here, in the outdoors, away from the police station and the tavern's upper room where its occupant lay in limbo, it was easier to be direct. 'What will happen now?' he asked. 'To Miss Malkon?'

The inspector turned back to him. 'That's for the courts to decide. How long before she reaches her majority?'

'Four, five months, I think.'

He shrugged. 'It'll take the courts almost that long to hear her case.'

'And meanwhile? She'll surely not go back to St Hilda's?' Redman shook his head. 'Returning her to the vicarage is unthinkable!' He shrugged and John frowned. 'She should remain with Celia Goodfellow, surely you must see that, either at her house, or back here in a place that's familiar.'

Redman's face gave nothing away. 'It's not for me to decide.'

'But in a case like this—'

Redman cut him off. 'I've made clear to you on several occasions, Dr Osbourne, that I can only work within the confines of the law. Her family has been informed that she's been found and—'

'Do they know where she is?' he asked, quickly.

'No, but I'm obliged to tell them if they ask.'

'In which case—' He broke off.

Redman gave him a dry look. 'Tell me, Dr Osbourne,' he asked, at his most urbane, 'when you were playing outlaw skulking in these woods, what was your plan then?' John looked away; the wretched man had read his mind. 'I imagine, beyond eluding me, it was to devise a way of getting Miss Malkon away from St Hilda's. Yes?' John remained silent; Redman had tripped him up once too often. 'Those amazons had previously planned to take her abroad, I understand. Had *you* agreed to that, or had you another idea?'

'It had not been decided,' John replied.

'And you'd not tell me anyway.' A glint of amusement appeared in his eyes and was gone. 'For the time being, as you and Dr Brandt consider it dangerous to move her, and Mrs Puckitt is willing to house her, I shall recommend to her family that she stays where she is. I can do nothing else as matters stand.'

Returning to The Ouse Bridge Tavern, John found Brandt reading quietly beside Olwen's bed. Olwen herself seemed not to have stirred, and Brandt confessed himself puzzled. 'It's as if she's in some sort of suspended state. She's not asleep insofar as she could be woken, nor has she a fever.' John lifted her limp wrist, and Brandt watched his face. 'Slow but steady, eh? No cause for alarm, and her breathing is regular if still rather shallow. It is as if she no longer inhabits her body but has left it marking time.'

John frowned. 'Are you concerned?'

Brandt shook his head. 'Intrigued. It's as if she has placed herself in a deep trance, as I might have tried to do with her consent. And yet I cannot reach her.' They sat and looked at her, at the uncanny stillness, the awful vacancy. 'If she doesn't rouse in the next few hours then we must see what we can do to bring her back, but not quite yet. While her mind is apparently untroubled, her body is restoring itself, and perhaps we should leave her for a little longer. But not, I think, through another night.'

'No.'

Brandt looked up. 'I forgot! Fraulein Celia has made an appointment with a gentleman she knows, a man from the museum who she said might be helpful, and hoped that you would be back in time to join them.' John looked again at Olwen's still form, unwilling to leave her, but Brandt waved him away. 'I will stay beside her, my friend, and make no attempt to alter her condition until you return. Go now, and see what you can learn.'

CHAPTER 47

C elia was waiting for him on the terrace outside the museum, gazing across at the ancient corner tower of the Roman fortress. And just behind it, John thought, as he walked towards her, a king's residence once stood.

The note she had left with Brandt simply said that she had contacted Dr Henly, a friend of Olwen's late father, and once a regular visitor to Swindale Hall, and she waved as she saw him approaching. 'Good. You're back,' and she searched his face anxiously. 'How did you get on?'

John told her about the bottles and Redman's intentions. 'Does Olwen need to know all this?'

He looked aside, and did not answer for a moment. 'I believe she already does. . .'

There was no time for more. The room to which they were taken was lined with books, their leather bindings faded and worn, and on higher shelves there were pottery vessels, dusty and looped with cobwebs, and there was that hush which museums engender, as if time itself was held in a moment of reflection.

A man appeared at the door. 'Miss Goodfellow! How delightful to see you.' He too looked as if he belonged to another era, his exuberant whiskers were dusted with grey and his suit was antique. Introductions were made, commiserations offered concerning the tragic events at Swindale Hall and sympathy expressed regarding Olwen's present condition. He gestured them to chairs around a table. 'Now tell me, if you will, what has brought you here.'

John left it to Celia to explain. 'Those fragments of carved stones found in the walls of the church at Kirkthorpe,' she began. 'You were excited about them, as I remember—'

'Yes, indeed! A very important discovery.' He embarked at once on a lengthy discourse promoting their undoubted antiquity and the possibility of their association with an early monastery.

Celia gave him his head for a few minutes and then asked, 'Is it possible to associate them with any particular individual, or specific period of time?'

He shook his head. 'Not very precisely but I'd hazard a guess that they are from a free-standing cross of late eighth or early ninth century date. The iconography is reminiscent of. . .' and he was away again.

John waited until the man paused for breath, then leapt into the gap. 'There appear to be fragments of some white substance, chalk or white quartz, in the eyes of the seated figure.'

The man looked delighted. 'Is that so? Well, well, well. I must come and have another look. You saw that yourself, did you? It's not unusual for traces of paint to be found on such monuments and suggestions have been made—'

'Do you know if a king by the name of Ælfwald ever ruled in Northumbria?' John ruthlessly interrupted him.

'He did indeed. But there's nothing to connect Ælfwald with the cross, other than being broadly contemporaneous. Has someone suggested this? It would be a very rash claim! Very little is known of these early kings, a few lines in the various sources, the odd coin, but further insights are rare.'

'But Ælfwald did exist?'

'Most assuredly he did, sir.' John exchanged a glance with Celia. 'Those were turbulent times in Northumbria, some dozen kings came and went in a single century, exiled or murdered in swift succession. It was a very unhealthy occupation!' They laughed with him, as was expected. 'Ælfwald was one of them. His reign lasted about a decade, a brief interlude in a very bloody time. He was succeeded, if my memory serves me right, by his nephew.'

'Osred.' John spoke without thinking.

'I believe it was!'

'What happened to Ælfwald?'

The man sank his chin onto the tips of his fingers and frowned down at the table. 'Now there's a question! Some were exiled, others murdered, some died and some, like Osred, took the tonsure—'

'They did what?'

'Took the tonsure. Became monks, gave up the throne, willingly or otherwise, eschewed politics. The Church was a powerful force too, of course, but sometimes also provided a refuge for former kings. A preferred alternative to death, I imagine.'

'And what was Ælfwald's fate?'

'I am endeavouring, sir, to remember.' The man closed his eyes and muttered a string of names and dates as if it were a litany and then opened them again with a smile. 'Murdered! That's right, he was murdered as the result of a conspiracy led by one of his ealdormen, a noble by the name of. . .' Sicga, John thought bitterly, the traitorous Sicga who had held up the bloodied head of his king in triumph. 'Dear me, my memory is not what it was.' He rose and went to the bookshelves and began thumbing through one of the leather-bound volumes, muttering as he turned the pages, and found the name. 'Sicga! Of course. Smithson's account describes it here: *Ælfwald fell foul of a conspiracy led by the patrician, Sicga, and was miserably slain at a place on the Wall called Scythlescester.*' John felt the hairs on the back of his neck rise. '*His body was taken to Hexham accompanied by a great many monks, chanting and praying, and he was buried in the church of St Andrew the Apostle. . .*' John stared, hardly able to credit what he was hearing, but Henly was continuing. '*And above the place where the killing took place, a light appeared in the night sky, hanging in the heavens, and was seen by many. . .*'

John drew a sharp breath and Celia looked at him with concern. A light, scarring the night sky. . . but Henly, absorbed in the book, was continuing. 'His burial place became the focus for pilgrimage and then. . . yes, here we have it. . . *his nephew, Osred, succeeded him, but after a year he was forced to assume the tonsure, and was subsequently exiled, from where he later returned, but was betrayed, captured and put to death.*'

The betrayer betrayed.

'Why did Osred become king?' John asked, feeling a stab of vicious pleasure to hear of his end. 'Had Ælfwald no sons to succeed him? Or daughters?'

'Presumably not.'The man was still turning the pages, unaware of the weightiness of the question. 'A daughter would be unlikely to rule anyway, except as consort to a king.' Celia pulled a wry face as Henly brought the book to the table, and leaned over it, continuing to skim the pages, engrossed in the detail. '*Æthelred I, son of the usurper Æthelred Moll, succeeded Osred. . .*' he muttered, 'some discrepancy about actual dates. . . ah yes, *and then he himself was murdered some six years later.* Ah! Yes, Ælfwald *did* have sons but, oh dear me, yes, I remember now. . . Let me read you the passage: *The sons of King Ælfwald, whose names were Ælf and Ælfwinne, having been drawn from St Peter's Church by deceitful promises, were taken from the city and miserably slain by Æthelred in the waters of Wonwaldremere.*'

CHAPTER 48

Later John could not remember how they managed to extract themselves from Dr Henly; Celia must have covered for him somehow. He had left the museum feeling nauseous, his head reeling, and descended the steps in a daze. So those lads, those innocent princes, had been murdered. But *drowned*. . . ? His mind roared as he took in the implications, for here might lie the key.

It made a sort of sense.

An imprint of the past, Gussie had said.

Celia led him to a bench under the spreading branches of an ancient beech, where he sat staring at the ground, grief-stricken and bewildered, and she sat beside him, saying nothing.

'Forgive me,' he said, straightening at last. He took out his handkerchief and blew his nose. 'What an absurd display.'

'We begin to understand, I think?' she said.

He nodded. 'These events happened, that much is clear. These people existed. . .'

'And their story has found its way into Olwen's mind – and through hers, to you.'

They sat a moment in silence. 'We must get back. Tell Brandt—'

Celia put out a restraining hand. 'No, sit a moment, John. I saw what a shock it was to hear what he said.'

Their bench was beside the Roman fortress wall, even now eloquent of an empire's power, a point that would not have been lost on Northumbria's kings. But those who had peopled that shadowy time, the kings and prelates who had tried to govern, their rebellious subjects who plotted against them, the traders too and the ordinary folk, they would only ever be faint, insubstantial figures. And the dead king's murdered sons survived only as a single entry in the records.

Their sister not at all.

Before they left the museum, Celia had asked Dr Henly if his book made any mention of a daughter Ælfwald might have had and the man, still engrossed in its pages, had shaken his head. 'It doesn't mean he didn't, of course, daughters would hardly get a mention.'

So Wyn had left no trace, John thought as they made their way back towards the tavern, although he was convinced now that she had once breathed the air of York, gazed across its river, and bestowed a smile upon a silver pin, and upon its giver.

They walked back in silence and found Gussie was waiting for them. John left Celia to describe what they had learned and went upstairs to the little room at the back where he opened the door to see Brandt leaning over Olwen's bed. He lifted his head and John saw from his face that something had changed.

'She's woken?' he asked, as all other thoughts fled.

Brandt shook his head. The bedclothes were disturbed, and Olwen lay less rigidly than before, her face turned away. 'Not woken, but stirring,' he replied. 'It began about half an hour ago. She made a little mewing sound and moved her head from side to side, and every now and then she fidgets and mutters.' A frown had appeared on her brow and John leaned close, saying her name. Brandt watched him. 'She made no response when I tried. Perhaps she will, for you.'

But she remained still and John straightened, looking across at Brandt. 'So what do we do?'

'We wait, I think. And while we do, you can tell me what you've learned.'

/

A deep sense of dread grew in Wyn as she contemplated her cousin, who stood awkwardly before her. '*Why* are you come, Osred?' she repeated.

He had arrived, not with his retinue but quietly, secretively, as darkness was falling. 'Do you bring word of my brothers?' But he avoided her eyes, commanding her to go outside with him, and bidding all others draw back. And he led her to the walled enclosure of the church and they stood alone, beside the tall cross, where none but the rooks could overhear.

The sun slipped behind the clouds.

'They are safe,' he replied, as a chill breeze reached them. 'They tired of their lessons and have gone hunting with some of my men.'

She stared back at him. 'They have *left* St Peter's! Left sanctuary? Are they with trusted men?'

'Aye. Amongst them are those who brought them from Modig.'

'They are with Heri and Bri?' She felt a rush of joy. Then they were safe if Heri was still here, watching over them, but Osred's eyes again slid away from hers. 'Do you come simply to tell me this?' But why had Heri not been to see her, as he had promised he would? 'You've left me here, telling me nothing of our futures. The abbess will say nothing either and treats me with contempt. She keeps me under watch as if I am a prisoner.' Her food tasted odd some days and she had seen the woman out gathering herbs and suspected that her lethargy and current confusion resulted from her handiwork.

'Abbess Emma is my kinswoman and she knows her duty is to keep you safe. But rest easy, your future is assured, and your former status will soon be restored to you. I come with good news! A marriage has been arranged, to a man of noble birth. An ally, an equal.'

She stared at him, unable to breathe. Heri was of noble birth, and was an ally. Could he possibly mean. . . But Osred was continuing, in a slightly petulant tone. 'I'd planned to wed you myself before you fled so impulsively and you would have been my queen, but now you must wed for the sake of the kingdom.'

/

When John told Brandt what they had learned the professor's eyes widened in astonishment. '*Unvorstellbar! Einfach unglaublich.*' He

turned to stare at Olwen. 'But this is quite *extraordinary*! It is docu-
mented, you say, this history, and it all accords with your dreams?'

'It does.'

Brandt sat down heavily, shaking his head in disbelief. He sat
silently for a moment then raised his eyes to John. 'So these
people actually *lived*. . .' John nodded. 'You realise, I think, that
the implications of this are immense.'

'I know.'

Brandt turned again to look at Olwen and then pulled from
his pocket a notebook and a pencil. 'Tell me again. As much as
you can remember, every detail of what the man said.'

And so John described what he had learned of Ælfwald's death,
the description of his burial, and of the light that had appeared in
the sky. . . A low moan came from the bed as he spoke and they
turned to see that Olwen had begun tossing her head from side
to side, her legs moving beneath the bedclothes. John leaned close
again and said her name again but still elicited no response and
after a moment she seemed to settle. Brandt took her wrist.

'Her pulse has quickened. It did that before. . . but I think we
can afford to wait a little longer before we try and rouse her. Go
on with your telling.'

/

'May I know who I am to wed?' Wyn straightened, tense beside
the cross, her fingernails digging into her palms, and in the strange
light of evening, the painted figures stood out in sharp relief.
Their drilled eyes, cold and starkly white, stared back at her.

'He awaits you in the church,' Osred said.

She took a step back from him. 'I am to marry *now*, with no
kin, no ceremony—' for if Heri was with her brothers, then it
was not he who awaited her inside the church.

An odd wheedling tone crept into Osred's voice. 'Now is only
the time to exchange vows, to plight your troth. . .'

'I refuse.' She took another backwards step and, looking at
him, she realised suddenly that he was afraid. Terribly afraid.

'You cannot refuse.' He spoke quickly, pleading with her. 'I am your cousin and your king and you must obey me—'

And she saw that there were others gathering beyond the enclosure wall, and knew then that all this had been carefully planned. The abbess was standing at the enclosure gate, blocking her retreat, and she saw armed men emerging from the shadows. The sun had lost its battle against the darkness and a blood red moon was rising to the north, casting an uncanny light onto the seated figure on the stone cross.

She was trapped.

But even as that thought struck her, the cross vanished and an image flashed across her mind – spring flowers nodding in the breeze, sunlit and lovely, and around the empty stone socket of the cross two ring doves dipped and bowed in courtship.

And, in her head, and as if from a great distance, she heard a voice speaking.

/

'Following his murder,' John continued, 'Ælfwald was succeeded by his nephew Osred, but his rule was of short duration and there was a conspiracy and he was forced to relinquish the throne. . .'

'Her breathing is quickening,' Brandt said, watching the still form on the bed. 'She may surface again. But go on with the story.'

/

'Aye, it *is* her duty, Osred. So tell her how it will be.' She swung round, confused, caught off-balance, and saw that a figure had emerged from the church. He approached slowly, almost leisurely, a tall man with a commanding presence, dressed in dark clothes with boots that laced up his calves. He made her a mocking bow. 'The Lady Ælfwyn, you do me great honour.'

Osred could no longer hide his fear. 'Let us go into the church.'

'*No!*' That fleeting image had impressed itself on her mind and she glanced back, seeing that the cross was restored to its proper place. What had that vision meant? The doves had vanished and only the rooks remained. Then from behind the church she heard the drum of hoof beats and spun round again, her heart leaping with sudden hope.

Heri! He had come.

But no. . . It was a riderless horse, a stallion, maddened perhaps by temperament or the dusk-risen flies, bucking and twisting as it galloped across the pasture, white as a ghost. Her eyes widened at the sight of it and then flew to the man beside her. '*You*! You were at Scythlescester, and at Catreath!' she cried.

'What of it?'

'You are Æthelred, son of the usurper!'

The horse came to a sudden halt and stood staring across at her and the man drew in his breath. 'I am Æthelred, son of a murdered king. And you are daughter to another such.' He took a step forward and gripped her arm. 'I ruled Northumbria until your father deposed me but it was Sicga, not I, who murdered him. I went to Scythlescester in good faith, to secure a lasting peace, it was others who brought with them a blood lust that sought to destroy the power of Northumbria, and restore the old kingdoms. But now Osred and I share a common purpose, and so it is your duty to wed, to help bind your father's kingdom together, to help it heal.'

She tried to pull away. Osred was a fool, this man would never share the throne, but her struggles only served to tighten his grip. She saw that the figures outside the enclosure had drawn close and put a trembling hand to her head as the voice inside grew stronger. And then she recognised it. It was not just any voice, it was Heri's! And he was giving an account of her father's betrayal. . .

She closed her eyes and strained to hear.

John saw Olwen's hand move and her head began making odd questing motions. He stopped to look across at Brandt.

'Go on,' the professor said, but he too was watching her.

'Henly assumed that Ælfwald was succeeded by Osred because he had no sons of his own.' He stopped again, staring at Olwen. 'I do believe that she's listening,'

Brandt nodded. 'I think so too. Go on, but carefully.'

'Henly found an account in one of his books that stated that he had two sons, Ælf and Ælfwinne. . .'

/

Strengthened by the strange, distant voice, Wyn turned back to confront Osred. 'I demand to see my brothers.'

But Æthelred pulled her back round to face him, his brows drawn together, and she sensed those around them stiffen. 'Osred has told you they are taken care of. Come now. You know now where your duty lies.' And he pulled her, resisting, into the church where she saw the abbot standing in front of the altar, his arms spread wide in welcome. She tried to turn back but the abbess was following close behind, with men falling in after. It had become a procession.

She sought Osred's eyes. 'Wait, cousin. I must consider this betrothal—'

'Betrothal?' Æthelred raised his eyebrows and laughed. 'Osred, you craven! This is no betrothal, lady, we wed this day, you and I. We seal the knot.'

'*No!*' Desperately she tried to free herself but he was too strong.

Osred stepped forward and took her other arm. 'You *must* obey me, Ælfwyn, you have no choice.'

The abbot was approaching them, a smile fixed on his face, but she continued to struggle. '*No*, priest! I will not,' she cried, and then, in desperation. 'For I am handfast to another!'

Æthelred pulled her round to face him again, flashing a furious look at Osred. 'What other?'

Beside her Osred quailed and spoke quickly, pleadingly. 'She means Oshere, Modig's grandson, the one they call Heri.' She shut her eyes, still hearing his beloved voice in her head, and strained to catch his words. 'He came to me to press his own suit but I forbade it and he is gone, Æthelred, he too is taken care of, I saw to it, he is gone with the young princes to. . .'

'. . . they were lured,' John concluded, 'or so Henly's book said, by deceitful promises from sanctuary at St Peter's Church, and upon Æthelred's orders, were miserably slain in the waters of Wonwaldremere. . .'

'*Monster*!' Wyn's anguished cry took Æthelred by surprise and his grip slackened. She struck out wildly at Osred, cursing him. 'Slain!. . . at Wonwaldremere.'

Æthelred grabbed her and pulled her round. 'Witch!' he hissed, gripping her shoulders and glaring into her eyes. 'How can you know this?'

Osred crossed himself as she struggled like a mad thing, kicking and biting. '*Murderer! Traitor!*' Heri too, and Bri. . . On a rising sob she saw their bodies, bloodied and cast aside along the track, and struck out at Æthelred in a frenzy of grief. He grabbed her hair, pulling her head sharply back against his chest. '*Devil*! You've had them all *slain*!'

'Aye, but how did you *know*?' he demanded, his voice hoarse in her ear. 'Tell me! Where sits the traitor?' She felt a clump of her hair torn from her scalp. 'Tell me ere you join them, and your precious Heri.' And suddenly she felt his blade cold against her throat and heard Osred cry out in protest.

But she had reached a place that was beyond fear. She had lost everything and turned her head towards him, this man who had done these terrible things, he had left her just enough play in her hair, just enough for her to look up into his murderous eyes – and spit.

Then moonlight from the open door lit the moving blade, it flashed and she let out a cry, arching against the piercing pain, and felt herself falling, falling, falling. . . and the beaten earth of the church floor came up to meet her.

/

John sprang to his feet in horror as Olwen suddenly contorted, her back grotesquely arching as she let out a strangled cry. Her eyes flew open, sightless in shock, her arms outstretched, the fingers splayed. Brandt rushed to the other side and between them they caught her as she crumpled, a rattle in her throat, and fell back against the pillow.

CHAPTER 49

They thought her dead. And perhaps for a moment she was. Desperately John searched for a pulse. 'No, *no*. . . !' but Brandt pushed him aside, locked his hands together on her chest, and began pressing hard and fast, entreating her to breathe. . . he paused and bent to blow into her lungs, pulled back to check for signs of life '. . . *um Himmels willen, atme*. . .' then repeated the process while John stood by, frozen.

'It was my words that did this!' he said. '*My* words.'

Brandt glanced at him, '*Mut, mein Freund*. Courage!' and he kept going, panting, then signalled to John to take over until at last Olwen's chest began to rise and fall and a flush of colour stained the pallor of her face. Brandt put his finger to her neck, and looked across at John.

A nod was enough.

It was sometime later that John sat silently beside with Brandt in the taproom on the tavern, neither of them speaking. Satisfied that her condition was stable, they had left Olwen with Celia watching over her.

John took a pull at his drink and stared into the fire, thinking that the moment she had opened her eyes would stay with him forever. She had looked up at him for a long time and then her eyes had flooded with recognition as they had that day outside the glasshouse in the vicarage garden, and she had simply said: 'Dr Osbourne?' He had clasped her hand and nodded, unable to speak, as she turned her head to the other side of the bed. 'And Dr Brandt. . .'

'I thought I'd killed her,' he said to Brandt, raising his glass again and noticing that his hand still shook. 'That what I was saying, that account of her brothers' death—' he stopped to correct himself ' – of those princes' deaths, could trigger such a reaction.'

But Brandt shook his head. 'It was, I think, only a part of it. She responded to that with a cry, but then. . . then something else occurred.' He took a drink. 'And for a moment, she left us.'

'You saved her life, Brandt.'

Brandt waved a dismissive hand. 'We did that between us, my friend. But whatever it was that happened to her, in whatever place she inhabited, it was catastrophic.' He glanced again at John. 'Perhaps, one day, she will tell you, or perhaps she will not remember and we will never know.'

They sat in silence again, looking out of the window, and watched a bluff-bowed barge manoeuvre into its moorings at the staithe, dropping its tan sail as men gathered, shouting out to each other as they tied up and began unloading the cargo. How many vessels had pulled up there, he wondered, in all the years since the Roman surveyors chose the confluence of two rivers to build their fortress. He lifted his gaze and looked across to the other side, remembering again the ships from Frisia, and how a silver pin with intertwined creatures had once raised a shy smile. And yet. . . and yet the memory was fainter now, the image had become two-dimensional, and the emotional burden was diminished.

Brandt's mind, it seemed, was running along a similar theme. 'You spoke once of folds in time,' he said, drawing on the inevitable cigar and blowing the smoke up to the rafters, 'when describing your encounter with that vagabond. A good analogy, my friend, and I have been considering it. But perhaps this goes beyond the simple warping of time, beyond what is defined within any dimension. We have here an extraordinary convergence of circumstance, of repeating patterns, a recalling, a retelling. . .' he paused, struggling to find the words. 'And because of this our young lady was not only traumatised by her own experiences but unwittingly became a conduit for some other powerful current, a resonance of past evil, an echo. . . and that too became her reality. Perhaps because her own situation was sufficiently similar to that of what you call her *alter ego* and, crucially, I think, because of the same physical context - that village church and this city – even the lowering of the river was to play its part.'

John nodded. 'And I wonder if, deep down, she suspected that her brothers' deaths were not accidental.'

'Or the possibility bled through from one frame to the other.' He gave John a slanting smile. 'And all was sparked by the arrival of the catalyst.'

It took John a moment. 'You mean me?'

'I believe so. Perhaps you had a context of your own, something deeply buried in your ancestral memory that meant that you too had a part to play in this little drama.' John looked aside, thinking of his mother's people, their roaming lives so closely bound to the land, forever wandering and restless, absorbing stories and keeping them alive. For how long, he wondered, had they come and gone through the lands of the Gododdin? Brandt paused to relight his cigar, and flicked another glance at John. 'I conjecture, my friend, I simply muse. But all this serves to confirm that there are forces beyond the dimensions of time and space with which we must grapple. Perhaps something more is to be learned, I hope, if Miss Malkon is able, one day, to tell us. But that there was once a strong emotional bond between two individuals, Wyn and Heri, is clear and that bond remained strong. Their tragedy remained unresolved and so, in consequence, Miss Malkon, a disturbed young lady, aided by opium, became consumed by it and drew you in.'

They sat a moment longer, watching as the last of the cargo was unloaded from the barge, then Brandt continued in a lighter vein. 'Two magnetic materials are needed, after all, to create a magnet, there must be a charge between them, an irresistible attraction. And that, I observe, has also endured.' He smiled at John's expression, wafting away the cigar smoke. 'Do not trouble to deny it, my friend.'

'I don't,' said John, returning his look.

*

Rain, long threatened, blew along the river in great swathes that dashed against the windows of the little room tucked under the eaves of the tavern. Celia sponged away the last traces of mud from Olwen's face, and gently combed through her knotted hair. 'You'll do for now, my love,' she said, smiling down at her, and Olwen took possession of her hand, and held onto it. She had so many questions to ask, but one thing was clear. She must never lose Celia again.

A little later, Gussie arrived with a bowl of broth. 'You look better, chick,' she said with a smile, then addressed Celia. 'John says come down for dinner. He's on his way up.'

A moment later there was a tapping at the door and Dr Osbourne entered, stooping to pass through the low doorway, and he looked across at Olwen and echoed Gussie's words. 'You look better,' he said.

'And she's even eaten a little,' Celia said, getting to her feet. 'I'll go now, my love, and leave you with John.'

She left and Olwen looked steadily across at him. 'I never think of you as John,' she said, 'how strange it seems.'

He came further into the room. 'Does it?' he asked, and took the seat beside her. 'I hope it'll get easier.'

'I think it will. . .' They sat looking at each other, without tension or awkwardness but with a sort of wonder, and the silence between them lengthened. 'Wyn is fading,' she said, eventually. 'I can feel her going.'

'Heri too.'

'He killed her, you see, that other Alfred – already I have forgotten his name.'

'Æthelred.'

'He stabbed her at the place where I faltered in the church.' She had been so fearful but the fear too had gone. He nodded, watching her, and she knew that soon the memory would be gone that she wanted him to know. 'I was being tricked, forced to marry him, but I was handfast to. . . to Heri and then. . . then I heard *your* voice, in my head, telling me that my brothers had been slain. . . at a place with a strange name. . .'

'Wonwaldremere.'

'Yes, that was it.'

'Rest now, Olwen,' he said, putting out a hand to her. 'We can talk some more later.'

She looked back at him. So Heri too was fading, he said. . . but leaving this man in his stead, and on a sudden impulse she took his hand and held it tight against her cheek lest he too might slip away.

An hour later she was sleeping with Brandt sat reading beside her, when Redman appeared, unannounced, at the door of the little snug where John was sat with Celia and Gussie considering what ought to happen to Olwen now. They invited him in and John brought him up to date with the situation. 'Dr Brandt and I are both optimistic that she's taken no lasting harm from her ordeals.'

In this world and another. . .

'I'm delighted to hear it, as will be her family.' John frowned and Redman blandly met his eye. 'They've been content so far to leave matters as they stand, but I'm here to tell you that a decision has been made regarding her future.'

Quick glances were exchanged between them. 'Which is what?' John asked.

The inspector took up a position in front of the fire, surveying them as he warmed himself. 'It has been decided that in the short term she should remain under professional care—'

'Decided by who?' Gussie demanded, but he showed no sign of having heard her.

' – and to that end, a place has been found for her at The Retreat.' He raised his eyebrows at John. 'There can be no objection to her having a recuperative spell there, I trust?'

They all spoke at once.

'There are very strong objections.'

'Has no one thought to ask *her*?'

'Dammit, man, surely—'

Redman waited until they had finished, surveying them with

the same dry expression, then continued. 'Her uncle is anxious that she be removed from here as soon as possible and, as you imply that she is doing well and since she will be under medical supervision once she arrives at The Retreat, I shall report back that she can be collected from here tomorrow.'

Gussie glared at him. 'She's not a bloody parcel!'

He waited, unmoved, for their further protests to cease. 'I charge you, therefore, with having her ready to leave.'

John made one last appeal. 'Inspector, she needs her friends around her, not more strangers, she needs to know she's safe. She should stay with Miss Goodfellow. Speak to Brandt, he'll say the same!'

Redman gave him a long considering look. 'To ensure a smooth transition I'll escort her family here myself tomorrow afternoon. . .' John turned furiously away '. . . as they'll be coming to the police station first, all of them, to answer some questions. I'd not expect to be here before mid afternoon.'

John turned back. 'What questions?'

'Oh, quite another matter altogether,' Redman replied mildly, picking up his hat, 'The questions concern the contents of some bottles recovered from Swindale Hall.' His eyes met John's and, for a moment, held them. Then he turned to address Celia and Gussie. 'And if you ladies should take it into your heads to whisk your friend away before we come to collect her – to Europe perhaps, as you once considered doing – then I can promise that you will be pursued, even to the ports themselves, wasting my officers, time chasing after you.' He turned at the door. 'The same applies to you, Dr Osbourne, although. . .' he paused, looking thoughtful as he placed the hat on his head. 'Although in your case you never did tell me your intentions, did you?'

CHAPTER 50

Two months later

John came down the valley in long easy strides, the turf cushioning his feet as he filled his lungs with heather-scented air. He descended quickly, following the course of the burn, until the low buildings of his mother's farm came into view around the bluff. Ah, the joy of being back here; he felt it more and more with each day that passed. He had arrived in time to help with the late lambing, even putting his medical knowledge to good use with one or two awkward births. And now the shearing too was done. He grinned as he remembered the mockery that had accompanied his efforts from those whose practised hands seemed to fly across the creatures, shearing the rise with a skill born of years' experience, releasing and grabbing the next animal all in the time it had taken John to hold onto a single struggling ewe. But he had improved and, since he was his mother's son, had been accepted by the shepherds. He liked this life, he thought, looking down the sweep of the valley, his skills were appreciated amongst the scattered community who had never had a doctor of their own, but also he liked working on the farm, working with his hands, stretching his muscles and letting his eyes drink their fill of the ancient hills of home.

He slept the nights up in one of the shielings, which both his mother and Olwen declared was quite unnecessary, and came down the valley once a day to eat with them. The nights were warm and it had seemed no bad thing to put a little space between himself and the young woman he had, most assuredly this time, run off with. And he knew he needed to give her time, there was too much at stake to rush things, but by God, sometimes it was hard to hold back.

Over the weeks he had watched her recover and begin to bloom. God, but she was lovely! There was colour in her cheeks now and that haunted look had gone.

She had been haunted indeed, he thought as he kicked aside a stone on the path, but now the whole business seemed so improbable! When they had first arrived and related the story, little by little, his mother had listened with the wisdom of the nomad in her eyes, nodding in that way of hers, and then taken Olwen firmly in hand. John reckoned she knew what she was about, keeping the girl busy, and Olwen soon declared herself proficient at bread making, proudly informing him that she was learning to make cheese from the rich creamy milk of her mother's herd.

Of the future beyond the day, he did not yet think. It was enough now that they both took time to recover.

When Redman had left the tavern that day, and was out of earshot, Gussie had leapt to her feet. 'What a *splendid* man! And it's a rare day that I say that!'

'Do you really think. . . ?' Celia had looked at John as he stared at the door, hardly daring to believe. But he too had seen the glint of humour in Redman's eye as he pulled down the brim of his hat.

'I do.'

After that Gussie had paused only long enough to see if Olwen approved her plan and had then driven them hard, sending John off to discover train times, Celia to pack and, that evening, had herself boarded a train for Knaresborough, returning on the milk train with Joyce, their housemaid, who had been drafted in and whose eyes flashed at the thought of the adventure. 'After all, you're doing nothing wrong, m'dear,' Gussie had reassured her, 'we're simply going down to Portsmouth for a holiday, and you're coming too. There's no law against that!' Amongst the baggage she had brought back from Knaresborough was a hat to which was attached a heavy veil, which Joyce would wear, and there was much discussion as to how best to lay the false scent without the ruse being uncovered too quickly.

'You must leave on the first train north,' Gussie had decreed, addressing John, 'but travel separately.' Brandt offered to accompany Olwen to the station to make sure that she arrived safely, leaving John to board the train on his own. They would travel second class, in the same compartment, but would sit apart and make no contact during the journey. Conveniently, it transpired that Olwen was seated beside a family who drew her into their fold, sharing their food with her, and so it would have appeared that she was one of their party, had anyone come through the train looking for a couple, or a solitary female. But no one came. And so John spent the journey silently offering blessings to Redman and watching Olwen from across the compartment. She slept for much of the journey, but when she woke she would look back across at him.

Later, they were to learn that the three women laying the false trail had got as far as Guildford before Jones, the constable who had been posted on the door in Knaresborough, had discovered that the veiled lady reported at various points along the way was not, after all, Olwen Malkon. The game was up then, Celia had gleefully written, but since there were no grounds on which to detain them, the three of them had carried on to Worthing and enjoyed some pleasant blowy days beside the sea before coming home.

By which time John and Olwen were tucked away in the hills where Redman, even if he was moved to try, would never find them.

He smiled again, imagining Gussie's triumph at the success of her plan, and, as he pushed open the gate to his mother's farm, he raised a hand to Olwen, who, with her skirts hitched up and her hair blown by the gusting wind, was feeding the hens in the courtyard. She scattered the last of the grain and came across to him, releasing her skirts as she did, a hand to her unruly hair as she smiled at him. 'Something's come for you from Celia. Your mother has it.'

She went ahead of him into the house, and his mother turned to greet him. 'It's a fat one, I'll say that,' she remarked, taking a small package from behind the clock on the mantelpiece and handing it to him. He turned it over, thinking he would have preferred to open it in private, but the two women had pulled out chairs and were sat, expectant, at the table. 'Is there a drink to be had?' he asked, stalling, and his mother rose to fill a tankard, which she pushed towards him.

The package he discovered contained several items. The first one was correspondence sent to Celia from Dr Henly and he skimmed it rapidly.

> *I searched in vain for further reference to Ælfwald and his sons (I found no reference to a daughter) but discovered only an account of the death of Earl Sicga; it would appear he committed suicide at Lindisfarne in 793. Does this suggest remorse for his misdeeds, one wonders?*

John paused a moment, remembering what Reagan had said: '. . . but you damned that blackened soul to hell. . .' and reckoned it had been no suicide.

> *I also found scholarly discussion concerning the deaths of Ælfwald's sons, equating Wonwaldremere with Windermere in the Lake District. This is disputed but there is a persistent suggestion that the boys were forcibly drowned and one must wonder at the use of the word 'in' Wonwaldremere rather than 'at' which would support such a claim.*

And suddenly it all came back to him, the horror, and the dreadful guilt that had consumed him. They had been deceived, he and Bri, and set upon, left for dead. . . He put the letter aside, sickened by the memory, not looking up and wishing that Olwen need not see it. He took up the next letter, which was from Celia herself, and in her usual way she came quickly to the point.

I discovered, to my relief, that the courts have put some sort of check on the vicar as regards handling the estate until Olwen is found, so her mind can be easy on that score – although it does make it impossible for the work on filling in the lake to be carried out as she had hoped. And please tell her that she must not be hasty regarding the generous proposition she raised.

John paused, wondering what this meant; Olwen had said nothing to him.

We've had a letter from Professor Brandt who tells us that Dr Linton has joined him in Zurich for a while. Both send best wishes and looked forward to being in correspondence with you as soon as that becomes possible. He says, as you can imagine, they have many questions!

He set aside the first page and began reading the second.

You will see Dr Henly's letter with the reference to drowning, which makes me wonder whether you have raised your suspicions with Olwen? One questions now whether you should? Read the cutting, and oh John, what must one think! Gussie says you must still tell Olwen, it is her right to know, but it seems that the fates have taken a hand and justice, of a sort, has been delivered.

Folded inside the letter was a newspaper cutting.

Tragedy strikes in Kirkthorpe. Alfred Malkon, elder son of the Reverend Malkon of St Helen's parish, was killed last Tuesday in a freak accident. The circumstances of his death were witnessed by the village blacksmith who reports that Mr Malkon was galloping past his smithy when his horse, a spirited Connemara, which he has raced on several occasions, reared up and threw him, its hoof catching Mr Malkon in the head as he fell. Death was believed to be instantaneous. When asked what had alarmed the white stallion, the blacksmith reported that a tramp, seen earlier in the morning close by the smith's pasture, had stepped out of the hedgerow, and must have startled the creature. Mr Malkon is the cousin of Miss Olwen Malkon, the missing heiress to Swindale Hall, whose whereabouts remain unknown. The tramp too has vanished.

Good God. Conscious of Olwen's eyes on him, he did not look up but went back to Celia's letter, seeing there was a postscript written on the back.

P.S. Redman summoned us to York the other day to ask what we could tell him about your whereabouts, but in a manner that clearly did not require an answer, and then remarked, in that way of his, that the end of the month was approaching. We think he was telling us that you would soon be able to reappear.

The end of the month! Olwen's birthday. He glanced at his mother's perpetual calendar. He had forgotten, lost all track of dates. 'John?' said Olwen. He looked up and saw her face was pinched and anxious.

'For goodness sake, son, tell the lass! Whatever it is.'

Silently he handed Olwen the first page of Celia's letter and watched her read, then passed across the one from Dr Henly and saw her blanch and swallow hard. Then he gave her the newspaper cutting, and her eyes flew to his.

And once again they shared a common thought.

Reagan.

He too had been caught up in this strange duality, this resurgence of the past: '*Who will avenge the innocents?*' he had asked, and John had left the job unfinished.

'And the other page,' she said, stretching out her hand for it. He saw her frown as she read and looked up. 'What suspicions are these that I should know of?'

'It's something better told outdoors.' He pushed the letters towards his mother, who nodded in reply to the look he gave her.

And so he told Olwen as they walked downslope towards the burn that ran along the valley bottom, he told her what Reagan had said, about the boat and the bottles, and then held her close while she wept, wondering what Redman's analysis of the bottles had revealed.

'We cannot be sure,' John said,

But Olwen shook her head, pulling away. 'I think we can,' she said, balling his handkerchief in her hand. 'I never understood how they came to drown, they were so familiar with the boat, and the lake was frozen that day. It nagged away at the back of my mind but nothing would bring them back, and so I buried it. . .' She pulled away and looked out across the hills. 'I imagine that Edmond was simply a stooge, I can't believe he was knowingly involved in such a cruel plan, but Alfred was persistent in his pursuit of me, so determined, toadying up to Papa, and it's true that Papa was always worse in the days that followed, tired by their visit, we thought. It would have been so easy. . . But *the boys!* Oh, God, I cannot bear it.'

He had taken her back to the farm and into his mother's care.

Olwen did not see John in the days that followed. His mother had suggested to him that he stayed away. 'It is better so, my dear,' she had said, taking Olwen's hand, 'just for a little while. You need time! These are terrible things to have to bear.' And she had looked at her with kindly eyes, dark like her son's, and Olwen had nodded and, as the pain of knowing the truth became gradually familiar, if no less acute, she found herself speaking at last about the boys as she went about her tasks with John's mother always close. She spoke haltingly at first but then more openly as the memories were released from a dark place in her mind and, as they hung up cloths full of rich sheep's cheese to drip, she described how sweet life had been once Celia had come and the boys had a tutor who understood that they needed their freedom every bit as much as book learning. And, in the thinking of them and in the telling, they lived again in her mind.

Occasionally she would see John out on the hills and once, when he rode past the farm on his way down the valley, she had felt again that panic which once consumed her, and had stood at the window watching him disappear over the brow. 'Where is he going?' she asked and his mother came to stand beside her. 'He's gone to see about a place in Yetholm to set himself up. Can't have the sick forever climbing up here to see him. But he'll be back, don't you fret.'

And so he planned to stay, she thought, as she had imagined he might.

Sometimes she would escape from the house and wander down the valley to sit beside the burn and watch the dipper vanish below the surface, its bright eye stalking nymphs and tiny minnows on the stream bed. And there, she felt again another presence and allowed Wyn to inhabit her once more, and so they shared each other's sorrow and she was comforted. And in the sharing she could imagine Olly and Will running wild here under the slopes of The Curr, climbing up beside the sikes that trickled down from Latchly Hill or panting their way up to the windy summit of White Law. And sometimes she imagined that she saw two shadows running beside them, glimpsing perhaps those few short weeks of summer a thousand years ago.

And slowly she began to turn her mind to the future.

It was on the morning of her birthday that she set off up the valley, her shortened skirt swishing over the heather, her stout shoes repelling the damp. The sun had climbed above the hills to light the far side of the valley, and she felt the need now to resolve matters between herself and John. She could never live at Swindale Hall again, that much was clear. Celia and Gussie could take it and outrage the vicar by establishing a place of learning for women, as Celia had always wanted. He would be powerless to oppose it, as he now owed his living to her. And Gussi had shown that she was more than a match for the bishop.

She tramped on, uplifted by the thought, noticing that last night's full moon could still be seen, pale and fading in the bright early morning light. By the time she reached the shieling where John slept the sun had risen above the rounded peaks and the little stone structure was in sunshine. Would she find him still abed, she wondered.

But no. . . As she approached, he appeared at the door, stretching and pulling on his shirt. He saw her at the same moment and raised a hand, tucked his shirt into his trousers and came down towards her.

'Today is my birthday,' she called up to him.

'I know it is,' he said, smiling down at her. 'I was on my way to offer my felicitations.'

'But I came to you.'

'Aye,' he said, smiling still. 'I see that.'

The sun was now flooding the valley and adding diamonds to the little burn as it tumbled downhill over moss-velvet rocks. 'I came with a purpose, John,' she said, 'as I'm now a free and independent woman.'

He raised an eyebrow. 'And what purpose was that?'

'To ask whether you intend to redeem a promise you made to me a long, long time ago. . .'

He looked back at her, then took her hand in his. 'And I was coming down to the farm to ask the same of you.' He put a hand in his pocket, closing it over something which he slipped over her wrist, his eyes never leaving hers as he pushed a bangle high onto the soft flesh of her upper arm. His hand clasped it there a moment, and then he pulled her to him, his hand cupping her head, and as the sun rose above the hills she felt its warmth on her back.

After a moment he released her and glanced back towards the shieling, but she laughed and shook her head at him. 'No, John, not there. There's another place – I think you know it – a grassy hollow in the fold of the land close by, where that promise was made. Between us, we could find it, don't you think?'

AUTHOR'S NOTES

This is a story, a work of fiction. With the exception of the historical figures, listed here, the characters are all imaginary: Ælfwald, king of Northumbria (ruled 779–88), his sons, Ælf and Ælfwinne (d. 791), Eanbald I (archbishop of York 779/80–796), Osred II (ruled Northumbria 788–90), Æthelred I (ruled Northumbria 774–9, was deposed and ruled again 790–6) and the patrician, Sicga (d. 793).

The dates have been compressed a little to fit the fictional storyline, but the main events relating to the lives of the historical characters are drawn from the limited historical sources for the period – although there is no evidence that Ælf and Ælfwinne ever left the city following the murder of their father until drawn away to their deaths in Wonwaldremere (location unknown). While it is recorded that King Ælfwald fell foul of a conspiracy at Scythlescester (believed to be Chesters on Hadrian's Wall) led by Sicga, named as a patrician (nobleman), the circumstances and nature of his death are not known. According to documentary sources, there were many sightings of a fiery light (a comet?) hanging in the sky over the place where he was killed, and his place of burial, St Andrew's Church at Hexham, became a place of pilgrimage. All that is known of Ælf and Ælfwinne is that they were lured from sanctuary in York's principal church by false promises and 'miserably slain' by Æthelred in Wonwaldremere; though whether by his own hand or at his command is a matter of speculation. In 792 Æthelred married the daughter of King Offa of Mercia at Catterick.

Ælfwyn (Wyn) and Oshere (Heri) are entirely fictional. The

name Oshere has been borrowed from the inscription on a spec-
tacular 8th-century helmet found following excavations at
Coppergate in York in 1984.

The battle of Catreath (Catterick) took place c. AD 600
between the pagan Angles and an alliance of (mainly) northern
kingdoms, sub-kingdoms and chiefdoms. *The Gododdin*,
Scotland's oldest poem, celebrates the battle's fallen heroes,
recorded by the poet Aneirin, who was reportedly the only
survivor of the people of the north. The village of Kirk Yetholm
lies amongst the Cheviot hills on the Scottish side of the border
and was the wintering home of gypsies from 1695 when one
of their number saved the life of the son of the local landowner
during the siege of Namur. The valley of Halterburn rises above
it into the Border hills.

Kirkthorpe village does not exist, but the small villages in the
Vale of York, along the winding course of the River Nidd near
its confluence with the River Ouse, have ancient origins. Some
have Anglo-Saxon churches, perhaps early monastic foundations,
and fragments of early stone sculpture have been found embedded
in the fabric of remodelled churches. St Hilda's House in York
is fictional but The Retreat, founded in 1792 by Samuel Tuke,
was a progressive, and well-regarded, mental health institution
established initially for the benefit of Quakers.

The River Ouse in York was temporarily lowered in the 1890s
to allow for the laying of water pipes, revealing the sloping
riverbanks not seen since York ceased to be subject to tides
following the creation of locks downstream in the 18th century.
York itself was established as a Roman legionary fortress in AD
71. In the course of the 5th century the city was abandoned,
but by the 8th century it had become an important ecclesias-
tical centre. There was commerce along the riverbanks and
somewhere, presumably, a royal residence; no trace of it has
been found but the site behind the Roman multangular tower
has been suggested, and was chosen for this novel. The bridge
that Wyn and Heri crossed would have been on the site of the
old Roman bridge, believed to be the only fixed river crossing

until c.900. Excavations in Church Street in 1972 revealed part of the Roman sewer system, a stone-lined tunnel still largely intact and wide enough for the archaeologists who found it to crawl along.

ACKNOWLEDGEMENTS

I am very grateful to all those who supported me in the writing of *The Awakening*. Special thanks go, as ever, to my brilliant agent, Jenny Brown and to my editor Lily Cooper and to all the team at Hodder and Stoughton. The story draws on the work of a great many historians, including those describing advances in psychotherapy, the Victorians' fascination with the mind and the psychic world, the reform of asylums and the treatment of the mentally ill. It also draws on discussions of the very patchy documentary sources for the Anglo-Saxon period, richly augmented by what archaeologists have discovered in York and the surrounding region.